To Steve + Lynn

BLOOD JUSTICE

Tim W. James

BLOOD JUSTICE

TIM W. JAMES

Jackson, WY

This is a work of fiction. Names, characters, businesses, places, events, locales, and incidents are either the products of the author's imagination or used in a fictitious manner. Any resemblance to actual persons, living or dead, or actual events is purely coincidental.

For permission requests, write to the publisher, addressed Attention: Permissions Coordinator

Sastrugi Press, P.O. Box 1297, Jackson, WY 83001, United States.
www.sastrugipress.com

Library of Congress Cataloging-in-Publication Data

Names: James, Tim W., author.
Title: Blood justice / Tim W. James.
Description: 1st United States edition. | Jackson, Wyoming : Iron Spike Press, [2022] | Series: The Roger Brinkman series ; 1
Identifiers: LCCN 2022010333 (print) | LCCN 2022010334 (ebook) | ISBN 9781649222442 (hardback) | ISBN 9781649222459 (paperback) | ISBN 9781649222466 | ISBN 9781649222473 (ebook)
Subjects: LCSH: Brothers--Fiction. | Revenge--Fiction. | LCGFT: Western fiction.
Classification: LCC PS3610.A4595 B57 2022 (print) | LCC PS3610.A4595 (ebook) | DDC 813/.6--dc23/eng/20220315
LC record available at https://lccn.loc.gov/2022010333
LC ebook record available at https://lccn.loc.gov/2022010334
ISBN-13: 978-1-64922-247-3 (Ebook)
ISBN-13: 978-1-64922-245-9 (Paperback)
ISBN-13: 978-1-64922-244-2 (Hardback)
ISBN-13: 978-1-64922-246-6 (Large Print)

Iron Spike Press is an imprint of Sastrugi Press LLC.
Interior design by Kelly's Book Layout, kellygaffney232@gmail.com

Printed in the United States of America when purchased in the United States
10 9 8 7 6 5 4 3 2 1

Foreword

The roar of a Colt .44 splitting the dense air of a Texas saloon to end a hate-filled argument conjures up stories of the American Wild West. The Western and its cowboys, seen by most as tough men with noble character, portray a time we'll never see again. Battles between the law and the outlaw have been the substance of many morality tales.

This story takes place in the 19th-century and depicts slavery, war, and the lawlessness of the Old West. It is the tale of a young man, Roger Brinkman, who is stricken by tragedy while attempting to follow in the footsteps of his father, a preacher. The tragedy leads him to become a Confederate sniper and later a U.S. Deputy Marshal, hoping to find the man who turned his world upside down. Driven by a vengeful heart, he confronts outlaws and renegades before being chastised by the woman he could have loved. He reunites with the Bible's Man of Peace, only to find he still cannot escape the violence of the Wild West.

This story's character was inspired by Pastor Douglas Jones of St. James Lutheran Church, Imperial Beach, California. Jones's creation is a traveling preacher in the American Southwest. His tales are based on family and friends, who lived that lifestyle in the Old West. However, any resemblance between "Blood Justice" and the pastor's writings is purely coincidental.

The author of this book grew up in a small "cow town" located along the Wind River in Wyoming's Rocky Mountains. Filled with all the flavor of the Old West, he expresses his faith, the joy, and memories of that time as both a writer and filmmaker.

Dedication

This book is dedicated to the memory of Thomas George Linsdau and his loving family. Tom passed away September 30, 2019, in Imperial Beach following his 80th birthday. He was surrounded by members of his family.

Tom was a devout Christian, who served as a Lutheran Lay Minister early in his life. He was forced to retire early due to rheumatoid arthritis that plagued him most of his adult life.

This book is also dedicated to his wife, Diane, daughters Trudy, Teresa and Tanya, son, Timothy, and Tom's grandchildren.

Written by Tim W. James, based on a character created by Lutheran Pastor Douglas Jones

Chapter 1

It was hot that day in Lexington, Missouri, but that did not keep a crowd from gathering along one of the town's side streets. A multitude had assembled, some to participate and others out of curiosity, to see what was attracting so much attention.

Not far from where the folks were congregating, a tall man dressed in a dark coat and black broad-brimmed hat was preparing his horse and buggy for a long ride home. He loaded his carpeted luggage into the carriage, removed his coat, folded it neatly and placed it on top of his bag. He also removed his clerical collar and placed it inside the jacket. He stroked the gray-flecked beard that ran from his sideburns down to his chin, as he moved to the front of the carriage to inspect the harness. As he ran his hand down the white patch that adorned his horse's face, he glanced over at the growing crowd and experienced a sudden feeling of uneasiness. He raised his hand to the brim of his hat to help shade his eyes and focus on the activity taking place just a short distance from the livery stable where he stood. He undid the top button of his white shirt and walked toward the crowd.

Pastor Douglas Brinkman was approaching a slave auction, an event not uncommon in this part of Missouri. The importing of humans for slave labor had been outlawed in America nearly a half-century before, but the sale of people as chattel continued. Brinkman, who opposed slavery, was unsure why he was being drawn to the spectacle. His instincts told him to return to his carriage and put the activity out of his mind. But as he scanned the makeshift stage, his eyes settled on a boy standing in line with the men chained together. The lad wasn't chained to the others and appeared far too young to be sold as a slave. However, there was a rope tied around his neck held by one of the white men standing on the auction block.

A rotund man wearing a light-colored straw fedora was center stage calling out to the folks encircling the platform. His fleshy cheeks were reddened by the heat of the day, and he frequently wiped the sweat from his face with a kerchief kept in his hip pocket. As Brinkman looked on, he noticed one adult slave was being led off the platform in the custody of his new owner. The heavyset man turned and motioned for the boy to be brought forward. The caller took hold of the child's rope and tugged him to center stage.

"What am I bid for this fine young specimen? Yes, he's just a lad, but he will grow into a strong laborer fit for any plantation or farm," boomed the auctioneer. "Start the bidding at twenty dollars, but I doubt he will go for less than fifty."

The going price for a slave was far greater than twenty dollars, but the slave peddler had been unable to draw any interest in the youth during previous auctions. He was running out of slave territory and decided he would give the child away if necessary.

"I'll give you five. He's just a boy," someone shouted from the audience. A slight murmur went through the crowd, as several nodded in agreement with the bidder.

"A boy, indeed, I can guarantee he will grow into a fine worker in no time at all."

As the pastor drew nearer, his six-foot frame gave him the advantage of peering over the heads of those in front of him. As the morning wore on, some folks lost interest and began to leave. Others departed with purchased slaves in tow.

The pastor had been in Lexington for a church convention and typically would have had no interest in a slave auction. But something about this event piqued his curiosity, and his interest was now riveted on the black child standing in the center of the stage.

"Five dollars! Don't insult me," shot back the auctioneer in the direction of the first bidder. "It cost me more than that just to get him here."

"Six dollars!" the pastor called out, surprised by his own actions. Brinkman was the minister of a small church in a western Missouri community known as Bordertown. He had never bid on a slave before, and he was not certain why he was doing it now.

"That's a little better, but too little," the barker answered. "I'll pull this future striver back if you can't do better than that."

"Ten dollars!" Brinkman said in response. The pastor had no more than twenty dollars in his pocket, but something told him to keep bidding.

"Now you're bidding against me. I like that," said the auctioneer with a laugh. The short but large man was beginning to work up a sweat that was now showing through his yellow-stained shirt. He again pulled his wrinkled bandana from his pocket and mopped his brow. "The boy is a prize, I tell ya'. You folks can do better than that."

"Twelve bucks, not a penny more," said a man wearing a straw hat, denim trousers and shortsleeve shirt, resembling that of most farmers from the Lexington area.

"Fifteen!" Brinkman countered. He watched nervously as the man in the straw hat slapped his open hand through the air and turned to leave the auction. The pastor whispered a small prayer of hope that no other bids would come forward.

The frustrated auctioneer took note of the bidder who turned away and looked down at the boy on the end of the rope. He rubbed the stubble on his ruddy face and again produced the kerchief. He held the wrinkled cloth out in the direction of Brinkman and called out "Sold to the gentleman in the black hat."

Brinkman approached the stage while reaching into his pocket for three-fourths of the money he had on him. The auctioneer handed Brinkman the rope tethered to the young slave's neck.

"What's his name?" Brinkman asked, taking a light hold on the rope.

"Nikkumbaba, but we just call him Nik," said the auctioneer, with some disappointment in his voice. "What interest do you have in the boy?" he asked, with a puzzled look.

Brinkman looked at the young lad, who had glanced up to see his new master. "I guess there was just something about the child that drew me to him. I'm sure my wife will be happy with him," the pastor added, not knowing why he made such a remark. He knew his spouse would likely be horrified to learn of his participation in a slave auction.

"Kind of a house boy, eh?" the auctioneer said, taking Brinkman's money and handing it to the man who had been holding the rope. "Not a bad idea, a gift for the wife. Maybe I'll use that the next time I have a child to sell."

"What about his parents?" the pastor blurted out, as an afterthought.

"No parents involved," the slave merchant replied. "The boy was given to me when I purchased these men from a trader down south."

"Do you have his belongings?" the pastor asked.

"He's wearing what belongs to 'im," the auctioneer said. "I'm just glad I won't have to feed him anymore."

As the crowd continued to disperse, the slave merchant told the pastor Nikkumbaba was purchased in New Orleans. The slave trader made no mention that "Nik" was among a shipment of Africans smuggled into Louisiana. The man did confide he tried peddling the boy while traveling the Mississippi River, but no one wanted him. He confessed to a certain joy over no longer having to look after the child.

Brinkman took the rope and placed the loose end into his pocket. He put his arm around the youth's shoulders and began leading him toward the livery stable. His purchase said nothing as they passed by the few remaining onlookers. The two walked in silence until reaching the pastor's carriage.

"I'm going to take this rope off of you," Brinkman said, looking down at the lad and hoping he understood. "Please don't run. I'm not going to hurt you. I just need you to get into the buggy."

Brinkman removed the rope from Nikkumbaba's neck and helped him into the carriage from the driver's side. Brinkman slipped in next to him, grabbing the reins. He snapped the leather straps and began the long journey home.

Pulling onto the road leading southwest out of Lexington, Brinkman's thoughts turned to the reception awaiting him when he reached home with his new companion. He did not approve of slavery but lived in a state that did. Buying and selling human flesh was something he abhorred but he could not turn his back on Nikkumbaba. The pastor pondered just how he would explain his decision to become a slave owner.

Chapter 2

The two passengers spent most of the first day riding in silence. Brinkman's heart held the reason for buying Nikkumbaba but not what to do with him. He did free the lad from bondage but certainly could not turn him out on his own. He knew his family would understand why he did it, but what would be their reaction to owning a slave?

Nikkumbaba rode quietly, gazing out over the countryside. It was pleasant, much like the areas along the Mississippi River, where the slave ship stopped to hold auctions. The man next to him was nothing like those who held him in chains, but who was he? Why did he want Nikkumbaba? Why him and not one of the adult slaves?

Nik's thoughts drifted back to how it all started: his village, his mother, hunter training, capture and a long nightmarish voyage shackled to others in the dark hold of a ship. When the vessel finally docked, those who survived were transferred to a smaller boat on a large river in a strange land. They sailed under similar conditions, stopping on occasion to sell those Nik had come to know, purchased by men he did not know.

Several times, he had been paraded off the ship, passed over and then placed back into the belly of the boat. Eventually, he was unshackled and led to the quarters of a man referred to as "captain." He was taught to serve the man each day, then taken below deck at night only to be fettered again. This continued until he was eventually sold to the man sitting next to him.

"Do you speak English … Nik?" Brinkman asked, interrupting the boy's thoughts. The pastor used his nickname to avoid stumbling over the lad's full name.

Somewhat startled, Nik looked up and said "Some."

Nik had been introduced to English through missionaries visiting his village. He also picked up more of the language serving the captain on board the ship.

"Where are you from?" the pastor asked in hopes of extending the conversation.

"Where from?" Nik responded.

"Yes. I am from Bordertown, are you from Africa?" Brinkman continued.

"Africa?" Nik queried. The youth knew what the meaning of the word was but didn't understand the question.

Brinkman dropped the discussion, satisfied that "some" English was at least a good start. He noted when Nik repeated his words he did so clearly, but he seemed troubled by the questions. The pastor decided on a different approach.

"I am Douglas Brinkman. What's your name?" Brinkman asked, wincing at the fact his new approach still ended with a question.

"Nikkumbaba," was the reply.

Listening to Nik pronounce his name made Douglas glad he did not attempt it.

"That's quite a name. Do you mind if I just call you Nik?"

"Nik, captain say," Nikkumbaba said. He did not like the shortened name. The people of his village took great pride in their names.

"Some folks call me Doug instead of Douglas," Brinkman added. "It's just easier for some people to do that."

Nik could follow what his new master was saying but was not confident to answer in English. He looked away and did not speak, so Brinkman decided to let the fractured dialogue rest for a while.

Douglas was part of a coalition of pastors who offered their homes for journeying clergy. Clerics did not travel that much, but they did fill in for one another when necessary. Brinkman's trip home took longer than usual, as he made stops along the way to visit and enjoy the hospitality of coalition members. The layovers also helped pastors finance their trips.

Brinkman carried a bedroll for sleeping outdoors but was aware

Nik would need one. He planned to stop in Greenton, Missouri, and pick up some suitable bedding for his companion and simple fare for a meal. Still in "Little Dixie" country, the pastor knew he would not be able to get Nik into a hotel.

But Brinkman was familiar with the area. He knew where they could camp near a creek and enjoy a small campfire. They shared the food and spent the night without incident. The next day, the pastor hoped to make it to Pleasant Hill where a member of the coalition had a church.

During the ride, Nik broke the ice with a question.

"Where going?" he asked.

"To my home," Brinkman answered, choosing his words carefully. "But we will make several stops along the way."

"Home?" Nik repeated.

"It's where I have a church. My family and I live on a farm in Bordertown," Brinkman explained, pleased with the communication progress.

Nik had little knowledge of "church," other than the mission located near his village. His understanding of "farm" was also limited. The captain had used the term "farm" during auctions but never explained what it was.

"What is farm?" Nik asked.

"It's a place where things are grown, like potatoes, tomatoes, fruit and other vegetables," the pastor said, not knowing if Nik understood any of that.

"Grow food." Nik said, offering the pastor relief that his young charge may be more informed than he thought.

As the afternoon shadows began to push back the daylight, the two riders came to a parish outside of Pleasant Hill. Douglas drew the buggy to a halt in front of Pastor Finn Kelly's adjacent home. He got out of the carriage and took Nik with him, afraid to leave him alone. When Kelly answered the door, he stepped out onto the porch.

"Doug, I would invite you and your young friend in for the night, but that could make things a little awkward for my congregation," the pastor said after Brinkman made his introductions. "I hope you understand."

"I'm not for driving away any of your flock, Finn," Brinkman answered, with an understanding smile. "But I do need some assistance. You see, I spent ..."

"I understand, Douglas. There's a spot where you can camp nearby, and Margaret will supply enough food for both. I'll also get you some hay and oats for the horse."

"I am grateful. God bless you, my friend," Brinkman said, hoping Nik did not realize his presence made others uneasy.

Nik paid little mind to what Pastor Kelly said, as he was unfamiliar with being given an invitation into an American home.

Graciously accepting the provisions, Brinkman drove the buggy to the described campsite. The area was remote but pleasant and not far from the Kellys' home. There was a campfire area encircled by stones and a stream nearby. The campsite was barren but surrounded by trees.

Douglas used the time to instruct Nik on the use of certain English words. He was surprised at how quickly his young charge grasped the basics of the language.

As evening settled in, the two ate and then retired for the night.

Douglas rose before daybreak, considering it prudent to travel through town while still dark. Nik did not wake up as early as he had the day before. The youth was sleeping soundly, so the pastor picked him up and laid him in the carriage. Brinkman climbed in, placed Nik's head on his lap and set out for the road.

As the carriage bumped along, Nik eventually woke and sat upright as if in shock, prompting Brinkman to bring the buggy to a halt.

"Are you okay?" Brinkman asked, with a smile of encouragement.

Nik looked about and then looked back at the pastor and said "Okay."

"Here, let me grab you an apple," Brinkman said while reaching into the basket. "You didn't eat much last night."

Nik ate the apple in big bites, giving Douglas a sense change was coming over the young lad. He had slept more soundly than the night before. He ate little at supper but was now eating ravenously.

"Careful, don't choke on that thing," Brinkman said. The sun was now barely clearing the trees lining the road and promising a day of good weather.

"Choke?" Nik said, turning to look up at the driver. "Apple is good."

"There's plenty in the basket," Brinkman assured. "Take what you want. I'll explain 'choke' later."

The last few stops made at homes of participating pastors met with mixed results, but none turned them away. They spent the night in a barn, on a porch and in an empty stable, along with Brinkman's horse.

They were on the last leg of their journey when they entered Hilltop, the last town they would visit before reaching Bordertown. It was the home of Pastor Bob Altman and his wife, Annie. Although the Altmans were nearly two decades older than the Brinkmans, their proximity led to a strong friendship between the two families.

It was late afternoon when Brinkman guided the buggy up a dirt street to Hilltop's church on the outskirts of town. Hilltop was about the size of Bordertown. Besides a livery stable and saloon, it also had a bank, mercantile, schoolhouse, hardware store and sheriff's office. The main industry was farming and employment at one of the small businesses. As the travelers approached the church, Douglas saw a horse tied to the chapel's hitching post, indicating Bob Altman was at work.

Douglas stopped the carriage, got out and signaled Nik to do the same. Normally, the pastor would have gone straight to Altman's home, but past "rejections" convinced him it would be best if Nik did not come as a surprise. However, knowing Pastor Altman, as he did, gave him a feeling this visit would somehow be different.

Once inside the church, Brinkman was about to escort the youth down the aisle when Nik stopped to look around. Douglas noted the wonder on the boy's face and his attire. The only clothes Nik had were a pair of single-strapped overalls that exposed his bare feet above the ankles. He wore a ragged cotton shirt at least two sizes too large over a dirty undershirt. For the first time, the pastor felt guilty about the child's clothes, or lack of them.

As they continued, Nik pivoted his head to take in his surroundings with an expression of awe. The church was not large, but something Nik was not used to. Along each side of the aisle were rustic wooden pews. Above was an arched ceiling and below small windows dotting the walls. Most were open to alleviate some of the summer heat. There was a small wood stove for winter near the corner of the platform at the front of the church. Its black, tin chimney ran up through the vaulted ceiling. On the platform, a wooden altar stood and above it attached to the wall was a roughly-hewn wooden cross.

Douglas and company made their way toward the altar and turned to approach a small door next to it. Brinkman knocked and a voice from inside answered "Come in."

Brinkman opened the door and placed his hand on Nik's shoulder, gently pushing him in before him.

"What have we here?" Bob Altman exclaimed as he rose from a worn cloth chair positioned behind a wooden desk.

Altman had a head covered with short white hair, but the years had been kind to him. His step was lively and his voice strong, even after decades of delivering sermons and singing hymns.

As Brinkman stepped into the office behind Nik he announced: "Hey, Bob, it's Doug from Bordertown. This is my traveling companion, Nik."

"Doug. Just getting back from Lexington?" Bob inquired. "I did not know you were traveling with anyone."

"I really had not planned on it, but circumstances changed a bit for me after the pastor's meeting," Brinkman said.

"How so?" said Altman, who was at least six inches shorter than Brinkman and his ready smile exaggerated the creases in his tanned face.

"Nik, here, was being auctioned off as a slave. He can't be any older than my boy, Roger. I simply could not let any of those plantation owners turn him into... well, you know...," Brinkman said, trying to choose his words carefully.

"I understand completely," Altman said. "Does Patricia know about Nik?"

"No, and I was kind of hoping you could help me come up with an explanation to use when I get home," Brinkman said.

"I don't know that you need any more explanation than what you just gave me, Doug. Patricia will probably tell you she would have done the same thing had she been in your position," Altman said.

"I hope so because I know of no other alternative than to adopt him into the family. There is no way we can let him go out on his own at this age," Brinkman responded.

"I could not agree more, Doug. I think this is a fine thing you are doing. I wish more pastors could do it, but I'm afraid the church doesn't have the money or power to buy slaves," Altman said.

"We do what we can, Bob," Brinkman said. "Nik understands some English, though our conversations have been brief. We've been doing our best to get to know each other. I just hope what I've been telling him hasn't gone over his head."

Nik only nodded in response to the conversation.

"I know what I'm doing is highly irregular and have no idea what I'm dragging my family into," Douglas said. "I'm sure they'll understand, but I have no idea where it will go from there."

"Never underestimate the power of the Almighty," Bob said. "But let's get you two fed and set you up a place where you can rest for the night. Is your buggy outside?"

"Yes," Brinkman answered.

"My horse is out front," Pastor Altman said. "You guys can just follow me back to my place."

After their arrival at Altman's house, the pastor's wife, Annie, was delighted to hear what Brinkman had done. She immediately took to the child and ushered him into her home.

The Altman house was modest but neat and clean. Bob Altman's talent was woodwork, adding furniture and fixtures to make the place more comfortable. After joining the traveling pastor's coalition, he remodeled their son's room to accommodate guests. Their son was grown and had moved to Kansas City.

Annie was a fabulous cook and housekeeper. She was even smaller than Bob but had the energy of six women. She was also an expert gardener, growing both vegetables and flowers. She would cut a bouquet every day for the kitchen table, giving the house a fragrance as fresh as the outdoors.

"I would not worry about what Patricia or your children will have to say, Douglas," Annie offered. "But I'm not sure how everyone in Bordertown is going to view this."

"I think I just have a way of inviting more trouble than I need," Brinkman said, not thinking how Nik might take his remark. "I just could not stand by and see Nik dragged around from auction block to auction block in those chains."

"Doug, you've got Christ in your heart and His Comforter to guide you," Bob offered. "Put them to the forefront and subordinate yourself. You'll do just fine, and God bless you for what you're doing."

Annie set out an excellent dinner for them and afterward showed their guests to their room. While Nik and Douglas brought in their things from the carriage, Bob took care of the horses. Following a brief after-dinner conversation, all settled down for the evening.

The room had a small bed that Brinkman dropped onto to take off his boots. Nik had not slept in a bed or in anyone's home before. He stood in the corner wondering if the pastor was going to fetch his bedroll and take him outside to sleep.

"Say, Nik, you don't have to stand there all night," Brinkman said. "Come on to bed." Brinkman sat up waiting patiently for Nik to respond.

"You say trouble," Nik answered, remembering the pastor's words earlier. "Nik trouble?"

Brinkman thought a moment, recalling his comment about inviting trouble. "Nik, I sent word to my family about you. I don't know if I can make you understand," the pastor said. "But time was against me. I had to do what my heart said was right. I think my family will agree."

After a short hesitation, Nik moved to the side of the bed and sat down. "Nice," he said.

"You bet," Brinkman replied. "And you're going to have one of your own once we get home. Now, Mrs. Altman has some night clothes here for you. Put them on," Douglas said, handing the nightshirt to Nik. "We will be home tomorrow," Douglas concluded.

"Home," Nik responded. He put on the nightshirt, as Brinkman swept back the top cover, gesturing for Nik to crawl in. His youthful roommate complied, and the two slept comfortably through the night.

The next morning, Annie Altman packed a lunch for the travelers. She also gave Nik a shirt worn by the Altman's son when he was about Nik's size. Bob Altman offered Douglas some money to help on the trip home.

"We're too close to home for that," Brinkman said to his friend, as he and Nik boarded the carriage. "I can't repay you for what you've already done," Brinkman said, turning to look down at Altman, who was standing by the buggy. "I'm sure the lunch Annie packed will see us through."

"Fair enough, but I won't let you go until you promise to ship me some of Patricia's canned peaches," Altman said, with a wide grin. He waved as Brinkman snapped the reins and the carriage pulled away.

Chapter 3

The carriage ride from Lexington not only drew Brinkman and his young companion closer but also gave the pastor a better understanding of prejudice. Nik seemed to be growing more comfortable and more open with the pastor. He was scared and knew very little about his circumstances other than the strange and cruel customs of slavery.

Although Nik's English was broken, Brinkman assisted him with words the youth found confusing. Eventually, Nik was able to describe his circumstances.

Nik told of his life in an African village near the coast. His people were peace-loving, but warring tribes made it necessary for young males to train as warriors and hunters. Warrior training was mainly for defense.

"Father hunter. Brave warrior," Nik related. "Die when Nik not old. Men teach to hunt."

Brinkman calculated that Nik had trained as a hunter-warrior around the age of ten. Nik stressed that he had killed an antelope and helped track a lion killed by his hunting party.

"Lion kill animals. Afraid kill children," Nik said. "I help hunt."

"Were you afraid hunting that lion?" Douglas asked.

"Lion kill father. Men kill lion," Nik replied. "I not show afraid."

"So how did you end up coming here?" Brinkman inquired.

Nik thought for a minute and explained that a hunting party he was with was attacked by men from another village.

"Kill two, take men, Nik," the boy said. "Take to big water. Men in small boat take men, Nik, to big boat."

While Nik described the voyage, Douglas could only imagine the horrific conditions Nik and his companions went through.

"Slave ships," Nik's mood was now solemn as he spoke. "Too bad to say."

"That's all right, Nik," Brinkman said. "Maybe in time, ... when you are ready. Just relax now and enjoy the ride. You won't have to go through that again, I promise."

Douglas could tell Nik was still troubled by it all. He shifted tactics to try and get his young companion's mind off the memory.

"Nik, how would you like to drive the buggy?" the pastor inquired.

"Drive buggy? Nik not know," was the lad's response.

"There's nothing to it. You take the reins and I'll be right here next to you," Brinkman instructed. "You've been watching me for several days now. Just do what I did and if there's any trouble I'll take over."

Douglas handed the reins to Nik and could see his passenger's eyes widen with excitement. The plan worked, as Nik focused on the horse. Brinkman put his arm around Nik to comfort him and soon the pair were riding along as natural as the serene countryside around them.

When Nik grew tired, Douglas took the reins and Nik seemed more at peace.

"We'll be home soon," Brinkman said. "Take it easy and think about life on the farm."

"Farm?" Nik questioned. "Slave land?"

"Heavens no, Nik," Brinkman remarked. "What do you know about slaves?"

"Work for bad men," Nik answered. "Nik not old, work kill."

"No need to worry now. That part of your journey is over, son," the pastor said, amused by the reference and wondering how the Brinkman family would feel about that. "You may encounter some hostility while you are here, but you will not be a slave."

"Counter hos-tilly?" Nik asked.

"Ah, it's when you run into someone not very nice, bad. Since Missouri is a slave state, no one can take you away without breaking the law," said Brinkman.

"Break law?" Nik again inquired.

"It's a sort of protection one has for property," Brinkman said. "You'll learn more as time goes along."

Brinkman explained, as best he could, what to expect as a member of the Brinkman family and life in Bordertown. He told the lad about Mrs. Brinkman, their daughter, Dolly, and son, Roger. Although the pastor informed his family by telegraph he would arrive with a guest, he gave no details. His hope was to soften the surprise and pray the Lord would take care of the details.

"You're going to like Roger," Pastor Brinkman said. "He's right around your age and he likes to hunt as well."

As the pair approached Bordertown, Brinkman was grateful his small farm was north of it. That meant not having to endure the quizzical looks as they passed through – for now. They had met enough resistance during their journey to know that not all thought his decision a good one. Brinkman took some comfort in thinking some of the Christians in his church would consider his actions appropriate but reminded himself of the negative reactions of Christians they visited along the way.

Douglas turned the horse onto a rutted path leading from the main road. They entered a small grove of apple and peach trees that drew Nik's attention.

"What trees?" he asked, scanning the hanging fruit.

"This is our orchard," the pastor replied. "Here, I'll stop and get you something."

Brinkman climbed out of the buggy and picked out a ripe peach. After plucking it, he lifted himself into the carriage and handed the fruit to Nik. The boy took a bite, and a smile crossed his face.

"Yeah, you like that?" Brinkman said. "It won't be long, and you'll be out here picking those off the tree," he added, rethinking his remark and amending it. "With Roger, I mean. That is if you want to."

Nik paid no attention to the pastor's attempt to cover what he thought was inappropriate. When serving as a cabin boy on a ship, he had no understanding of what slave labor entailed. He quietly chewed on the peach and gazed as stands of corn, plowed fields and a house came into view.

As they neared Brinkman's farmhouse, Roger and Dolly began running toward the approaching rig. Roger was growing and was twice as tall as his little sister. The pastor was pleased with how well his children got along and their eagerness to help with the farming and housework. Roger's hair was dark, like his father's. He had a crop that kept sliding down his forehead, falling just above his eyes. No matter how often his mother let out his clothes, it took no time at all before he had outgrown them.

Dolly's hair was more auburn, like her mother's. Her clothes always appeared neat and clean, despite her willingness to assist with housework and romp with her friends at church. Like her brother, she was smart and an excellent student.

Patricia Brinkman, the pastor's wife, remained on the porch as the travelers approached. Her shoulder-length red hair flowed around a lightly freckled face that needed no makeup. She was small in stature but strong and resourceful. Her canned foods were well known throughout the county and that, which wasn't given away, helped bring in extra money.

"Pa, man it's great to see you," Roger called out between breaths, as he approached and eyed Nik. "Who is this you have with you?"

Pastor Brinkman could see the enthusiastic reception surprised Nik, so he tried to calm the situation.

"Now, take it easy, Roger. Let me pull up to the porch and I'll do the introductions," Brinkman said.

With that, Roger jumped onto the back of the buggy next to the luggage and helped his little sister do the same. In a short while, they pulled up in front of the porch where Mrs. Brinkman stood. The pastor stepped down from the carriage, while Roger grabbed his father's travel bag. He and Dolly gathered behind their father as he hurried around to the other side of the coach where Nik was sitting.

"You can climb down now, Nik. This is your new home," Brinkman said. Nik was wide-eyed, as the pastor took from him what was left of the peach and assisted his exit. Brinkman turned to his wife and children.

"This is the 'guest' I wrote to you about. His name is Ni-koom-bay-ba," Brinkman said, struggling to mimic Nik's pronunciation of the name, "but you can just call him Nik,"

"He's only a boy," Patricia Brinkman said, as she moved toward the steps leading down from the porch.

"I realize this comes as a bit of a shock," Pastor Brinkman began. "But something told me I could not let him be taken into slavery, and I happened to have enough money to prevent that."

Patricia Brinkman descended the porch stairs and approached her husband. She gave him a quick kiss, gazed into his face and said, "Douglas, you did the right thing."

She then walked past her husband, put her arm around Nik's shoulders and turned to Dolly and Roger. "Children, meet your new brother."

Nik looked up at Mrs. Brinkman and tears began to fill his eyes.

"Is something wrong, Nik?" Patricia said, turning to look at her husband who drew near.

"Nik mother," the newest Brinkman answered, recalling his biological mother.

Patricia gave Douglas a knowing smile anticipating the work that lie ahead. But on that day, Nikkumbaba officially became a Brinkman.

Chapter 4

The Brinkmans wasted no time incorporating their new "son" into the family. They retrieved a bed from the utility room where guests usually stayed and moved it into Roger's room. Knowing Roger's clothes were "shrinking," Mrs. Brinkman shifted some of his over to Nik's side of the closet. Nik was slightly smaller than Roger and fit right into his "brother's" hand-me-downs.

Patricia and her daughter went into town to select new materials to outfit both boys and picked up something lacy for Dolly. Patricia eyed some flower-patterned cloth for herself but decided to hold off until after the harvest. She found a pair of boots for Nik's bare feet and a straw hat for his head. The Missouri sun was still in summer mode, and days could get hot.

Now aware that Nik's inclusion had triggered memories of his life in Africa, the family encouraged him to talk about it.

"What was your mother like?" Patricia asked.

"Nice, like you," he said. "Sad father killed."

"Do you remember him, your father?" she inquired.

"No, Warriors knew father. Tell Nik stories," Nik answered. "Nik be like father."

Nik did himself proud by readily applying himself to farm chores. Roger taught him to milk the cows, and they spent many days picking apples, peaches, and shucking corn. The potatoes had already been harvested and Nik helped with the plowing to prepare the land for the next crop.

The gap between Roger's early life and that of Nik's was as wide as their ages were close. But the two narrowed the background differences rather quickly through a fascination each had for the other's stories. Although a good student, Roger knew very little about slavery and even less as to what it was like living in Africa. Nik's interest was stirred by the Brinkman family's love and the fact he was now part of the very life Roger took for granted.

It did not take long before Nik was speaking English almost as well as any Brinkman. Words that hindered communication at the start were now a standard part of his growing vocabulary. Pastor Brinkman and Patricia planned to officially adopt Nik, but Missouri law forbade it, complicated by the fact the state considered him "property" and not family. The Brinkmans circumvented the problem by referring to Nik as "son" and "brother" until it became natural.

After a year living as a Brinkman, Nik and Roger became very close. Douglas Brinkman had taught Roger to hunt and frequently accompanied him but gladly turned that role over to Nik. Roger was skilled with a long rifle, and largely unrivaled by anyone in Bordertown. He was the proud owner of several blue ribbons earned while shooting at community events.

The gun was new to Nik. Roger taught his brother the safe and proper use of a muzzle-loader, but shooting a rifle was foreign to the former African hunter. His shooting improved over time, but he was never able to match Roger's accuracy.

"Did you ever shoot a bow and arrow," Nik asked, after missing a distant target frequently hit by Roger.

"Never," Roger answered. "Would an arrow actually carry as far as that target is?"

"No," Nik answered, as he looked over the rifle at Roger. "I had to learn to get much closer to my game before shooting an arrow at it. You could hunt on the back of an elephant with this weapon."

Nik was an accomplished tracker. He had an awareness of his surroundings Roger could only admire. Dangerous game in Missouri did not compare to the predators of Africa.

Although Nik was included in family devotional Bible studies, he was allowed to decide for himself what he wanted to believe. The Brinkmans did not encourage church right away. Pastor Brinkman spoke to the congregation about Nik, but the feedback was mixed. Douglas wanted Nik to attend church but feared a negative reception could discourage both him and the congregation. He and Patricia agreed it was best to gradually introduce Nik to the community. They did so by inviting church members and close friends to family celebrations, especially during the holidays. They encouraged everyone to bring their children to meet Nik and introduced him as a Brinkman, not a slave.

During that time, the Fenton family brought their daughter, Gloria. Gloria and Roger were near the same age and had known each other most of their lives through attending the same school and church. There were also the O'Learys and their son, Todd. Todd was a year younger than Roger and occasionally accompanied him on his hunts. Todd was an athlete and was considered the fastest student in school, winning almost every race he entered. Anthony and Karla Carrossa also brought their young sons. The boys were pleased to meet Nik but were closer to Dolly's age and viewed Nik as too old to play with. The Carrossas were devout Christians and instructed their sons not to treat Nik any differently than Roger.

Greta Bagget came to meet Nik and brought her daughter Emilia. Emilia was also slightly younger than Gloria and Roger but was a close friend of Gloria's.

"Roland could not make it?" Pastor Brinkman inquired of Greta. Roland Bagget was Greta's husband and the president of Bordertown's bank. After Roland and Greta were married, Roland's efforts at farming failed. He was hired on at the bank by Greta's father, who owned the bank. After her father's death, Greta inherited the bank and Roland became its president.

"He insisted he had to work and sends his regrets," Greta said, answering the pastor. "He was very surprised when you brought home Nik. You say he is your son?"

"Unofficially, yes," Douglas answered. "Missouri is a slave state and adopting him was more complicated than owning him."

"So, he does not work for you?" she continued.

"He does his share of work around here, just like the rest of us," the pastor said. "He's a Brinkman and no less is expected of him than of Roger or Dolly."

"That is remarkable and rather mature, I would say," Greta responded.

"God willing, I hope everyone sees it that way," Brinkman answered. He could not help but feel there was more to Greta's excuse for Roland's absence than she let on, but since the meetings were being done on Nik's behalf, Douglas put it out of his mind.

As the months passed, the four children Nik's age befriended him and included him in whatever they did. The five planned a fishing trip, but Emilia's father would not give her permission to go. Gloria, who did not want to be the only girl on the trip, decided to spend the day in town with Emilia.

The two teenage girls spent the afternoon strolling about town in bonnets and ankle-length dresses. Emilia's dress was new, and store-bought, while Gloria's somewhat older and homemade. There were material differences between the Fenton and Bagget families, but they did not matter to the two girls. They became friends when they first met at the Bordertown School. A year older, Gloria was taller and less refined, being the daughter of a struggling farmer. She did her share of farm work, as well as helping her mother with domestic chores. She was pretty, with short blonde hair and blue eyes.

Emilia was not as attractive as Gloria, but she was the apple of her father's eye. She always had nice clothes and practiced piano as opposed to doing chores. On the other hand, Emilia was not allowed the freedom Gloria enjoyed. Roland Bagget was particular about who his daughter was allowed to spend time with, but he did approve of Gloria. This despite his elevated perception of the class difference between the two families. As a former farmer, Roland was painfully aware of how difficult farm life could be.

"Emilia, I have not seen your father in church lately. Is he okay?" Gloria asked as the two walked along the boardwalk of downtown Bordertown.

"I guess so," Emilia said, looking down at her patent shoes as she spoke. She raised her head and looked at her companion. "Do you remember when all of us asked Pastor Brinkman to put Nik in my mom's Sunday School class?"

"Yeah, and I'm glad we did. Nik has done so well," Gloria responded.

"Well, my dad was not at all happy about that and threatened to make Mom quit teaching the class," Emilia had a look of hurt in her eyes as she spoke.

"Did Nik do something to upset your father?" Gloria asked with an expression of both bewilderment as well as sympathy for Emelia. Gloria was aware of how her friend's father lorded over her.

"Not that I know of, he just said Nik was one of 'them' and that he was not at all happy with Pastor Brinkman," Emilia continued.

"One of them? You mean like a slave?" Gloria prodded, almost regretting the word.

"I suppose," Emilia began. "You know, my father tried to get a loan from my grandfather to buy some slaves to run his farm. Grandpa turned him down, said he wanted nothing to do with buying slaves. I think Dad's borne some kind of grudge about such things since then."

"So how does your mom feel about this?" Gloria asked.

"She did not like it and told father she would not give up teaching her class, but ever since then he has refused to go to church," Emilia again looked down as she spoke, this time at the wooden planks in the boardwalk. The two girls had reached the edge of town and stood facing each other.

"Do you think Nik knows about this?" said Gloria, whose eyes did not reflect the hurt Emelia's did.

"I hope not," Emilia answered. "I know Pastor Brinkman felt he did the right thing buying Nik, and all. But it seems it may have caused more trouble than it cured, at least with our family."

"I don't know, Emilia. I'm going to have to talk with Roger about this."

"If you think that's best," Emilia replied. "I just hope things don't get worse."

With that, the two girls reversed direction and started back through town, ducking to avoid the dust thrown up by a wagon rolling past on the village's main street.

***

Meanwhile, once the boys learned Gloria and Emilia were not going to go fishing with them, they decided to go hunting instead. Nik and Roger typically hunted smaller game, such as rabbits, squirrels, and turkeys, but this time they were on the trail of a deer.

"I would not go that way," Nik said in a hoarse whisper to his companions. The boys had been tracking the larger animal and Roger and Todd had turned toward a small path leading through the underbrush.

"Why not?" Roger asked, using the same low tones and putting his hand on Todd's shoulder to hold him back.

"Because that's the way the animals go. If you follow that path, you will merely chase the game away. We must plan a strategy to intercept our prey rather than just follow it," Nik advised. "When I learned to track, I was told following directly behind the animal could be dangerous. Depending on the beast one was after, it could backtrack and start hunting the hunter."

Roger and Todd listened as Nik plotted a path that would take the boys in a circle placing them where the deer would likely be feeding. After traveling about two hundred yards, they spotted a young buck grazing about one hundred yards from where they were. Nik put his hands on the shoulder of each friend and slowly pushed them into a kneeling position. They were positioned behind some tall grass growing between them and the deer. After each caught his breath, Nik signaled Roger to prepare for a shot. The young Brinkman slowly raised his rifle and took aim. Roger squeezed the trigger and fired. The buck dropped instantly, and Nik sprang to his feet and raced to where the deer was lying. Within seconds, he had his knife out and was beginning to dress the kill.

"I thought I was fast," Todd said to Roger, as the two followed behind Nik. "That guy runs like a deer."

When the two reached Nik, Roger put his hand on Nik's back.

"Take a moment, Nik, to give thanks for this deer," Roger said. "This blessing will help feed our families for quite a while."

After the prayer, Nik finished dressing the deer and the three dug a hole in which to bury everything but the heart and liver.

The three hunters set about cutting down a pole they used to fashion a litter. After they fastened the deer's legs to the pole, Nik placed the organs inside their kill. He and Todd then hoisted the litter onto their shoulders, while Roger followed along with rifle in hand. The proud hunters made their triumphant journey back to the Brinkman farm.

The story of Nik's trek from Africa to America and, eventually Bordertown, infatuated Roger. It gave the young Brinkman a better understanding of his brother and a deeper feeling of gratitude toward his father for rescuing him. Roger once remarked to his Pa that he'd always wanted a brother, but never thought he would buy him one. Douglas Brinkman corrected the record by saying the purchase of a brother for his son's benefit was not the reason for his action. However, he was glad it worked out that way.

As Nik grew into his teen years, the hold his former life had on him faded and he began to feel more "Brinkman" every day. He thoroughly enjoyed life on the farm and, like Roger, having a brother his age was a terrific bonus. Besides their fondness for hunting, they shared chores and Mrs. Bagget's Sunday School class. Nik's eventual transition to Christianity was not solely because of the Brinkmans. He had been introduced to the Gospel of Jesus Christ while attending a missionary school near his village. However, it was his admiration for the Brinkman family that fortified his faith.

Roger also proved to be a great teacher, describing life in America while contrasting slavery with the country's growing sentiment against it.

"America is about hope," Roger said. "We have problems like any other nation. The difference is, we believe we can fix them."

"Do you think America will fix slavery?" Nik asked.

"It's really only a matter of when," Roger stated. "The how is what worries me."

"How so?" Nik questioned, smiling at his play on words.

"There are rumors it will take a war," Roger acknowledged, crafting his answer. "We fought for our independence. Now, some say, we will have to fight for yours."

***

One day during recess at school, Gloria took Roger aside and told him what Emilia Bagget said about her father no longer attending church.

"I heard Pa ask Ma if she knew why Roland was no longer attending church," Roger said thoughtfully. He peered out across the field where the younger school children were playing, as a strained look crossed his face. "I guess I just don't understand anyone feeling that way."

"I've noticed a few other church members missing, too," Gloria offered. "I don't know if that's because of Nik, but it is discouraging."

"I had best let Pa know what Emilia said," Roger countered, bowing his head and shaking it in disappointed disbelief.

"Don't let Nik know," Gloria said. "None of this is his fault. Mrs. Bagget's parents moved here from Germany of their own free will. Nik was brought to this country against his will."

"It's a crazy, mixed-up world," said Roger. "It gives me a sick feeling in my stomach."

"I hope your father is able to work this out," Gloria said. "On a brighter side," Gloria interjected, changing the mood, "the school dance is this weekend. Would you like to go with me?"

"You know I'm a terrible dancer, Gloria," Roger said, offering a look of embarrassment and frustration.

"It's time you learned, Roger Brinkman," Gloria demanded. "There is really nothing to it."

"Okay, okay, but if you end up with sore toes it's your fault, not mine," Roger said.

"I'll take my chances," Gloria responded, with a slight scowl. "We'd better get back to class," she added, as the younger children started running toward the schoolhouse in response to the teacher's handheld bell.

That evening, Roger told his father what Gloria had related to him about Roland Bagget. Douglas Brinkman was not surprised, as he listened to what Roger had to say. He then lowered his head and ran his fingers through his gray-streaked hair searching for a reply to his son.

He then lowered his hand, raised his head and said, "I was afraid of something like this. I had given the folks of Bordertown more credit than this and hoped they would eventually all understand, but apparently, I was wrong.

"I haven't told your mother," Pastor Brinkman continued, "but your teacher, Isaac Muddleman, told me he could not admit Nik into the school."

"Pa," Roger exclaimed, as the pastor raised his hand to remind his son to keep his voice down. "That's not fair. Nik's plenty smart enough to be in school," Roger continued using a heavy whisper.

"I know, son, I know," Douglas Brinkman said, "but it's not Muddleman's fault. He cited a law that forbids Negroes to go to school. It makes me sick, but apparently it's the law."

"It stinks, Pa," Roger blurted out.

"What stinks?" Patricia said, as she walked into the room. "I hope you're not talking about what I've cooked for dinner."

"No, dinner smells great, Dear," Douglas said. "We can talk about it later. Right now, I'm famished and ready to follow my nose into the kitchen."

Roger tightened his lips and went to find Nik and let him know dinner was ready.

Douglas Brinkman had approached Isaac Muddleman, Bordertown's teacher, about enrolling Nik in school. Muddleman apologetically explained that Missouri law would not allow a black child to attend public school. However, he offered to assist should the family choose to homeschool Nik. After discussing the situation with Patricia, they decided to sit down with the family and come up with a plan to educate Nik.

"Nik, we've spoken to the teacher at Bordertown School, and he is going to help us teach you right here at home," Patricia said.

"I had hoped I could go to school with Roger and Dolly," Nik said. "Am I not smart enough for school?"

"It's a little more complicated than that," Douglas chimed in, looking over at his wife. "We have no doubt about your ability to learn, but the school cannot take you at this time."

"I guess I am too far behind," Nik said, looking down at the floor. "Can I still learn this way?"

"Mr. Brinkman and I believe you will learn fast no matter how the schooling is done," Patricia said, leaning over the table to draw Nik's attention. "There are rules we, as a family, must follow for now. But I believe the day will come when Bordertown School has someone like you as its teacher."

Nik smiled at Patricia's remark and said, "I want to learn like Roger and Dolly, no matter how we do it."

Using the lesson plan Muddleman laid out, Nik advanced rapidly. It was not long before the newest Brinkman was only a little more than a year behind Roger academically.

Nik also learned a great deal about America through his new parents and came to understand the real reason why he could not attend school with Roger and Dolly. The thought of being a burden to his new family was troubling for Nik.

"Nik, it took pioneers to build this great nation and you must resign yourself to being one of those pioneers," Douglas said. "The challenges you will face may be different from Davy Crockett's or Lewis and Clarke, but there is no reason on this earth that you can't overcome them. All we ask is that you follow the Good Lord and give it your best effort."

"I guess I'm just feeling a little sorry for myself, Pastor Brinkman," Nik replied, lowering his eyes.

"Whoa, hold it right there, son," Douglas reprimanded. "I am your

Pa and Mrs. Brinkman is your Ma. Do not refer to me as pastor or mister, unless you're introducing me to someone."

The tone of his Pa's voice shook Nik somewhat. "Yes, sir," Nik responded in surprise. "I'm sorry, is that okay?"

"I will accept sir," Douglas said with a smile. "As long as I only hear it out of respect. However, I prefer to be addressed out of love."

"Yes, Pa," Nik said, with a broad smile.

That was all the reassurance Nik needed. He knew where he stood as a Brinkman, and as an American. He decided he would put God first, family second and America would have to earn third.

Accepting his role as one of the family, Nik seldom missed an opportunity to help Ma, who did most of the teaching. He also assisted her in the kitchen, helping with the cooking and cleaning. During the canning season, Patricia put him in charge of cleaning the canning jars. He would build a fire outside and boil a large pot of water in which to place the jars. Using tongs to pull the jars out to cool and dry, he would transport them into the kitchen where Patricia and Dolly were busy cooking. After the jars were filled and sealed, he would label them and carry them into the cellar.

He used the experience to write an essay on planting, harvesting, and canning. He gave it to his brother to read, and it so impressed Roger that he persuaded Muddleman to allow him to read it in class.

After school, the teacher asked Roger and Dolly to stay over for a few minutes before leaving for home.

"Please tell Nik that is one of the finest term papers I have heard in some time," Middleman said. "It is a shame he cannot be here to do it himself. Perhaps, one day, that will all change."

"We really appreciate what you are doing for him, Mr. Muddleman," Roger said. "It is hard for me to understand it all."

"Nik is really smart," Dolly chimed in. "Ma said he learns so fast it's hard for her to stay ahead of him."

"Come on, you two, I'll take you home," Muddleman said, standing up and smiling at Dolly's remark. "I think you Brinkmans just may set new standards for this country."

Nik's progress was such that he was able to help Dolly with her schoolwork and he became more involved in the church. In Sunday School, he delighted other classes with his tales of what life was like as a boy growing up in Africa.

As Christmas approached, Pastor Brinkman determined he had waited long enough for Roland Bagget to return to church, so he rode into town and strode into Bordertown's bank. He walked straight to the president's office and knocked on the door. He heard the shuffle of footsteps, and the door suddenly opened.

"Pastor Brinkman," Bagget said. "What brings you here?"

"I believe you know, Roland," Brinkman said, removing his hat and holding it in front of him with both hands. "It has been a while since I've seen you in church."

"Oh, that," Roland said, turning and retreating to his desk. Once he sat down, he continued: "I've been real busy, lately, Reverend. A lot of folks are struggling with their mortgages."

"I'm struggling with something too, Roland," Douglas deadpanned. "I think you stopped coming to church because of Nik."

"Well, I've got to admit his presence came as somewhat of a shock," the banker said, as he leaned back in his chair. "It is highly irregular, you understand."

"Look, Roland, I'm willing to meet you halfway on this. I know this is a slave state, and you once tried to buy slaves to run your farm. That was your right, but it didn't work out," the pastor began. "I bought a slave for a different reason, to raise him as one of our own to show our children, and yours too for that matter, that he's no different than they are."

"That's where you're wrong, Pastor," Roland said, his hands folded across his stomach, while still reclined. "There will always be a difference."

Pastor Brinkman stared at Bagget for the better part of a minute and then asked: "Roland, how long have you been going to my church?"

"I became a member about the time that church was built. In fact, it was this bank's money that financed it," Bagget said. "That's almost ten years ago."

"Then it makes sense why you are no longer in attendance," Brinkman remarked, keeping his eyes on the banker as he spoke. "In all that time I haven't taught you a damn thing." Brinkman restored his hat to his head and turned to walk out.

"I'm one of your biggest donors, Pastor," Bagget said, as he leaned forward placing his folded hands on the desk. "You know that church has a mortgage to pay. I hope you have a plan on how to do that now that you're losing memberships."

Brinkman stopped, and when Bagget finished speaking, he turned around and said: "Like we always have…, with God's help. Good day, Roland," Brinkman opened the office door and walked out.

Chapter 5

Nik Brinkman was never told of the prejudice Roland Bagget held for him, but he was not naïve to his circumstances. There were places and people he was to avoid and given half-hearted explanations as to why. The issue of slavery went beyond bonded labor; it also involved the shade of his skin. He learned what troubled some folks was that he did not fit the stereotype of a black slave. He was smart, quick-witted, hardworking, and loving. He not only could quote parts of the Bible, but he personified them as well. He did stand out but that was because he was the only Negro in Bordertown.

In response to those who considered it poor practice to have a former slave as a member of the family, the Brinkmans let it be known that would not change. As more local children got to know Nik, his circle of friends grew substantially, and some adults who had defected from the church started to return. But one who did not was Gloria's father, Tom Fenton.

The Fentons were struggling to keep their farm out of foreclosure. Tom told Pastor Brinkman he had to work weekends to keep his farm solvent. However, Douglas suspected Tom was being pressured by Roland Bagget to defect or fall out of favor with the bank.

"Pa, does it bother you that Nik Brinkman attends church?" Gloria asked her father one day, as they worked together.

Tom Fenton paused a moment, removed his hat, and wiped his forehead with a handkerchief. "Gloria," he said, turning to his daughter, "I like Nik well enough, but his coming here has stirred up trouble. I cannot give up my Sundays for church."

"But Pa, it's only a few hours out of your day," Gloria said, half pleading. "It makes Ma and me uncomfortable the way folks ask about you."

"Sweetheart, it pains me to say this, but things have not been the same since Nik showed up," Tom answered, with a look of hurt on his face. "I don't blame Nik, but the Brinkmans have done something folks think ain't natural, and I can't afford to go against 'em."

"It's Roland Bagget, isn't it, Pa?" Gloria said.

"Girl, let it go. I've said all I'm going to say," Tom responded, putting his hat back on. "Now let's get back to work."

To keep the church from financial difficulties, Patricia Brinkman increased her canned produce sales, thanks to help from Nik, Gloria and most of Greta Bagget's Sunday School class. Greta Bagget also secretly drew on her inheritance and donated the money to the church to help keep it out of debt.

Roger helped whenever possible, but after graduating with honors from the Bordertown School, he was kept busy studying and corresponding with Concordia Seminary in St. Louis, which he planned to attend. He also spent as much time as he could with Gloria, and they often hinted of sharing their life together after Roger became an ordained minister.

As Nik matured, he learned to cope with the bias some held toward him. The fact no one in Bordertown owned a slave helped him keep the issue in perspective. His heart ached for those like him who continued to live in slavery. But most folks in town grew to accept Nik, not only as a Brinkman, but as a young man willing to help others in any way he could. Still, he could not help but feel responsible for the sacrifices the Brinkmans made on his behalf

"I regret I have caused hard feelings in Bordertown by being here," Nik said, after building up his courage to speak of the subject at the dinner table.

"Why would you say that?" Roger asked, looking over at his brother.

"I know how some have reacted to me, and I believe they are blaming you for it," Nik replied, glancing at Roger and giving Pastor Brinkman a woeful look.

Douglas dabbed his mouth with his napkin and laid it on the table. "Nik, those negative feelings are not confined to Bordertown," the pastor said. "Some may be expressing dissatisfaction with us for making you a Brinkman, but that's just an excuse. Their ill will runs much deeper than that."

Douglas explained how slavery had poisoned the country and why those imported from Africa were seen as being of a lower class.

"Dark skin became a symbol of racial hatred and there are some who think it improper for you to be the son of white parents. But it's important you realize we are all in this together," Douglas continued. "They may pick on you, but they dislike this family for what we have done."

"It's important you stay grounded in the fact that you are a Brinkman, period," Patricia assured. "We know you were not born in America, but that makes no difference to us or to God. None of this is a problem unless you see it that way."

"You're our brother," Dolly said, tears welling up in her eyes. "You're not thinking about running away or something, are you?"

"Nik's not going anywhere," Roger said, answering Dolly and turning to his brother. "As Christians, we must finish what Pa started and without you that would not be possible."

"Jesus once said to his disciples, 'If the world hates you, you know it hated me before it hated you,'" Douglas concluded. "Nik, when you turned your life over to Christ, you no longer belonged to this world."

Nik was sitting up straight and looked each Brinkman in the eye. "I guess I was just going through another episode of poor me," he said. "Without me, your problem would not exist. But I understand Roger's point as to my role. What you have done illustrates how a change of attitude can break down racial barriers and bring people together."

"Well put, Nik," Douglas concluded. "As Christians, we have to stand together."

Over the years, Roger grew slightly taller than Nik, but his African brother was broader in the shoulders. Nik was lean but strong and was becoming increasingly more self-assured. He supported Roger's career move and accepted that he might never be given a chance to attend college. Besides, he considered the Brinkman farm to be his future and rarely thought otherwise. He had grown comfortable referring to Douglas and Patricia as "Pa" and "Ma," and though he held fond memories of his mother in Africa, he thought of himself to be no less of a Brinkman than Roger.

As summer faded into fall, the time drew near for Roger to leave home and go off to seminary. He had long made up his mind to follow in his father's footsteps and had no trouble getting accepted into Concordia University in St. Louis. He felt saying goodbye to Gloria to be a private matter and asked that she not be at the station when he boarded the train. Instead, he spent the evening before his departure with her.

"I'm going to miss you, Roger," Gloria said, as they strolled about the Fenton farm, hand in hand. "A lot," she concluded, giving Roger's hand a slight squeeze.

"Don't make it any harder for me than you have to," Roger said, with a pained expression on his face. "You will be here with family and all our friends, and I'll be in a place I've never even seen before."

"Don't worry, Roger, we'll all be here when you get back," Gloria answered. "Besides, you're the one going off on a new adventure while the rest of us are back here doing the same old thing."

"Sorry, I guess I'm just getting too much into myself," Roger replied, as the two sat down on a bench in the front of the Fenton home. "It's just that I've never been out of Bordertown before and already I'm feeling powerful lonely."

"Lonely?" Gloria said, with a small laugh. "You'll be in a city full of people and a university, besides. There's probably a lot of pretty girls back there, I'm sure." Gloria turned her head and gave Roger a smile that begged for reassurance.

"Oh yeah, I hadn't thought about that!" Roger said, breaking into a wide grin and then laughing. Gloria gave him a hard slap on the arm, followed by a "wrong answer" look.

"You know that's not going to happen," Roger consoled. "My folks would kill me if I didn't spend my spare time studying or helping the pastor where I'll be staying. Besides, I plan to write you every day."

"Don't promise that, Roger," Gloria responded. "I certainly can't promise to answer you every day, not with the work I will have to be doing here."

Roger stood up and extended his hand for Gloria to join him. "We've known each other too long to be thinking crazy ideas," the college-bound Brinkman said, as Gloria took his hand and stood beside him. "I'm going to miss you so much. I just hope I can keep my mind on my studies."

"Roger, just promise me you'll pull yourself together and do the right thing," Gloria said, in a mildly demanding tone. "I am counting on you." With that, she pulled Roger close and kissed him hard. "Just remember that!" she concluded.

Roger stared at her for a moment and said, "Wow, after that how could I forget?"

They both laughed, as the two slowly strolled back to Gloria's front porch and said their goodbyes.

The next day, the dreaded moment of saying goodbye to his family arrived. His bags were packed and placed in the carriage where his father sat waiting to take him to the train station. Roger patted his coat pocket to assure himself he had his train ticket, as he stepped onto the porch.

Patricia Brinkman had prepared some food items for Roger to take with him, and Dolly had given him one of her favorite possessions, a white stone. It was something she had found by the river during a family picnic. It had been polished by the flowing water and was of little value other than what it meant to her.

"Are you sure you want to give me that, sis?" Roger questioned, knowing how much she treasured the keepsake.

"That's why I want you to have it," Dolly answered. "When you are lonely, it will let you know how much we love you."

Roger had stoically prepared for this moment, but his sister's gesture ripped a big hole in his bravado. Roger choked back his emotions, put the stone in his pocket, and kissed his sister. He quickly pulled his mother close to avoid seeing the tears in her eyes, and then quickly turned to Nik.

"Well, brother, it's time for you take over all the duties I'm leaving behind," he said, struggling to keep his voice steady. "Somehow it doesn't seem fair, but I know you can handle it."

"I may not be able to shoot as well as you do, but I'll do my best to handle the rest," Nik replied. Nik felt more pride for his brother than sorrow. He embraced Roger in an effort to ease his brother's obvious distress. "I can't replace you, so I'll just hold your place until you get back. I know you will do well at seminary," Nik continued. "We will miss you but do us proud."

Tightening his lip, Roger nodded his head and turned to go down the stairs where his father was waiting. He climbed into the buggy and took his place next to his father.

"I'll be back this afternoon," Douglas called out, waving to his wife and children. He then snapped the reins to get underway.

Roger turned and waved, while still struggling to keep his composure.

"I can't tell you how proud I am of you," Douglas said, as they rode along. "Seminary doesn't accept everyone, but you earned your admission by excelling in your studies and your parish activities."

"Thanks, Pa, I just hope I'm up to it," Roger said, his voice cracking with the sadness of separation.

"It's tough leaving home for the first time, son, but you will soon get settled into your schoolwork, and life at home will become a fond memory until you get a chance to return," Pastor Brinkman assured. "As you know, I have arranged for you to stay with Pastor Tillotson and his family, where you will be expected to help at his parish in St. Louis, as well. It's a big church, so he said it was possible he could give you some spending money, from time to time."

"Thanks, Pa, but I think I will be too busy at school to need much spending money," Roger said.

"Then save it for a rainy day or a trip home once in a while," his father responded. "It'll help you learn a little about managing your money, and it's a good lesson to know when you have a church of your own one day."

The two continued the journey to the train station lost in their own thoughts. Pastor Douglas was quietly pleased about his decision to buy custody of Nik that day years ago in Lexington. It now meant he would still have a capable son at home while one was away at college. He was also concerned about the rising hostilities between the proponents of slavery and those who opposed it. He had tried to remain neutral on the subject, though he was repulsed by the practice.

Roger's thoughts were miles away from Bordertown, even as they rode through it with people smiling and waving as they passed by. He had been preparing for this day when he was still a student attending the community's local school. But he, too, was worried about the skirmishes that were taking place along the Missouri-Kansas border fueled by the slavery issue. There had been fatalities on both sides. The hostilities meant there was a chance Nik could be mistaken for a slave in one of those raids, rather than a member of the Brinkman family. He tried to put the growing specter of civil war out of his mind and concentrate on the college experience lying ahead of him.

Douglas Brinkman eventually pulled the carriage up to the railroad station, where he and Roger climbed out and gathered the soon-to-be student's belongings. They said little as they climbed up to the depot platform and Roger checked in with the station master. The train was at least a half-hour away, so Douglas Brinkman decided to say his goodbyes and return home.

"I should be getting back, Roger. Are you okay waiting here by yourself?" Pastor Brinkman said.

"Of course, Pa, it's something I need to get used to until I reach St. Louis and my new family," Roger said, again choking back his emotions.

With that, Douglas Brinkman hugged Roger and said, "God be with you, son. Make your mother and me proud."

Pastor Brinkman then turned and left Roger standing alone on the station platform. He climbed into the coach and turned his horse to make the journey home. He gave a brief wave as he did so, hoping his son would not see the tears welling up in his eyes.

Roger simply stood and watched his father's carriage pull away, eventually disappearing behind a row of trees along the road leading back to town. He dragged his luggage over to one of the benches located on the platform. Roger sat down, put his face in his hands and let go of the tears he had been holding back. Because of it, he was delighted he chose to say goodbye to Gloria the night before.

"It's a hard thing to have to say goodbye, even when you're going off to do a good thing," a gentle voice said, as Roger wiped away his tears the best he could before looking up. There standing next to him was a woman in fine dress, complete with parasol and bonnet. The sweetness of her fragrance lifted his spirits, and her face looked like a combination of his mother's, Dolly's and Gloria's all rolled into one. "You need not be ashamed of your tears. They come only because you have great love for those you must leave behind."

"Sometimes I wonder about myself," Roger responded, regaining his composure. "I try to be strong in front of people and half the time I'm falling apart inside."

"You're not born with the strength you wish you had," said the woman. "It's the suffering you endure that helps your strength to grow. Even the suffering you feel when doing the right thing, like now."

"I don't know," Roger responded. "I guess I'm also scared about going to college. What if I fail? What will my folks think of me then?"

"You know the answer to that, Roger," the lady said in a comforting tone. "They will love you just the same, whether you succeed or fail. In their minds, your failure would not concern them. What would concern them is how you respond to it."

"I guess I'm just so darn afraid I'm going to let my family down, and I love them so much," Roger said, just as a train whistle blew. Roger turned his head to watch an approaching locomotive chug into the station. He looked back to thank the lady, but all he saw was an empty platform. The woman was gone.

His tears were gone as well, and he returned to thinking of his future in St. Louis. As the steam hissed from the engine, Roger climbed on board and before long he was seated and ready to make his way east.

A short way from Bordertown, Roger was so lost in his thoughts that the train conductor had to shake his shoulder to get his attention.

"Ticket, sir," the conductor said.

"Oh, sorry, sir, I guess I wasn't paying attention," Roger replied.

"First time away from home, son?" the conductor asked.

"Yes, yes, I'm on my way to St. Louis to attend seminary. This will be my first time there," said Roger.

"Seminary, my, an aspiring preacher, are you?" said the conductor

"Yes, sir, my father is the pastor of the church in Bordertown, where I was raised," Roger said.

"I think you're going to like St. Louis. It's considerably bigger than Bordertown," the conductor added, with a smile. "And I'm sure you will make a fine pastor, one day."

"I certainly hope so – I certainly hope so," Roger repeated, responding to the conductor's remark about becoming a "fine pastor."

"Well, if you will excuse me. I have to get along to the other passengers," the conductor concluded, as he turned and approached another traveler seated in the same car as the young Brinkman.

Roger turned to look out the window of the train and a thousand mental pictures flooded into his mind. For a time, the landscape passing by was familiar, but then it began to fade into a countryside he had not seen before. Before long he grew accustomed to the rocking of the train car, and soon he was enjoying some of the food his mother had packed for him.

The trip was long, wending its way to eastern Missouri, and Roger spent much of his time in deep thought or reading his Bible. He did engage some of the other passengers in brief conversations but mostly sat by himself. He was delighted when the locomotive pulling his car finally chugged into the St. Louis Depot.

Pastor Tillotson and his wife, Edna, were at the train depot to greet him, along with their youngest son, William. He was also a seminary student and a couple of years older than Roger.

"You must be Roger Brinkman?" Pastor Tillotson said, approaching Roger as he stepped off the train. "I'm Glen Tillotson, and this is my wife, Edna, and son William."

After introductions, Roger's luggage was loaded into the Tillotson's coach, one much larger than the one owned by the Brinkmans. As they rode along, Roger was amazed by the size of the buildings in St. Louis, and the sheer number of them. He could not take his eyes off the enormity of the city. He often had to ask the Tillotsons to repeat their questions because he could not pull his attention away from his new surroundings.

They eventually arrived at a huge stone church, something his father had often spoken about. It rose almost to the point that Roger could not see the top of it without craning his neck out past the roof of the buggy. Pastor Tillotson drove the carriage around the church and then into an alley, where the Tillotsons' home was located. The house was considerably larger than the one the Brinkmans had in Bordertown. It also was made of stone and was a perfect match for the church. There was a small front yard and a well-maintained wooden, three-foot-high fence around it. They turned onto a small lane that led to the back of the house where a small stable and carriage house stood. William told his parents to take Roger into the house while he took care of the horse and buggy. Glen and Edna then led Roger into their home and took him straight to his room. The room they had for him was well beyond what he had imagined.

His room contained a bed flanked by a dresser and nightstand, each adorned with a kerosene lamp. Against one wall were a desk and chair. There was a small fireplace with plenty of wood stacked on a wrought-iron stand next to it. A crucifix was fastened to the wall above his bed, and a Bible was placed neatly on the desk. There was a window between his bed and the adjacent wall where his desk stood. The scene from the window was partially blocked by tall buildings, but it did give Roger a limited view of downtown St. Louis.

"I hope you'll find this room to your liking," said Pastor Tillotson. "You also have the run of the house, with the exception of the other bedrooms."

"The bathroom is down the hall and on your left," Edna said. "You will be glad to know that this home and the church have modern plumbing facilities. I do not know what you're used to in Bordertown, but our bathroom should meet all your needs. There are plenty of washcloths, towels and such under the cabinet containing the sink."

"Thank you," Roger said, while looking about the room with almost the same fascination that greeted him when he first laid eyes on St. Louis.

After settling in, Roger satisfied his curiosity by visiting the bathroom. He was amazed to find that a turn of a faucet handle produced clean water and a pull on the cord of the water closet flushed the toilet.

The wonders of life in the city soon began to crowd out the sadness of leaving home. The Tillotsons were extremely gracious, and William began telling Roger all about life at a seminary and what to expect. Roger also mentioned his plan to write to his family daily, and Edna suggested he write one short letter a day and then mail them all together each week. Roger took her advice and saved his daily tomes chronologically. He would turn over his "diary" of notes to Mrs. Tillotson, who would put them in an envelope and mail it for him. He wrote to Gloria once a week.

After a few days had passed since Roger's arrival, William Tillotson treated Roger to a tour of the seminary. Concordia University in St. Louis was barely ten years old but had an enrollment of more than five hundred students.

"This is a lot to take in. We had just fifteen students in our school at Bordertown and not all were of the same age," Roger said to William, as they climbed the steps leading into the seminary.

"I'm sure it is a bit overwhelming for someone coming from a small town in western Missouri," William said. "It wasn't as much of a transition for me. My high school had more than fifty students, and I was able to watch this college being built. As soon as they broke ground for this place, I knew I would be going here."

"I'm fortunate to have friends like you and your family," Roger said. "I don't think this would have been possible if it weren't for that."

"Your father and my Pa have been friends for quite some time," William said. "They began planning for you to attend seminary several years ago."

"I just hope I can live up to expectations," Roger said. "I only wish there wasn't all this trouble going on in the country. This slavery thing has a lot of people upset."

"It's a terrible thing, all right," William responded. "I just think Missouri ought to be opposed to it."

"There's been a lot of trouble along the Kansas-Missouri border where I grew up," Roger said. "I guess being on the border is how our town got its name."

As they talked, the two entered the school library. The sight of its cathedral ceiling with rows and rows of books leading up to it was a sight Roger could not have fathomed.

"Wow, look at all the books," Roger said, awed by the massive number of volumes lining the walls of the facility.

"Don't let it frighten you. You aren't going to be required to read all of them," William said, with a laugh, "just most of them." He gave Roger a playful push on his shoulder.

"Actually, this is a great place to study in between classes," William said. "You'll find studying at university to be a lot different than it was in your local school."

"It is a lot to take in, but I think I'm going to like it here, William," Roger responded. "It just feels like a place filled with the spirit of the Lord."

"That it is, Roger, that it is," William said.

As Roger and William continued their stroll about the campus, William would occasionally greet a passing classmate. It intrigued Roger to learn where each student they met called home. A small number came from overseas, and it stretched Roger's imagination to think anyone would travel that far to attend college. The young Bordertown resident could not help but feel a little overwhelmed, but the thought of being a student in such a magnificent setting fascinated him. After the two completed their tour, they returned to the Tillotsons' home.

Chapter 6

"Dear Pa, Ma, Dolly and Nik," Roger's letter home began, as he approached the end of his first semester at Concordia.

"If it were not for the Lord Almighty and this wonderful Tillotson family, I think I should die of homesickness. The first month was not so bad, and my studies took my mind off things at home. However, as I near the end of my first term, it is like I should be coming home, but that will not happen until spring.

I am doing well in school, and my work at the church also keeps me busy. It took time to get used to Pastor Tillotson's parish because it is so large, much like the edifice itself. It took me a week to learn where everything was, and I fear there are still some areas I have not yet found. In the beginning, I was not much help, but now I am beginning to understand the system. It is a good experience for me should I be called to be a pastor at a church of similar size. I do believe I would prefer one no bigger than Bordertown, but I will serve where the Good Lord sends me. I have even been considering missionary work.

I hope all is well at home. I try to stay out of discussions about civil war in America, but it now seems secession by some Southern states is going to happen. A student here at seminary said his state of South Carolina could trigger the secession before the end of the year. A few of the boys have even been talking about leaving school and joining the army, but they avoid saying which one. I think most here do not look favorably on slavery, but they do talk about upholding states' rights. I hate to think of any of my classmates fighting one another over such contentious issues. The election of our new president, Mr. Lincoln, seems to have not set well with those from the South and Missouri seems to be leaning that way. I am disappointed.

I have heard that Jayhawker groups from out of Kansas have stepped up their raids on those populations in Missouri that continue to hold slaves. It is a conundrum, considering there are slave holders in Kansas, as well. I hope Nik is well and none of this affects him. He is a Brinkman and belongs to no man.

Give Dolly a hug for me. Tell her I have the stone she gave me on my desk, and I take it to school with me each day. And tell her I miss her sorely, as well as all of you.

With Love, Your Son and Brother, Roger"

The letters Roger received from home were either written by his mother or Gloria Fenton. Nik would sometimes add a small note to put in Mrs. Brinkman's envelope, that mostly had to do with the farm, church, or schoolwork. Roger got the impression Nik did not venture out much since he left.

One letter was accompanied by a shipment of Patricia's canned fruit for Mrs. Tillotson to use in her baking. After receiving the goods, Edna wasted no time in baking delicious pastries and fruit pies that rivaled those of Roger's mother. The tasty treats reminded the young Brinkman of home, which fostered a mix of both comfort and melancholy.

Gloria's letters always contained words of encouragement for Roger and how much he was missed, but the letters could not hide her concern for the Fenton farm. The missives also included hints of her family moving west.

The Christmas season activities helped Roger take his mind off his homesickness, although he could not dismiss the memories of the holidays in Bordertown. In St. Louis, there was a different function at the church almost every night during December. When Roger was not busy with his schoolwork, he helped arrange special services and, when able, participated in the yuletide pageantries sponsored by the church. He sang in the choir, functioned as an usher, served meals to the needy and even traveled about St. Louis with a youth group singing carols and helping others wherever there was a need.

The campus at Concordia was also replete with scenes and activities of Christian worship for the birth of Christ. William had a part in the annual Christmas pageant and invited Roger to join in. He declined, saying he was too busy. In truth, he wanted to be free to soak it all in. He had never witnessed the joy of Christmas on such a large scale and did not want to miss any of it.

By the semester's end, Roger's grades at seminary put him near the top of his class, thanks in part to William's help. William was careful not to help Roger too much, as he was aware of the negative consequences of doing that. However, he had already taken several of the courses in which Roger was enrolled. William helped the freshman to better understand his professors and what they expected from their students.

What was most helpful, and a joy for Roger, were the Tillotson family discussions concerning theology and philosophy. What he learned helped him stay ahead of a majority of those in his class. Roger shared that knowledge during organized study groups held in the library from time to time.

Meanwhile, North vs. South tensions were growing. Roger buried himself in his studies and church work to help block out news of the nation's mounting hostilities. Staying busy did ease his mind, but he could not escape the growing concern for his family. They lived on a Missouri border that came to be known as Bleeding Kansas.

Seven southern states had seceded from the Union by the time Fort Sumter, South Carolina, was overrun by Rebel forces – the nation was officially at war.

As summer approached, Roger prepared to return to Bordertown to spend a couple of months on the Brinkman farm. He wondered if his hometown would be different now. He wondered if those he knew would view him differently. If seminary had changed him, he was not aware of it. He missed everyone, especially Gloria, but that opened a brief feeling of dread. What if something about her had changed, or worse, what if there was something about him she would not like?

Finally, Roger chuckled at himself for entertaining such self-important thoughts. His insides ached counting the hours until he would see everyone again. Did he really think Gloria would not be Gloria or the family would be overwhelmed by his "new maturity?" Or that Nik wouldn't chide him for such ideas? He silently prayed to have such notions purged from his head and quietly laughed at his folly.

Upon departure, the Tillotsons said their goodbyes and William drove Roger to the depot. The air was warm and muggy, fed by the steam of locomotives traveling in and out of St. Louis.

"I know you're anxious to get home," William said, as they approached the ticket office. "But I hope you'll be equally anxious to return. My family has really enjoyed having you, and you're rapidly becoming a star pupil at Concordia."

"I will be happy to see everyone in Bordertown again," Roger answered, flashing a smile William's way. "But it would be foolish of me to turn my back on my future now. You and your parents have become like family to me."

Roger was sincere, but he could not deny his anxiety over the civil unrest threatening the very foundation of the country. Though highly unlikely, he secretly hoped the war could be over before school began again.

"Wonderful," William said, returning the smile. "We shall look forward to your return."

The two young men shook hands, and Brinkman boarded the train for home.

Roger was surprised to find Nik waiting for him at the Bordertown Depot. They hugged and laughed, almost embarrassed struggling to find words to express their joy over being together again. They quickly loaded the Brinkman buggy and set out for the family farm.

"Whooee, is everyone anxious to see you," Nik said, turning to Roger in the seat next to him. "Especially Gloria, she is fit to be tied waiting for you."

"How do I look, Nik?" Roger asked, his anxiety catching up to him again.

"How do you look?" Nik fairly shouted with a laugh. "You look like Roger Brinkman, and that's a fine way to look right now. Everybody's busting a gut to see you."

A good deal of Roger's apprehension melted with Nik's comment, as the returning seminary student felt a wave of comfort come over him. He knew if Nik were aware of any of the self-doubts, he imagined about returning home he would never hear the end of it. He quickly changed the subject.

"So, how have things been, brother? Any big changes?"

"The biggest change will be having you here," Nik said, casting a reassuring glance at Roger. "If there's anything you don't recognize it's because your memory isn't as good as it used to be."

The two boys, now almost fully grown, had a good laugh over that one.

"So, has everything been okay with you and all?" Roger asked, his words rolled out awkwardly as he fumbled for the right words.

Nik looked over at his brother for a moment and spoke. "You mean, have I had any trouble being a black member of the family?" Nik said.

"I feel stupid for bringing it up," Roger stammered, "but I do worry about such things."

"Well, brother, every now and then I hear a comment I don't like, but I brush it off," Nik started. "I can't change that about some people, it's just the way of things. Sometimes I feel like bustin' a head or two, but Pa cautions me about such things, and I listen to that man."

Roger's face grew serious. "I just hope I can show the same restraint if I ever witness such bigoted rudeness," he said. "What, in the Good Lord's name, is wrong with some people?"

"Relax, Roger," Nik said, with a slight grin. "This world is like that. When those things happen, I fill my mind with you, Ma, Pa, Dolly and all the good folks that treat me no differently than they treat each other.

"They killed Jesus, brother," Nik said, turning to look straight ahead. "Why in heaven's name would anyone want to do that? It's just the world we live in," Nik concluded.

The two rode the rest of the way mostly more subdued, chatting about mundane issues like the weather. Gloria was at the Brinkman's farm when Roger arrived and, with a big hug, squeezed out whatever remaining doubts he had. Although everything was pretty much as he remembered, the serenity was tarnished by the growing echoes of battle. It affected nearly all those living in America, including Nik.

During Roger's summer break, he and Nik curtailed their love of hunting together for fear the gunshots could be mistaken for an attack. Kansas Jayhawkers and Missouri Bushwhackers had clashed several times, each representing an opposing side of the war. But not all marauding Jayhawks were true to their free-soil claim. Although the Kansas territory was considered anti-slavery, not all Jayhawk raiders viewed it that way. They often took slaves under the guise of freedom, only to hold them in bondage as "servants."

Roger also spent days working on the Fentons' farm, discerning the family's troubles by reading between the lines of Gloria's letters. Their crop production had been terrible, and the farm's water supply dropped, as the summer days grew warmer.

"Curse this ground. Curse the day we bought this farm," Tom Fenton said, while he and Roger worked to improve the irrigation system. Unfortunately, the Fentons' water table was unpredictable, and there were times the family had to borrow water from their neighbors just to have enough for themselves.

"It's been tough for you, hasn't it, Mr. Fenton?" Roger commented.

"Too tough, Roger. I think if it were not for the help you and your family have given us, we would have walked away from this farm long ago," Tom added. "I think myself a fool for buying this place simply because it was the cheapest in the area. I thought I was getting a deal, but I did not thoroughly investigate why the price was so low. I'm paying for that now and struggling just to meet our mortgage payments."

After each day's work, Roger had a standing invitation to stay over for dinner. Roger would bring food from home to supplement the meals, but his main reason for volunteering was to spend more time with the Fentons' daughter.

"I think your Pa is worried you folks might lose this place," Roger said, while he and Gloria sat on the bench in front of the house enjoying the cool evening air.

"He has mentioned selling it and maybe moving west to try homesteading," Gloria said, as she lowered her gaze onto her bare feet. She had shoes for school and social events, but in summer she wore weather-beaten boots and took them off at day's end to cool her feet.

"I get your letters at school and worry you might not be here the next time I come home," Roger said, leaning forward to prop his elbows on his knees and placing his chin into the palms of his hands. "It might be hard finding you if you moved out West," he added, turning his head to look at her.

"We can stay in touch, Roger," Gloria said, as she returned his gaze. "I'm nearly old enough now to set out on my own if Ma and Pa do leave."

"What would you do? Where would you live?" Roger inquired.

"Oh, I don't know," Gloria said, wearing a sly smile. "Maybe I would move in with your folks."

"What?" Roger said, straightening up and looking at Gloria while trying to smile back. "And have you hanging out with Nik while I'm gone. Next thing you know I'll be coming back to find out you're his girl."

Gloria laughed out loud. "I'm just kidding," she said. "I like Nik, but not the way I like you. Besides, with this war going on, a beau like Nik would only stir up trouble with those who do not know Nik like you and I do. We have enough problems as it is."

Roger felt embarrassed by his sudden display of sheepish jealousy. He managed to smile through it as he looked down at his own scuffed-up boots. "You're right about that. It seems some folks are having trouble accepting Nik as a Brinkman. This war is tearing families apart. Every time I think of it, it reminds me of how different things would have been for Nik were it not for Pa."

"Just stay out of that terrible war if you can, Roger," Gloria said, now staring into Roger's eyes. "Stay in school and become a man like your Pa. Who knows, it could mean doing something like Pa did for someone else."

Roger managed a slight grin. He reached his arm behind Gloria to grab her shoulder and gently pull her head against his. They sat lost in their thoughts while a full Missouri moon rose silently over the horizon, making it a night they wished would never end.

When fall rolled around, Roger's anxiety returned. But what was troubling him now was being away from his family in these uncertain times. His departure the previous year was one of sadness, but now the feeling had turned to concern. The only comforting circumstance was that most of the fighting was in the southeast, although tensions on the Kansas-Missouri border could not be ignored.

"Pa, I can't help but think I ought not return to St. Louis with this war breaking out," Roger said.

"Son, I know this is troublesome, but we need to put the Lord's work ahead of our own fears," Douglas Brinkman answered. "Just think, where we would be today if Jesus had decided to hide out in Nazareth rather than travel to Jerusalem knowing what awaited him there. Besides, the Tillotsons sing your praises, telling us how much you have grown in your faith and preparation for the future," Douglas concluded.

"But it's hard, Pa," Roger lamented. "Hardly a day goes by I don't think and worry about all of you, hundreds of miles away."

"I understand, Roger." Pastor Brinkman said, thinking "son" could make leaving even harder for him. "But until this terrible scourge in America is eliminated, we need all the help the Lord can give… and He needs ours. Comfort yourself through prayer and we will do the same."

Roger Brinkman did just that over the few nights before again boarding that train for St. Louis. He knew Nik was more than capable of helping Pa on the farm. Still, it bothered Roger knowing Nik's race was a focal point in the war.

"Nik, how do you feel about all this?" Roger asked as the two sat on the front porch together.

"Roger, you cannot know how it felt to be captured and brought to a foreign land to be sold as a slave," Nik answered, looking out over the fields and orchards. "I had so much fear in me that I eventually accepted it as normal, thinking it was going to be that way for the rest of my life," Nik continued, hoping to find the words necessary to comfort his adopted brother. "This war is a terrible thing, but it does not compare to what I felt before Pa stepped in to rescue me. This fighting is bad, but slavery just ain't natural."

Just hearing Nik refer to Pastor Brinkman as "Pa" eased the ache in Roger's heart. It was obvious his year away at school had served to draw Nik and the pastor even closer. Roger also felt Nik was beginning to understand the depth of the family's commitment to him. If there were any doubts as to Nik being a true Brinkman, they were Nik's alone.

"If it were not for this 'Bleeding Kansas' issue, I would feel better about going back to school," Roger said, turning to look at Nik. "You've grown to be more able-bodied around here than I was. Why can't I take more comfort in that?"

"Because I'm black?" Nik said, continuing to stare across the landscape.

"It kills me to hear you say that," Roger replied, leaning back in his chair and following Nik's gaze. "Why do I see you as a target for trouble?"

"Perhaps I am, Roger," Nik said, turning to look at his companion. "But we can't worry about that now. We knew years ago this would be tough, but we worked through it. Yes, this war makes it tougher, but we'll get through that, too."

"Thanks, Nik. I just have this raging battle in my head to deal with," Roger sighed, turned toward Nik and grinned. "Oh, and just for the record, its slavery 'isn't' natural," Roger added, as both laughed over the silly grammar correction, which did lighten the weight of their conversation.

The day came for Roger to return to seminary, and the departure this time was a little easier than the year before. The Brinkmans' pride in Roger's progress lessened the anxiety, making the sadness heartfelt but brief. Roger forced himself to accept that Nik and Bordertown were too removed from the war to be in harm's way, but he could not dismiss the raids along the Kansas-Missouri border.

Roger felt better, as he boarded the train for St. Louis, but what he witnessed reminded of the growing calamity in America. Upon entering his car, he saw several Confederate soldiers dressed in gray uniforms headed east. There were some men in civilian clothes, about Roger's age, talking earnestly with the soldiers about joining them. There were also young civilians who glanced at the conversationalists but sat in silence. Perhaps, they were thinking if they wore a uniform it would not be gray. Then there was Roger, trying to focus on eventually wearing the black robe of a pastor.

As the train rumbled on, Roger came to realize the trouble with riding the rails was it allowed too much time to think. Conversation may have helped, but he was too deep in thought to even try.

Chapter 7

With Roger away at school, Douglas and Nik Brinkman were hard at work completing the fall harvest. Patricia and Dolly, along with help from Marie and Gloria Fenton, were working on preserving produce for sale and charitable distribution.

As the two men strolled over the final pasture of plowed potatoes surveying what work remained, they drew near the forest where Nik and Roger had done much of their hunting. The leaves on the white oaks were just beginning to adorn their autumn colors.

There was a knoll not far from where they were walking that held one of Pastor Brinkman's favorite oak trees. During the farm's early years, he and Patricia discussed removing the tree to prepare the area for future farming. However, the tree had stood for so long they decided to keep it as a symbol of their life together. There was also the fact they could not afford the time or labor necessary to cultivate the field that contributed to their decision. What they did grow without the added land was more than enough to sustain them, as well as helping to feed others in the church and community.

"It's beautiful out here this time of year, don't you think, son?" said Douglas.

"Yes, it is, Pa," said Nik, whose memories of the distant past had faded to the point his concerns now were mostly about the Brinkman family, their farm, and church.

Nik's initial feelings of being an outsider were stirred when the war started. However, the Brinkmans reassured him the war did not involve him because, as a Christian, he was not a part of this world.

His lot in life was to help with the chores, be responsible, pray and expect no special treatment.

It was tough at first, not everyone in the community accepted him. But Pastor Douglas made it clear that with Jesus' help he could rise above life's travails, no matter what others thought.

Nik had learned to accept why he could not attend the local school with Dolly and Roger and came to appreciate the effort made to tutor him at home. Patricia explained that his circumstances were a part of a plan known only to God.

"We do not always know why God does things the way He does," Mrs. Brinkman said. "When the pastor brought you home years ago, we could not give a reason for it but knew in our hearts it was the right thing to do."

She added that Nik could either see himself as a problem or apply himself to become a part of the solution, the choice was up to him.

He was not to forget his past and the Brinkmans encouraged him to talk about it if he felt so inclined. The family also made it clear that when he was old enough, if he wanted to return to his village in Africa, he could do so. As far as they were concerned, he would go with their love and encouragement, and as a Brinkman.

By the time Roger was ready to go off to seminary, Nik's attitude and behavior had become so Brinkman that his past had been nearly forgotten.

As father and son worked their way through the fields enjoying the cool, crisp, and invigorating fall, Missouri day. Despite a war raging between the Union and Confederacy, most living in Bordertown were able to temper news of the conflict by turning their minds to the upcoming holidays. The town had a tradition of making the most of harvest time and the busy work that led up to Christmas. The battles were mostly in the East, but being a slave state, Missouri was virtually surrounded by free states.

As Nik and the pastor approached the oak tree, there was an uneasy shift in the atmosphere. Douglas Brinkman stopped to look around and spotted a small band of riders on horses rapidly making their way toward them. Nik glanced over at his father and noticed a change in his expression. He followed the pastor's gaze and caught sight of the fast-approaching group, numbering six in all.

"Stay by me, Nik," Pastor Brinkman said, "and do just as I say."

"Yes sir," said Nik.

As the horsemen drew nearer, the one in the lead was wearing a blue jacket and a dark slouch hat. Both items were noticeably ill-fitting and threadbare. His trousers were without an officer's stripe and tucked inside unpolished boots, while his troops looked more like refugees than soldiers.

"Can I help you?" Douglas Brinkman asked, as the ragtag cavalry drew near.

"I'm Colonel Curtain of the United States Army and I see you have a slave with you. How many slaves do you own?" said Curtain, using a matter-of-fact tone. He placed one hand on the back of his saddle to help turn his overweight body, as he rose in his stirrups. He scanned the area to determine if the two men on the ground were alone.

"I don't own any slaves," Brinkman answered.

"Then who is that with you?" Curtain said, leaning forward in his saddle and nodding toward Nik. The move exposed a scar on the man's neck that resembled a rope burn.

"That's my son, Nik Brinkman," Douglas said without hesitation.

"Son? Is his mother a slave, too?" Curtain said.

"Like I said, there are no slaves on this property," Brinkman answered.

Like Roger, Nik was no longer a boy and well on his way to adulthood. His frame was lean and muscular, and his countenance mature. His vigorous appearance was unlike that of the downtrodden, melancholy slaves Curtain was used to.

Pastor Brinkman could tell the colonel's interest in Nik was not to set him free. Jayhawk raids were not uncommon, but slaves were rarely the beneficiary of them.

"I was not aware of any Union patrols in this area," Brinkman said. "There are no slaves here, so state your business and be on your way."

"I would say the evidence says otherwise," Curtain noted, growing impatient with a discussion he did not understand or care to. He again scanned the horizon. "I am afraid I am going to have to relieve you of this..., ah, 'Nik,' did you call him?"

"Nik isn't going anywhere, especially with you," Brinkman said.

"According to the Confiscation Act, I am under orders to do this," the portly rider said, while laying his fingers on the handle of his holstered pistol. "We can do this easy-like or by force, however you wish."

Realizing the gravity of the situation, Brinkman turned his head toward Nik and said in a subdued voice "Run, Nik!"

"But, sir ...," Nik responded in a hoarse whisper.

"Run! Dammit, Nik, RUN!" shouted Brinkman.

With that, Nik was off like a deer heading for the woods. His father's tone and swearing frightened him, and he was now running on adrenalin. He was aware the situation was dangerous and literally flew across the field.

"Damn!" shouted Curtain. "Jake! Fetch that boy!" he called out.

A rider mounted next to the colonel's side spurred his horse to give chase. As his steed sped by Brinkman, the pastor grabbed the animal's rein and jerked its head around. The horse stumbled and threw the rider from his saddle. Curtain drew his pistol and fired. Douglas crumpled to the ground, as the shooter quickly looked around.

"Well, what are you waiting for!" he shouted at the remaining squad. "Go after that colored boy. I want him!"

Pastor Brinkman lay on the ground with blood flowing from his chest. Curtain fidgeted in his saddle and stared down at the dying man with a menacing expression.

The four horsemen still mounted, startled by the sudden turn of events, regained their composure and rode after the fleeing youth, now lost among the trees.

Patricia Brinkman was in the kitchen when she heard the shot and started out the front door onto the porch. She could see the oak tree in the distance and the mounted man near it. She saw four riders galloping across the field, but neither Douglas nor Nik were in sight. Seized by terror, she hurried back into the house. Without saying a word, she grabbed Dolly and headed into the cellar.

Nik had a significant head start on his pursuers and knew the forest well. He stripped off his light-colored shirt and discarded it. He soon came to a large tree that had been a favorite of the Brinkman boys to climb. It was tall and thick with autumn foliage, and an excellent place to hide. In an instant, Nik scaled its trunk and disappeared in a covering of leaves. He climbed up to a large limb and sat on it, out of sight from below. Nik pulled his knees up with his arms and buried his head between them. His heart was pounding as he struggled to control his breathing and remain as quiet as possible.

Curtain's riders found it difficult to navigate through the thick underbrush. One, spotting Nik's shirt, called the others over where he found the garment resting among the brambles. After a brief survey, he ordered the men to spread out and continue searching. Nik could hear the horses crash through the thick brush, but he did not move. The men stopped frequently to observe and listen, but there were only trees to see, and the sound of leaves rustling in the wind. After a futile search, they heard Curtain call out. He had reached the edge of the woods where he waited. The man called "Jake" had remounted and was riding up behind him.

"Well, did you find him?" the large man inquired as his men surrounded him.

"No sign of him, colonel," the lead rider replied.

"Damn, I would like to have that boy," Curtain said under his breath. "Surely he could not have gone far. He must be hiding somewhere," he called out. "Jake, send three men back into the woods after him. The rest of you come with me."

The men were now some distance away, but Nik could still hear their voices. He quietly climbed higher in the tree for a better view of the surroundings. He saw the man referred to as "colonel" ride back toward the knoll, taking two men with him. The disturbance the three riders made as they re-entered the woods told Nik they were now moving away from him. Once their sounds diminished,

Nik quietly descended onto the original limb he was on and listened.

Curtain and his group put the pastor's lifeless body on the back of one of the horses, and the three rode off in the direction of the farmhouse. They circled behind the house near the woods and called the three searchers to rejoin them.

"Sorry, colonel, we couldn't find any trace of the kid, other than that shirt," the first rider exclaimed, emerging from the forest.

"That doesn't matter, now," Curtain replied. "We put the farmer's body in the house and need to burn it down."

"Is there anyone else inside?" Jake questioned.

"We don't have time to worry about that," the colonel replied. "We just need to make sure we don't leave any witnesses behind. After that, we hightail it out of here."

Nik's mind raced as he sat in the tree. Having heard the shot, he was certain he could not help Pastor Brinkman. He was anxious to reach the house to make sure Mrs. Brinkman and Dolly were all right. He strained to hear any new sounds, only to be startled by the sudden smell of smoke.

Nik's immediate thought was that the horsemen had set the woods on fire to drive him out into the open. He lowered himself to another branch but did not detect fire. He again listened carefully and could hear a crackling sound in the distance. If it were fire, why was it started so far from where he entered the forest?

His courage began to push back his fears, and he dropped down out of the tree. He quietly edged his way toward the field, while staying out of sight. Nik saw all six riders galloping back toward the knoll where the great oak stood. He ducked low and watched as they sped over the hill and disappeared.

Unbeknown to Nik, Patricia Brinkman and Dolly had descended into the cellar, locking the door behind them. They found some barrels containing produce and used them to hide behind. Patricia held her hand over Dolly's mouth to quiet her while trying to control her own breathing. She heard some men enter the home but quickly leave. She heard shouts coming from outside and patiently waited for them to disappear when a new terror welled up inside her.

"Mommy, I smell smoke," Dolly said in a muffled voice behind her hand.

"Just stay low, honey," Patricia said. She could tell the smoke was flowing from beneath the locked door and was paralyzed knowing it was their only means of escape.

"Mommy, I'm scared. It's hard to breathe," Dolly said, as her mother removed her hand.

"I know, baby. I'm scared, too," Patricia Brinkman said, "Just keep your head down and pray."

Patricia Brinkman was now aware the only chance she and Dolly had to survive was to stay below the fire. By grace, the smoke overcame them before the flames did.

Convinced the riders were gone, Nik stepped out of the woods. To his horror, he could see it was the farmhouse that was on fire!

He raced toward it, but the flames were too intense to approach. He began to sob uncontrollably and dropped to his knees. Blind with grief, Nik regained his footing and stumbled back into the forest.

Numb with fear and misery, the young Brinkman made his way back to where he had left his shirt and retrieved it. All he could think to do was go deeper into the woods and run away. Without the Brinkman family, he was all alone in the world with nowhere to go. As tears ran down his face, Nik continued working his way deeper into the forest.

Nik stumbled as he went, oblivious to where he was going or where he would end up. Behind him was a love and joy he once thought he would never experience in this new world, but he did. Now it was gone, destroyed by an evil he believed he had escaped.

***

Several hundred miles away, at Concordia University, Roger Brinkman was again deep into his studies to block out the nagging fears he had for his family's safety. But the joy of education was quickly eroding, as stories of battles and bloodshed were fast becoming the lessons of the day. Many of the holiday wonders he had enjoyed the previous year were now minimized through default or decree. As he sat in the library trying to concentrate on his schoolwork, William Tillotson approached.

"Roger," William said. "I'm afraid it may be time for you to go."

"Is the library closing?" Roger asked.

"I think you may be needed at home, actually," William said, choosing his words carefully.

"At home?" Roger asked, unsure of what he was hearing. The urgency in William's voice and his noticeable effort to say as little as possible told Roger something was wrong.

"Yes, I will give you a lift back to the house," William continued. "I think my dad has something to tell you."

Roger sensed he was not going to get much more information out of William. He saw urgency in William's face but uncertainty as well. The young Brinkman gathered his books and followed his friend to the Tillotsons' buggy. They rode in silence and the intensity with which William drove made Roger's uneasy feeling even worse. Soon they arrived at the parish home.

When Roger entered the house, Mr. and Mrs. Tillotson were waiting for him. They had his bags packed and were standing in the middle of the living room floor.

"What's going on?" Roger inquired.

"Son, I think you had best go home. We've gotten word that there's been trouble in Bordertown, and we took the liberty of securing your train ticket," Glen Tillotson said, as he and Edna picked up his bags and herded him back out the door. "I'm sorry I don't have more information for you, but the telegram from home said 'urgent,' and nothing more."

Pastor Tillotson was not telling Roger the whole truth about the telegram, but he and his wife felt the train ride back to Bordertown would be easier if Roger did not know its entire contents.

Unfortunately, that left Roger to his fears and imagination. He questioned the Tillotsons as he climbed back into the buggy with William, but they offered nothing but their goodbyes. The Tillotsons loaded his luggage into the back of the carriage and William popped the reins. Roger leaned out of the carriage and looked back at the couple now standing motionless and fading from view.

"William, I have to say this is strange and frightening," Roger pleaded. "Please tell me what you know about this."

"I really don't know, Roger. I was just told to bring you back to the house and get you to the train station," William answered, glancing over at Roger and noting the worried look on his face. "This damn war has everyone in an uproar. It may-be it has become necessary to close the schools and send everybody home."

"Couldn't they just say that?" Roger inquired, not really knowing who he meant by "they."

"Roger, we may all end up in the army before this is all over," William said, now staring straight ahead. "I just hope guys like you and I never have to meet on a battlefield somewhere. Please, just pray for an end to this thing."

Roger turned his gaze onto the road ahead, as the carriage sped along. He fought the temptation to think the worst and tried to say a silent prayer. Lost in his thoughts, he was almost unaware that William had stopped the buggy and was unloading Roger's bags.

After just a short wait, Roger boarded the first west-bound train that came through and offered an uncertain goodbye wave to William standing on the platform. His friend appeared as strained as what Roger felt in his stomach.

After finding a seat, the bewildered Brinkman sat down and fought to control the terrors preying on his mind. He reached into his pocket where Dolly's stone should have been, only to realize he must have left it behind in the rush to leave. He hoped the Tillotsons had packed it for him. He tried to comfort himself by envisioning how upset his sister would be discovering he came home without the gift she gave him.

Chapter 8

Roger Brinkman's mind had been in a whirl after saying his goodbyes to the Tillotsons and boarding the train. He stared out the passenger car window sorting through all the reasons why he was on a train headed for Bordertown. Normally, he would be delighted to be going home, but not like this. There were too many unanswered questions. In fact, there were no answered questions, just an urgent telegram from the sheriff in Bordertown. Why not a word from his parents or a reason why he was the one urgently asked to return home?

He did not have time to wonder how Concordia would view his sudden disappearance. He could only hope the Tillotsons would explain to the college his unannounced departure unless more students were getting the call to return home. There was no official word of that happening.

He did his best to dismiss answers to those questions for fear of what they could be. He was battling to keep his thoughts under control and did not want the answers to be left up to his imagination.

Similar to when Roger first left Bordertown on the train, the conductor had to shake him out of his trance to punch his ticket.

"Sorry, sir, but I have to have your ticket," the conductor said, raising his voice each time he repeated the phrase.

"Oh, I'm sorry, sir," Roger finally answered, his thoughts coming back to reality. "Here you go," he said, fumbling through his jacket to find his ticket, which he then handed to the conductor.

"I understand, son," the conductor said, aware of the changes that had come over travelers since the war started. After punching Roger's ticket, the conductor handed it back to his young passenger with a friendly, but inquisitive, smile and moved on.

With Roger's thoughts now more in focus, he noticed there were considerably more Confederate soldiers than civilians in the rail car he occupied. There were far more than there were a few months ago when he left Bordertown for St. Louis. As he looked about the car at all the gray uniforms, his eyes came to rest on a soldier in the seat across the aisle from him. Roger recognized him to be an officer by the broad-brimmed hat he was wearing. However, he appeared quite young, perhaps not more than four or five years older than Roger. The man did not have the rugged look of many of the soldiers Roger had encountered, his appearance was more refined, like that of a southern gentleman.

As he looked on, the soldier turned and looked back at Roger.

"Traveling alone?" the man in the broad-brimmed hat asked.

"Ah, yeah," Roger said. "I'm heading for home."

"And where might that be," the officer said.

"Bordertown," replied Roger. "I live in Bordertown."

"Bordertown," the officer repeated. "I heard there was an incident in that town a couple days ago."

"An incident?" Roger spoke in a voice that sounded as if he didn't understand what the word meant.

"Yeah, apparently some Jayhawkers hit the town. The number of such incidents has been going up on the western border of Missouri since the war started," said the officer and Citadel graduate. "This detail is headed that way, assigned to put an end to the Kansas Jayhawk raids inside Missouri."

"I certainly wish you well, officer...," the young Brinkman replied.

"Captain Ashley Baumgartner, at your service. And you are?" the captain inquired.

"Brinkman, Roger Brinkman," was Roger's answer.

"A pleasure to meet you, Roger," said the captain. "I hope your trip home proves to be a pleasant one."

Following the exchange, Brinkman fell silent again. As the evening shadows fell over the landscape outside the train, Roger tried to let the gentle rocking of the train offer him sleep, but it was of no use. Now he had the fact that an incident had taken place in Bordertown to grind away on his already unsettled stomach. When the conductor came around to lower the lights in the passenger car, Brinkman, though weary, could not sleep.

Much of the trip back to Bordertown continued that way for Roger. He would occasionally dose off to sleep, either to be awakened by the conductor, boisterous conversation or nightmarish dreams that now haunted his slumber. It was usually well into the early morning hours before sleep would come and then not for long.

While still several miles outside of Bordertown on the last leg of the train ride, Brinkman was jolted out of a fitful slumber by gunfire and the shouting of men. As his wits returned, Roger could see Confederate soldiers, with rifles ready, taking up positions along the rows of windows that lined the passenger car. A quick glance outside revealed several men on horseback riding alongside and firing indiscriminately.

"All passengers get down on the floor immediately and let the soldiers man your window seats," the Confederate captain called out.

Roger slipped from his position onto the floor and attempted to roll under the seat he was sitting in. As he adjusted himself to stay out of the way, a soldier fell in the space next to him, bleeding from a bullet wound to the head. All thoughts of safety left Brinkman's mind, as he almost instinctively grabbed the wounded soldier's weapon. Roger rolled out from under the seat with the rifle in hand and placed himself in a shooting position. He put the rifle barrel through the window that was now opened and fired. A horse fell from beneath one of the riders, sending the man sprawling. Roger then reached into the fallen soldier's ammo pouch and pulled a buck and ball cartridge from his belt and bit off the paper tip. He rapidly reloaded his musket, tamped the cartridge in place, took a cap from the soldier's pouch and was again ready to fire. The scene repeated itself when another horse crumpled to the ground.

The attack seemed to end almost as quickly as it started. The assailants began to disperse while the soldiers on the train remained at their posts. Baumgartner stooped to pull the wounded soldier from beneath the space between the seats where Roger was positioned and called to see if there was a doctor aboard the train. Soon, a man with a black bag was at the soldier's side examining the fallen Confederate.

"I'm sorry, captain, but this man is dead," said the passenger doing the examination.

"Jones, Carpenter," Baumgartner called out, "remove this man to the baggage car at once."

Two soldiers rushed to the scene. They bound the man's wound, carefully lifted his body into a carrying position and soon disappeared from the train car.

After giving the "all clear," the captain ordered his men to stand down and assist those needing help following the raid. Some passengers were badly shaken, but there were no other casualties. Roger handed the fallen soldier's weapon to the captain.

"That was some pretty good shooting, Roger. We appreciate the help," the captain said. "Where did you learn to shoot like that?"

"I used to hunt quite a bit while growing up on the farm," Brinkman said. "It sort of came natural to me."

"I noticed you shot the horses. Is that what you intended to do?" Baumgartner asked.

"I ain't never shot a man before," Roger said, letting his grammar slide due to the stress of the moment. "I was tempted, but I just couldn't bring myself to do it."

"Desperate times like these can change a man's thinking about that," Baumgartner said. "You know, we could use a man with your skills. I've been asked to create a sharpshooter unit and you would be a prime candidate."

"Sorry, captain, I'm a seminary student," Roger replied. "I don't think I would make a very good soldier."

"Well, in case you should change your mind, let me leave you some information on how you can get hold of me," said the officer. "We could use young men with the shooting skills you have. If you change your mind, get in touch with me."

"Much obliged, captain, but I'm not sure what this war is all about,"

Roger said. "My intention is to finish my education and become an ordained minister."

"It's about rights, Roger, the right for a state to do its own choosing, Lincoln and his Union boys see things differently," the officer said. "You are Missourian, are you not?"

"Yes, like I said, I'm from Bordertown," Roger answered.

"I would hate to see this new president take away your right to become a preacher," the captain cautioned. "Best you take my information, all the same."

Brinkman took the captain's contact note and stuffed it in his pocket. Just then the train began to slow for its stop in Bordertown. The change in speed took Roger's mind off the events he just experienced and turned his thoughts to the dread he feared awaiting his arrival. The knot in Roger's stomach had grown so tight he thought he was going to be sick. The train slowly came to a halt at the depot, and Roger gathered his luggage and made his way through the car's exit.

"Take care now, you hear," the captain said, as Roger passed. "You're a good man."

"Thank you, sir," Roger mumbled incoherently. His mind was fixed on what awaited him.

The returning Brinkman stepped down onto the wooden platform and his senses numbed when he did not see his family waiting for him. There to greet him were Sheriff Gus Perkins and a few members from Roger's church.

"Why aren't my folks with you?" Roger said in a cracking but loud voice, his stomach now churning in anticipation of an answer he could not bear to hear.

"I'm sorry...," Perkins began.

Roger's knees gave out and he dropped to the platform floor. Two men accompanying the sheriff quickly rushed to his side and helped him up. Although the men were speaking, Roger did not hear a word they were saying. They helped him over to one of the benches on the platform and, though his eyes were red from fatigue and worry, they produced no tears. The words of consolation and explanation could not penetrate the deep trauma, as he tried to process the tragedy. He consciously knew something terrible had happened to his family, but something would not let him confront it. He just stared straight ahead while the chatter of voices continued.

Finally, dear friend and church deacon Anthony Carrossa sat next to him, put his arm around Roger and gently rocked him.

"Roger, you are going to stay with us for a while," he said, repeating the words. "We will work through this. Just keep your faith in God and we will work through this."

When the consoling voices faded, Anthony helped Roger up and gestured to the others to help escort him to the Carrossas' carriage. One of the sheriff's associates put Roger's luggage in the back, and all crowded around to help him into the passenger's seat. Sheriff Perkins reassured the grief-stricken man that the town was there for him whatever he needed.

Anthony Carrossa was a man of slight stature and a small head that made his nose appear larger than it really was. He was strong for his size and a solid member of Douglas Brinkman's congregation. He and Douglas had become close friends over the years. His wife, Karla, and Patricia spearheaded many church functions together, and Dolly was a good friend of the Carrossa children.

Once in the buggy, Carrossa reached over and grabbed Roger's forearm and nodded before taking the reins to urge the horse forward. Roger acknowledged Anthony's gesture and looked ahead at a familiar corridor of trees that now appeared surreal. Every thought he wrestled with during his long journey home had come crashing down on him like a bad dream. It was as if he had stepped out of reality to retreat into a different world. Oddly, the only words he could recall were Captain Baumgartner's. Nothing spoken after he stepped off the train could he remember.

Carrossa was also at a loss. The kind words he had rehearsed with Karla, simply seemed totally inappropriate now. He, too, stared straight ahead and hid behind his silence.

As they rode along, Roger carefully allowed his mind to probe reality. Sheriff Perkins must have described the situation, otherwise

Anthony would have related it to him by now. That allowed him to process the gravity of the circumstance, while not really being a part of it. It was as if he were outside himself watching something surreal. Finally, Carrossa broke the silence.

"You can come and stay with us if you'd like."

Roger heard Anthony's words, but they did not stir any sensation.

"No, take me home, please," Roger said in a monotone.

Carrossa again retreated into his silence and continued steering the buggy.

Roger hardly noticed as the carriage passed through town. There were men removing their hats as the buggy went by, and many women were weeping. No one made any attempt to approach the carriage and appeared to revere it like a hearse. Roger thought prayer appropriate, but nothing came to mind.

As the road left town, it began to wind toward the Brinkmans' farm. After following the main road leading to the farmhouse, Carrossa made a slight turn away from the road to the house. When the coach rolled up a gentle slope, Roger could see the large white oak at the top of the hill, a favorite of the Brinkman family. As they drew closer, Roger could see three distinct mounds, each marked by a white cross.

Roger had allowed in enough reality to prepare him for the pain this scene would bring, but the pain never came. Perhaps fighting the terror that raged in his head during the train ride had drained his soul. Maybe the unanswered questions in St. Louis, Captain Baumgartner's comment about an incident in Bordertown or the attack on the train were now taking their toll. Why had it not done so before his collapse after he stepped onto the depot platform?

***

"What happened?" Roger deadpanned, as the carriage approached the graves.

"We figure it was a raiding party from Kansas," Carrossa said. "If you look off yonder, you can see there isn't much left of the farmhouse.

"The best we can tell, they must have spotted Nik and mistook him for a slave," said Carrossa. "It appears an altercation broke out and, well, Sheriff Perkins said it probably ended almost as fast as it started. The raiders were gone by the time anyone from town arrived to investigate where the smoke was coming from."

That comment made Roger wonder if those who attacked the train were the same men who killed his family. Was that why he instinctively took up that fallen soldier's rifle and joined the fight? Such ideas made him regret shooting only the horses.

Carrossa halted his horse on the crest of the hill, and both he and Roger stepped down from the carriage. Staring blankly at the graves, Roger said, "I see only three graves. Why not four?"

"There were no remains of Nik," Carrossa said. "Thought is, Nik was either run off or kidnapped by the raiders. No one in town has seen hide nor hair of him since."

"Any idea who those raiders were?" Roger asked, still staring at the three marked graves.

"Sheriff Perkins received a report from Jackson County's sheriff saying a Union patrol passed through there heading south. A Colonel Curtain was leading them and claimed they were a unit freeing slaves under the Confiscation Act," Carrossa said.

"What is the Confiscation Act?" Roger inquired.

"Just some law allowing the federal government to seize private property, including slaves," Anthony responded. "Perkins thinks they came upon Nik and wanted him."

"You mean the U.S. Army kidnapped Nik?" Roger said in exasperation.

"We don't really know," Carrossa replied. "Sheriff Perkins is trying to find that out."

"But why would they kill my family?" Roger said, nearly shouting.

"Nobody knows, Roger," Anthony said, looking down at the ground and shrugging his shoulders. "I am sorry, but that's about all we know right now.

"Do you want to go down to the farmhouse?" Carrossa asked.

"No. If that offer of staying at your place still stands," Roger interjected, "I believe I just need some time to think."

"You're welcome to stay with the Mrs., me and the boys as long as you like," Carrossa said.

"Much obliged," Roger answered.

The two men boarded the carriage, and Carrossa reversed his course.

After arriving at the farm, Karla greeted Roger with a hug and condolences. Roger acknowledged her good graces, but her words only went as far as his ears.

Karla was not a large woman, but life on the farm had toughened her. She was feminine and well-versed in social graces and never seemed to have a bad day.

The Carrossas showed him to the room they had set up for him. He sat down on the bed and looked around as if nothing made sense.

"Can I get you anything?" Karla asked. "Anything at all?"

"No, I just need some time alone, I think," Roger said, looking into Karla's face, almost as if he did not recognize her. "I'll be okay, thanks."

"Well, if you need anything, one of us will be just beyond that door," Karla assured.

Roger just nodded. Karla retreated and quietly closed the door behind her.

Roger lay down and stared at the ceiling, as tears suddenly filled his eyes. They ran past his temples, settling in his hair and running onto the pillow. Exhausted, he was soon asleep.

Chapter 9

Roger woke up the following morning with a shout. He sat up in bed and looked around the room with fear and confusion, not knowing where he was. Anthony Carrossa burst through the door.

"Are you all right, Roger!?" Anthony asked.

"Oh, Mr. Carrossa, I'm so sorry. I must have been having a bad dream," Roger said, sitting up and holding his head with one hand.

"Would you like some coffee or some breakfast?" Anthony asked.

"Ah, not right now, thank you," Roger answered. "I don't think my stomach could take it. Just give me a bit to collect myself."

"Take as long as you like," Carrossa said. "I'll be right outside the door if you need anything."

With that, Anthony stepped out of the room and closed the door.

Roger tried to recall his dream, thinking it might give him relief from the emptiness and anger he still felt inside. Besides the grief over losing his family, including Nik, he languished over the senselessness of what had happened. His family murdered and their home burned to the ground, why? Why wasn't this colonel and his gang more notorious? Why massacre innocent people – for what purpose? Were they after Nik, someone not yet a man, even if they did think him a slave? Roger again felt like shedding tears, but they would not come.

Roger got up and went into the Carrossas' family room, where Anthony and Karla sat in silence.

"Mr. Carrossa, could I borrow your buggy?" Roger asked, bearing a slightly pained expression on his face.

"Of course, Roger," Anthony answered. "I won't be needing it or the horse."

"Perhaps my husband could take you somewhere," Karla suggested.

"Oh, no, thanks," Roger replied. "I'd like to borrow the buggy and take a ride… alone… if you don't mind."

"Of course. Anthony, would you get the carriage ready for Roger?" Karla said, turning to her husband.

"I will certainly do that," Anthony responded. "I'll bring it around front." He then went out the main door to fetch the horse and buggy.

"Would you like some breakfast?" Mrs. Carrossa asked.

"Not just now," Roger said. "I just need some time to be alone, if I may."

"Whatever you need, Roger," Karla said. "We have plenty to do around here, so take your time."

"Thank you," Roger responded and went outside, where Anthony was waiting with the buggy.

As he rode along, Roger avoided going into town and rode instead out past the train depot and pulled up in a grove of trees not far from the station. He got out of the carriage and walked into a stand of oaks among a scattering of pine trees. He stood just listening to nature's sounds when the blast of a train whistle filled the air. Roger wheeled about to see a locomotive pulling into the depot. The knot in his stomach tightened, nearly causing him to double over. When the line of cars came to a stop, Roger's mind flashed back to the moment he stepped off the train, only to have the horror of his fears come crashing down.

He was becoming obsessed with Colonel Curtain. Why wasn't the law hunting him down? Would Captain Baumgartner's unit catch up to him? Did Baumgartner even know who Curtain was? He didn't mention his name. Was his family's death destined to be written off like a casualty of war?

That thought seared Roger's mind like a hot knife. What about Nik? Where was he? Roger's frustration rose to the point he let out a violent, screeching scream. Just then the engine's whistle blew, as if on cue. Was it an omen? The beleaguered youth wondered as he watched the train chug out of the station. Was it taking all his hopes and dreams with it? Although there was no one on that train he knew, he felt as if he were being abandoned again. He watched as the sights and sounds of its last car faded away. Tears, again, rolled down his face.

"Wish you had a ticket on that train, young man," a voice came from behind him. Roger wheeled about to see what appeared to be a rail conductor. He was dressed in the familiar uniform with a friendly face, though nondescript.

"Did you get left behind?" Roger asked, trying to regain his composure.

"No, but I think you're feeling that way," the conductor answered. "Just so you know, your family is not on that train."

"Well, I kno…," Roger began, but his sobbing returned in mid-sentence. He knelt down, reminiscent of when he collapsed on the depot's loading area.

"Go ahead, get it all out. It's a lot for a young man like you to have to take in," said the stranger. "It's going to be tough for a while, but you will get through it."

"But I can't just let this thing go," Roger pleaded, looking up at the unexpected visitor while wiping the tears away with his sleeve. "I'm torn in so many ways."

"Those torn parts will heal once you've had time to mend," the stranger consoled, "but it will happen. Then you must decide on your next course of action."

"But how can I do that?" Roger questioned.

"Pray, Roger. It is the greatest tool you have for guidance," said the stranger. "It will turn out a longer road than you may imagine, but vengeance always does."

"So, am I to seek revenge?" Roger said, probing the uniformed man.

"Oh, I did not say that, Mr. Brinkman," informed the conductor, "but your heart does. Like I said, it's a long journey so choose well.

"I think your horse, there, is waiting for you," the man added, looking over Roger's shoulder.

Roger turned in the direction of the carriage and saw the horse nibbling on grass. Roger turned back.

"I'm still not sure...," Roger started, but the stranger was no longer there. The forlorn student stared at the vacant space for a moment, then returned to the buggy and drove back to the Carrossas' home.

Anthony came in a short time later, with some more uncertain news.

"Roger, I ran into Sheriff Perkins, and he said he received a wire from the U.S. Army," Anthony began. "Apparently some maverick soldiers did try to seize slaves, but there was no evidence anyone was killed."

"What about this Colonel Curtain?" inquired Roger. "Any news about him?"

"The federal report indicated someone by the name of Gabriel Curtain did submit a request for a commission in the Kansas Regiment but was turned down. They think he took his offer to another state."

"But do we know he was the same Colonel Curtain?" Roger asked.

"The sheriff had no way of connecting the two," Carrossa said. "Sorry, I couldn't be of more help."

"Perhaps you have been more help than you know," Roger said, his mind now turning. "At least I have a name and rank to go on."

Roger spent the next few days close to the Carrossa farm. He would sit for hours in his room or go for long walks. His appetite slowly returned, but he could not subdue his increasing anger.

After a week of living with the Carrossas, Roger became more open with the family. His brooding had diminished, and the Carrossas stopped treating him as if he would break.

"Would you care to join us in church this Sunday," Karla asked, with hope in her voice.

"Thank you, Mrs. Carrossa, but I do not think I'm ready for that yet," Roger replied. "Too many memories there. However, would you tell Gloria Fenton that I do plan to come see her? Tell her I'm not avoiding her, it's just that I still have some healing to do."

"I understand," Karla said. "I will be glad to let Gloria know. She asks about you all the time."

"I do regret that, but I'm a little too unsettled yet," Roger explained. "But I would be grateful if you would do that for me."

Roger began taking more frequent trips to the Brinkman burial site, borrowing the Carrossas' horse and buggy. He would talk to the graves and pray as if his deceased family was praying with him. During his visits, a strange feeling began to overtake him. He imagined his family was hiding behind the white oak tree, and it grew stronger with each trip. So strong was the feeling that he took comfort in thinking it, but he did not have the courage to look.

One day, while he was praying, Roger thought he heard voices. He looked up and stared at the tree until overcome with an uncontrollable desire to approach it. Hesitant out of fear of disappointment, he suddenly broke into a run and leaped behind the tree, but no one was there. He was heartbroken.

He fell back against the tree in bitter disappointment and slid into a sitting position. His faith was strong enough to tell him his denial could not restore him. He had to face the situation with resolve, but resolve to do what?

There was something primeval growing inside, a hate he had never experienced before. He gazed out over the back portion of the Brinkman property and began to breathe deeper and more rapidly. The words of the misplaced train conductor began to run through his head. There was something he must do, but what?

It was almost as if he had been infused with a renewed strength, and he slowly rose to his feet. He circled the tree until he stood between it and his family's graves.

"Ma, Pa, Dolly, I swear I will kill the men who did this," he said in a deep reverberating voice. "I can find no peace until I do, so help me God."

He then strode past the last resting place of those he loved more than anything in the world, boarded the carriage and rode off.

He rode back to the Carrossas, went into his room and found a piece of paper he had placed in his drawer. In passing, he told

Mrs. Carrossa he would be back soon and again climbed into the carriage and rode to the Bordertown Train Depot. He went to the telegraph office and sent the following wire.

To: Captain Ashley Baumgartner

101st Missouri Detachment

Third Confederate Regiment

General William Joseph Hardee, Command

Little Rock, Arkansas

Considering your offer. Please respond.

Roger M. Brinkman

Bordertown, Missouri

After that, Roger returned to the Carrossas' farm, where he would wait for an answer from Major Baumgartner. He also knew he had another big job to do before committing to the military.

With his newfound conviction, he resolved to call on Gloria Fenton. He again borrowed the Carrossas' buggy and rode to the Fenton farm.

When Gloria saw the carriage coming, she walked toward it somewhat timidly, knowing this time had to come.

"I am sorry I did not meet you at the train," Gloria said, as Roger lowered himself from the carriage. "I simply did not have the strength to face you and the Carrossas told me at church you wanted to wait, too." Tears welled up in Gloria's eyes as she spoke.

Roger certainly felt compassion for Gloria's pain, although it was a pain he no longer felt. He simply looked at her and then hugged her as she cried in his embrace. Finally, he spoke.

"Gloria, I'm going to join the army," he said in an almost hypnotic deadpan. "I cannot stay here."

"But why would you do that?" Gloria said, looking somewhat bewildered.

"This may sound strange, but the horror that has infected me seems to be getting worse," Roger continued, staring at Gloria as if some answer freeing his soul would emerge from her. "I think I have to experience something even worse to find myself again. It's hard for me to explain."

"So, surrounding yourself with those who love you is not an option?" Gloria's tears had dried rather quickly, and it was now as if she were speaking to someone she barely knew.

"I want to kill the man who did this," Roger said, still looking for some imagined resolution to come out of Gloria. "I think the army will help me to do that."

"Roger, that's no answer," Gloria said, looking at her friend as if he were a stranger. "You're not a killer. You're a preacher's son, for heaven's sake."

"I'm no one's son, now," Roger muttered. "It's as if I don't belong anywhere anymore. Maybe time in the army will help me find my place again. I would like your support in doing that."

"Have you abandoned all the plans we made together? Does that not mean anything to you?" she questioned.

"Part of me wants to ask you to wait, Gloria. Give me a little more time," Roger said, his words now coming more into focus.

"But we may not be here when you get back," Gloria implored. "We are going to lose this farm, and I'm not sure where we will end up. Without you, there is nothing to hold me here.

"And how do I know you will be coming back?" Gloria said, almost as an afterthought.

"I'll write," Roger offered.

"And send your letters where? Roger, my family is all I have," said Gloria, flinching at the words, knowing Roger no longer had his. "I do not know where I'll be."

"Then I'll find you," he said.

After a long pause, Gloria searched Roger's eyes to try and make sense of their conversation. Finally, she said, "Goodbye, Roger. May God go with you and keep you. I apparently can't." Gloria turned and walked back into the Fenton farmhouse, not wanting Roger to see that her tears had returned and were now running down her cheeks. Roger watched her disappear into the house and wondered if the words he spoke were truly his. He wasn't certain he liked this new person he was becoming, but it felt better than the old one.

He stared at the Fentons' closed door for almost a full minute before turning and climbing aboard the Carrossas' coach and returning to their farm.

As time passed, Roger's depressed state faded into a sense of purpose. Resolve replaced his anger and with it came renewed energy. Anxious to hear from Baumgartner, he took long walks in the woods, plotting a new course. To complete his challenge of finding Curtain would mean greater discipline and preparation. He would use the army to give him the confidence and ability to fulfill his mission. He prayed for guidance, as well as forgiveness, all the while knowing he could not forgive the man who had done this to him. It ran against everything he once held dear, but he had no answer for why God dealt him the hand He did.

Roger wasn't at all sure he was making the right decision, but heard Jayhawkers were being conscripted by the Union. It was also possible Curtain was serving in the Northern Army.

While pondering his prospects, Roger received a telegram delivered to the Carrossas' home. It was a wire from Major Baumgartner offering instructions on his recruitment. Travel arrangements via rail would take him from Bordertown to Little Rock, Arkansas. There he would be transported to the Confederate enlistment office for further instructions. The telegram concluded with a welcome note from now Major Ashley Baumgartner, Commanding Officer, CSA Sharpshooter Training Center.

Roger sat down with the Carrossas to tell them the news.

"Is this what you think your father would want you to do?" said Anthony, responding to Roger. "How about your mother?"

"I can't honestly say, Mr. Carrossa," Roger said, sitting at the Carrossas' table. "I have been following a certain path most of my life and did not expect it to take the turn it did. I am not sure I would have made this decision had I not met Major Baumgartner during my trip home."

Roger explained how he helped the former captain and his soldiers ward off some raiders attacking the train. He described how he instinctively grabbed a wounded soldier's rifle and began shooting at the men riding alongside the car he was on.

"I only shot the horses, though. I could not bring myself to shoot someone I did not know," Roger said. "When I discovered what had happened to my family, my life totally changed. The captain wants me for a special sharpshooting unit, and I believe that is what I was meant to do."

"You could, instead, help us restart your father's church," Anthony Carrossa said, standing to place his hands on the table and leaning forward. "We've been like lost sheep since the… since the incident. We've put out a call for a new pastor, but we've not yet received a response."

Anthony said they asked Pastor Altman to assist, but Altman sent back his regrets, saying he had retired.

"And, what about the farm? It's yours now, you know," Anthony added.

"I couldn't make a go of it there, not just now. I think it's going to take some time before I could even consider that, beings how it would be a constant reminder of what happened there," the young Brinkman responded. "As for the church, I'm just not ready for that, either."

"But you feel you're ready to go off to war, and fight for the Confederacy, no less," Carrossa said.

"I've given that some thought," Roger responded. "But Colonel Curtain has been described as wearing a Yankee uniform. I could not wear blue considering that."

"We really don't know who or what he was, other than being a cold-blooded killer," Anthony said, standing upright. "I'm sorry, Roger, I guess maybe I shouldn't have put it that way."

"It's okay, Mr. Carrossa, those are my sentiments, exactly. I need to find that man and make him pay for what he did," Roger responded.

"Well, give it some more time," Carrossa said. "You know, you would be fighting with those that would have made a slave of Nik."

Roger just looked up at Anthony Carrossa with very little expression in his face. "No one can tell me what happened to Nik," Roger said. "I hate to say this, but I may never see him again." Roger looked down at the telegram on the table and let the conversation fade into his personal thoughts.

By morning, Roger had packed his bags and asked Anthony Carrossa to take him to the station where he would catch the next train to Little Rock. He had been up all night considering Carrossa's comments, but his passion to avenge his family had grown too great.

Carrossa took his time driving the coach to the train station, still hoping to change Roger's mind. But Roger was so lost in what lay ahead, he barely heard a word. All he knew was he no longer had a real family, the army wanted him, and Curtain's whereabouts were still unknown. What few efforts Roger made to answer, he did with a deep sigh and few words, uttered more out of courtesy than understanding.

At the train station, Roger presented the telegram he received from Major Baumgartner to the depot clerk. It had information explaining that Roger was a potential recruit and that the train fare to Little Rock would be covered by the Confederate States of America.

"Oh, and one more thing, Mr. Carrossa," Roger said, returning to the coach to say goodbye. "I would like to keep in contact with Gloria Fenton. I'm afraid I've kind of let her down, and the Fentons are not at all sure they'll remain in Bordertown. If you would, could you let me know where they might go?

"I intend to write, but my letters may not find them."

"I'll do that, son," Anthony said. "Just take care of yourself," he added and rode away without looking back.

Chapter 10

After entering the rail car, Roger Brinkman discovered he was not the only one on the train heading for Little Rock with enlistment in mind. He was placed in a car that had Confederate recruits only. Another car had been designated for those young men planning to join the Union Army. Little Rock was a duty station for both sides.

"So, are you ready to fight for the cause?" said a young man about Roger's age, who took a seat next to Brinkman hoping to engage him in conversation.

The comment brought Roger out from his personal thoughts, and he said "Yeah, I guess so."

"No guessing about it, I say. We need to set those damn Yankees straight. This is supposed to be a free country without one side telling the other what to do and how to live," said the young man.

"Where are you from?" Roger asked.

"Macon, Georgia. I tried to sign up there, but they put me on this train for Little Rock, instead," the recruit said. "My name is Preston, Billy Preston. What's yours?"

"Roger, Roger Brinkman," he answered.

"Pleased to meet you, Roger, maybe we'll end up in the same outfit together," Preston said.

"Perhaps," Roger replied. "I'm afraid I don't know much about the military. I just happened to meet a Confederate Captain named Baumgartner, whose influence put me on this train."

"No matter," Preston replied. "We'll be fellow soldiers, just the same."

Roger gave an affirmative nod of his head and then turned to look out the window and bury himself into the recesses of his mind once again. Preston bid Roger a brief farewell and moved next to another recruit to strike up a similar conversation.

Once the train rolled into Little Rock, the soon-to-be soldiers were loaded onto recruitment wagons for transportation to the enlistment station.

It was late fall in Arkansas, and the air was cool, but the weather pleasant. That was fortunate, considering the number of men crammed into each covered wagon, some nervous and others enthusiastic. After a rough and dusty ride, the men were dropped off at a small building where others were already gathered waiting to sign on the dotted line.

"Listen up!" a sergeant called out loud, enough for all to hear. "For those of you who have not heard this message, fall into either of three single-file lines. Lines one and two are for new recruits, and line three is for those who have enlisted for a specific duty, job or service. Wagons for enlistees who have finished their paperwork are located in the back of this recruiting station. Those from line three will receive instructions from one of these five non-coms standing here, once they've reviewed your paperwork – that is all!"

Roger stepped into line three, uncertain if it were the correct one. He would offer Baumgartner's name hoping it was enough for proper processing. As he stood waiting, every so often a recruiter would direct an enlistee to get into a different line.

"I'm here on behalf of Cap… er, Major Ashley Baumgartner," Roger replied, with his telegram in hand.

"Sharpshooter, eh," the recruiter remarked. "Full name?"

"Roger Douglas Brinkman," he responded.

The recruiter finished filling in Roger's information and then had Brinkman sign at the bottom of the page.

"Sergeant Able," the recruiter called out. "I think this one is yours."

A soldier stepped forward and was handed Roger's paperwork. "Brinkman, we've been expecting you. What took you so long?"

"I recently lost my family and…" Roger started.

"Sorry to hear that, private," Able said. "I hope you will find this family of Confederates to be to your liking. Please, follow me."

The soldier turned and exited the small building. Roger trailed behind as he walked across a courtyard filled with others waiting to be processed, finally reaching a small buckboard. Roger climbed up and sat next to the sergeant since no one else was on board. The sergeant snapped the reins to begin rolling.

"Shouldn't we wait for some others?" Roger asked.

"There are no others," the driver said. "The sharpshooter unit is new and rather exclusive."

They first rode in the direction of where a sea of white tents sprawled across the landscape. The wagon then turned and headed into a grove of trees that spread almost entirely around the tented encampment. After a brief ride through trees decorated in late-autumn colors, the wagon entered a clearing where three tents stood. The driver pulled up in front of one larger than the others and a soldier standing guard at its entrance called out that the wagon had arrived.

As the sergeant stepped down from the buckboard, he motioned to Roger to do the same. Before responding, Roger saw Major Baumgartner emerge from the tent.

"Roger, so good to see you," Baumgartner said, as he returned the salute of the wagon driver.

Roger attempted to salute but wasn't sure how to do it.

"Don't worry about that now," Baumgartner said, with a broad smile. "You'll learn about all that soon enough. For now, come into my tent and I'll explain what we discussed some time ago on the train."

Roger followed Baumgartner into the tent and stopped in front of a makeshift desk. The major moved behind the desked and dropped into a wooden chair.

"Roger, I've been assigned to form a new unit of sharpshooters. We discovered the Union rascals have already done this and their riflemen have been raising hell with our troops," Baumgartner began. "When I suggested to my commanding officer that you and marksmen like you would be an asset, a counter-measure against the Yankees, the general not only agreed, but after speaking with General Hardee about it, he suggested we form a special unit to combat the North's sharpshooters."

"Yes sir," Roger said. "I just hope I can measure up to your expectations."

"Oh, you will, Roger, you will," Baumgartner said with a smile.

The major ordered one of his aides to outfit Private Brinkman with a uniform, be given a weapon and assigned to a tent. He was also introduced to his training officer, Sergeant Benjamin Rathman.

Roger's uniform consisted of a pair of lightweight boots, cotton trousers and jacket, plus a Confederate cap. He was also given a Springfield rifle and told ammunition and powder would be distributed during training. Brinkman was assigned to one of the two other tents located behind Major Baumgartner's headquarters. Inside the tent, Roger was assigned a cot, two blankets, a pillow, and a footlocker in which to keep his possessions. He was also introduced to his tent-mate, Ambrose Tucker, a large black man and former slave.

When Tucker rose from his bunk where he sat polishing his rifle, he stood more than a head taller than Brinkman and outweighed the new recruit by at least a hundred pounds. He was muscular and his face held little expression.

"Pleased to meet you, Ambrose," Roger said, extending his hand.

Tucker accepted Roger's hand and gave a nod of his head. Roger noted the size of Tucker's hand and wondered how it was he could fit his finger through the trigger guard of a rifle. After the handshake, Tucker sat back down and continued polishing his weapon.

"I'll give you soldiers some time to get acquainted," Sergeant Rathman offered. "When I return, Brinkman, I will give you a quick rundown on your training." With that said, Rathman turned and exited the tent. Roger made a feeble attempt to salute the sergeant, but Rathman paid the salute no mind.

"He's enlisted," Tucker said.

"What?" Roger responded, surprised at hearing Tucker's voice.

"Sergeant Rathman is enlisted. You don't salute enlisted men," Tucker answered.

"Oh, I'm sorry. I'm new at this." Roger said.

"Most all of us are, 'cept for Major Baumgartner," Tucker remarked. "Him, you salute."

"You know, I forgot to get my bag out of the wagon," Brinkman said, realizing he did not bring it with him.

"They'll bring it in," Ambrose said.

"Oh, okay," Roger replied, as he sat down on his cot to contemplate his decision to join the military.

After a short time, Rathman returned.

"Attention!" Rathman called out as he burst through the tent door. Tucker was up and at attention quite fast for a man his size. Roger followed suit, watching how his tent-mate responded. Major Baumgartner came in just seconds behind Rathman.

"At ease, men," the major exclaimed upon entering.

Again, Roger watched out of the corner of his eye to see what Tucker did and then mimicked the big man.

"Gentlemen, you have been selected to begin a new branch of our Confederate Army," Baumgartner started. "It will be comprised of sharpshooters, like yourselves, to support our ground troops. The Union Army has already done so, unfortunately, with great success. I'm not surprised the Northern devils would divert from conventional warfare to gain an unfair advantage. This requires us to do the same.

"But let it be known," the officer continued, "they have forced our hand, and we will do whatever is necessary to uphold the Confederate way of life."

Major Baumgartner paused to let his words sink in. "Sergeant Rathman will now give you instructions on the special training you are to receive," Baumgartner concluded and then departed the tent, returning Rathman's salute.

"Okay, you men fall out with your weapons," Rathman ordered.

Tucker picked up his polished rifle and was the first one out, behind Rathman. Brinkman picked up his rifle off the cot and trailed behind Tucker. He kept pace with the big man, who walked toward another soldier already standing at attention. Tucker then struck a similar pose, and Brinkman fell in just as Ambrose had.

"At ease, men," Rathman said. "You are here for a special reason, and because of that, your training will differ considerably from what the other recruits are going through. Most of them will be reassigned by the week's end, but you will be asked to remain here a while longer.

"Private Swain, here, has already been introduced to much of what the two of you will be learning," Rathman said, directing his words toward Tucker and Brinkman. "Therefore, he will spend some of his time assisting me in your training before he is reassigned.

"Your training will begin at oh-six-hundred hours tomorrow morning. Be dressed and ready to fall out at that time. Dinner is at eighteen-hundred hours today. You will all be transported by wagon to the mess tent at that time – dismissed!"

Swain turned toward his tent. Tucker headed for the one he and Brinkman occupied, but Roger hesitated.

"Sergeant, sir, if you have a minute," Roger quietly called to Rathman.

Rathman was no more than five and a half feet tall. He had been a Union soldier from South Carolina but came over to the Confederate side when that state seceded. He was slender and spoke with a deep southern accent. He also had a speech impediment that made understanding him a challenge.

"Yes, Brinkman," Rathman responded, "what is it?"

"What is eighteen-hundred hours?" Roger said, half embarrassed.

"Sorry, Brinkman. If you were infantry, you would know by now," the sergeant explained. "This corps is new, so there are going to be things crop up that you will not learn here. Be patient, you are not alone."

Rathman then explained the 24-hour clock to the new recruit and added why he was to be referred to as sergeant, not sir. Roger thanked the man and returned to his tent.

Later that day, the small unit rode the buckboard over to the outdoor mess hall, located in the middle of the large field of white tents. There were several campfires burning and hundreds of Confederate soldiers gathered about them. Many men were seated and eating in the mess area, while others were by their tents either talking or playing cards. Roger noticed a couple of soldiers engaged in a game of keep-away with a Confederate cap taken from a smaller recruit. The taller soldiers tossing the cap back and forth laughed, while the shorter, frustrated soldier scrambled to get it back.

Roger, Ambrose and Swain climbed down from the buckboard and joined the line of soldiers passing through the mess tent. The food consisted of chicken cooked over an open grill, hominy grits and collard greens. The meal was tasty enough, except some of the chicken was either undercooked or burnt. However, the soldiers could have all the grits and greens they wanted. As they came to the end of their meal, Sergeant Rathman spoke to one of the cooks, who left and returned with a full plate wrapped in a white cloth. Rathman signaled to the men to get aboard the wagon for the return trip to sharpshooter camp.

Later that evening, while still daylight, Rathman taught his recruits close order drill and discussed military courtesy. Swain, though a rather seedy-looking character wearing a uniform too large for his thin frame, performed the drills well. He did so while looking totally disinterested.

Swain had a thin face and a crooked nose that nearly stretched to the point of his chin. His lips were thin, and when he spoke, it was hard to tell if he had teeth. His voice had a honking quality to it, and his southern drawl made him as difficult to understand as Rathman. Still, he was skilled with a rifle.

After the drills, Rathman looked at his pocket watch and said, "Okay men, stand at ease until taps are played."

After a short pause, a bugle could be heard in the distance. Rathman turned toward the main camp at attention and saluted. Roger saw Tucker and Swain do the same, so he followed suit. After taps, Rathman released the recruits but asked Roger to wait.

"Brinkman, I know a lot of this is new to you, but you will catch on in time. You'll grow to appreciate military protocol. It just takes a little getting used to."

"Yes sir, ah sergeant," Roger said.

After being dismissed, Roger entered his tent and noticed that Tucker was lying flat on his back on his bed staring up at the top of the tent. Roger wondered how a cot that small could hold up under the weight of a man so large.

Brinkman sat on the edge of his bunk and decided to engage Tucker in conversation.

"How long have you been here, Ambrose? Roger asked.

"Three days," was Tucker's answer.

"You must be a fast learner. You seem to be quite at ease here, already," Roger continued.

"Not much else to do, not yet anyway," Tucker said. "Besides, I was assigned to a military company before being sent here."

"Where?" Roger asked.

"Mississippi," was the reply.

Roger thought it odd that a black man from Mississippi would join the Confederate Army, but he held his tongue on that question.

"Are you a pretty good shot?" Roger said, feeling a little foolish to have even asked.

"Yeah," Ambrose said.

"So that's why you joined the army?" Roger said.

"I joined so's to kill Yankees." Tucker spoke rather matter-of-factly and did not take his eyes off the top of the tent.

The evening shadows had grown into the night. Each cot was equipped with a small lantern, so Roger used the light of it to make up his bed. He couldn't think of anything to do after preparing his bunk, so he asked Ambrose if he wanted the light left on.

"No," was the reply.

So, Roger put out the lantern and undressed in the dark. He then lay down on his cot. He reclined on his back and stared up into the darkness. It was the first time he had stopped to think about what all had transpired. When the thoughts of his slain family flooded his mind, tears again filled his eyes.

Roger did his best to control the weeping, as his emotions seemed to come out of nowhere.

"You crying?" a voice said in the darkness.

"I'm sorry, Ambrose. My recent past kind of caught up to me," Roger said, struggling to recover.

"It's okay, Roger. I'd cry too if I wasn't so empty inside," Ambrose said.

Somewhat relieved to hear Tucker speak his name, Roger's tears subsided. "What happened to you?" he asked.

Tucker paused a moment and told Brinkman his story.

Before trying to enter the army, Tucker said he was a young slave in Mississippi. His father and mother were bought by a modest farmer, a Mr. Latimore.

"Master Latimore was a good man," Tucker said. "He had no wife and no kids, and he was able to buy my momma and daddy at a good price,"

Tucker continued, saying Latimore had acquired his parents to help on the farm. Ambrose's mother cooked and kept house, and his father helped with the farming. After Ambrose was born, Mr. Latimore helped raise him and, as Ambrose grew, the farmer taught him how to hunt and shoot.

However, Latimore fell into debt and had to take out a loan funded through a northern bank. Because of Latimore's meager means, he had to use Tucker's parents as collateral. As the farmer's troubles continued, the bank foreclosed on the loan, and Mr. and Mrs. Tucker were sold. Ambrose was not included and was separated from his parents.

"I was about sixteen then," Tucker said. "As much as my folks did not want to leave me behind, they knew I would be better off staying with Master Latimore on the farm."

Although heartbroken at the loss of his parents, Ambrose said he worked hard for Latimore in hopes of raising enough money to buy them back, but that never happened. Over time, Ambrose's hate for the North escalated, largely because of the bank's actions.

"They was hypocrites," Tucker said of the northern bank. "They talk righteous-like when it comes to slavery and then force the sale of my family so's they can get their money."

As Ambrose continued, he said he grew to the point his stealth at hunting became difficult, so he studied where the animals gathered to feed or water. He would conceal himself near that spot and wait until his game came into view.

"That was something about me the Army was interested in," Ambrose said. "A man my size hiding in plain sight."

Ambrose continued, saying Latimore took ill and offered Tucker manumission. Upon Latimore's death, Ambrose offered his services to the Confederate Army.

"At first, they wouldn't let me soldier, but since I was a free man and hated Yankees, they tried me out as a game hunter," Tucker said. "That worked at first, but before long, the animals got scarce."

Tucker said the fighting frightened away larger game and the best he could do was harvest a few squirrels, small game birds and an occasional rabbit. The army concluded such small fare to be of little help and considered Tucker for other duties. Impressed with his marksmanship, he was recommended to Baumgartner for the sharpshooter corps.

"There was some controversy about slaves being soldiers, even freed ones, but the major appealed and I was allowed in as an exception.

Tucker's story helped calm Roger's grief and he eventually fell asleep. In the morning, Ambrose shook Brinkman awake.

"Time to get up now," Tucker said. "The horn will be blowin' soon, and we need to be ready to fall in."

Roger quickly dressed and had his rifle at his side. He and Ambrose moved out of their tent and took their place alongside Swain before reveille. Roger noticed Swain looked like he had slept in his uniform. Swain never said much, but he followed orders and proved to be extremely accurate shooting a rifle. He was from the Deep South, but exactly what state no one in camp seemed to know. It was said he spent much of his time hunting squirrels and could drop a rabbit running at full speed.

The day's activities consisted of calisthenics, breakfast, rifle practice, military strategy, lunch, a long hike and camouflage training before returning for the evening meal, free time and lights out.

The camp had an area on the rifle range set up specifically for shooting long distance, up to fifteen-hundred feet. Under Rathman's watchful eye, and Swain's help, they trained to adjust trajectory depending on distance and how the amount of powder could affect the flight of the ball. All three men proved capable of hitting a target at long range, and Roger was not surprised to see Ambrose's rifle had no trigger guard, unlike his issued weapon.

Most sharpshooting was from the prone position, whereas infantry was from a variety of positions, including standing and walking forward. The sharpshooter's hikes consisted of walking several miles into the Arkansas hills with full gear. Although fall was slowly turning to winter, the days warmed considerably by afternoon. Each day they would hike to a location where the terrain differed. They learned to conceal themselves using whatever means available, including brush, tree branches, moss, grass and even mud and dirt. Rathman would take notes following Ambrose's suggestions since the unit was still in its infancy.

By the end of the first week, Swain was reassigned to a regiment back East and two new men showed up and occupied his tent. Before the end of Brinkman's second week, Roger was called to Major Baumgartner's tent.

"Private Brinkman, I've recommended you for duty with one of General Lee's regiments. You will function as a general attaché and be given top secret assignments when called for," Baumgartner said. "You may also be called upon for moral support with your seminary training. I know you will do the Confederacy proud. Good luck."

Roger never saw Baumgartner after that, and a day later, he was saying goodbye to Ambrose Tucker. Both men were told to say nothing about where they were being assigned, even to each other. If either were to be captured, they would have no knowledge of the whereabouts of other sharpshooters.

Two weeks from the day Brinkman had arrived in Little Rock, he was again on a train headed back East. His biggest disappointment was the feeling he would not be in a position to search for his family's killer, Colonel Curtain.

Chapter 11

Before leaving Little Rock on the train, Roger was told his destination would be Petersburg Train Station in Virginia. He was dressed as a civilian and given a small packet wrapped in a cloth tied with twine. He was told to keep the package wrapped and in his possession at all times. He was to be met by a small team of Confederate soldiers at the Petersburg Depot who would ask for someone named Winkleman. Roger was to claim to be that person and wait for the officer to approach and specifically ask for a "signal." When hearing that word, Roger was to respond with the word "lantern." The officer must then request the package and refer to Roger as "Mr. Brinkman."

If the officer failed to follow any of those precautionary steps, Roger was to claim he mistook the name requested for his own and keep the package in his possession. He was to then disembark, take local transportation into Petersburg and report the failed mission to Confederate Command.

The train ride proved long and arduous, with several stops and transfers along the way. Roger was traveling alone and was under orders to give no indication he was a soldier. He spent several nights of fitful sleep and days of boredom before entering the train's last leg to Petersburg.

"Ticket please," the conductor called out, looking down at Roger. The undercover soldier fumbled through his jacket, being careful not to expose the wrapped packet. Using two fingers, he extracted the ticket and handed it to the conductor.

"It does get boring on these trips, doesn't it, son?" the conductor said. "Not many civilians ride these rails anymore."

"How far are we from Petersburg?" Roger asked.

"Only about a half-hour out, if we don't run into trouble," the conductor said, patting Roger on the shoulder.

Roger was getting nervous. The secrecy had not bothered him in the beginning but whenever uniformed soldiers entered the car, his anxiety increased. He was now only minutes away from discovering what his role was in all this and worried he could make a mess of it. The sequenced code words he was given, routine at first, now seemed complex and foreign. He quietly rehearsed, only to realize he could not remember his code name.

Finally, the train pulled into Petersburg. As it screeched to a stop belching steam, a Confederate company-grade officer and two soldiers without rifles boarded the train and entered Roger's car. With his anxious mind now blank, the undercover soldier prayed he would recall his code name when spoken.

"Is there a passenger Winkleman onboard?" the officer called out.

"Are you looking for me?" Roger answered, suddenly recognizing the name.

Identified as a captain by his uniform, the officer and his fellow soldiers formed a semicircle around Roger to shield their conversation. Several passengers made their way to the exits, but none seemed to take much interest in the meeting

"What's the signal?" the captain asked, in a low voice.

Roger stared at the officer, speechless.

"What is the signal, Winkleman?" the captain repeated.

"Lantern," Roger blurted out almost without thinking.

The officer put his finger to his lips to advise Roger to keep his voice down.

"Please give me your orders, Mr. Brinkman," the officer said, using Roger's correct name, assured he had the right man.

Roger reached into his jacket and pulled out the cloth package. The officer untied the twine and removed the wrap. Inside were two sheets of paper, one with Roger's description. The officer quickly scanned both.

"Everything seems to be in order. Brinkman, come with us,"

the officer said.

Roger slid from his seat and followed, as the two enlisted men fell in behind him.

"Can you ride, Brinkman?" the captain asked.

"Yes sir," Roger answered. "I grew up on a farm..."

"That's all I need to know," the captain interrupted.

Brinkman glanced at the sign reading Petersburg Railroad Station, as the four men quickly crossed the station platform and descended the stairs. Another soldier was waiting there with five horses.

"We've got a long ride ahead and not a lot of time to do it in," the officer said.

The five men mounted and began riding at a brisk pace.

With the captain in the lead, the unit traveled on the main road leading from the station. After a short distance, the unit turned and disappeared into the forest. Although they followed no path, the captain seemed to know exactly where he was going and rode at a rapid pace. The woods helped conceal their journey and whenever they came to a clearing, they would stop and survey the surroundings. Once satisfied, they galloped across the open area.

Roger thought it a strange way to report for duty, but since this was his first assignment, he kept his mouth shut. He took it upon faith he was following the orders he'd been given but had no idea where he was or where he was going. His companions were also silent and spoke only in hushed voices when they stopped to check the surroundings. As night descended, they stopped, dismounted, and removed bedrolls attached to the backs of their saddles. Roger followed their lead and retrieved his bedroll, as well.

"Sorry I cannot tell you more about where we are headed, Brinkman," the officer said, using a hoarse whisper, "but our orders are simply to escort you to your duty station. In truth, we know little more about this than you do."

Roger found the secrecy unsettling since no one seemed to know why. They dined on dried food contained in each soldier's saddlebags.

"We can't risk a campfire, so we'll have to do with cold rations until we reach our destination," said the officer. "If you need to address me, just say captain or sir. As for the other men, call them what you like. But remember, this is not a pleasure ride. The less conversation the better."

"Yes sir," Roger said.

The captain gave orders dividing the night watch among his soldiers and told Roger to sleep by him. It was early December, and evening temperatures were near freezing. After wrapping up in his bedroll, Roger spent much of the night wondering where he was, why him and why all the secrecy?

The five were up before daybreak, and it was cold. After a small helping of rations, they prepared the horses and continued riding in the confines of the forest.

After several hours, they came upon a small encampment of Confederate soldiers where they received fresh horses. Soon, the detail was riding once again. As night approached, the captain stopped the group at the inside edge of a grove of trees.

Roger noticed the captain was listening for something. Roger strained to hear anything above the sound of a slight breeze blowing through the trees. He detected a sound resembling distant river rapids, but the noise continued to increase. The captain turned and gave a signal to dismount. Once on foot, the officer gestured quietly, leading their horses deeper into the forest.

After reaching a dense stand of aspen, the officer stopped and put his hand over his horse's muzzle, nodding for everyone to do the same. It was now evident the growing sound came from a troop of marching soldiers. Just beyond the tree line, Roger could make out blue coats passing where they had first stopped. Unaware, Roger discovered he had been holding his breath and could hold it no longer. Although he exhaled as softly as he could, the officer gave a cautionary glance and put his finger to his lips. Roger closed his eyes and concentrated on breathing as normally as he could.

Following what seemed like hours, the echo of marching started to fade. Once it disappeared, the officer turned and signaled his men to quietly escort their horses back to the edge of the trees. The detachment remained at the forest's edge until the sound was completely gone.

"We'll stay here for the night," the captain said. "I don't want to risk going any farther with Union soldiers in the area. However, keep your mounts saddled in case we have to make a hasty retreat."

The camping routine was the same. The next morning, they awoke early, but the captain delayed departure until daybreak. Roger's appetite for rations was growing thin, but hunger took precedence over taste. At daybreak, they rode.

Within minutes, the captain gave the order to slow the horses to a walk.

"Halt, who goes there?" came a voice from somewhere in the forest.

"Captain Ladd, reporting," the officer said.

"Approach and be recognized," the voice stated.

After riding a couple of paces, a soldier came into view.

"Captain Ladd, we've been expecting you," the post soldier said.

"We are to report to General Jackson," said Ladd. "I do believe he is expecting us."

"Yes sir, pass," the soldier replied.

Roger realized he had not known the captain's name or that of the other soldiers. His first assignment began in such a blur he never bothered to ask. He had to assume it was all a necessary security precaution.

They soon entered a large clearing where many white tents dotted the landscape. The five riders headed toward a large tent where two men stood guard. Once they reached the tent, Captain Ladd signaled his men to halt.

"Brinkman, you come with me," Ladd said and turned to the others. "You men take care of the horses and report to your duty stations."

Captain Ladd dismounted and gave his reins to one of the soldiers. Roger did the same. The captain then led Roger into the tent.

"Captain Ladd reporting, sir," the officer said, as he took the package he'd received from Roger and gave it to the general.

Behind the desk was a general sporting a thick black beard. He had a rather rigid face, black hair and was muscular in build.

"I assume this is Private Brinkman?" the general inquired, looking at the only one wearing civilian clothes.

"Yes sir, reporting for duty as ordered, sir," said the captain.

"Thank you, captain. You are dismissed," the general said.

Ladd then saluted, did an about-face and left the tent.

"Clark, dismiss the guards at the door and then take leave," the general said to his aide standing by.

Clark did so and soon Brinkman and the general were alone.

"Sit down, private. I want to learn a little more about you," the general said. "Where are you from?"

"Missouri, sir. Bordertown, Missouri," Roger replied.

"And what were you doing before joining the army?" the general asked.

"I was a student at seminary in St. Louis," Roger said.

"A student at seminary?" the general said quizzically. "Why did you join the army?"

"My family was killed by a band of Union raiders. At least I was told they were Union. Colonel Curtain was the name I was given as to who led them," Roger said.

"I see," the general responded. "And I assume you hope to meet up with this Colonel Curtain?"

"I do, sir," Roger replied.

"I'm afraid I can't help you there, but I do have an assignment for you. I caution you that it is risky. Your skill with a rifle has brought you here, and your use of it could bring a quick end to this war," said the general. "Are you prepared to kill?"

Brinkman did not say anything. He knew joining the military meant his job would be to shoot the enemy. His intent was to learn to kill, but he had not thought about doing it on a large, indiscriminate scale. That matter he put in the back of his mind to delay coming to grips with it. He held a vague hope Colonel Curtain would be the man they would ask him to kill. He used his hate for Curtain to fortify his duty as a soldier. As he sat facing the general, he knew he was in too deep to tell the general he was not up to the task.

"You hesitate, son. Is there something wrong?" the general inquired, leaning forward from behind his rather crude desk, consisting of four legs and a surface that resembled a wooden door.

"It's just that I have never killed anyone before," Roger answered. "I have only thought of killing Colonel Curtain."

"Brinkman, I probably have more than ten thousand soldiers who could have said something similar, before joining my command. For most, it is not something wished for, but something thrust upon each for the reason of survival," the general said. "We fight wars because governments know little or nothing of its horrors. And it is the business of a soldier to do the fighting. It is best if we are vigorous in our swiftness to make this war a success for the Confederacy."

The general's manner was so direct Roger quickly realized the officer was in no mood to tolerate a soldier who would not fight and kill, if necessary. The general even used a few biblical examples noting that war is man's nature, but victory belongs to God and the soldier who fights on God's behalf.

"Obviously, you are familiar with David and Goliath," the general began. "The young shepherd went out to slay the boastful giant on his people's behalf. It was not his intention to become a soldier, but he was eventually celebrated in song: 'Saul has slain his thousands and David his tens of thousands.'

"You are a soldier of great skill with a rifle," the general concluded. "Use that skill to the glory of the Almighty and no blood will be on your hands – only God's victory."

The general's words helped Roger feel more like a soldier than a former seminary student. He had joined the military determined to avenge the death of his family and used that to justify his decision. The general had now given him the inspiration to do so. He sat up straighter and paid much closer attention to the general's speech.

"Understand, if you are ever going avenge your family and kill this Colonel Curtain, you had better have the resolve to do it when the time comes," the general said. "Are you ready to fight, son?"

"I am, sir," Roger said, staring straight into the general's eyes.

"Good. Now here is your assignment," the general started.

Brinkman's services had been requested when Richmond, the capital of the Confederacy, was being threatened by a specific Union officer. The Southern command felt eliminating that officer could mean a quick end to the war. That is when a top-secret request for a sharpshooter was generated.

"Thousands, perhaps hundreds of thousands, of lives could be spared by this one heroic act," the general said. "You could help prevent a great deal of needless bloodshed."

The officer explained the reconnaissance that went into scouting the area and the painstaking effort it took to devise a plan.

"I won't lie to you. This is a dangerous assignment, as the area will be crawling with Union soldiers," the general said. "However, we have devised good cover and a proposed escape route once you have completed your mission."

Roger tried to draw parallels between the assignment and hunting deer in the woods near his family's farm. He convinced himself it was something God had prepared him for, much like David's triumph over Goliath, using the general's analogy.

"You will be assigned to two of our reconnaissance men, who will instruct you on your location and how to conceal yourself. They will also brief you on the terrain and potential escape route," the general said. "Any questions?"

"No sir," Roger answered.

"Good. Do the Confederacy proud, soldier," the general stated. "May God go with you."

With that, the general stood up and summoned his staff officer. He briefed the officer and turned Brinkman over to him.

After leaving the general's tent, staff officer Clark weaved his way among the tents, saluting soldiers as he passed by. Roger, still in civilian clothes, followed and only nodded his head or smiled. Eventually, the pair reached a tent near the outskirts of the camp, where two guards stood back for Clark to enter.

"Lieutenant Stanton," Clark said, ducking inside. "This is Private Brinkman, one of our sharpshooters."

Roger was introduced to the lieutenant, who in turn introduced him to his reconnaissance staff, Sergeant Gomer Thompson and Corporal Leroy Taylor. Thompson and Taylor were both skilled in tactical terrain, strategy and battlefield concealment.

After introductions, Lieutenant Stanton spoke of Roger's mission and how it was to be carried out.

"These two men will give you instructions on the expertise needed to fulfill your task, private," Stanton said. "You will only have a day of instruction and then these men will accompany you to where you will be stationed. You will be instructed as to your target, the distance and your escape route once you have made the kill."

The word "kill" briefly jolted Roger out of his call-to-duty mindset, but he pushed the feeling toward the back of his mind, as Stanton continued.

"You will likely have time for only one shot, so make it good," the lieutenant concluded.

"Yes sir, I will do my best, sir," Roger said, almost subconsciously.

"Thompson, Taylor you know what to do. Take Brinkman and instruct him well," said Stanton.

After leaving the lieutenant's quarters, the two men took Roger to a tent, which was to be his billets and classroom. Once in the tent, Taylor produced a map and gave Roger a layout of the mission. He pointed out where Roger's position would be and the approximate yardage to his target. The target would emerge from a tent located in the Union Army's compound. Taylor also pointed on the map to a grove of trees not far from where Roger would be positioned, which would be his escape route.

"Speed of evacuation is your greatest asset," Taylor said. "Whether or not you have time for a second shot, should you need one, will be up to you. All I can say is the Confederacy is counting on you to complete this mission."

"Is it really that important?" Roger asked as the unexpected magnitude of his assignment started to chip away at his confidence.

"It is important if we want to end this war quickly," Sergeant Thompson said. "If this mission fails, we will fight on and, I'm afraid, many more lives will be lost.

"If it helps to relieve some of the pressure," Thompson continued, "this mission is a long shot, no humor intended. But if it succeeds, you likely will go down as a hero."

Coming out of this as a hero was not something Roger had considered. It spurred him to immerse himself into his instructions and block out all thoughts of failure, or worse.

Thompson then produced a rifle.

"Private Brinkman, this is the Whitworth Rifle, complete with a telescopic sight," Thompson explained. "This weapon has been shown to be effective shooting at targets a mile away. It is the Confederate's most prized sniper rifle, so take good care of it, as there are not many to go around.

"Shooting it will be part of tomorrow's training."

The Whitworth Rifle was something Roger had never seen before. He would discover its sheer power to be almost overwhelming and took great pride in it being entrusted to him. Still, he could not completely erase from his mind what he was being asked to do with it.

After looking the rifle over, Brinkman was drilled on how to load the muzzle-loader and cock it. Roger was quite familiar with that but had no experience shooting through a telescope. However, the two soldiers assured him he would receive full instructions on the Whitworth before being released to apply its deadly force.

After instructions, the two men took Roger around the camp. At each stop, he was shown the training areas prepared for what he was to learn at each. Roger was then taken to the mess tent for supper and afterward returned to his quarters. The two men told him to get plenty of rest, for they would be back to get him at daybreak to begin training. They also informed him his day-use uniform was folded and on his bunk.

The next day, Roger, now in a uniform of drab brown, followed the two men to the sites he was shown the day before. Some instructions were similar to what he learned in Arkansas; however, these were location-specific, mimicking the actual mission.

After shooting the Whitworth rifle, at close range and extreme, he learned to adjust the scope and powder load depending on distance and wind.

"The rifle has been prepared based on our reconnaissance," Thompson said. "However, we cannot guarantee nothing has changed. It's important you have a solid understanding of the Whitworth's capabilities."

"It's an arsenal unto itself," Taylor chimed in.

Following training, Thompson gave him the exact distance of his intended target, and both watched as he adjusted the rifle for that range.

"If you have any questions, ask them now because there won't be anyone to help you tomorrow," the sergeant said. "We've described for you what our scouting has shown, but you might find the intended target altered once in position."

Taylor cautioned that if either the position or objective had been compromised, or both, he must be prepared to amend the plan.

"If the situation turns out too serious to remedy," Taylor said, "the mission may have to be called off."

As disappointing as that could be for the Southern Army, Roger thought, he felt it to be the desired option.

It came time to practice firing the Whitworth at the distance prescribed through field reconnaissance. Thompson scanned the range through field glasses, while Taylor hid in safety near the target. After each shot, Taylor would approach the target and indicate where the shot hit. By the third shot, Roger was hitting the mark. Although he had limited success adjusting the rifle for the wind, the sharpshooter's instincts kept his shot patterns near the target's center circle. Both men were pleased with Roger's ability, and Roger was quite pleased with himself.

He was put into a prone position and given a small tripod on which to rest the rifle barrel. Thompson covered the rifle with brush and other material to determine if it affected his accuracy; it did not.

"Roger, we will use small shovels to dig a trench about body depth for you to lie in," Taylor said. "Gomer and I will then cover you with foliage. This will be done under the cover of darkness, where you will be left to wait until dawn."

"Our intel indicates your target will exit the tent shortly after daybreak," Thompson added. "Your window of opportunity will be brief, so do not hesitate to shoot."

"Once you have taken your shot," Taylor chimed in, "it will be up to you to either reload, in case of a miss, or evacuate. That will be entirely up to you."

Near the end of the day, Roger was given the specifics on his intended target. He was told how to identify the tent and the object of his mission. The sergeant and corporal said they knew only those facts and not who his target would be. He would recognize the target by the markings on the uniform.

"That sounds like a general," Roger observed.

"It is," Thompson said. "That's all you need to know."

After supper, Roger retired to his tent. He was told to sleep well since the trio would be moving out well before daybreak. Lying in the dark, Roger ran the plan through his head. Move into position, prepare the site, and Taylor and Thompson would provide concealment. When it was light enough for visual, he was to locate the tent in question. He would set his scope on the exit and wait for the target to emerge. Roger was to shoot as soon as his mark was in his sights, otherwise his objective could move out of range. There would be danger in having to wait for a second chance.

Chapter 12

Roger's attempt to sleep turned out to be a struggle, dealing with thoughts and emotions much like those he felt on the night he first learned of his family's death. Thinking of that helped steel his resolve.

Whether or not he ever fell asleep by the time Thompson and Taylor entered his tent that morning, Roger did not know. However, he felt fully awake as soon as he rolled out of bed. It was dark, cold and the two men spoke in a resonance just above a whisper. The knot in Roger's stomach ached.

"Here, put on this sweater and long coat," Taylor said. "It's specially designed for concealment and long-term wear. The sweater is for added warmth, as well as these mittens," the corporal continued, "but you'll have to remove the one on your trigger hand."

Roger gratefully slipped on the sweater. The coat was lightweight and did not fit him all that well. The mittens were also a welcome addition against the early morning chill.

The three men ran through a checklist to make sure they had everything needed. They would proceed on foot to the site where Roger would be stationed. Thompson and Taylor produced small shovels, plus hatchets and knives to cut brush for camouflage. Once the checklist was complete, the three men left the tent and made double-time until they reached the edge of the forest, totally blanketed in darkness.

"Stay right behind me and make as little noise as possible," Thompson said in a voice just above a whisper. "It will take us about twenty minutes to reach enemy lines, where there may be Union sentries on patrol. If we're spotted, abort the mission and do your best to make it back across Confederate lines."

"We would make our escape together, right?" Roger asked.

"Not necessarily," Thompson whispered. "Now move out."

Roger's heart sank. He had no idea where he was and would be totally lost in the dark. His only comfort was he carried the rifle.

During reconnaissance, Taylor and Thompson had scoped out the area meticulously and were able to move through the trees with little or no sound. Roger followed as closely as he could so as not to create any greater disturbance than that of his companions. However, his additional gear and the Whitworth rifle did not make the effort any easier.

Suddenly, Thompson came to a halt and raised his hand. Although it was still quite dark, Roger's eyes had grown somewhat accustomed, and he could see the sergeant's gestures. The three men stood still for several seconds before Thompson gave the sign to continue. They came to a spot on a small stream that was easy to cross and shallow enough to prevent water from flowing into their boots. Before long, they reached the other side of the forest where a large clearing lay before them.

"We will now move at a low profile," Thompson said in a full whisper. "Follow me closely. Stop when I stop and get face down on the ground. Get up when I get up and move forward – any questions?"

Roger shook his head to indicate "no," before considering the possibility Thompson could not see that in the dark. Thompson apparently did, or didn't care, as he took off at a quick pace, keeping his profile as low as he could. About every twenty paces, Thompson dropped face down on the ground. Taylor and Roger did the same. Then the sergeant rose again and was back on pace for another twenty steps. Thompson continued this tactical practice for about thirty minutes until they came to the edge of another group of trees.

"We'll set you up here," Thompson whispered. "We were able to survey this site with field glasses and picked this spot as the most advantageous. If you look down below, you can make out some white tents. That's the Yankee compound. The tent you want is visible from here and within range.

"There are some low-lying bushes here. We will dig a small trench and cover you up," the sergeant said. "You are to lie here until morning. You know the drill."

The men quickly dug a small trench allowing Roger to bury most of his body below ground level. Roger began setting up the tripod upon which to rest the barrel of the Whitworth rifle. Taylor and Thompson cut some small brush to cover the sharpshooter as best they could without interfering with his field of vision.

Preparations progressed much like they had rehearsed the day before, but at that time they were not behind enemy lines. Roger did not begin to realize his fears until Thompson and Taylor completed their camouflaging efforts and prepared to leave.

"It's almost daybreak, Brinkman," Thomson said. "We'll be moving out. I think you're going to be in great shape to be a hero in this war."

"Thanks," said Roger, desperately gulping in air to say it.

"Good luck, Buddy," Taylor said.

Within seconds, the sounds of Roger's companions moving away disappeared. He was now all alone. At least, he hoped he was.

When hunting, he could remember the agonizing times he had spent in a blind waiting for the sun to come up. This time, he hoped it never would. His breathing quickened and he could hear the beating of his heart. Before long, darkness slowly turned to dawn until it was light enough to see the Union camp and soldiers moving about. Roger peered through the scope on his rifle, putting the crosshairs on various targets. He could see some of the sentries moving out of the woods and being replaced by others. It made him wonder how three intruders ever got past them.

As the creeping light of day revealed the enormity of the task before him, a lump began to swell in his throat. He tried to picture his escape route but had no real knowledge of that terrain. He had seen it on a map, but never in reality.

Making every effort to push his fears down to meet the butterflies in his stomach, Roger trained his sights on the tent containing his target. Oh, how he hoped he would later learn that the officer he was to shoot would now be General Curtain. He did a quick survey of the area and spotted a flag hanging limp on a flagpole – terrific, no wind.

There was a soldier standing near the opening of the tent containing the objective of his mission. The soldier was at ease and looking down at his rifle. Roger centered his scope on the soldier's chest to determine his range. The scope had been preset for the approximate length of his shot, and Roger decided it was too far to attempt any adjustment to his sight. He was probably going to get off just one shot. If he hit his target, the chaos in camp would be to his advantage, if he missed – Union advantage.

As he focused, using the guard by the tent for his range, the soldier suddenly snapped to attention. Roger's heart began to race, but what he saw nearly stopped it completely.

"Oh, my God!" Roger said under his breath. The soldier snapping to attention was Nik Brinkman!

Roger froze; he lowered his head in confused disbelief.

Meanwhile, Sergeant Thompson and Corporal Taylor had stationed themselves about five-hundred yards behind Brinkman to confirm the kill. Thompson had his field glasses trained on the tent and Taylor scanned the terrain to better determine the enemy's activities.

As Roger looked up and peered through the scope, a tall, bearded man in civilian clothes and a towering top hat came out, bending over to clear the tent exit. He stepped past Nik and turned to face the man following him. Coming out of the tent next was a general. The officer stopped to talk with the tall civilian with Nik right in the middle – Roger could not shoot.

***

"Why doesn't he shoot!" Thompson said in a hoarse voice while peering at McClellan and President Lincoln through his field glasses. "He's got a shot."

***

As Roger lay there, frozen with fear, he heard footsteps approaching his location. Now his heart was pounding so hard he thought his ears would bleed. Suddenly, the footsteps stopped, and Roger could hear someone cocking a gun. Afraid to move his head to see, he decided to defend himself. Roger rolled away from the direction of the sound and pulled the Whitworth into position. Bursting forth from his hiding spot, he surprised a Union sentry who had stopped only to check his rifle. Just as the soldier raised his weapon to take aim, Brinkman fired!

The extra-load of the Whitworth's recoil was so hard the weapon flew from Roger's grasp, cutting his hand. The bullet hit the Union soldier square in the chest and knocked him back and off his feet. Overcome by regret after realizing what he had done, Roger scrambled over to assist the heavily bleeding soldier. He heard shouts coming from the Union camp aroused by the shooting and knew he was in imminent danger. Desperate, Roger spotted a pistol tucked in the dead man's belt. He grabbed it knowing it could prove his best chance at defending himself.

"God bless you and have mercy on your soul," Roger said softly over the fallen soldier, "... and on mine."

Roger then fetched the Whitworth and disappeared into the woods opposite the one from which he came. He ran in the opposite direction of the Union encampment, only hoping he was going the right way.

***

"What the hell was that?" Thompson said, responding to the gunshot, while still peering through his field glasses.

"Brinkman shot a sentry," Taylor said. "I think he's making a break to escape."

"A sentry!?" Thompson responded. "What about the general?"

"Too late now, Sarge. We had better clear out ourselves," said Taylor.

With that, the two men grabbed their gear and headed for the woods.

***

Deft at moving through forests, Roger made excellent time despite the unfamiliar surroundings. Having arrived at his sniper location in the dark, he had no idea where he was or which way he should go. He could remember crossing a stream with Thompson and Taylor, but he knew not where. Although it was possible he could outrun the Union soldiers, Roger concluded it would be best if he hid and waited. If necessary, he would surrender.

Spotting a tree with thick branches, but few leaves due to the advancing winter, he placed the Whitlock in some bushes and began to climb. It was then he noticed his bleeding hand. He tried to climb with his good hand to keep blood off the tree trunk, but he was not sure if he was successful. He found a suitable spot high in the tree where his uniform would blend in. He had a good view of the landscape but put his head down, prayed and waited.

Detecting the sound of movement, he slowly raised his head to see a figure approaching. He held his breath and put his hand on the pistol he had taken from the fallen soldier. Through the underbrush, he could tell the movement was a soldier traveling stealthily through the forest. His only hope was that the soldier was alone. He put his head down and waited.

Eventually, the footsteps stopped. He was afraid to lift his head, but knew if spotted, he was a sitting duck.

"Come down from there," a voice called out.

He recognized the voice and slowly raised his head.

"Nik, is that you?" Roger called out in a hoarse whisper.

"Roger? Roger Brinkman? What are you doing up there?" Nik said in a bit stronger voice than Roger was using. The emotions of that fateful day in Bordertown came flooding back to Nik. The joys and fears of seeing Roger again rendered him almost speechless.

"Be quiet. I'm the one you're looking for," Roger answered.

"My God, come down from there," Nik called, trying to control the tenor of his voice. Nik loved his brother, but he could not help but wonder how that tragedy in their past may have affected their relationship.

Roger climbed down out of the tree and was going to embrace Nik, but Nik backed away.

"Whoa, Roger, why are you in that uniform?" Nik said, shocked by what he saw. "What in tarnation have you done?"

"Nik, it's a long story. Please don't turn me in," Roger pleaded.

"Turn you in? Roger, you don't know how I've longed to see you again," Nik blurted out the words, struggling to hold down his voice. "Roger, I am so sorry."

"I'm sorry too, Nik, but I can't tell you how happy I am to see you."

Roger's words comforted Nik, who for a long time worried that Roger might think him responsible for their family's death. The emotion of this unlikely reunion brought them together in an embrace that neither wanted to end. Suddenly, Nik pulled away.

"My God, Roger, you've joined the Confederacy," Nik said. "What were you thinking?"

"I did it because I thought they would help me find Colonel Curtain," Roger said.

"Colonel Curtain? I don't understand," said Nik.

"I was told he and a group of Yankee soldiers killed Ma, Pa, Dolly and maybe you, too, for all I knew. Because of what they did, I became a Reb in hopes of finding him and killing him," Roger said.

"That man was no colonel and no soldier. He was a rogue outlaw looking to steal slaves and resell them to an underground market," Nik said. "Had it not been for Pa, I would never have escaped. It was horrible, my brother...," Nik's voice faltered as tears filled his eyes. "Afterward, the only thing I could think to do was join the Union cause."

"I know I messed up, Nik, but I didn't know what to do, either. I,

I…, I joined up to learn how to kill," Roger said, hanging his head in bewildered shame. "The army wanted me to shoot your general and then I saw you and, in the confusion, ended up shooting that poor soldier," Roger lamented, shaking his head as tears filled his eyes.

"Shoot the general? You mean McClellan? That would have been a waste," Nik said, putting his hand on Roger's shoulder. "President Lincoln fired him. Why did they pick you to do the shooting?"

"I was assigned to the Confederate Sharpshooter Corps, and they sent me here for this assignment," Roger answered. "When I saw you by the general's tent, I couldn't shoot. Then that soldier showed up and… well, here I am."

"Look, Roger, it might be a good thing if I brought you back as a prisoner, but I'm not sure what kind of treatment you would get. I'm here because I followed your trail of blood. The other soldiers can't track like you and I can.

"It might be best if you get back up in that tree and make good your escape tonight," Nik concluded.

"But I don't know where I am, Nik. I'm lost. I don't know this country," Roger said, exasperated at the situation.

"Look, there'll be a sliver of a moon tonight shortly after nightfall. Just follow it and it will lead you to the Confederate line," Nik said. "Just be careful the Rebs don't shoot you by mistake."

"And here, take my bandana and keep that hand wrapped," Nik continued, helping to wrap Roger's wounded hand.

"I'm afraid I got blood on your jacket, Nik…," Roger noted.

"it's all right. I'll just say it's from that man you shot," Nik responded. "I did stop to see if I could help him, but there was nothing I could do."

"Nik, my brother, I'm sorry about all this," Roger said. "Please stay safe and hopefully we'll meet up again under better circumstances."

"I will pray for it and you, brother. Now, Godspeed and get back up that tree," Nik said.

Roger did just as Nik said, while his brother turned and retraced his steps back toward the Union camp. Roger sat in the tree watching Nik until he disappeared into the forest. Then, Roger's tears began to flood down his cheeks. He buried his face into the partially bloodied bandana and sobbed, wondering how in the world his life had come to this.

As darkness fell, Roger slipped down out of the tree tired and hungry. Just as Nik had said, a sliver of the moon was setting in the western night sky. He made sure to retrieve the Whitworth Rifle and then set out in the direction of the crescent moon.

Chapter 13

Nik's directions led Roger back to the Confederate camp, as the tired and hungry soldier knew they would. He did not encounter any trouble along the way and even made sure the camp picket he came upon did not shoot him by mistake. Once he identified himself, the guard called for assistance. The mess tent was closed, but a sergeant among those who came to help was able to round up some grub for the famished sharpshooter. The word was that if he made it back, he was to report to the general's tent at eight-hundred hours the next day. Roger was grateful for that, as he needed some sleep and time to think. He thanked the soldiers for their help and retired to his tent.

Roger slumped down onto his cot, and with his elbows on his knees he put his face into his hands. He had intended to pray, but the ordeal of the last twenty-four hours kept running through his head, upsetting his concentration. He was dog tired and wanted to sleep, but images of what he'd just been through kept flashing in his mind's eye.

"So, you killed a soldier, did you?" Roger hesitated and then slowly looked up. He stared at what appeared to be a battle-weary soldier sitting on the cot across from him. The man's eyes seemed sunken and appeared vacant. He was unshaven, somewhat disheveled and looking fatigued. "How does that feel?" the soldier asked.

"How do you think it feels?" Roger answered. "But if you want to know the real truth, I really can't tell how it feels."

"Did you ever think you would be a soldier involved in a war?" the old warrior asked.

"Of course not," Roger shot back. "And I didn't think I'd lose my family, either."

"Yeah, that was a shame, all right," the old soldier said. "I'll bet it was nice to see Nik again, though?"

"I really thought I would never lay eyes on him again, then finding him here no less," Roger said, letting out a sigh.

"Yeah, it was nice of him to help you. Being as how you two are on the opposite sides in this war," the visitor said.

"In one way we are opposites," Roger said pensively, "and in another way we're… well, we're brothers."

"That you are, son, that you are," said the soldier.

Suddenly the duty officer burst into Roger's tent. "I heard a voice, who were you talking to?" said the officer.

"Oh, ah…," Roger said, looking over at the cot where the soldier had been sitting, "ah, nobody. Just mumbling to myself, sorry, sir." Roger stood up at attention and offered a salute.

"You okay?" the officer asked, returning the salute.

"I'm fine, sir, thank you," Roger said. "Just a little tired."

"Okay, goodnight, then," the officer replied and then departed.

Roger lay down on his back and, while looking at the ceiling of his tent, continued retracing all the events of the recent past. Despite the disturbing visions that kept racing across his memory, he drifted off to sleep.

He was awakened by the rat-a-tat-tat of a drum calling the soldiers to fall in for roll call. Roger slid his legs off the bunk to put his feet on the floor of his tent. He still had his boots on, and the bandana was still wrapped around his wounded hand. Just looking at it reminded him that Nik was still alive, and that gave him a feeling of near euphoria. As he sat on the edge of his bunk trying to gather himself, Thompson and Taylor came into the tent.

"We have a report to give at oh-eight-hundred hours. Best not be late," Thompson said. "Glad you made it back."

"What happened out there?" Taylor asked. "We saw you shoot that Yankee soldier."

"You saw that?" Roger asked.

"Yes. We were stationed about five hundred yards behind you to record the kill," Taylor added. "Did that sentry spot you?"

"I figured he had and at first I did not move out of fear. Then I thought maybe he had not spotted me and so I remained still, so as not to give myself away," Roger said, surprised to hear that Thompson and Taylor saw the whole thing. "But when I heard him cock his gun, I knew I had to act fast."

"We'll be anxious to hear all about that at report," Thompson said.

"Yes, I'll see you there," Roger answered. "First, I've got to get myself something to eat."

The two soldiers left Roger, who took off the field jacket they had given him and put on his jacket of issue. He was mulling over what Thompson and Taylor saw, or thought they saw. He was hoping his story would match theirs. During his breakfast of bacon and cornbread, he decided he would tell it just as it happened, including the part about being discovered by his brother, Nik.

At eight-hundred hours, he was ushered into the general's tent, came to attention and saluted. Thompson and Taylor were standing off to one side.

"Private Brinkman, Thompson and Taylor have briefed me on the operation and the unfortunate fact it did not succeed," the general stated, looking up from the table that served as his desk. "Naturally, I'm glad you're back safe, and I understand you managed to keep the Whitworth rifle in your possession."

"Thank you, sir," Roger said.

"At ease, soldier," the general ordered. "I should like to hear your side of the story."

"Thanks to the training and assistance of both Sergeant Thomp..." Roger began.

"No need for the gratuities, private," the general interrupted. "Let me hear what happened from the point you had McClellan in your sights."

A segue would have helped give Roger some time to calm down and gather his thoughts, but that was not going to happen.

"I... I saw something, ... someone that caused me to hesitate with that shot," Roger said.

"President Lincoln? Or do you mean the sentry coming up on you?" the general asked.

"No, sir, my brother, sir," Roger said

"Your brother? What was he doing in your sights?" the general inquired.

"Standing guard at the entrance to the Union general's tent," Roger answered.

"Gentlemen," General Jackson said, addressing Thompson and Taylor. "Can you confirm this?"

"Sir, there was a guard," Thompson said, "but the only one I saw was a black man."

"Can you explain this, Brinkman? Just where did you see your brother?" the general questioned, somewhat confused.

"The guard, sir, the black guard was my brother, Nik Brinkman," Roger said. "I simply could not take the chance my shot might hit him. He was standing right next to the general."

"You have a black brother? Was your father twice married?" the general continued.

"It's a bit of a long story, sir, but he is the reason I was unable to take that shot," Roger offered. "It was at that time the sentry happened to stumble upon my location."

"Gentlemen, you may be excused," the general interrupted, speaking to Thompson and Taylor. "Brinkman, I want you to tell me that long story. And you may sit down to do so."

After Thompson and Taylor left, Roger sat down and explained to the general about Nik, how he came to be a Brinkman and his escape from the so-called colonel who killed his family.

"That's a touching story, Brinkman," the general said. "I cannot say I am not disappointed. This mission could have saved a lot of lives had it been successful, although we generals knew the probability of its failure was great, indeed. Was there a chance you could have shot when your … brother was not in the line of fire?"

"From the time I saw Nik, until the sentry was on me, I think was only a matter of seconds," Roger answered. "Once I fired at the sentry, I sort of panicked."

"Have you been in a situation like this before, private?" Jackson questioned.

"No, sir, this was my first assignment, sir… I am sorry…," Roger began.

"No need to apologize, private," the general cut in. "Apologies are not a part of this inquiry. "Tell me of your escape."

Roger related his escape into the woods after shooting the Union soldier and how the cut on his hand left a trail of blood that Nik followed. Roger told of the brief reunion between the brothers and Nik's assistance in helping him find his way back to camp.

"And how did… this Nik, feel about you being a Confederate soldier?" the general inquired.

"He was surprised by it, sir. He suggested taking me prisoner, but he was not certain I would be treated well. We parted as brothers, though," Roger concluded.

"As difficult as this may be for you, your brother is a Union soldier. You could have shot him from your vantage point in the tree, could you not?" the general asked.

"No, sir. Like I said, sir, he is my brother," Roger answered. "Besides, I had hidden the rifle, not wanting to climb with it." Roger thought it best not to mention the pistol.

"I see, private," the general said. "I will pass this report on to headquarters. There are mitigating circumstances, and your story was corroborated by Thompson and Taylor. However, your hesitation to shoot may require disciplinary action. Confederate soldiers are required to shoot Union soldiers, brothers or otherwise. You will be confined to your tent under guard. If you try to escape, you will be shot. Is that understood, private?"

"Yes, sir," Roger responded weakly, looking at the dirt floor of the tent with regret.

"However, we have orders to move out tomorrow and I will have to turn your case over to General Lee for review. The Commander will decide if he wants to take any further disciplinary action."

"Yes, sir," Roger said, relieved that his story at least matched that of Taylor and Thompson.

The general called in his attaché and instructed him as to Roger's confinement.

"You are dismissed, private," the general said.

Roger stood up, came to attention and saluted, but before departing he hesitated.

"Permission to speak, sir," Roger said, still standing at attention.

"What is it, private?" the general allowed.

"Sir, my brother told me Lincoln had fired General McClellan," Roger said, remembering Nik's comment.

"Lincoln fired McClellan?" the general responded, piqued by Roger's comment. "Are you sure?"

"I can only say my brother would not lie to me, sir, but he did not say it in confidence," Roger answered. "He was only needling me on the irony of my failure."

The general rose from his chair and placed his fists on his desk and leaned forward. "If you are lying to mitigate your circumstances, private, it will go worse for you if this is not true," he warned.

"I can only relate what he told me, sir," Roger acquiesced. "I cannot confirm it nor expect favor because of it."

"Very good, soldier," the general said thoughtfully. "This will be passed on to General Lee, as well as the rest of your testimony."

"Yes, sir," Roger responded, saluting again.

"Dismissed," the general repeated.

Roger left the tent in the company of the attaché.

The general orders were being given throughout the camp to prepare to move out in the morning. Soldiers were taking down their tents and packing up their gear. There were those who would be left behind to defend the position, but most infantry and artillery units were getting ready to move.

Under guard, Roger was escorted back to his billets. His tent was inspected for weapons, and he was told he and his escort would follow the troops to Lee's command the next day. A guard was stationed outside his tent.

He packed his gear and lay down on his bunk, only to hit his head on something under his pillow – the Colt Army pistol. A sudden flash of fear ran through him. He said a quiet prayer of thanks that his guard did not think to look under the pillow. Afraid he would be caught with it, he used it to quietly dig a small hole near the edge of his tent, buried it and returned to his bed. He again whispered a silent prayer, giving thanks that he did not mention the pistol to the general and added a request it never be found.

***

The march to Lee's winter headquarters took less than two days and General Jackson's unit arrived in General Lee's camp late the next morning. Roger remained under guard but was not bound. One of Lee's lieutenants caught up with the sergeant leading Roger's escort.

"Is this Private Brinkman?" the lieutenant asked the sergeant.

"Yes, it is, sir," the sergeant answered.

"Sergeant, you and the prisoner are to come with me. You soldiers may report to your units," the lieutenant said. He then led Roger and the sergeant directly to Lee's headquarters, where he dismissed the sergeant and spoke to the guards outside Lee's tent.

Upon entering the general's headquarters, the lieutenant presented Roger to the general.

"At ease, private," Lee said. Two officers flanked the general, standing at ease. "General Jackson has informed me that you are a trained sharpshooter. Is that the case?"

"I trained at Little Rock under Major Baumgartner, sir," Brinkman said.

Lee continued "I understand you have a brother fighting for the Union?"

"Yes, sir. He was a part of McClellan's staff, I believe, sir," Roger said.

"And your brother is black. Was he a slave?" the general inquired.

"He is black, sir, but he was really never a slave," Roger said.

Following Lee's request to continue, Roger explained how Nik became a part of the Brinkman family and how they were separated when Roger went off to school. After the death of the Brinkman family, Nik ended up in the Union Army while Roger enlisted with the Confederacy.

"I have read your report and regret your mission failed. I have to decide if further discipline is necessary," the commander of the Army of Northern Virginia began. "I could use a sharpshooter, but I need one willing to shoot. What do you have to say for yourself?"

"As I told General Jackson…" Roger started.

"I have read the report private," the general interrupted. "I want to know if you have what it takes to be a soldier or do I have to brand you for cowardice."

"I was not a coward, sir," Roger said straightaway, shocked by the accusation. "I was surprised by what I saw, and circumstances made it impossible for me to carry out my assignment as requested."

"Can you convince me of that?" Lee asked.

"Sir, I killed a sentry making an immediate decision that I was about to be shot. The sound of that Whitworth going off alerted the entire Union camp. I knew my only option was to escape, sir," Roger replied, struck by the determination in his voice. "I…"

"Hold on, private," the general said. "Setting aside the failure of firing your weapon in order to fulfill your mission, I have to know if you have what it takes to serve in the Southern Army."

Roger paused for a short time to gather his thoughts. "If I may speak freely, sir," he said.

"Please do, I need to get to the bottom of this as soon as possible," Lee said, showing impatience at having to adjudicate the issue.

"I joined the Confederacy to learn to fight, sir," Roger began. "I did kill a Union soldier, although he was not my assigned target. I cannot deny my duty as a soldier comes in conflict with the life I once led, but I do want to put that behind me. I need the army as much as I hope it needs me."

Lee stared at Roger for a few moments, then said, "Is it true your brother told you McClellan had been fired?"

"He did, sir," Roger responded.

"Would your brother, … Nik, give you more information if you asked?" the general inquired.

"No sir, I do not believe he would," Roger answered.

"Why not, if you're brothers?" Lee asked.

"He would never betray the trust of the Union Army," Roger added. "My brother considered the information he gave me ironic and unimportant."

After contemplating Roger's reply, the general leaned forward and folded his hands on the desk.

"Private, I need good men and I am inclined to accept your explanation – providing you continue to serve with distinction," the general said. "You will serve me as an attaché, a guard, sharpshooter and soldier. If you fail me in any way, your punishment will be severe. Do I make myself clear?"

"You do, sir," said Roger. "I will make it up to you, sir."

"See that you do," said the general. "I do not have time for soldiers who will not fight or follow orders."

Lee told the lieutenant to instruct Roger on his duties and get him the proper gear to do so. He was assigned to the attaché tent and dismissed.

Lieutenant Connor Rickman escorted Roger to his quarters and began relating the details of his new assignment.

"General Lee is under a lot of pressure," Rickman confided. "I think you got off easy because of it. If you perform your duties properly, this will all blow over. I suggest you do not push your luck around him."

"Yes, sir," Roger answered, still somewhat shaken by Lee's words.

"General Lee is a good man and highly respected by his men." Rickman said. "I hope you will serve him in that capacity, private."

"I fully intend to do that, sir, and thank you for the assistance," Roger said.

After Lieutenant Rickman departed, Roger sat on his cot and tried to sort out all he had been through. He was surprised at the gravity of military justice, but pleased his reprimand was light. He wanted the army to mold him into a man willing to fight, even kill, but his confidence had been shaken to the core. He was used to things going his way but now had doubts. Would he emerge from this war the man he imagined he would? – time would tell.

As the colder months approached, Roger had time to recuperate in Lee's winter camp. He had planned to write to the Carrossas and Gloria but learned his letters would not likely be delivered. He was told terminating federal postal service was one of the hardships the Union had placed on the South. The other hardships were poor rations and inadequate clothing against the wintry weather. Many in his outfit became disillusioned and more than one soldier deserted Lee's command during that time. He was reminded of Rickman's words about the pressure Lee was under. Roger resolved to serve Lee to the best of his ability.

Without any contact with the life he once knew, Roger turned his attention to Colonel Curtain. During guard duty, he would imagine Curtain charging into camp intent on killing General Lee. He used the vision to help fortify his conviction that he would shoot even if the attacker wasn't Curtain.

When winter edged into spring and the fighting increased, Lee began using Roger as a sharpshooter. Roger exercised a similar strategy to bolster his courage when assigned to carry out a mission. His targets were far enough away that he simply imagined each as being one of the men who killed his family. Seeing the Union uniform helped raise his contempt and determination to aim and fire. The blast and smoke from his rifle gave away his position, prompting him to make a hasty retreat. That also eased his conscience by limiting visual confirmation of the kill.

Roger's renewed commitment to the general prompted Lee to promote him to corporal. Awareness of Roger's seminary training also led the commander to confide in him.

One day, while on guard duty, Roger snapped to attention and offered his best salute as General Lee approached. The Confederate commander was returning from a strategy meeting.

"At ease, Brinkman," the general said, returning the salute. "Step into my headquarters for a moment, if you will." Roger entered the tent behind the general. Lee removed his hat, laid it on his desk and continued, "Please, have a seat."

"What are your thoughts on slavery, corporal?"

"I cannot say that I am in favor of it, sir."

"And why is that?" Lee inquired.

"After spending a good part of my life living with someone who would have been a slave under different circumstances, I cannot see him as being any different than I, sir," Roger said, knowing the general preferred honesty over discretion.

"Really, I come from a state that sees the Negro slave as being in the position God intended. I do not favor the practice, myself, but I can empathize with Virginia's position," Lee began. "I am here because I am sworn to defend my state's right to follow the path it has chosen."

"You are a man of higher learning and greater responsibility than I, sir," Roger replied. "I have to believe your convictions are based on things I cannot know, at least not now."

"Sound answer, corporal," Lee said. "I believe you were attending a Lutheran seminary, right?"

"Yes, sir, it was the faith of my father," Roger answered.

"I believe the Lutherans do not support slavery, is that right?" the general's eyes narrowed as he spoke.

"I am of the mind that is the case, sir," Roger answered. "But I cannot say if it is church policy."

"Odd how we differ there," Lee mused, leaning back in his chair. "You see, my church holds the practice to be biblical. You do know that Hebrews held slaves?"

"And were slaves, at times," the corporal answered. "But I do not believe they were enslaved because of their color."

"Perhaps you're right, soldier," Lee said, bending forward in his chair. "I hope circumstances offer us a chance to speak again. You may return to your post now."

"Yes, sir," Roger replied. He rose from his seat, saluted and returned to his duty station.

Late that spring, Lee and Jackson won a decisive battle at Chancellorsville. Since the charge that broke the Union defenses was made by Jackson, Roger was not called into action from Lee's command. However, he felt he would one day be asked to fight on the front lines, and he tried to mentally prepare for it.

After the battle at Chancellorsville, a small Rebel unit accompanied General Jackson on a reconnaissance mission. As the detachment returned to camp that night, they were shocked when a Confederate picket mistakenly fired on Jackson. The general's wound required the amputation of his arm and he later died of complications. General Lee was devastated.

Whether driven by the success of Chancellorsville or the loss of his most trusted general, Lee made a poor decision for a three-day assault on the Union at Gettysburg, Pennsylvania. Roger was assigned to an infantry unit in that campaign, but Lee held back his sharpshooter for the final day. Heavy losses during the first two days of fighting forced Lee to scrap the attack on the third day and retreat into Virginia. Although he never fired a shot, Roger saw firsthand the carnage of war, as Lee lost up to a third of his manpower.

To add to the general's blunder at Gettysburg, Union General Ulysses S. Grant's troops had overrun Vicksburg, Mississippi, gaining control of the Mississippi River waterway.

Taking his regular post at the defeated general's tent, Roger learned that Lee offered his resignation to Confederate President Jefferson Davis, but Davis refused to accept it.

Chapter 14

As the war again entered the winter season, Lee spent those months trying to bolster the morale of his Northern Virginia Command, but time and enlistments were running out. However, those who remained were determined fighters.

Before the campaign of 1864, Roger was called into the commander's headquarters.

"Son, I'm going to need you to join the riflemen on the front lines," Lee instructed, relating those fateful words Roger had been dreading but expecting. "We have been able to hit Grant hard, but we cannot seem to stop him or mount a successful offensive. We'll dig in at Cold Harbor and see if we can't turn this thing around."

"Yes, sir," Roger said. "Where should I go?"

"I'm assigning you to General Porter," Lee said. "His is an artillery unit, but he can use your skills as a rifleman to help ward off assaults on his position."

After reaching Porter's emplacement, Roger found it well-bunkered, offering good cover from which to fire. Most of the other soldiers there manned the cannons under Porter's command.

"Are you one of the replacement recruits?" a soldier asked, crouching down behind the stone wall next to Roger.

"More of an add-on," Roger answered, as the two leaned their backs against the dust-covered stones of their bunker. "I'm one of General Lee's attachés," the corporal continued. "I was recruited as a sharpshooter, but that job has kind of disappeared."

The other soldier was older than Roger by maybe 10 years. He was gaunt, and his uniform reflected the many campaigns in which he had likely fought. Roger noticed he was still a private and wondered if he was among those forgotten soldiers who were now numbers without names.

"A sharpshooter, eh?" the soldier said, giving a little glance over the wall and then looking back at Roger. "Seeing through the cannon smoke of this battle will be a real test for you. I recommend you stuff some cloth in your ears to help keep your hearing sharp, as well." The man smiled as if telling a joke, although it proved to be sound advice.

"Thanks, I'll do that. I'm Roger, by the way."

"Vince Puckett, Mobile, Alabama," the soldier said. "If I don't make it out of this war, maybe you can look up my family and tell 'em we fought alongside each other."

"Sure, I'll do that," Roger said, dismissing the suggestion of "not making it." He ripped off two pieces of cloth from his bandana, rolled them up and stuffed them in his ears. As the afternoon shadows began to grow, a Confederate lieutenant ducking below the stone wall moved along telling everyone to fix bayonets. Roger did not have a bayonet and his stomach began to ache in anticipation of such a battle. Shortly after the officer moved on, the sounds of Union troops breaking out across the clearing just beyond the wall could be heard.

"Let it begin," Puckett muttered, rising to his knees, and positioning his rifle on the wall. Roger followed suit, rolling into position, and firing at the distant blue line of soldiers running toward them. He then squatted back down to reload.

"Hold your fire until I give the signal," the lieutenant called out.

Roger paused, slightly embarrassed realizing he was out of his element as an infantryman. But it was only a moment later when the officer gave the order to shoot, and the cannons exploded in a barrage of firepower. Roger finished reloading and popped up to shoot once again. And like Puckett said, all he could see was smoke, but he fired anyway. He slipped down to reload when a streak of blue flew over his head. A Union soldier had breached the wall.

Roger looked up as the soldier turned and charged with his bayonet aimed at Roger's chest. A shot rang out and the Union soldier collapsed face-first at Roger's outstretched feet, his musket beneath him.

"That was close," Puckett called out. After reloading, the older soldier had raised up in time to see the soldier clear the abutment. He instantly spun around and shot the intruder. Roger could hear bullets whizzing over his head as he fumbled at trying to load another cartridge. Puckett took just seconds before he was back in shooting position and quickly dropped back down with blood pouring across his face from a small hole above his left eye. The sight drove Roger into a trance-like state, reminding him of the first soldier he saw fall during that fateful train ride home. However, he continued to reload, rise, shoot, and drop back down to reload again. He was unaware of how often he had repeated that action when he was shaken back to his senses.

"Ceasefire, corporal, ceasefire," said the officer rocking him by the shoulder. "The Yanks have retreated." Roger merely stared at the officer as if coming out of a bad dream. He looked down at Puckett, who was lying dead beside him.

"Do you know that man, corporal?" the lieutenant asked.

"Ahh, yeah, his name is Vince Puckett," Roger replied, "from Mobile, Alabama."

"Thanks, corporal," the officer responded. "We'll try to notify his family."

Roger looked up at the officer and said, "Would you do me a favor?"

"Sure, corporal, what can I do for you?"

"Would you tell his family that he saved my life?" Roger's voice was without emotion as he continued to stare at the officer.

"I will, corporal. Perhaps you should move to the rear and get something to eat and rest awhile," the officer continued. "We'll begin rotating posts so everyone can get a break. You'll be notified when to return."

The evening shadows were descending into darkness and the officer called two men over to help Roger find his way back to camp. Roger used his rifle to pull himself up and the officer could see it had no bayonet attached.

"Here," he said, reaching down to remove the bayonet from the fallen soldier's rifle. "Better take Puckett's bayonet. You may need it before this is all over."

Roger took the blade from the officer and locked it in place on his rifle. He joined the two men, who weaved their way through a wooded area back to camp. Upon reaching the camp Roger departed from the two soldiers and went straight to the attachés tent, now empty, and lay down. He had no appetite, and all he could see in the dark was the image of Vince Puckett's wounded face.

Roger was unaware of what time he was awakened to return to his post. There were other soldiers moving back to the front, gliding like silent shadows against a starry sky. Roger fell in line and followed, numbed by the specter of death that now hung in the air.

When he reached his post, he realized he was not in the same location he had been the previous day. Roger followed the dark figures ahead of him into a trench where he promptly stumbled over a dead body. The man following dragged the body out of the trench and returned to fill the fallen soldier's position. The shallow ditch had no stone wall and through the early hints of dawn, Roger could see there were only riflemen, no cannons. He realized he was now just another soldier on the front lines. His job was to help turn back an anticipated attack and, if fortune was on his side, survive. After sliding down and leaning his back against the wall of the trench, he tried closing his eyes to wait for the sun to rise behind him, but that effort was again greeted by Puckett's bleeding face. There would be no rest that day.

At daybreak, there was very little gunfire, mostly in the distance, and Roger could see battle-worn soldiers next to him with their rifles in position simply scanning the landscape. He turned to do the same and saw nothing but a quiet field covered with blue-clad bodies and ravens picking at exposed flesh. The air was acrid, filled with the smell of gunpowder, death and decay. It was June in Virginia, but it could just as well have been a late-spring morning in hell.

For the better part of the day, the soldiers waiting in the trenches seemed almost relaxed. The sounds of occasional gunshots in the distance continued, but little else broke the silence. As the day moved into the late afternoon, the call came for the troops to evacuate the trench and move out.

When the orders came down, the word on the frontline was that Grant had decided to end his attack on Cold Harbor and do an end-run for Richmond via Petersburg. Lee then called for a forced march into that city for what would be the last major battle of the Civil War.

Roger returned to the camp at Cold Harbor, where he found the attaché tent being taken down. One of the soldiers informed him that Lee was moving his headquarters to Violet Bank overlooking Petersburg. After helping load the tent and supplies onto a wagon, Roger climbed on board for the long ride to where the Army of Northern Virginia would make its final stand.

To assist in countering the siege Grant brought against Petersburg, Roger was pulled from the front lines and assigned reconnaissance duty.

"Corporal, you have served the South well, and I am now reassigning you to serve as a scout and sharpshooter, should that opportunity present itself," Lee said, now occupying the mansion at Violet Bank Farm. "We are under siege and need to find out as much as we can as to Grant's movements and weaknesses, if he has any."

"Yes, sir," Corporal Brinkman answered. "Will I have orders or reconnoiter on my own?"

Roger was asked to find strategic locations from which to observe Federal troop movements and was given a map to outline areas where he saw Union soldiers gathering. He was to carry a notebook to record information and a pair of binoculars. He also had a Whitworth rifle, just in case one of Lee's "opportunities" came his way.

Roger put most of his efforts into gathering intelligence, and that proved to be of great assistance to Lee. The Army of Northern Virginia was about half the size of the Union forces and Roger's reports helped Lee to counter Grant's moves. Recalling the stealth tactics

Nik had taught him, Roger was able to find strategic observation locations close to federal lines, where he would sometimes spend hours. Once he stayed in the same position too long and was driven away after being spotted by a Union sharpshooter. He chose to escape with his information rather than return fire.

The coming of winter weather made life miserable for the Southern soldiers manning the bunkers surrounding Petersburg. Soldiers were sitting in cold water wearing clothing inadequate for the conditions. The men virtually welcomed combat because it took their minds off the misery, hunger and sickness exacerbating their situation. Desertions were not uncommon on either side, but for Lee, they were particularly damaging.

Roger also had to contend with the weather during the day, but at night, he could return to Violet Bank where a dry bed in the attaché tent awaited him. What bothered him most about his job was the probability his efforts were prolonging the war. He sensed the end of hostilities was drawing near, but Lee was not about to give up.

The commander of the Southern Army had great hopes Confederate General Joseph Johnston would arrive in time to rally the Rebels once more. But news of Union General Tecumseh Sherman decimating Georgia meant that Confederate hope for Johnston's return was becoming wishful thinking.

Grant's successes in cutting off Confederate supplies to Petersburg also contributed to Lee's growing problems. After a near ten-month siege, the word came down that Richmond had fallen, and the Confederate Capital had been abandoned. Lee had little choice, but to consider moving the Army of Northern Virginia into North Carolina to meet up with Johnston.

The month of March was now spilling into April, and the climate was improving. Roger's reconnaissance assignments continued, and one spring day he was perched on a ridge overlooking the battle lines northeast of Petersburg. Like the Confederates entrenched below him, he was unaware of Lee's pending orders to move out. Roger scanned the area with his field glasses and spotted some Union activity north of the Appomattox River. A Federal detachment was moving a cannon into range with plans to shell the bunkered soldiers. Without thinking, Roger reached for his Whitlock rifle and peered at the embattlement through his scope. He could see the Union soldiers preparing the artillery and knew the Confederates below him were totally unaware of the impending bombardment.

Roger rolled onto his side, loaded the Whitworth, and rolled back into position to shoot. As he peered through the scope, he set the crosshairs on the cannon's fuse and did his best to adjust for range. He could see the artillerist approaching, while the other soldiers moved back. Roger put his sights on the soldier holding the torch.

As the soldier approached the fuse to light it – Roger fired. The artillerist and torch dropped from view.

Almost immediately following the shot, bullets began whizzing over Roger's head with one striking the hill just below his position. He determined the gunfire was coming from the Confederate trench, where the soldiers must have assumed his position was that of a Union sharpshooter. He put his head down to avoid being hit when suddenly the shooting stopped. He slowly looked up and saw Rebel troops pouring out of the trenches and retreating from the battlefield. Unbeknown to Roger, Lee had given his order for those soldiers to move out. Not knowing this, the sharpshooter maintained his location to offer cover fire if needed.

Roger then scanned back to the embattlement and saw the cannon was receding. In response, he slowly began to crawl backward from his position, thinking it best if he joined the retreating Confederates.

"On your feet, Reb," a voice called out from behind him. "Get up slowly and leave your weapon where it is." Roger let go of the Whitworth and did as he was told, with his back to whoever was speaking.

When told to turn around, the sun was in his eyes, but he could make out four men surrounding his position with shadowy images of rifles pointed his way.

"Why don't we just shoot him, Sarge?" one soldier suggested.

"No," the sergeant said. "If he's a sharpshooter he may have special orders, information we could use."

"Roger?" said one of the men.

"You know this man?" the sergeant asked.

"I do," came the reply.

With the sun behind the large man, Roger raised his hand to shade his eyes and recognized the soldier was Ambrose Tucker.

"Ambrose?" Roger said, a smile crossing his face. "You're Union?"

"Enough with the small talk," the sergeant cut in. "We have to get this man back to camp."

One of the men patted down Roger for other weapons and a second retrieved his Whitworth and binoculars.

The sergeant ordered the men to flank Roger on both sides with Tucker in the rear. Once in position, the five men made their way off the ridge, with Roger holding his hands behind his head. After a twenty-minute walk, they approached a small clearing where a federal officer stood with a group of men. The officer turned when he saw the detachment approaching with Roger.

"This is the man we found that fired that shot from the ridge, captain," the sergeant said. "He may be a sharpshooter or a spy. He was carrying this." The sergeant took the Whitworth from the soldier carrying it and presented it to the captain. "Corporal Tucker knows this man."

"We were in sharpshooter training together, sir," Ambrose said. "He's a good man and a hell of a good shot."

"Take him and this Whitworth to command," the captain said. "They may want to question him."

Ambrose and the two Union soldiers were ordered to escort Roger, while the sergeant remained behind with the officer. Roger's hands were tied, and the four men set out on an hour's march behind Union lines.

"Permission to speak, corporal," Roger requested.

"Sure, Roger," Ambrose said.

"How did you end up with Grant's army?" the prisoner asked.

"Got fed up with the way Johnny Reb treated us," Ambrose began. "There was too much objection to me having a gun. I was assigned to a work detail worse than anything I had done before. One night I slipped away and gave myself up to the Yanks. They kept me in confinement for a time and when they learned I was a trained sharpshooter, they put me in a uniform. Before long, I was promoted to corporal."

The four men arrived at an encampment north of Petersburg containing three tents. They approached a tent where two guards were on duty.

"Corporal Tucker reporting," Ambrose said, approaching the guards. "We have a prisoner that may be of use to the Union cause."

"One moment," one of the guards spoke out and entered the tent. He emerged and held the tent flap back as a higher-ranking officer appeared. Ambrose explained Roger's circumstances, including their acquaintance. The officer directed Tucker and Brinkman to enter his tent for interrogation.

Colonel Kinkaid had the two men sit opposite him, with nothing in between.

"So, you were spying," Kinkaid directed his inquiry to Roger. "You could be shot for this.

"Corporal," Kinkaid was now addressing Tucker. "Since you know this man, you can help verify his answers."

Roger's responses were direct and to the point. Whenever the interrogator looked at Tucker, Ambrose would nod his head in the affirmative. Roger eventually convinced the colonel that he was telling the truth.

"Do you know if Lee intends to surrender?" Kincaid queried.

"I do believe the general recognizes his situation is… let's say, grave," Roger responded. "But he is a man of great pride. I do believe he is hoping for reinforcements, but there is no guarantee they will arrive in time."

"If you are referring to General Johnston's forces, that is highly unlikely," said the colonel. "And what were you doing when you were captured?"

"Providing cover for the retreating Confederates," Roger said.

"And spying?" the colonel quizzed, lifting an eyebrow as he spoke.

"Simple reconnaissance," Roger said with a straight face. "I feel I made a mistake joining the Confederacy, but I have tremendous respect for Lee," Roger added, casting a glance at Ambrose. The large man did not respond.

"Corporal, do you have any questions for our prisoner?" Kinkaid said, looking at Tucker.

"I would only say that Corporal Brinkman and I will end up on the same side again. He is no slave man," Ambrose said, staring straight at the colonel.

"I tend to agree, corporal," Kinkaid said. "Brinkman, we shall have to keep you in confinement until the conclusion of this miserable war. I hesitate to send you to a prison camp if the end is near.

"Corporal, please place our prisoner in the compound."

"Yes, sir," Ambrose said, rising and saluting. "Roger," he concluded. Roger stood up and led the big man out of the tent.

Roger was placed in the compound, where his hands were untied.

"Maybe we'll see each other again," Ambrose said. "If not, I hope all goes well for you."

"And you, too," Roger replied. "You're a good man, Ambrose. I'm glad we were able to meet again. May God go with you."

Roger watched Tucker and his fellow Union soldiers depart from the camp. He turned his eyes on the other prisoners and joined in their wait for further orders. Roger noticed many of his fellow prisoners looked sick enough to be in a hospital bed. None were wounded, and Roger learned most had either surrendered or were picked up after deserting the Confederacy. For the most part, there was little conversation and even less food.

After about a week, word came down that Lee had surrendered at Appomattox. It was April 9, 1865.

The next day, the prisoners were released from the compound with the requirement they take a loyalty oath and swear allegiance to the United States. All agreed and afterward were given vouchers for train fare. Those headed in Roger's direction were taken to a wagon complete with a driver and armed guard.

"What now," one of the former prisoners asked the Union soldiers.

"Go home, if you still have one," the guard answered.

For the first time in his life, Roger Brinkman now faced a time when no one was telling him what he should do. In fact, there were few who said much of anything. There were no prison uniforms, so the only clothes Roger had were those he was issued as a sharpshooter. Fortunately, they were not readily recognizable as a Confederate uniform. Roger wore brown wool slacks, a wool jacket lacking corporal stripes, a hat, and the worn boots on his feet.

He climbed into the prisoner's wagon to begin the long journey home.

Chapter 15

Roger was again lost in his thoughts after boarding a train to make the arduous trip back to Bordertown. As so often did on trains, he would gaze out the window, only this time to be greeted by his reflection. He studied his face, knowing he was not the same person who left Bordertown for St. Louis several years ago. His features were essentially the same, but he was no longer the boy who peered out from those eyes back then. His life had been turned upside down. He was to pursue a life for God and instead was dragged through Hell. First, it was the devastating loss of his family and then three years trying to survive a war.

He had battle scars, but unlike thousands of others, he had amazingly few physically. The eyes he saw in his reflection said his biggest wound was the one left on his soul. He had so looked forward to seminary as a student but now had no desire to return. The life he once embraced would need redeeming if he were ever again going to follow in his father's footsteps. How could he preach to a congregation telling them to remove the splinters from their eyes when he had a log protruding from his?

He was aware of the forgiveness offered through the death and resurrection of Jesus Christ and the need to be born again. But he did not see himself as a man rising from the ashes; he felt more like someone buried in them.

He thought about his return to Bordertown but had no idea where his life would take him. The only one left of his family was Nik, and he had no idea where his brother was or if he had survived the war. For all Roger knew, he was all alone, but he was too empty to feel lonely. Instead, he wondered if he had the capacity to again experience the wonderful emotions he once shared with family, friends and Gloria.

He looked about the car and noticed how different it now appeared. Passengers seemed melancholy and despondent, as if on a train bound for nowhere. Not like the excitement he vaguely remembered on that first trip. The travelers then were enthusiastic and inviting, but that memory had faded. Perhaps it was his mood back then. He was young and idealistic, thinking life would always be like that – how naïve. He laughed silently to himself thinking of how wrong he had been.

After stops at various stations and a couple of rail line changes, he came to the final piece of his journey. After the transfer, the former soldier found an open seat and sat down. His inclination to lose himself in thought was interrupted when he noticed a tall, middle-aged man board the train and enter his car. The man approached and took a seat across from Roger, one row ahead. Roger wasn't sure what drew his attention to this man wearing a broad-brimmed hat. He was nicely dressed, complete with a jacket complemented by a leather vest. What piqued Roger's attention was a badge pinned to the gentleman's vest.

Brinkman stared absentmindedly at the back of the man, momentarily escaping his personal thoughts. He had done it before with other passengers. Who was the man with a badge? What was he? Where was he going? This exercise helped Roger avoid contemplating his own bleak and uncertain future.

Almost as if on cue, the man slowly turned and looked back at Brinkman.

"Is there something I can help you with, son?" the stranger asked.

The encounter surprised Roger and partially jolted him from speculating about the passenger wearing a badge.

"Oh, ah, no. Sorry, I did not mean to stare," Brinkman said.

"Where are you headed?" the man inquired.

"Ah, Bordertown… Bordertown, Missouri, sir," Roger responded.

"Back from the war, are you, son?" the fellow traveler questioned.

"Yes, yes I am," Roger answered. "How could you tell?"

"You're much too quiet for a man your age," the stranger said. "I've seen behavior similar to yours before."

"Like I said, I'm sorry about that. I..." Roger started.

"No need to apologize," the passenger said. "Mind if I come over and sit by you?"

"No, not at all," Roger responded while straightening up as the passenger exchanged seats.

The man introduced himself as Ned Borchers, a United States Marshal. He was headed for Kansas and then wherever his next assignment took him. Roger also introduced himself, mentioning his service as a Confederate soldier.

"What do you plan to do now that the war is over?" Borchers asked.

"I honestly don't know, Mr. Borchers. I..." Roger replied.

"Please, just call me Ned, unless you prefer marshal," Borchers said. "I answer to either one. Mr. Borchers sounds much too formal."

"Yes, sir, that would be fine," Roger continued. "I really don't know what I'm going to do. I was a seminary student before the war, but my heart isn't into that now."

"I'm sorry to hear that, Roger," Borchers said. "War can certainly alter a man. What was it you did as a soldier?"

"I was a sharpshooter and did reconnaissance. I learned to shoot when I was younger and hunted near our farm," said Roger. "In the army, I was used largely in that capacity."

"What about returning to the farm?" Borchers asked.

"It isn't there, anymore," Roger said, looking away from the man beside him. "Neither is my family. They were killed shortly after the war started, while I was away at school."

"I am powerful sorry to hear that, Roger," Borchers offered. "For what reason are you returning to Bordertown, then?"

"I don't know. It is just where I grew up, I guess," said Roger. "I know a few folks, maybe something there will pan out."

"Do you think you could consider a career in law enforcement?" Borchers said nonchalantly.

"A lawman?" Roger questioned. It was a profession Roger had never considered.

"It's not a bad life. We deputy marshals do a lot more than just hunt for bad guys," Borchers said. "We're federal agents and take care of a lot of the government's needs.

"With that being said," Borchers continued, "your skills with a shootin' iron would not be overlooked if you're interested."

"You say you're heading for Kansas? Are you familiar with Kansas?" Roger asked.

"I know my way around that territory pretty good, there and Oklahoma," Borchers replied.

"You wouldn't happen to know a man named Curtain, would you? A Colonel Curtain," Roger asked, checking the emotion that name evoked in him.

"Curtain?" Borchers said. "No, I can't say as I do. Did you serve under him?"

"No, just a man I knew from Kansas," Roger said. "Well, I really didn't know him, just someone I was told about. Sorry I asked."

"Not at all, Roger," Borchers said. "But give my suggestion some thought. We're always looking for good men to join our ranks, and I would be happy to put in a good word for you to your local congressman. Let me give you some information on how to get in touch with me if enforcing the law may be something you would want to consider."

Borchers took out a card from his jacket, scribbled down some information on it and gave it to Roger. Roger glanced at the card and slipped it into his shirt pocket. Borchers went on to explain what life was like as a U.S. Marshal, covering new territory as the country continued its expansion westward.

When Roger's train pulled into the Bordertown Railway Station, he peered out the railcar window and was pleasantly surprised to see Anthony Carrossa and his wife, Karla, waiting for him. Roger had sent a telegram to the Carrossas asking if they would meet him on the date of his return, but he had left Virginia before receiving a response. The Carrossas' sons, now both of high school age, were not with the pair waiting at the depot.

As the train came to a stop, Roger slid out from his seat, gathered what few belongings he had and began to walk down the aisle to exit the car.

"Think about what I said," Marshal Borchers offered as Roger passed.

"I will, sir," Roger answered, turning to face the lawman. "I still have some soul searching to do for now."

"I understand, Roger. But you have my information, and I would be happy to help you in any way I can," Borchers said.

"Thank you, sir, and good luck the rest of the way," Roger said, as he turned away thinking his final remark a bit out of place.

The Carrossas enthusiastically greeted Roger as he stepped off the train. The overwhelming emotion Roger felt over being in his hometown and in the company of people he loved was almost enough to bring tears to his eyes. However, his mixed feelings of emptiness and relief left him showing almost no outward emotion, as he simply stood and grinned at the Carrossas.

"No need to say anything, Roger. We know you've been through a terribly tough time in your life," Karla Carrossa said, nudging her husband to take the small bag Roger was carrying. "There'll be plenty of time for talking when you're good and ready."

"The buggy is right over there," Anthony Carrossa said, tilting his head in the direction of the horse-drawn rig. "You just come on with us, and we'll help you get settled in."

After boarding the coach and heading toward town, Roger spoke. "It's awful nice of you folks to look after me like this. I'm not sure where I would have gone after the war had it not been for you."

"Nonsense, Roger. This whole town loves you and certainly loved your family, as well," Karla said. "If not us, some other local family would have taken you in, just as well. Your father was well respected in Bordertown."

At the mention of his father, Roger felt the pain of how long it had been since he last laid eyes on his Pa or any other Brinkman. With that thought and the emotion he had bottled up during the war, a tear ran down his cheek.

"Oh my, we've upset you," Karla said. "I'm so sorry."

"You must be more careful of such things, Karla," Anthony interjected.

"No, it's all right. I'm okay," Roger said, not wanting the Carrossas to feel it necessary to act delicately around him. "I'm sorry about my reaction. It's just that my mind has been a million miles away from Bordertown the last few years. I guess the memory of it all sort of came rushing back to me. Please forgive me."

"Not at all, Roger," Karla consoled. "There will be some tough times ahead, but you'll get through it. Anthony and I, these town folks, and the Good Lord will see to it. Don't you worry."

"You're too kind," said Roger. "Thank you." Roger then turned away and gazed at his old surroundings, wiping away a few more tears as they rode along. By the time they reached the Carrossas' home, Roger's eyes had dried, and darkness had again flooded his insides.

***

As time passed, Roger began to adjust to civilian life. He ventured from the Carrossas' home and began visiting folks he had not seen for years. They all greeted him with a "welcome home," but avoided saying anything about the Brinkman family. The Carrossas had taken it upon themselves to caution Bordertown residents in advance, as to the grief Roger still felt for his loss.

"You're welcome to come to church with us, Sunday," Anthony offered. "We have a young pastor who fills in here and at Hilltop since Bob Altman retired."

Roger thought a moment and then looked down at his weather-worn boots. "I think I will pass for now," he replied. "I need to get reacquainted with Bordertown before I do that. But I think I will eventually come around."

"The invitation is always open. You proceed as you see fit," Anthony responded. "Whether you do or don't is up to you. You just get settled in."

"Thanks, Anthony," Roger said. "But I do feel more like myself than I did when I headed off to war."

For reasons Roger did not fully understand, he felt attending church would complicate his struggle to reconcile the person he had become with the one he once knew. Something was pushing him to put both lives behind him and emerge as someone entirely different. But trying to separate himself from what had gone before proved difficult.

Time spent with the Carrossas did soften his fear of the past and helped him consider a proper course for his future.

As his confidence grew, he decided to accept Anthony's offer and attend church. The first time Roger arrived he was given a special welcome. As familiar members of the congregation came up to express their joy over his return, his fear of being reminded of his family began to fade.

Over time, the dread turned into fond memories, and he slowly allowed himself to recall his years growing up in Bordertown. The church was where he remembered many of the good times from his past.

Roger did not see Gloria or the Fentons in church and brought it up with the Carrossas.

"Tom finally lost the farm, and he and Marie loaded what few belongings they had in a wagon and set out to homestead somewhere in the West," Anthony said.

"Gloria had considered staying in Bordertown, but she felt her folks were going to need her help getting started again," Karla chimed in. "She was torn hoping you would return, but when she did not hear from you, she made up her mind to leave."

"Our mail was cut off by the United States Postal Service. I wanted to write to you folks, as well, but there was no delivery service for Confederates," Roger said. "I'm powerful sorry for all the trouble I've caused. I just hope the Fentons do well. Do you ever hear from them?"

"Marie wrote once, while they were still traveling," Karla continued. "Since they had no address, I never wrote back, hoping when they were settled, they would send word as to how to get in touch. It's been a while now and still no word."

"Did she mention where they were headed?" Roger inquired.

"She said they were still heading west. Some folks took them in for a time, but nothing permanent," Karla concluded, shaking her head at the disappointment in Roger's face.

"The bank took over their farm, but could not sell it," Anthony said. "That reminds me, the bank leased your folk's place to a young family that moved here. Greta told me to tell you they have the lease money in an account under your name. I don't know if you know, but Roland died of a stroke, and Greta now runs the bank."

"I saw Mrs. Bagget and Emilia in church," Roger responded. "I figured Mr. Bagget was still mad about Nik."

"No, Roland had apparently been involved in some shady land deals and the stress of trying to correct the problem up and killed him," Anthony said.

"Now Anthony," Karla cut in. "I think Roland just worked himself to death. Once he left the church, I think making money was all he thought about."

"We elders kept Sunday services and Sunday school going until the new pastor arrived," Anthony said. "He's a young fella named Layton Epperson. But he splits duties between us and Hilltop since Bob Altman retired."

Relieved the church issue was settled, Roger took a job at the local hardware store owned by Peter Williams, where most guns in town were sold. Roger had learned about firearms while in the military, and Williams was happy to have him onboard.

Roger described the Army Colt he took from a soldier but held back on how he got it.

"I have one you may like even better," Williams said. "It's an 1860 Colt .44 pistol." Williams described the improved features of the new pistol over the Army's older version. "I would be glad to sell it to you at an employee's discount and throw in some ammunition, holster and gun belt," Williams offered.

Roger's interest in firearms dated back to when he was a boy. He had also read literature about postbellum expansion and tales of the Old West. He bought the 1860 Colt and enjoyed wearing it when strolling around the Carrossa property.

Besides working at the store, the former soldier also assisted with the Carrossa farm. Laboring there increased his strength, and he used his free time to hone his skills with the new pistol.

One day, Roger was on the outskirts of the farm practicing with his pistol, as Anthony Carrossa approached.

"You're getting mighty good with that shootin' iron," Anthony said. "Is there something you have in mind to do with it?"

"I'm not sure, Mr. Carrossa, but I know I'm drawn to this thing," Roger answered. "Maybe it's a carryover from my hunting days as a boy."

"You know, many here in Bordertown have been talking about raising the money to send you back to seminary," Carrossa said. "We'd sure like to see you do that."

"I appreciate that, sir, but I'm not inclined that way right now," Roger responded. "I'm sorry. I kind of wish I was."

"What are your plans, if I may ask?" Anthony replied.

"I'm considering becoming a lawman," said Roger, somewhat surprised at having said it.

"A lawman? Why would you want to do that?" Anthony asked.

"A U.S. Marshal I met on the train said the agency was looking for men like me," Roger said. "I guess my time in the army impressed him. As for seminary, too many things have happened since then."

"Are you still thinking about the man that kill…, ah, raided your family farm?" said Anthony, trying to curb mentioning the Brinkman family's fate.

"I don't know, Mr. Carrossa, but if I ran across him, I would not hesitate to use this gun on him," Roger said, "and that's no way for a preacher to feel."

"Do you really think you could still find him?" said Carrossa.

"I'm not sure, but I did find Nik," Roger said, "even when I wasn't looking for him."

"You found Nik!? Where?" Anthony asked.

"He was wearing a Yankee uniform and came looking for me after I shot a Union soldier," said Roger, wincing at the memory.

"My Lord, that must have been horrible," Carrossa said with a quiver in his voice.

"Yes, the killin' was bad," Roger confessed, "but it brought Nik and me together in an awkward sort of way. I was in a tough spot, and Nik helped me escape."

"Where is Nik is now?" Carrossa inquired, grabbing Roger's arm, and peering into his face.

"Sadly, I don't know," Roger replied, lowering his eyes, and then reversing to match Anthony's gaze. "We were on opposite sides, so I don't know what happened to him. But seeing him again kind of restored my soul."

"That's quite a story. It sort of explains why you're doing this," Anthony said. "I just hope God goes with you whatever the circumstances."

"Thanks, Mr. Carrossa. You and your family have done everything possible to help me rebuild my life," said Roger. "Now I'm in need of finding redemption on my own."

Chapter 16

Roger's urge to become a lawman brought with it doubts if he was ready for such responsibility. He had no real knowledge of being a U.S. Marshal, other than what Borchers had offered. He had read about marshals, sheriffs, and Texas Rangers, but realized much of it was embellished. Still, he did not know much about being a soldier, either, but served honorably.

Roger's time in Bordertown had healed much of the past for him but a certain anxiety remained. He was experiencing a need to bring one chapter of his life to a close and open another. He found Marshal Borcher's information and penned a letter. He folded the pages, stuffed them in an envelope and placed it in his drawer. He was ready but not yet satisfied.

The people of Bordertown had become accustomed to Roger, and no longer felt it necessary to mollify him. He discovered Pastor Epperson had been a student at Concordia in St. Louis about the same time he was there. Although his attendance at church was sporadic, Roger would seek out Epperson to discuss seminary and the Bible.

His work on the Carrossa farm became more intense and included helping the Carrossa boys with their schoolwork and Bible study. He also stopped by the bank to talk with Greta Bagget about the sale of his family's farm.

"The Allen family leased the farm, putting down enough to pay off your family's mortgage," Greta said. "To ensure the equity you are owed, I set up an account for them to pay into. I was lenient so they could rebuild the house and re-establish the farm. Of course, that money, including interest, is yours."

"You did a wonderful thing, Mrs. Bagget," Roger said. "Handle that account as you see fit. I have no desire to add any burden to the new owners. By the way, I'm powerful sorry to hear about Mr. Bagget."

"It was tough at first," Greta said, "but with some help, we got the books straightened out, and now we feel we're helping folks again."

Just then Emilia entered her mother's office. She was not dressed as elegantly as she had been when her father was still alive. She seemed more natural now, and Roger thought more attractive than when he went off to war. Most of the curls her father had adored were now gone and her brown hair flowed freely. Roger always felt Emilia looked a little too regal the other way.

"Roger, I've wanted to talk to you. I had seen you at church, but it seemed we were always going in opposite directions," Emilia said. "Mother, I just dropped by to take you to lunch. Perhaps Roger can join us."

"I've got to get back to the store," Roger said. "I'm sorry I can't join you but thank you for asking. Perhaps we can get together another time and talk about how things have changed."

"I would like that," Emilia said. "I guess you know Gloria left with her family when the Fentons lost the farm."

"I heard," Roger said. "I regret she and I were not on better terms when I joined the army."

"She really missed you and would have waited for you," Emilia said. "But she felt her parents needed her more than she thought you did."

"I can see why she felt that way," Roger said. "I have not been the same since my family was killed."

"That was a tragedy," Greta Bagget said, rising from behind her desk and moving out where Roger and her daughter were standing. "I'm sorry you cannot join us, Roger, but I need to get something to eat. I'm famished."

As they walked out, Greta gave the bank teller a note as to the money owed Roger. Brinkman thanked Greta again and told her to give the Carrossas access to the lease account. He also told her when the lease payments equaled the equity owed to grant deed the farm over to the Allens. He told Emilia he would get in touch.

After drawing out his money and before returning to the store, Roger visited the post office and mailed his letter to Borchers.

By the following week, Roger began calling on Emilia Bagget, hoping time with her would ease his guilt feelings toward Gloria. However, Emilia's presence only served to remind him of his former girlfriend. Emilia, on the other hand, grew fond of Roger but wasn't convinced he felt the same way.

During a picnic together, Emilia gently prodded Roger as to his plans.

"You know, Roger, my mother wants to send me away to school. She wants me to take over the Bordertown Bank, one day," Emilia said, casually starting the conversation, while the pair spread out their picnic blanket by the river.

"Do you want to do that?" Roger asked as he picked a sandwich out of the basket and unwrapped it for his companion.

"Mother feels if I learn the banking business, she could retire," Emilia answered. "What do you plan to do?"

"I've been reading about the lawlessness that has grown since the war, especially out West," Roger mused, unwrapping a sandwich for himself. "I've been thinking about taking a job in law, perhaps with the United States Marshal Service."

"But what about seminary? Folks think you ought to finish and pastor Bordertown's church, like your Pa did," Emilia encouraged. "You ought to, you know."

"I cannot do that just now," Roger said, sensing Emilia was trying to make up her own mind on something. "My desire to find my folks' killer still burns inside me."

"So, you would abandon seminary for law in hopes of finding this man?" Emilia asked, setting aside her sandwich to sip on a cool drink. "Hasn't your life been interrupted enough by tragedy and a war? Do you not want to put any of your old life back together?"

"That's just the point," Roger explained. "I am trying to put my life back together. Restoring law and order, finding Colonel Curtain and Gloria are things I feel I need to do."

"Finding Gloria? I knew you wanted satisfaction concerning this colonel," Emilia responded, with frustration entering her voice. "But I was unaware you planned to go after Gloria, too."

"I'm sorry I mentioned that," Roger said, sheepishly looking down as he spoke. "As you know, Gloria and I did not part on the best of terms. I just feel I need to make that up to her."

"Then you still love Gloria?" Emilia asked, her voice softening. "I'm glad you mentioned it, otherwise I might never have known."

"If it's any consolation, I don't know if I still love her," Roger said, looking up at Emilia. "I've been juggling these feelings of hate, love, betrayal, redemption and maybe even fighting for the wrong side," Roger continued. "I'm so mixed up inside, half the time I don't know what I'm doing – or what I'm going to do."

"You've gone off to war, and now you're thinking of becoming a lawman," Emilia replied, aligning her thoughts. "Is it danger you seek? Would that be redemption for you?"

Roger turned his head to look out over the river and said nothing for a time.

"I wanted war to teach me to kill," he said absentmindedly. "It did, but that did not satisfy me. Now I want to kill someone specific hoping that will relieve my burden."

"And Gloria?" Emilia asked.

"Closure," Roger said. "God is about love and forgiveness. I do not feel either right now, not even for myself."

"What would you have to forgive yourself for?" Emilia questioned.

"Making a lot of bad decisions, I guess," Roger answered. "Helping to restore law and order might help me restore my soul. It's like providence is pulling me in that direction."

"Roger, I hope in some way this all will help you," Emilia said, placing items into the picnic basket. "As children, we led pretty sheltered lives. It makes me wonder if we're not paying for that now."

"You too?" Roger said, looking into Emilia's eyes.

"Me too, Roger," she responded. "I was hoping you could restore the world father built around me, but that's not going to happen. You have your path to follow, and now I have mine. I always knew it. I just did not want to face it."

"It's all been so ugly these past few years," Roger said. "If it had not been for folks like you and others in this town, I might have considered becoming an outlaw rather than a lawman."

Emilia laughed. "Whatever you do or wherever you go, Roger, I truly hope a guardian angel goes with you," Emilia said.

"Thanks, Emilia," Roger replied, looking into his friend's comforting eyes. "Who would have thought our sheltered childhoods would lead to this?"

"Someone up there knows why," Emilia said, turning her eyes up to the sky.

"Let's hope so, Emilia. Let's hope so," Roger concluded.

The two gathered up their picnic belongings and boarded the carriage Roger borrowed from the Carrossas. They rode in silence until they reached the Baggets' home.

"I've truly enjoyed your company, Emilia," Roger said, as he helped her down from the buggy.

"We can stay in touch until one of us leaves for who knows where," Emilia said. "I would like to know if you do join the Marshal Service if you're still here before I leave." Though a little saddened by the way things worked out, Emelia was also relieved.

"I'd like that," Roger said. "Thanks for being a true friend, Emilia."

With that, Roger climbed back into the buggy, tipped the edge of his hat, and drove off.

After reaching the Carrossas' farm, Roger unharnessed the horse, fed and watered the animal and entered the house. It was about time for dinner.

"Oh, glad you're here, Roger," Karla said, coming out of the kitchen. "There's a letter here for you."

"A letter … for me?" Roger said, taking the envelope from Mrs. Carrossa and using a pocketknife to open it. He pulled out the letter and read it.

"Roger Brinkman,

I received your letter inquiring about a position with the U.S. Marshal Service. I would be delighted to meet with you and begin processing your entry into the agency. I sent a letter to your congressman, and he said the Federal pardon you needed as a former Confederate was granted, making you eligible for the Marshal Service.

There are a few matters necessary to settle, but after talking with you on the train, I do not believe there is any reason why the agency would not accept you. Either way, the expenses of your trip will be reimbursed.

I will be on assignment in Wichita next month and can meet with you there. I will be expecting you.

Sincerely,

Ned Borchers

United States Marshall

Kansas/Oklahoma Territory"

It was like a load was lifted from Roger's shoulders. He was now convinced a career with the U.S. Marshal Service would be his next step in life.

"Come and eat, Roger, dinner's ready," Karla called out from the kitchen.

"Be right there," Roger said, as a smile spread across his face.

***

With the time Roger had left before reporting to Marshal Borchers in Wichita, Kansas, the former Confederate sharpshooter decided to make the best of his final weeks in his hometown.

He had worked through many of the issues that had weighed on him since returning from the war. Roger also managed to put Colonel Curtain and his band of murderers into the back of his mind. He tired of it lingering in the background of every conversation he engaged in. If God would someday lead him to Curtain, so be it. When he prayed, he avoided expressing a desire to kill the man, observing the fifth commandment.

He looked up his former schoolmate Todd O'Leary and invited

him to go hunting. Todd did not participate in the war, and Roger did not burden him with any of his tales of combat.

The Carrossas were appreciative of the game Roger brought home, and they salted away much of it. Roger also informed them their names were on the bank's lease account for the Brinkman farm.

"You did not have to do that," said Karla. "You've helped us out in many ways, and we'll be just fine after you're gone."

"I guess I'll just have to get used to not having a Brinkman around," Anthony responded. "Bordertown just won't be the same."

"Very little about the Brinkmans is the same," Roger replied. "Maybe it's time Bordertown accepted that. The tragic memories of this place no longer haunt me, and I will take the pleasant ones with me wherever I go."

Roger terminated his employment at the hardware store but had plenty of money to purchase a horse. He named the animal Brinker, in honor of his family. He had already picked out a saddle and tack at the hardware store, which Williams sold him at a discount.

"Roger, not having you around is going to leave a big hole in the town," Williams said. "I was hoping you would take over this store for me, one day."

"Thanks, Pete, but there's a hole in me I have to fill," Roger said. "I'll never forget what you and this town have done for me. Had you not done so, I would be in a lot worse place."

"I admire what you're doing," Williams said. "I just wish you didn't have to go so far away to do it."

Roger also bought a broad-brimmed hat, mimicking the one Borchers wore when Roger met him on the train. He decided not to buy more clothes, since he was unaware of what deputy marshals wore when on duty.

Finally, as the end of the month drew near, Roger saddled up Brinker and said his last goodbyes to the Carrossas and their sons.

"If you're ever back this way, you know where our home is," Karla said. "You know it's also your home, as well."

"If I weren't a Brinkman, I would be going by the name Carrossa," Roger said, climbing aboard Brinker. "Hospitality does not begin to describe what you've done for me."

"Write when you can," Anthony requested. "You are family to us now."

Roger could only touch the tip of his hat and ride away, battling the same emotions he struggled with when he first left Bordertown.

He stopped by Emilia Bagget's home, knowing she too would be leaving soon. Emilia would be attending a prestigious women's college in Massachusetts, where the ravages of war had little effect.

"We'll, pretty much, be worlds apart," Emilia said, content now with Roger's friendship. "Will I be reading about you in the newspapers?"

"I didn't make the newspapers as a soldier, so I doubt I will as a marshal either," Roger answered with a laugh and removed his new hat. "There's a better chance I'll be reading about you once you finish school."

Emilia approached Roger and kissed him.

"There's something to remember me by in case I don't make the news," Emilia said, pulling away. "I know I will remember you. Now go before I end up missing my train."

Roger offered a weak smile, turned and stepped off the porch while placing his hat on his head. He mounted Brinker, nodded to Emilia, and rode off.

After Roger and Brinker reached the outskirts of Bordertown, he made a small detour to visit the farm where he had grown up. Roger stopped by the new farmhouse to tell the Allens he was leaving. They came out onto the porch as he rode up.

"I'm sorry I haven't been more sociable, but I'm leaving Bordertown and wanted to pay my respects," Roger said, remaining in his saddle. "Everything's been settled at the bank, and Mrs. Bagget will fill you in on the details. I cannot say how pleased I am with how well you've done with the place."

"We've already spoken to Greta and want you to know we're grateful for what you have done," Mr. Allen said. "We also want to assure you that spot under the white oak will never be disturbed as long as we are here."

"Much obliged," Roger said. He touched his hat in a salute and rode away.

After departing the farmhouse, Roger rode out to visit the graves located under the white oak tree on the knoll. After reaching the site, Roger dismounted and took off his hat to say a few words.

"Well, Pa, Ma, Dolly, I guess this is it," Roger said out loud. "I done my part in the war, as did Nik. We just happened to end up on different sides for different reasons. Anyways, I plan to become a U.S. Deputy Marshal and perhaps one day catch up to the man who did this to you. I've never been able to forget about what he did, and I simply have been unable to forgive him. I know I should, but it has never settled for me.

"I'm sorry I did not follow the path you all wanted for me, but you being there and me here changed all that. Maybe someday…," Roger's voice broke off, and he wiped his tears with his sleeve. "So long for now, I know you are all in heaven where we'll all meet again one day. Until then, God bless."

After a small prayer, Roger mounted Brinker, tipped his hat farewell, and continued on his way to Wichita.

It was nearly mid-summer, and the days were hot. So, Roger took a route that followed along the rivers and streams he was familiar with. He also had a map he picked up at the hardware store. The traveling, although warm, was rather pleasant, and he encountered very few people along the way. Those he did meet were friendly. One wagon train he came across invited him to dinner.

Because of his frequent stops to enjoy the countryside, his trip would take him a day longer than planned. But having built in extra time by leaving early, he had occasion to enjoy the serenity of the outdoors. It lessened the excitement he felt about becoming a deputy marshal, but it did not diminish his motivation.

Roger eventually came to the Neosho River in Kansas and found an area where previous cattle drives had crossed. After fording the river, he headed west toward Wichita. Although Wichita was not that big of a settlement, the population temporarily grew as each cattle drive passed through on its way to Kansas City. Whenever meeting up with a cattle drive, Roger would inquire about Colonel Curtain. The answers were always no. Although disappointing, Roger's obsession with the man slowly waned.

"Where are you headed?" one trail boss inquired of Roger.

"Wichita," Roger answered.

"Well, be ready for some exciting times," the cowboy remarked. "Wichita can turn into a wild town."

"How so?" Roger questioned.

"After watering down in the local saloons, cowhands from differing drives like to mix it up a bit," the trail boss said, with a laugh.

Roger thanked the cowboy for his advice, and the two parted company.

Chapter 17

When Roger reached the Arkansas River near his destination, he decided to bed down for the night and head into Wichita in the morning. He figured if the town was as wild as the trail boss had suggested, it would probably be worse at night.

At the river, Roger crossed over and camped in a small grove of trees along the riverbank. Having killed a rabbit earlier in the day, Roger roasted it over an open campfire for dinner.

As he was laying out his bedroll, he heard horses approaching. He stopped to stroke his sidearm to make sure it was handy.

"Can I help you gentlemen?" Roger asked as two men rode into the camp and stopped short of the campfire.

"Well, that all depends," one of the riders said. "What do you have that we might be able to help ourselves to?"

"Coffee is about it," Roger said, as he watched the two men. Both appeared to be cowboys and slouched in their saddles. The pair were middle age and Roger figured either tired, drunk or both, especially if coming from Wichita.

"Coffee? We don't need coffee," the other cowboy said, grinning as he said it. "Got anything, like… say, whisky or money?"

"Sorry, none of one and too little of the other," Roger said, as he readied his hand by his pistol.

"You look kind of young, pardner," said the first. "What are you doing out here? Is your herd nearby?"

"No, I'm to meet someone in Wichita," Roger said, withholding mention of meeting with a U.S. Marshal.

"Wichita, that's a pretty tough town. What do you plan to do there?" the second remarked.

"Get a job," Roger answered. "Like I said, I haven't got much money."

"Come on," the first said to his companion. "There isn't anything here of interest. We'd best be getting back to the herd."

With that, the two turned their horses toward the river and plunged in.

"Good luck to ya, boy," one of the cowboys called out, as they splashed their way through the water.

Roger's heart was pounding, but he wasn't sure why. He had been in uneasy situations before. Despite what he'd heard about Wichita, the two cowboys did not appear threatening. Although one asked about money, Roger got the impression the cowboy was more interested in whisky.

Perhaps it was the thought of drawing his gun that excited him. Although he could handle the weapon and had killed during the war, the encounter did feel different. He wasn't under orders to shoot anyone. Drawing on those two men would have been his decision alone. It didn't happen, so he tried putting the entire incident out of his mind. Still, he spent most of the night with his hand near his pistol and his ears trained for any further intruders.

In the morning, following a fitful night's sleep, he brewed some fresh coffee and chewed on some of the bread Karla Carrossa had baked for his journey. The bread was hard and crumbly, but it complemented his coffee. Despite the lack of sleep, he felt wide awake with thoughts of the previous night's encounter.

Roger saddled up and headed toward Wichita. As he approached the growing community, he could see a large tower being constructed. There were several herds of cattle headed north out of Wichita and some grazing nearby. After the war, Wichita had become a way station for tired cowboys out of Texas and Oklahoma driving herds to northern markets.

As Roger rode into the Kansas settlement, the place appeared overrun with people. He saw fur traders and Indians bargaining with each other, and cowboys peering into the storefront windows.

Despite the mid-morning hour, there was still plenty of activity in the saloon as he passed by. He noticed a blacksmith shop just past the tavern and stopped there for directions to the U.S. marshal's office.

"You're looking for the marshal?" the blacksmith said, his head still bowed over the anvil he was pounding on. "They usually occupy a room at the hotel across from the saloon you passed back yonder," the man continued, pointing with his hammer. "I don't know if the marshal's there or not, but that's the best place to find him."

"Thank you, sir. I appreciate your help," Roger said, turning Brinker around to return to the hotel.

After reaching the hotel, Roger dismounted, tethered Brinker to the hitching rail and stepped up to the wooden walkway that lined the town's main street. He turned to look at the saloon where loud voices and music were emanating. There was also the odor of cow manure scattered in the street. It was in sharp contrast to where he camped the night before and a far cry from the streets of Bordertown.

"Excuse me. Do you have a Marshal Borchers staying here?" Roger asked as he entered the hotel lobby and approached the front desk.

"He does stay here," the hotel clerk said. "His room is 101. I don't know if he's in or not, but you can knock on the door. It's just down the hall."

Roger turned and entered the narrow, pinewood-paneled hallway, coming almost immediately to room 101. He knocked and heard a voice say "Come in."

As he entered, Marshal Borchers was sitting behind a desk going over some papers.

"How can I help you, young man?" Borchers asked, looking up.

"I'm Roger Brinkman. We met on the train," Roger said, leaning forward on the desk to shake the marshal's hand.

"Oh yes, you sent me the letter of your intent to join our agency, right?" Borchers said, grasping Roger's outstretched hand.

"Yes, sir, that's me," Roger answered, releasing his grip and standing upright. "I hope I'm not interrupting anything."

"Not at all, Brinkman, come in, take a seat," Borchers said, shoving some papers aside on his desk. "You'll have to forgive my makeshift office. The agency supplies us with this room and some furniture. They plan to build us a permanent office, but they're waiting to see if Wichita grows enough to warrant it. Until then we'll have to make do with this hotel room."

"Suits me okay, sir," Roger said, sitting down in a wooden chair in front of the marshal's desk.

"So, you want to be a U.S. Deputy Marshal?" Borchers asked.

"That I do, sir," Roger answered. "I rode all the way from Bordertown, Missouri, to get here with that being the purpose of my journey."

"You seem to have grown a bit, and I see you're wearing a pistol. I would say you appear to have come prepared," Borchers said.

"Yes, sir, and I've been practicing quite a bit, ... should I need to use it," Roger said.

"I would hope you wouldn't have to, Roger. You don't mind if I call you Roger, do you?" Borchers replied.

"Roger is fine, sir," he said.

The two men talked for a while. Borchers repeated that the congressman from Roger's district had cleared him for hire, despite Brinkman's service in the Confederacy. The marshal then had Roger read over some official paperwork and sign his name to it if satisfied. Following Roger's signature, Borchers pulled a Bible from a drawer in his desk and had Roger place his right hand on it. The chief deputy then swore Roger into the United States Marshal Service. Once the preliminary ceremony was over, Borchers pinned a U.S. Deputy Marshal badge onto Roger's shirt.

"I'm a bit overwhelmed," Roger said. "I'm not sure what I'm supposed to do."

"Oh, you'll learn," Borchers counseled. "I have another deputy arriving today who will take you under his wing and show you all the ropes you're going to need. Out here, experience is the best training.

"So, do you have a rifle?" Borchers asked.

"Ah, no, I don't," Roger said. "I wasn't certain what I was going to need."

"Not a problem, Roger," Borchers said. "The agency does supply them. Let's head over to the local hardware store and get you one."

The two departed the small hotel-room office and walked over to the local mercantile, where Borchers introduced Roger to the Winchester .44-40.

"I noticed you were wearing a Colt .44," Borchers said. "The beauty of this rifle, besides its accuracy, is that it uses the same cartridge as your pistol.

"By the way, a lot of our deputies carry a second pistol, fully loaded, just in case. And a shotgun isn't a bad companion, either. Unfortunately, I don't have the budget to get you either of those," the marshal concluded.

"That would be quite an arsenal," Roger said, with a grin. "I didn't carry that much as a soldier."

"As a soldier, you knew your enemy and what it would take to defeat him – plus, you had an army with you," Borchers responded. "Out here, you're sometimes on your own and may have to reach for all the help you can get.

"Come on, let's get this paid for," Borchers said, changing the subject. "I saw a chuckwagon pass by. I think my deputy has arrived."

After returning to the hotel, Borchers and Roger entered room 101 to see a man sitting in the chair Roger had occupied. He had on a large, grayish-green hat that covered his eyes and most of his face, but Roger could see the man was sporting a rather large handlebar mustache.

"Brinkman," Borchers said, "meet Deputy Marshal Brinkman."

The introduction kind of puzzled Roger, until the man stood up and pushed his hat back to expose a wide grin.

"Nik!? Roger blurted out. "Is that you?"

"None other, brother," Nik answered, now laughing out loud.

The two embraced, and then Roger stepped back.

"Nik, I can't believe it's you. You're now a deputy marshal?" Roger continued.

Borchers cut in, "I kind of thought the sight of your brother, here, might come as a surprise to you. I probably should have told you when we were on the train. But I wanted to talk to Nik first, and we decided to surprise you."

"Good Lord, I can't believe it," Roger said, smiling as broadly as his face would allow.

"Me neither, Roger," Nik said. "When Marshal Borchers told me about meeting a Brinkman on the train, I just knew it had to be you. Then when the letter arrived with your name on it, I told Ned I wanted to be your training officer."

As the three men continued their conversation, Nik explained that after Lincoln fired General McClellan, he was sent by the Army to New York to train with Colonel Berdan's sharpshooters. Nik said he was proficient enough with a rifle, but it was his ability to track that caught Berdan's attention.

"Rather than send me back to the infantry, my name was submitted to the president's office as a possible recruit for the U.S. Marshal Service," Nik continued. "Lincoln liked the idea, and before I knew it, I was in Arkansas tracking down renegades and outlaws. Since then, I've been assigned to Chief Marshal Borchers' territory."

"So, what's up with the lip duster?" Roger asked.

"I decided to see what it would look like on me and afterward decided to keep it," Nik said. "It also seemed to fit my new lifestyle as a deputy marshal," Nik said with a wink.

As the conversation wore into late afternoon, Borchers set Nik and Roger up in a hotel room across from room 101.

"I still can't believe my luck," Roger said. "I'm now a U.S. Deputy Marshal and you are my training officer."

"Luck or providence, Roger, which do you think it was?" Nik asked.

"Now that you mention it, providence, I hope," Roger answered.

"I hope that, too," Nik said. "Tomorrow, we'll meet up with Charlie Blue Feather at the chuck wagon and be on our way."

"Who is Charlie Blue Feather?" Roger asked.

"He's a Wichita Indian. He serves as my cook and my interpreter,"

Nik said. "He's been a god-send."

"Nik, do you ever think about that so-called colonel that killed our folks and sister?" Roger asked.

"I think about him nearly every day," Nik answered. "My prayer is that I meet up with him again, sometime."

"Would you kill him?" Roger asked.

"I would certainly do that," Nik said. "What I don't know is just how I would go about it."

"What do you mean," asked Roger.

"I mean, it would have to be a killing worthy of erasing that man and that incident out of my mind," Nik said. "I just haven't come up with a means of doing that yet."

"Do you think he's out here somewhere maybe running from the law, even today?" Roger inquired.

"There is no record of the man in any of the U.S. marshal's files that I know of, so I can't say that the prospects are good," said Nik. "But I intend to keep on praying."

"Yeah, me too, Nik, me too," Roger said. "But I'm not sure I would know him on sight. Do you remember anything about him?"

"I remember everything about him," Nik said, almost with a growl. "He was fat, pretended to be someone he wasn't and had an ugly scar on his neck."

"A scar on his neck?" Roger repeated.

"Yeah, like a rope burn," Nik replied. "Like someone tried to hang him once."

"Too bad they didn't succeed," Roger commented, shaking his head.

"Yup, too bad," Nik added. "But one thing I have to get off my chest, brother," Nik said in a matter-of-fact tone. "Whatever possessed you to join the Confederacy?"

"Like I said the last time we met, I could only envision Colonel Curtain in a Yankee uniform," Roger said, his eyes expressing the regret of that decision. "I was heartbroken to find Ma, Pa and Dolly murdered. I could not think of anything other than being on the side that would shoot him on sight. I tried mixing that with the 'states rights' thing to justify my decision, but fighting on the side of slavery depressed me almost as much as my hate for Curtain."

Roger continued, "I often thought of desertion or defecting and felt relieved when I was captured."

"You were a prisoner of war?" Nik replied.

"For about a week, is all," Roger said. "Being a sharpshooter made me feel less of a soldier, and I tried to imagine it was you, me and Todd out hunting again. I do thank the Lord I met Major Baumgartner, who got me into the corps. And I did admire General Lee, somewhat, but my time in service of the South still haunts me."

"I'm glad to hear you say that, Roger," Nik offered. "I have to admit seeing you in that Rebel uniform did take me by surprise. But now that we're on the same side of the law, we can put that behind us."

"I would like that, brother," said Roger. "You're my only family now. I think losing you would be more than I could bear."

Nik smiled at Roger's comment. "As your mentor, you may want to eat those words, someday," Nik said, then laughed out loud and Roger smiled knowing he could not have a better teacher than Nik.

Roger leaned forward, and his expression turned from mirth to one of interest. "Nik, how did you go from our family's massacre to end up as a sentry for General McClellan?" he asked.

Nik's face softened a bit, as the echo of his laugh faded into the seriousness of Roger's question. "Roger, I know you cannot fully grasp what I am about to say, but that horrible feeling I felt when placed on that ship bound for America could not match the horror I endured that fateful day in Bordertown. I literally watched die all I considered wonderful in life. I stood helpless while evil triumphed over good."

Nik said all the dread he knew before Pastor Brinkman "rescued" him from slavery came flooding back that fateful day. All he could think of was to run as far away from it as he could. He explained it wasn't just the fear, but the guilt of hopelessly turning his back on a life he would have never dreamed possible. A life better than had he remained a proud hunter-warrior in his homeland.

"I didn't know if I was running from hell or toward it," Nik continued. "And when I had to stop running, I simply wandered, trying to bury the terror of that day."

The young deputy marshal said he stumbled along, lost and hungry, until coming upon a church he recognized.

"It was the church ministered by Bob Altman, Pa's friend," Nik recalled, as his mind drifted back to that time. "Bob and his wife, Annie, were the only ones to take Pa and me in on our trip back from Lexington – what beautiful people," Nik said, slowly shaking his head at the memory of the Altmans.

Nik related that the church was empty, but he found it open so he went inside and fell asleep on the floor. The next day he was awakened by Pastor Altman, who took him home. Nik said he lived with the Altmans until he was able to open up and face what had happened, thanks to the Altmans' help.

"I think just sleeping again in that bed Pa and I shared that first night helped promote my healing," said Nik, as tears began to well up in the eyes of both men. "Pastor Altman taught me Jesus wasn't there only in the good times, but in the bad, as well. Once I accepted His forgiveness, the Altmans were able to get me back on my feet," Nik straightened up and said, "Shortly thereafter, I made up my mind to join the Union Army."

Nik described how Bob Altman, who had retired as a pastor, got in touch with a recruiter, who inducted him into the service. Negroes could not serve in combat at that time, so he was taken back East and ended up as a sentry for General McClellan.

"The rest is history," Nik concluded. "If you have not already guessed, I was too filled with guilt to face you after the tragedy. I even begged the Altmans not to give away my whereabouts, especially to you. I knew you would be returning from school, and I simply did not have the fortitude to tell you the story. All I could think about was hiding in the woods like a coward. I'm sorry, Roger."

"No need to apologize, Nik. Had there been anything you could have done, you would have done it. I know that," Roger assured, releasing a sigh. He leaned forward, folded his hands, and placed his forearms on his knees. "I'm sorry, too. At least you fought for the right side," he added. "We're human. We're not perfect."

"I did see the Brinkmans that way," Nik replied, focusing on Roger, "but somehow never quite saw myself in that same light. Running away didn't help, either."

"You acted no differently than I would have in your place," replied Roger, speaking almost in a whisper while looking into Nik's eyes. "You're a Brinkman, whether you like it or not. And you're the only one among us who earned that distinction."

The two men sat without speaking for a time, lost in thought. Afterward, they quietly retired to their beds for the night.

Chapter 18

Both Roger and Nik slept soundly, being treated to a bed with a mattress. However, Nik's sleep was not quite as restful since he had spent nearly a year sleeping on the ground. Beds in the Oklahoma Territory were rather scarce. Roger, on the other hand, fared better during that time since he hadn't been subjected to sleeping outdoors, until he left Bordertown for Wichita. Regardless, both men woke up early and prepared for a day of riding south along the Chisholm Trail. There was a knock at the door.

"Are you two awake yet?" the sound of Marshal Borchers' voice could be heard coming from other side of the door.

Nik opened the door to see Borchers' smiling face, with a little bit of irony etched in it.

"What's up, Ned?" Nik asked.

"Not much. I know you guys are anxious to get started so I wanted to fill you in on what you will be dealing with for the next coupla' weeks," Borchers said, as he entered the two deputies' room. "We have reports Iron Bear and his band of renegades could possibly be persuaded to turn themselves in if handled right. But we have to find him first."

"And you think we could do what the U.S. Army has been unable to do?" Nik quizzed.

"Iron Bear is too clever for the army," Borchers answered. "A military patrol is too easy to avoid. So, it's been suggested a small party, of say two or three, may be able to draw him out of hiding."

"The strategy for finding him sounds reasonable," Nik continued, "but two deputies bringing him in would be a stretch, don't you think?"

"Strategy number two is to offer him a flag of truce," Borchers began, adjusting his hat. "If we can get him to return to his tribe in peace, that should keep him from raiding settlers moving into the territory."

"And you think he would go for that?" Nik responded. "There is a price on his head, you know."

"We could only hope," Ned replied. "The government feels it's worth a try, and we don't think he would deliberately kill two innocent marshals trying to do him a favor."

Roger choked a little on Borchers' remark but kept silent.

"Other than possibly exposing his whereabouts," Nik remarked. "Iron Bear is no fool."

"And neither are you, Nik. You just hit on strategy number three," Borchers said, pushing his hat onto the back of his head and smiling at both deputies. "You're my best man, and it would be great training for Roger, as well. However, go with caution and abort the assignment if there's any trouble."

"Trouble is Iron Bear's middle name," Nik said, picking up his hat and giving Ned a reassuring smile. "We'll be back, but I can't guarantee it will be with Iron Bear."

"On the lighter side," the marshal added, "a couple drunken cowboys had a shootout in the street last night. Neither could shoot straight enough to hit the other, and they ended up wrestling in the middle of that dung-filled street until they passed out. I drug them both over to the side of the road, so I caution the two of you to watch your step this morning. They're probably still out there sleeping it off."

"Welcome to Wichita," Nik said over his shoulder to Roger. Roger nodded, as he finished pulling on his boots.

"And Iron Bear country," Roger said, in a voice barely audible.

"Would you guys like some breakfast before starting out?" asked Borchers.

"No thanks, Ned, Blue Feather will be waiting for us and it's a good bet he'll have breakfast prepared in anticipation of our arrival," Nik answered.

"Suit yourselves," Borchers said and led the deputy marshals back to his office for a briefing. The chief marshal spread a map out over his desk and went over the territory they were to cover on their journey. Borchers also identified areas where Iron Bear had been seen and estimated where he might be in hiding.

After the meeting, Nik and Roger checked out of the hotel and stepped into the street. Sure enough, they spotted the two cowboys sitting on the ground and leaning against the boardwalk. Both were working to shake off the after-effects of the previous night's escapade. The two deputies continued walking in the direction of the livery stable when one of the town merchants hurried up to the two men, with a concerned look on his face.

"Are you U.S. Marshals?" the merchant asked.

"We are," Nik said.

"I want you to arrest those two cowboys," the merchant demanded. "One of them shot out my store window and I want restitution."

"Sorry, we're deputies on assignment and haven't time for local matters," Nik said.

Unfamiliar with such an encounter, Roger just listened.

"But those two ought to be in jail," the merchant said. "They should be held until they pay for my window."

"As best I know, there's no proof they are responsible for your window," Nik said, "and proving it would take too much time. Besides, Wichita doesn't have a jail yet."

The two brothers left the merchant standing in the street exasperated, as they continued on to the livery stable. Upon reaching the stable, they paid the livery proprietor and retrieved their horses.

"What do you call your horse?" Nik asked.

"Brinker," Roger answered. "I named him that to honor our folks. What's your horse's name?"

"I couldn't think of anything better than calling him Mr. Lincoln," Ned said, patting his horse on the neck. "He's solid, like the president was."

After mounting up, the two deputies rode out of town. They eventually left the trail and headed toward a grove of trees near a fork in the Arkansas River where Charlie Blue Feather waited with the chuck wagon. Sure enough, as they approached, they could smell bacon cooking and Roger's stomach leaped for joy. It had been a while since he had a decent breakfast.

"You're going to like Charlie's cooking. He's a magician with a Dutch oven," said Nik. "He's also very imaginative when it comes to what he cooks. So don't ask what it is, because Charlie may tell you, and it could be something you don't want to hear."

Roger wasn't sure how to take Nik's comment concerning Blue Feather's menu. He knew he had plenty to learn, including what life was like in the Wild West. Something told him it wasn't going to be as romantic as the novels he'd read.

When introduced, Roger was pleased to discover Charlie Blue Feather had an excellent command of English. Nik also mentioned that Charlie was fluent in all the Native American languages spoken in the area. Blue Feather was one of the Wichita Indians relocated when the town of Wichita was established. After signing on with the U.S. Marshal Service as an interpreter, he was also instrumental in Nik's early training as a deputy marshal. After Nik was ready to go out on his own, Charlie offered his services as the traveling chef.

Charlie Blue Feather appeared to be in his fifties, with a few strands of silver among the wind-blown dark hair that hung to his shoulders. He wore an old cowboy hat with the feather of a Great Blue Heron sewn into the band. He did not look like a warrior but was quick in his step, despite his heavy-set frame. The Wichita Indian wore tall moccasin-style boots with dark denim pants tucked inside. He wore an old, black leather vest over a red long-sleeved shirt. His face had the classic high cheekbones of his ancestors, covered with light ruddy skin.

The breakfast turned out to be quite traditional with bacon, biscuits and eggs. The eggs were a treat Charlie found when he came upon a duck's nest down by the river. After breakfast, they loaded the chuck wagon, and the three men headed south into Oklahoma Territory.

"Iron Bear is a Comanche," Nik said to Roger, as they rode beside the wagon. "He heads up a small band of warriors intent on avenging some of the false promises and broken treaties he claims were made by the government to protect settlers in the area."

Nik added that Iron Bear's spouse was said to have died of cholera, a disease spread by the arrival of the white man. Cholera devastated the Comanche.

"His band is too small to take on the army, so he raids small groups of settlers and then retreats to the Llano Estacado area."

"Yano esta, what?" Roger asked.

"I've been told the words are Spanish and mean Staked Plains," Nik responded. "It is an area most people avoid because of its harsh landscape. It gets hot in summer and cold in winter and water is scarce. It covers much of western Oklahoma and the Texas Panhandle."

"So, you think Iron Bear is hiding out there?" Roger questioned.

"It is an area where a savvy Indian can survive, and travelers unaccustomed to such difficulty, like us, do not do well," Nik answered. "That's why it's a good place for renegades and outlaws to hide."

"So, what are our chances of finding him in a hostile environment like that?" Roger asked.

"Not good," Nik stated, "but I'm placing my hope on the possibility that he will find us."

The idea was not a comforting thought for Roger. He knew what it was like being targeted by Union soldiers, but not by Indians. However, Nik seemed self-assured that being found by Iron Bear would be a step in the right direction. It also did not help when the land west of the Chisholm Trail became barren, forsaken and foreboding. An attack there would mean no one coming to the rescue.

Was this the life of a U.S. Marshal? Roger thought, as he touched his badge and failed to feel the same exhilaration he did when it was pinned on.

Suddenly, Roger's horse reared up and made a sharp turn. The move sent Roger tumbling to the ground. Without taking a moment to assess his wellbeing, Roger sat up to see a large rattlesnake coiled not more than a few feet away. Without thinking, Roger drew his pistol and fired. The snake flew into two pieces, with the lower section thrashing on the ground. Roger jumped to his feet as Nik rode up with Brinker in tow.

"Are you all right, Roger?" Nik shouted.

Roger looked up at Nik momentarily, as he gathered his wits.

"I think so. That snake must have spooked my horse," Roger said, still a bit shaken. "I think I got him."

"You got him, all right," Nik exclaimed. "That was a good shot, even from close range."

By this time, Charlie Blue Feather had jumped down from his wagon and had a hold of the snake's tail. Charlie held the snake up to allow the blood to drain from its nearly six-foot-long body. The chef then carried the section of snake over to his wagon where he retrieved a knife and started carving on the serpent's carcass.

"What's he doing?" Roger quizzed his brother.

"He's preparing tonight's supper," Nik said. "We shall feast tonight."

Roger's uneasiness started to return.

After a couple more hours riding, they came upon a river.

"This is the upper fork of the Canadian River," Nik said. "We'll camp here for the night and cross in the morning. We'll soon be in Oklahoma Territory and entering the Llano Estacado."

The sight of the river was comforting for Roger. It was in sharp contrast to the surrounding landscape. The trio pulled into a grove of trees that lined the river and the riders dismounted to make camp. Roger and Nik set about gathering firewood, while Charlie laid out what he needed to prepare the evening meal. Charlie also used a circle of rocks to define the campfire and set up a tripod on which to hang his cooking pots. After bringing in a night's supply of firewood, Nik started a fire in the area laid out by the camp chef, and soon a rattlesnake stew was simmering over the flames.

Nik and Blue Feather exchanged a short conversation in what Roger assumed was Charlie's native language. As Nik nodded to Charlie's words, Roger figured the chef was telling Nik what else was in the pot besides snake. Roger took Nik's advice and showed no interest in knowing what it was.

When the stew was done, Charlie began ladling out each proportion. After scooping a single portion of stew onto one of the plates, Roger called out, "That's enough for me. I'm really not that hungry."

Roger could see Nik was smiling and when Charlie brought Roger his plate, he was sure the Indian chef was smiling too. However, it was not that easy to tell. Roger paused to pray, but kept an eye on Nik, who took a generous helping. Nik started in on the stew like someone every bit as hungry as Roger was.

Roger took a spoonful of stew and was amazed at how great it tasted. And when his thoughts turned to what he was actually eating, he concentrated on one of Mrs. Carrossa's prepared meals to help clear his mind. After finishing his first ladle of Charlie's broth, Roger boldly asked as if he could have some more.

"Not bad victuals, right Roger?" Nik said.

"I've got to admit, best snake stew I've ever eaten," Roger quipped, knowing Nik was aware it was the first snake stew Roger had ever eaten. All three laughed at the remark, as Charlie filled Roger's plate with a second helping.

Later, as the three men sat around the campfire enjoying some coffee and conversation, a distant howl could be heard. Roger looked around anxiously, having read how Indians used animal sounds to communicate. He looked at Charlie and saw the Wichita took no notice of the sound. Roger glanced at Nik and discovered his brother was staring at him.

"That's a critter," Nik said. "Iron Bear and his warriors would not venture this far out of the Llano Estacado just to keep an eye on us. We'll likely hear more from them the deeper into the Staked Plains we get."

"I guess that's comforting," Roger said. "What happens if we do encounter Iron Bear's band?"

"We do what we have to," Nik replied, "whatever we have to. Don't worry, Roger. Just remain calm, show no hostility, and never lie – Indians can tell. It's all a part of your deputy marshal training.

"Right now, I suggest we get some shuteye. We've got a long ride in the morning," Nik continued. "We'll load up our barrels with water from the river after we cross. There won't be a lot of water where we're going."

The three men turned in, and in the morning, Charlie whipped up some biscuits and gravy using some of the leftover rattlesnake stew. The men enjoyed some black coffee, biscuits and gravy and afterward loaded up the wagon. They crossed the river, loaded their barrels with fresh water and were soon on their way to the Llano Estacado.

The three traveled southwest and soon came to the main Canadian River. They found a place where the chuckwagon could safely cross and rolled through to the other side without incident. They entered a land that seemed to stretch for miles, dotted with patches of tall grass that sometimes came up to the horses' knees. There were also scrub trees spread out over the terrain, like mesquite and juniper, with groves of cottonwoods by rivers and streams that often dried up during the warmer months. For the most part it consisted of dirt, sand, and mesas.

"It gets a little hot out here during the day," Nik said to no one in particular, "but it cools down considerably on the plateaus during the evenings.

"We have some extra clothing and blankets in the chuck wagon," Nik added, turning to Roger, "depending on what you packed and brought along from Bordertown."

"I did bring a jacket and poncho, not knowing what to expect when I got to Wichita," Roger said. "And I'm still not sure what to expect."

"Charlie's an expert on this part of the country," Nik continued. "The temperatures in this region can vary considerably, so we have to be prepared for almost anything. They don't get a lot of rain here and the land sucks up the water awfully fast. That's why it's smart to bring one's own water supply."

"Sounds like a fun place. A bit different from Missouri, but you and I are not unfamiliar with the outdoors," Roger commented.

"No, but we are rank amateurs here, compared to Charlie and the Plains Indians," Nik said. "This territory belongs to whatever is native to the area. Whoever or whatever is new to this land can find it quite hostile when trying to survive out here – and some don't.

"I know it sounds strange that this would be a place to hide out," Nik said, "but it's a favorite for renegades and those who run afoul of the law because very few law-abiding citizens want to venture here."

"Right up our alley as deputy marshals, right, Nik?" Roger quipped, allowing himself a little pride.

"Yeah, but this place is not our alley," Nik commented.

Later that afternoon, the team found a decent spot to camp and set up for the night.

Roger and Nik again gathered up some firewood and cut a few branches, as loose wood was not in abundance. Charlie also carried wood in the wagon, used mostly for kindling. The chef set out his pots and pans and began baking biscuits. Charlie took some salt-preserved snake meat, cleaned it, and boiled it in flour and water to make gravy. When the campfire had provided enough red-hot coals, he had dinner cooking.

The evening air was considerably cooler than it had been during the day and a slight breeze blowing against their sweaty clothes made it even more so. Roger strode over to his bedroll to pull out his jacket.

"Wait until you're bone dry before putting on that jacket," Nik said. "The evening will get cooler, and you don't want to perspire more with that jacket on."

Nik pulled a blanket out of the chuck wagon, took off his shirt and wrapped himself in the blanket. He hung his shirt out to dry. Charlie seemed content working over the fire and soon had a meal of biscuits, gravy, potatoes and beans ready to serve. He also pulled out some honey from the chuck wagon to put on the biscuits for dessert.

Again, Roger ate his fill and was delighted at how tasty the food was. Although food cooked outdoors always seems to taste better, Charlie's meals had an extra flavor that Roger relished.

After dinner, the men chatted over cups of coffee and soon laid out their bedrolls and turned in for the night.

The next day they began a three-day trek farther into the Llano Estacado. As they traveled, they came upon a small trading post once used by trappers and Indians to exchange wares, which had long since been abandoned. There were occasional signs of campfires, either made by outlaws or those chasing after them but, for the most part, they found few signs of civilization.

"Since it is not likely we'll find Iron Bear, exactly what do we hope to accomplish out here, Nik?" Roger said, after hours of riding in silence.

"It's really just part of your training, Roger," Nik answered. "I'm not sure we'll accomplish anything of significance, but you need to become familiar with this territory. You'll find this job can get boring at times, but when things heat up you need to be prepared for anything."

"Even running into Colonel Curtain," Roger said, almost absent-mindedly.

"Yeah, that and beyond," Nik responded.

After reaching the main fork of the Canadian River, the three men headed west, staying near the river. Although day temperatures were hot, spending time near the water offered relief to both the men and animals. At the spot they crossed into Texas, they again filled their water barrels before heading farther south.

"Things get a little rough in this territory now," Nik said. "We'll pretty much be traveling survival style until we reach the Red River. There are generally mixed settlements of Indians, trappers, cattlemen and ne'er-do-wells out here. We might be able to resupply if we run across one of them, but after that, we'll follow the river and head due east."

"Survival, you say. Like you indicated, I guess that's part of my training, right?" Roger inquired.

"It will likely be a lot more than simply learning how to travel," Nik mentored. "That's one thing about this job. One never knows what 'training' might be in store from one minute to the next, especially out here."

"So, will we be living on jerky, biscuits and beans for a while?" Roger asked.

"For the most part," Nik said, "but keep your eye out for a possible turkey or deer. They're not plentiful out here, but occasionally it's possible to run across one. They also have wild pigs in this barren, high desert. They're not that tasty, but Charlie is good at doctoring up those beasts into something edible.

"There are antelope out here, as well, but they are very wary and very fast. Getting a good shot at one is rare, but if you bag one, they're good eatin'."

"I know there are snakes," Roger commented. "Charlie certainly knows how to doctor up a snake for dinner.

"How do animals survive out here without water?" Roger concluded.

"Generally, they don't," Nik answered. "That's why you see so few of them. That's why I say this is survival training. However, the animals are a lot better at finding water than we are. They can smell it."

As the sun rose in the sky that day, the traveling slowed a bit. There were few trees in the area to offer shade and the afternoon sun proved especially brutal. For the most part, the riders remained silent, lost in thought, and using an almost hypnotic state to take their minds off the heat. The landscape was spreading into a vast high desert allowing one to see an almost uninterrupted view of the horizon. Several mesas dotted the landscape with plateaus beyond that. The trio rode almost aimlessly with no goal in mind, other than to introduce Roger to the Llano Estacado.

Day one on the Staked Plains ended without incident, other than chasing down a couple of sage hens for supper. Sagehens were slow birds and not terribly wary. Nik suggested chasing them until getting close enough for a head shot, since a shot to the body would destroy much of the meat. That strategy worked.

They ate well again that night and chatted around the campfire before turning in.

"What is the success rate of ever finding anyone out here?" Roger questioned, to no one in particular.

"It depends on how soon you start your pursuit," Nik said. "The more distance an outlaw, or group of outlaws, can put between themselves and a posse the greater the chance they have of escaping, especially if the outlaws know their way around out here.

"Now, Indians are a different story. Although they are more adapted to this area, they don't care anymore for this Godforsaken place than the rest of us."

"When chasing Indians, they find you," Charlie Blue Feather said.

"Somehow, I just do not find much comfort in that," Roger quipped.

"There are some bad ones, but for the most part Indians will give you a fighting chance, even the hostile ones," Nik answered. "A war party is the exception to that, but there isn't much out here to go to war over. Still, there is the occasional military patrol that runs into trouble. But many of the tribes in this territory live in a rather uneasy peace with the white man."

Chapter 19

The next morning, the men rose early and started out without eating breakfast. The plan was to take advantage of the cool of the day and they would wait until later before taking food. As the day wore on, the men again fell into a silent stupor as they rode along.

"Party being watched," Blue Feather said, snapping the two deputy marshals out of their drowsy state.

"Did you see something?" Nik asked.

"No, but feel eyes on us," Charlie answered.

"Do you think it is Iron Bear?" Nik continued.

"Not sure, will know by sundown," Charlie said.

"Do we need to take cover?" Roger stated.

"No, just keep riding," Nik said. "It is likely they know we are aware of their presence, but it is necessary we do not do anything to provoke whoever it is that's out there."

After riding a couple more miles, Nik suggested the team stop, rest, and have a little to eat. It was time to water the horses and see if they had attracted enough attention to warrant a visit.

"We'll head southwest to indicate we're looking for something, or someone," said Nik. "That way, whoever is out there will either make a move or go on about their business satisfied we pose no threat."

For the rest of the day, there was no incident or sign of anyone approaching the travelers. By late afternoon, the three stopped in a dried-up wash. They used the banks of the gully for shade from the setting, but still hot, sun. They made a campfire to boil some coffee and dined on leftovers for dinner.

The night was without incident, but the next morning they woke to find three Indians standing over them. They appeared determined in their intentions but not overtly hostile. One had a rifle pointed at Nik and the other two were armed with bows with arrows on string. Charlie spoke to the three of them in Comanche.

"Warriors ask why here," Charlie said to Nik.

"Tell them were looking for Iron Bear," Nik said.

Roger wondered if it was wise to tell them their intent and soon had his answer.

"Say take us to Iron Bear, but long ride and cover eyes so we not see," Charlie said. "We leave weapons behind."

"Tell them we will do it because we come only to talk, not to fight," Nik said.

After a brief conversation between the three Indians an agreement was reached. All weapons were to remain in the wagon and the three men would be blindfolded. Their horses would be led by the warriors.

"Is this a good idea?" Roger asked Nik.

"It is the best we can do if we want to see Iron Bear," Nik replied.

One of the braves asked Charlie to translate the Brinkmans' conversation. After Charlie spoke, the braves laughed while blindfolding the men.

"What was so funny?" Roger said, directing his question to Charlie despite the blindfold.

"I say you are new," Charlie said.

It was hard for the men to tell just how long they had been riding, but by the time they reached Iron Bear's camp, it was late afternoon. The Indians had them dismount and then led them on foot over some rocky terrain. Once the blindfolds came off, Nik, Roger and Charlie found themselves standing inside a small, covered rock shelter with a fourth Indian sitting near the back. He was dressed in an eclectic array of army-issue pants, a dark shirt and wearing moccasins buttoned along the ankles with silver studs. He was draped in a blanket and wore a beaded band on his crown with braided hair hanging over each shoulder. He appeared older than his companions, and his face was expressionless.

"I am Iron Bear. You look for me?" the sitting warrior said, using reasonably good English.

"I'm here to ask you to give up your warrior ways and return to your tribe in peace," Nik said.

"And you are, dark man?" Iron Bear asked.

"My name is Nik Brinkman. I'm a U.S. Deputy Marshal," Nik said.

"And they?" Iron Bear said, gesturing to Roger and Charlie.

"U.S. Deputy Marshal Roger Brinkman and Indian Scout Charlie Blue Feather," Nik said.

"Blue Feather. Iron Bear know you, Blue Feather," said the renegade. "Both Marshal Brinkman?"

"We're related," Nik said.

"You say return to tribe in peace, marshal," Iron Bear said, dismissing Nik's remark about being related. "You here because you think Iron Bear and braves kill settlers? I say not Comanche, white man kill settlers. The man Sockeye and his men."

Nik turned to Roger. "Sockeye is a nefarious character and it's been said he hangs out in these parts," Nik explained.

Nik then turned back to Iron Bear. "My request is for you to turn yourselves in and return to your tribe as peaceful warriors," Nik said. "As for the killing of settlers, I know nothing of what you speak. I am here to ask you to return to your tribe."

"You not know of settlers?" Iron Bear inquired. "Three days past, lone wagon attacked. Two killed. Woman taken."

"We've been riding for several days. We have not received word of any wagon attack," Nik said.

"White outlaws make attack look Comanche. Take horses and woman," Iron Bear was speaking louder now. "Iron Bear and warriors not part of it."

"As I said, Iron Bear, I am here only to request you return to your tribe in peace," Nik stated. "I have been sent to make that offer to you and your braves."

"Sit," said the notorious renegade. "Iron Bear happy here far from tribe and white man's lies."

Charlie sat to Iron Bear's right to serve as an interpreter if needed. Roger sat next to Charlie, and Nik sat off to Iron Bear's left.

"You will continue to be hunted," Nik said. "There are army patrols out here and they will eventually find you. Iron Bear and his warriors would do well to come peacefully with us."

"No, marshal, not go with you. Soldiers not find us," Iron Bear said. "We live here. We stay."

"Then we shall go," Nik said.

"No go, dark man, not 'til nightfall," Iron Bear said. "You cannot know Iron Bear camp."

"Your braves are going to take us back, right?" Nik said. "They can blindfold us again."

"No. You go back at night, law man," said Iron Bear. "Braves keep horses."

"You're going to send us back in the dark on foot? We have no idea where we are," Nik said, turning to Charlie. "Charlie, do you know where we are?"

As Iron Bear and his warriors turned to look at Charlie, Nik drew a pistol hidden in his boot and pointed at the warrior holding a rifle.

"Drop your weapon," Nik demanded.

Just then, Iron Bear pulled out a knife and made a backhanded slash across Charlie's cheek and cut off the tip of his left ear. Nik fired and killed the armed warrior and then turned his weapon on Iron Bear, who was lunging at Roger. Another shot rang out and Iron Bear sprawled face first in front of Roger's feet.

The two remaining braves made a break for the shelter entrance as Nik fired off another shot in their direction. However, the two Indians were able to make it to their mounts and rode off toward the horses belonging to the three men. Nik bolted after them.

"Look after Charlie," Nik yelled at Roger.

Nik fired at the retreating Indians, who turned their mounts away from where the three horses were tethered. Soon, they were out of sight and Nik returned to the shelter.

"How is Charlie?" Nik inquired.

"He's cut pretty bad. I'm having trouble stopping the bleeding,"

Roger responded, applying his bandana to the cut across Charlie's face.

"We'll have to burn the cut," Nik said, and stepped over to where Iron Bear's body lay and picked up the renegade's knife. "I'll start a fire to heat this knife."

Nik began to talk to Charlie in the Indian's native tongue. Charlie nodded and said a few words in response. After that, Nik exited the shelter and proceeded to get a fire going.

"Bring Charlie out and set him by the fire," Nik called out to Roger. "We'll need to get that cut taken care of."

Roger helped Charlie up and walked him out by the fire. Charlie then sat down, crossed his legs and began to quietly chant.

"What's he doing?" Roger asked.

"He's preparing himself for the branding of that wound. He'll soon be in a trance that will keep him from resisting what I have to do," Nik said.

Before long, the fire was going, and the knife blade was beginning to glow. Charlie had stopped his chanting and was now sitting as still as stone.

"Remove your wrap from Charlie's face," Nik said.

Blue Feather's blood had started to coagulate, forcing Roger to have to tug the bandana from Charlie's face. Roger winced when he pulled on the cloth. However, Charlie did not move or change his expression. Nik then applied the hot blade to Charlie's face and the smell of burning flesh filled the air. Nik reheated the knife and continued until the bleeding from Blue Feather's face and ear had stopped completely. Nik stepped back, sweat dripping from his face.

"We'll let that take effect before disturbing him," Nik said to Roger. "He'll come to when he's ready. Now, go down to our horses and bring them up here," Nik instructed. "Retrieve the rifle of Iron Bear's warrior and take it with you."

Roger removed the rifle from the dead Indian's body and approached the horses cautiously so as not to spook the animals. He scanned the terrain just in case the two runaway warriors were still lurking in the area. Roger was able to rope-halter the horses and added the two apparently belonging to Iron Bear and his rifleman. He brought them up to the shelter where Nik was keeping an eye on Charlie.

"We need to keep these animals close. Iron Bear's warriors will likely return for them because the Comanche place a high value on horses," Nik said. "I'm debating whether to take the bodies of Iron Bear and his warrior or leave them for his braves to retrieve and bury."

"Why would we need to take them with us?" Roger asked.

"As evidence that Iron Bear is dead. The army and marshal service would like that confirmed. Iron Bear has made quite a name for himself in these parts," Nik said. "On the other hand, Indians prefer to bury their own, even renegades."

"What was that thing about attacking a settler's wagon?" Roger asked.

"I'm not sure about that. Iron Bear seemed adamant that he was not to blame for it," Nik said. "He blamed an hombre nicknamed 'Sockeye.' I know very little about him, other than the fact he's a bad one. Attempts to pin something on him have failed. I think he has others do his dirty work for him.

"At any rate, we'll stay here for the night and try to find our way back in the morning. In the meantime, we need that warrior's rifle, and any other weapons Iron Bear may have."

After a quick search and using the Indian's blankets to cover the bodies of Iron Bear and his rifleman, another rifle was found, apparently belonging to Iron Bear.

"We'll build a campfire and try to find the water that must be around here. These renegades could not have survived here without some source of it," said Nik.

Each took a rifle and Nik climbed onto the rocks behind the shelter. Roger stayed behind to keep an eye on Charlie and the horses. Not only were the rocks the best place to find a hidden springs, but they also gave Nik a better view of the sprawling plain below him. After locating the spring, Nik drank his fill and filled the canteens the men brought with them. Afterward, Nik returned and set about finding a spot to corral the horses for the night.

The evening meal was venison jerky kept in Nik's saddlebags and some of the dried fruit and nuts Charlie brought along. Blue Feather remained in his trance-like state and did not eat.

Nik took the first watch that night, finding a spot on the rocks well above the campfire. The horses were tethered nearby and visible from Nik's position. Nik fought sleep for several hours before waking Roger to finish the night watch. Roger was having trouble sleeping after what they had been through and gladly gave his brother a chance for some shuteye.

By morning, Charlie had recovered full consciousness and had replenished the campfire with wood. He claimed not to be bothered by the pain of his wound and helped himself to a little of the previous night's supper. Charlie then prepared the horses for the trek back to the chuck wagon, not at all certain they would find it. After Nik woke up, he and Charlie tried to piece together what their captives did to disguise the route to the shelter. They determined they had taken the long way around the mesa to get there. They also discussed where they felt the sun was positioned during different parts of their trip. From there, they hoped to pick up some tracks, although they knew the Indians would attempt to erase them.

Nik and Charlie thought it best to leave Iron Bear and his warrior behind for their companions to bury. They did not want to damage Comanche relations any more than necessary. They did gather materials in hopes of proving Iron Bear was, indeed, dead. They found scalps and an amulet the renegade had worn around his neck. They also had Iron Bear's horse, his rifle and the knife used to slice Charlie's face. They placed the bodies on rocks to keep them off the ground.

They began their uncertain journey keeping the two Comanche ponies in tow. They circled the mesa and found where several horses had passed. Judging from the sun, they set out in the direction they believed they had come.

They rode east for several hours and saw what looked like a small dust storm in the distance.

"Horses," Charlie said.

"How many do you think, Charlie?" Nik asked.

"Many," Charlie responded, "maybe patrol."

With hopes it was an army patrol kicking up the dust, the three men rode toward it. When still some distance from the dust cloud, the three could see it was a cavalry of soldiers. The trio continued to where both groups could see one another. Nik told Charlie and Roger to hold up while he approached the mounted soldiers.

"U.S. Deputy Marshal Nik Brinkman," Nik said to the leading officer, after reaching the soldiers.

"What brings you out here, marshal?" the officer asked.

"We were led out here by a band of renegade Comanche. They blindfolded us so we could not tell where we were going. When we left, we took a chance on which direction to go and fortunately ran into you and your patrol," Nik answered.

"Those two men with you, who are they?" asked the officer, looking at Roger and Charlie waiting about one hundred yards away.

"One is Deputy Marshal Roger Brinkman and the other our Indian scout, Charlie Blue Feather," Nik said. "They were in my party."

"You were taken by renegades you say. Any idea who they were?" the officer asked.

"A small war party led by Iron Bear," Nik said.

"Iron Bear? How is it you're still alive?" the officer inquired, with a look of surprise.

"We came in peace, but that deteriorated when Iron Bear decided to take our horses and hold us until nightfall." Nik explained. "I took exception to that, and Iron Bear and his warrior are the dead ones. Two other braves escaped."

"You have proof of this?" the officer asked.

"We do," Nik said. "We have some of Iron Bear's belongings and his horse."

"Let's take a look," the officer said and signaled to his men to wait while he followed Nik back to where Roger and Charlie were waiting.

After inspecting the items, the officer introduced himself as Lieutenant George Holbrook. Holbrook was young and his uniform looked fresh enough to be new. However, he appeared confident, modest, and comfortable leading soldiers. He reminded Roger of how Major Baumgartner carried himself.

After viewing the items taken from Iron Bear, Holbrook asked if Nik could point them in the direction of the renegade's hideout. Nik turned the lieutenant's attention on the mesa where the three men had been and outlined the whereabouts of the shelter.

"I doubt you'll find the bodies," Nik said. "I imagine his braves returned to bury them by now."

"Too bad," the officer said. "I think there is a reward for Iron Bear's capture, but I'm not sure you can collect it without the body."

"We felt it wasn't our place to dishonor the dead and we didn't want to have to hasten their decay in the hot sun," Nik replied. "A reward would be nice, but I think we're all just happy to be alive."

"Your scout doesn't look too well," Holbrook said. "Is he alright?"

"He received a nasty cut across his face from Iron Bear that cost him the tip of his ear. I cauterized the wound and he's recovering, but he's still a bit weak," Nik answered. "So where are you headed, Lieutenant?"

"We're just a patrol. We, too, believed Iron Bear was out here somewhere, but we had little hope of actually finding him," Holbrook said. "However, we did find an abandoned chuck wagon a few miles back. Any idea who that might belong to?"

"Yes sir – it's ours," Nik answered. "Can you direct us to it?"

"Yes. In fact, I left a small detachment of soldiers to guard it," Holbrook said. "We found holstered pistols in it and did not want to leave those for the renegades."

"Were there rifles, as well?" Nik asked.

"Not that we saw," Holbrook said.

"The two Indians that got away from us must have wasted no time getting back to the wagon to confiscate our weapons. They were both armed with bows and probably only wanted our rifles to do battle with us, but to our knowledge, they never returned," Nik said.

"It's possible we got there in time to force them into making a hasty retreat," said Holbrook. "Otherwise, I'm sure they probably would have burned your wagon."

"I'm sure you're right, Lieutenant," Nik said.

"By the way, Officer Holbrook," Roger interjected, "have you heard of a settler's wagon being attacked recently?"

"I have," Holbrook said. "A couple of days ago a small family was attacked, and their wagon burned. A patrol found the bodies of a man and his wife, both scalped. I believe they were later identified as a Mr. and Mrs. Fenton out of Missouri."

"Fenton!?" Roger blurted out. "Were there three bodies?"

"No, just the two," Holbrook said. "Did you know them?"

"It's possible. Nik and I grew up in Bordertown, Missouri, where a family of Fentons lived," said Roger. "However, they had a daughter."

"No other body was found," Holbrook said. "However, one of our soldiers came across two scalps not far from where the bodies were. Throwing away scalps is not typical of an Indian raid."

"That must be why Iron Bear insisted the killing was done by an outlaw, if it's the same wagon he was referring to," Roger said, holding back his grief with the hope that the wagon didn't belong to the Fentons. "Oh my God, I can't believe this," Roger said to himself, but was overheard by the others.

"Take it easy, Roger. We can't be certain those Fentons were the ones we knew in Bordertown. Besides, there were only two, not three," Nik advised. "Let's not jump to conclusions until we know if it was an Indian attack or the work of some outlaws."

"I'm sorry if it was someone you knew," Holbrook said. "But I have to continue my patrol. Do you need any assistance getting back to your camp?"

"No," Nik said. "We'll head in the direction you showed us. We should be all right."

"The soldiers with your wagon will direct you to the nearest military camp, where you can get some help for your scout and replenish your supplies," Holbrook said.

With that, Lieutenant Holbrook motioned his men to continue in the direction of the mesa, and the two deputy marshals and Blue

Feather set out to rediscover their chuck wagon.

After reaching their former location, Nik told the soldiers guarding the site in which direction Lieutenant Holbrook was headed. He then requested directions to the nearest military outpost. After the exchange, the soldiers rode off to catch up to their patrol. Nik, Roger, and Charlie took the time to eat and then set out for the outpost.

Nik harnessed Charlie's horse to the wagon and tied his horse and the two Comanche horses to it, as well. Nik took over driving the chuck wagon and insisted Charlie ride in back and rest to help speed up the scout's recovery.

As directed, they came to the Brazos River and followed it until arriving at Camp Cooper. They spent a couple days resting and replenished their supplies for the return trip to Wichita. They informed the outpost commander of Lieutenant Holbrook's intent to investigate the mesa where they had left Iron Bear's remains. They also turned over the two Comanche ponies to the commander, who said he would wait for Holbrook's report and then pass along the evidence concerning Iron Bear to have his death confirmed.

The following day, Charlie was ready to assume his position driving the chuck wagon and the three men departed Camp Cooper for Wichita.

Chapter 20

Charlie Blue Feather had made a complete recovery but bore a terrible scar across the left side of his face and he was missing the top of his left ear. His strength came back quickly during his short period of recuperation at Fort Cooper in Texas. He was now back at the helm of the chuck wagon, with Nik and Roger riding Lincoln and Brinker, respectively, alongside. They were headed for Wichita, Kansas.

The trip was long but uneventful, for the most part, and they were now just a few hours away from reaching their destination.

"You know, Nik, you never told me how you came up with that pistol you used to get us out of that situation with Iron Bear," Roger said. "Now that I've had time to think about it, just how did you do that?"

"Simple enough, my brother, I always keep a loaded pistol in my boot. All I needed during our discussion with Iron Bear was a diversion, which you gave me," Nik replied. "Marshal Borchers recommended the 'hidden pistol' when I came on board with the service. I devised a holster to hold it inside my boot and I've taken the time to practice drawing it when needed. I am certainly glad I took his advice."

"We're all glad you did, or we might not have survived to tell the tale," Roger remarked. "Now that you mention it, Borchers suggested carrying a second pistol. He even said a shotgun wasn't a bad companion, either."

"The hidden gun is a must in this business," Nik continued. "I was a little afraid Iron Bear's braves would try to frisk us after we agreed to leave our guns in the chuck wagon. However, Indians never seem to suspect such things. I guess it's a part of their culture."

"No boots," Charlie Blue Feather said. "Indians carry knife in tall moccasins, seldom wary of gun in boot."

"I have to admit, I'm glad they were satisfied they could trust us to come along totally unarmed," Roger said. "I'm surprised by that considering all the treaties that have been broken."

"Good point, but if they had discovered the gun in my boot before we left for Iron Bear's hideout, I was prepared to go for my Colt and shoot it out with that bunch," said Nik. "I really wasn't going to face Iron Bear knowing we had no way to counter a betrayal on his part. He was a known killer."

"I certainly was not prepared for such a situation and shudder to think of what would have happened if I had been on my own," Roger replied.

"That's why the U.S. Marshal Service trains this way," Nik remarked. "And, like Borchers said, there is no teacher-like experience."

The trio reached Wichita in late afternoon and tied up in front of the hotel where the U.S. Marshals Office was located. After checking in with the hotel clerk, they were informed that Borchers was out. They were given the key to Room 101 and told there was no telling when the marshal would be back. They checked to see if Borchers had left a note, but none was found.

"I think we'd best find a spot by the river to camp for the night," Nik said. "We'll check to see if Borchers has returned tomorrow morning."

"Can't we just stay here in the hotel like we did the first time?" Roger asked.

"No," Nik said. "Without Borchers' authority, the hotel would never let Charlie stay here. It's best if we all three sleep under the stars tonight."

"Really? Charlie's not welcome here despite working with the Marshal Service?" Roger inquired.

"The local Indians were driven out of Wichita when the whites settled the town," Nik said. "Kansas, and the Federal Government, wanted them south of the Kansas border in Texas and Oklahoma, where so many tribes are located."

"With that kind of attitude, I'm not sure I would now want to stay in this hotel, either," Roger replied. "It's a little too exclusive for me."

"Get used to it," Nik said. "You'll find that attitude is the rule out here, not the exception."

The men left the office, thanked the clerk, and mounted up to find a place to camp near the creek. They selected a little plateau just below a hill that led down to the water. There was a group of trees downhill from their camp, standing between them and the creek. The late-summer evening was warm and muggy. Heavy black clouds could be seen gathering on the horizon, but they were far enough away to not cause any concern. Lightning flashes could be seen in the distance, but the rumble of thunder was barely audible.

"We might catch a little rain tonight," Nik said. "Charlie can sleep in the wagon, and you and I can put our saddles and blankets underneath it to sleep. With any luck, if the rain heads this way it won't amount to much."

That evening, the men had just settled in when a light rain began to fall but the heart of the storm was still miles away. The sound of falling rain soothed the campers as they began to drift off to sleep. As the night approached early morning, a sudden bright flash and clap of thunder jerked the men awake. They awoke to a heavy downpour and a runoff that was now flowing down the slope above them. The water was soaking their bedrolls and running toward the creek. The stream was beginning to overflow and flooding the area where the stand of trees was located.

The rain was now coming down hard and the force of the water rushing down the hill threatened to push the wagon in the direction of the trees.

"Roger!" Nik shouted. "We'd best get out from under here and try to move the wagon to higher ground."

Charlie was awake and had jumped from the wagon. He ran down to gather the horses, loosely roped in and left to graze near the grove of trees. Charlie quickly released the rope corral and used it to halter the horses and lead them up to the campsite. Blue Feather then tried to harness his horse to the wagon, but the rushing water was making it too difficult for one man to do.

Roger had followed Nik's lead and was loading gear into the back of the wagon.

"Roger, put a rope around your horse and tie it to the wagon wheel in order to keep the rig from sliding," Nik shouted. "I'll help Charlie get his horse harnessed up."

Roger was able to calm Brinker enough to put a rope around the animal's neck. He attempted to tie the other end of the rope to the wagon wheel. But the wheel pulled free and nearly pinned Roger to the ground, which by now was an oozing mass of mud.

"Charlie! Cut that horse loose from the harness," Nik shouted through the roar of the deluge. "The wagon is caught in this mudslide, and it'll pull him down with it."

Meanwhile, Nik's horse was loose and began heading for higher ground. Charlie freed his animal from the wagon and was leading him uphill above the flow of water, as well. Nik grabbed Charlie's horse by the tail and followed. The wagon was now beginning to slide toward the trees and the creek was overflowing its banks.

Roger managed to hang onto Brinker, as he wrestled to get out from under the wagon wheel. When free, he and Brinker climbed together up the slope with the others.

The trio, with two horses in tow, eventually made their way to the hilltop and out of the torrent of water. However, the ground was a mass of slippery mud and the rain continued to fall, unabated.

"We'll have to make our way back to Wichita on foot," Nik said. "We'll spend the night in Borcher's office and come back in the morning to salvage what we can. I'm sure my horse will be okay, if we can ever find him."

The rain was starting to let up as the three men made their way through the deluge back to town. Upon entering Wichita's main street, they could see light still emanating from the local saloon. Otherwise, the town had virtually shut down after the storm hit. The three reached the hotel and tied the two horses to the outside rail and made their way inside to dry off. They did not bother to wake the night clerk and simply slipped behind the counter and grabbed the key to Room 101. Once in the room, they sat in silence for a moment pondering what had just happened.

After assessing the situation, they went out to take their horses to the livery stable. They wiped down the animals and placed them in stalls with plenty of hay. Upon their return to the hotel, they stayed outside to empty the mud and water that had collected inside their footwear.

Inside the hotel office, they removed their shirts and hung them on the backs of chairs to dry out.

Nik removed his pistol, emptied the cartridges, and began drying his weapon with a cloth. He walked behind Borchers' desk and withdrew a key from the drawer and approached the gun cabinet. Nik unlocked the cabinet and pulled out a box of shells.

"Expecting trouble?" Roger asked almost in jest.

"In this business, you never know when it's going to show up," Nik said over his shoulder. "I suggest you do the same and load it with fresh ammunition from this box."

Roger leaned forward from where he was sitting, pushing his chin forward and nodding his head in agreement. He rose to his feet and followed Nik's lead, doing the same with his Colt.

Afterward, thankful to be out of the storm, they each found a comfortable spot in the office to recline and get some sleep. But despite their efforts to do so, they were soon interrupted by a sharp knock at the door.

"Marshal, marshal come quick. There's trouble a-brewin'," said a loud voice from behind the door.

"What now?" Nik said, almost half asleep.

Roger was closest to the door and sprang to his feet to open it. He was confronted by a man who identified himself as the bartender of the saloon that had its lights on when the three men reached town. The man stepped into the room, obviously agitated.

"You the marshal?" he asked, looking at Roger.

"I'm one of the deputies," Roger answered. "What's the problem?"

"Two men are fighting in my place, and I think there's going to be gunplay," the bartender said in an excited voice.

"Just what we need on a night like this," Nik commented, getting up and putting on his shirt and gun belt. "Roger, strap on your iron. You might as well come along.

"Charlie, you stay here and get some sleep," he added.

Roger and Nik followed the man back out of the hotel and into the street. The rain had let up considerably, but it was still enough to keep the main street a mass of mud under their feet. The three men headed for the saloon, where they could hear shouting coming from inside. The bartender stepped aside to let the two marshals enter first.

There were five men in the saloon and two seemed to be causing the ruckus. Four were dressed like cowboys, and the fifth wore a Confederate soldier's cap and was doing his best to goad one of the cowboys into a gunfight.

"Okay, what's going on here?" Nik inquired, raising his voice, attempting to be heard over the confrontation.

"Just a friendly disagreement," said the man wearing the Confederate cap. "Who are you?"

"We're with the U.S. Marshals Office, charged with keeping the peace in these parts," Nik said. "It's been a long night, gentlemen. Can't you settle this in the morning?"

"You're a marshal?" said the man in the Confederate cap. "I ain't seen your type as a marshal before. Shouldn't you be pickin' cotton somewhere?"

"It's a little late in the evening for that, don't you think?" Nik said, noting the man's contempt. Nik figured the stranger was a former Confederate foot soldier left over from the war. His demeanor was that of a drifter who used ridicule to elevate his status above those around him.

Roger picked up on the man's obvious negative attitude toward Nik but was impressed at how well his brother handled it.

"However, if you don't want to see my 'type' again tonight," Nik emphasized, "I suggest you make your peace for now and allow the barkeep, here, to close up for the night.

"Do all of you have a place to stay?" Nik added, looking at the four cowboys. "It's a pretty nasty night."

"Why don't you just throw us in jail, … marshal?" said the Confederate antagonist.

"Wichita doesn't have a jail yet," Nik answered, squaring his shoulders and facing the Confederate.

"So, if we don't stop fighting, what are you going to do then, … marshal?" snarled the rebel-capped man, sarcastically hesitating before referring to Nik's title.

"I guess I'll just have to shoot ya," Nik said, losing patience with the man's condescension.

Roger glanced over at Nik, picking up on the mounting tension building between his brother and the stranger in familiar gray headgear. He wasn't sure if Nik was sincere but knew his brother would not let another's arrogance intimidate him, regardless of color.

"Now, are you two going to behave or do things have to get ugly?" Nik continued.

"I'm going, marshal," interjected the cowboy in question, who had been silent during the conversation. "I didn't want this dang fight, anyway.

"C'mon boys," the cowboy said to the other three men, "let's get back to our outfit."

With that, the cowboy and his companions headed for the saloon door.

"Go ahead and run, you damn Yankee cowards," the Confederate called out.

The four cowboys left without looking back.

"And you?" Nik said to the remaining troublemaker.

"I'll go," said the Rebel. "Just let me finish my drink."

Nik motioned to Roger to move toward the exit. Roger did so, pushing through the swinging doors and stepping onto the boardwalk. Nik backed out, while keeping an eye on the man in the cap. The two deputies then crossed the boardwalk together and stepped into the street.

"Man, that was close, Nik," Roger said. "What was that all about?"

"Shhh," Nik said. "Don't talk."

The rain had stopped, as the two marshals headed in the direction of the hotel. Roger could tell Nik was listening for something, and it came when they heard the creaking of the saloon doors swinging open.

Nik wheeled about while drawing his gun and fired a shot that sent splinters flying from two slats lining one of the swinging doors. The Confederate, whose gun was drawn, flinched when Nik's bullet hit the door and his shot flew wide of the deputies. Nik's second shot found its mark and the man staggered forward and fell into the street. His Rebel cap tumbled from his head and came to rest in a puddle of mud. Nik, with his gun drawn, approached the fallen man while Roger stood in almost disbelief as to what he had just witnessed. Nik checked for a pulse and found none.

"We'll just leave this guy here until morning," Nik shouted to the bartender, who had now come to the door. "Shut down and go home."

Nik started back toward Roger.

"What just happened?" Roger said, still staring at the dead man in the street.

"Couldn't you tell?" Nik said, as he passed by his brother. "He was going to shoot us in the back."

"How did you know that?" Roger asked, turning to follow Nik.

"I didn't, for sure," Nik said. "That's why I wanted you to be quiet so I could listen for the sound of those swinging doors when he followed us out."

"But how did you know he was going to shoot?" Roger said.

"I didn't," Nik answered. "That's why I missed with my first shot. If he had not intended to shoot us, I would have just scared the hell out of him with that initial shot. But when he fired his gun, I knew not to miss the second time.

"C'mon, let's go get some sleep," Nik said, as he continued walking in the direction of the hotel.

Chapter 21

Early the next morning, Ned Borchers walked into Room 101 to find three men fast asleep in various locations about the office. Uncertain why two of his deputies and a scout decided to spend the night there, he quietly backed out of the room. He left the hotel and hurried across the street to the local eatery, just opening its doors for breakfast.

"Luke, can you get me a pitcher of coffee and three cups? I've got a room full of hombres, who appear in need of something to wake them up this morning," Borchers said to the diner's proprietor. "They'll likely want something to eat when they get up, as well."

"Sure thing, marshal," Luke said. "Do you need any sugar or cream?"

"Nope, just black will do," Ned answered.

"Nasty storm last night," Luke said, as he retrieved three coffee cups from the cabinet.

"It was a gully-washer, all right," Ned said.

Ned left the establishment and returned to the hotel with the cups and pitcher in hand. When he entered the office, Charlie Blue Feather was awake, but Nik and Roger had not moved from where they spent a short night.

"Charlie, can you get the boys up? I'm anxious to hear what's been going on," Borchers said.

Blue Feather began shaking the two men awake. Both rolled over with a groan and began rubbing the sleep from their eyes.

"You boys want some coffee," Ned asked, "or do you plan to sleep all day?" With that, Ned poured three cups of coffee. Charlie did not drink coffee. His morning brew was made from the yaupon holly berry, which had been left behind in the wagon.

After the deputies consumed enough coffee to wake up, Ned asked "What happened last night, fellas? I returned to find some men dragging a dead body out of the street. Nik, one of the men told me you shot him?"

"I did, Ned, had to," Nik said. "Roger and I tried to break up a fight in the saloon, and this guy decided to take the fight to a different level, involving Roger and me."

"Well, I think you did the territory a big favor. That guy was a troublemaker," Ned said.

"Who was he?" Roger asked.

"His name was Jedediah Southland," Ned said. "They also called him Jed South or Jed Reb. He fought for the Confederates in the war and was powerful bitter when the South surrendered. He was run out of Mississippi when it was discovered he was part of a plot to assassinate General Lee. It seems a few of these soldiers weren't willing to give up the fight."

"So, what was he doing here?" Nik inquired.

"Southland hightailed it west when the assassination plot was uncovered and became a hell-raiser and possible murderer."

Ned said Southland would pick fights with northerners and Union supporters. His victims often ended up dead, but Southland was long gone before the bodies were discovered.

"Other than the arguments, no evidence was left behind linking Southland to the murders," Borchers continued, "and witnesses were mixed about who started the altercations."

Borchers said the bartender at the Wichita Saloon told him Southland came in with a few cowhands running a herd nearby. Southland had been part of the outfit, but he was such a poor cowhand the trail boss decided to cut him loose.

"The cowboys with Southland brought him to town for a couple drinks," Ned concluded. "When they told him he was done, Southland turned the situation ugly."

"So, why did you boys sleep in here last night?" Ned asked, changing the subject.

"Had to," Nik said. "I knew the hotel wouldn't let Charlie have a regular room, so we decided to camp down by the river for the night. But when that storm blew in, I lost my horse and possibly Charlie's wagon in the deluge."

"I had to wait out the storm, myself," Borchers said. "I was on my way back from Kansas City when all hell broke loose."

"What was going on in Kansas City?" Roger asked.

"I was picking up some new assignments. That's where I heard about Southland and was told to look out for him. I guess you boys took care of that problem for me.

"And, on an even brighter side," Borchers said with a grin, "I got kicked up a couple of notches in my pay grade, which means I can buy you boys breakfast and Charlie can join us on my authority."

The four men enjoyed a full breakfast before beginning their day. After eating, Borchers stopped by the saloon where Nik had the run-in with Southland. The marshal informed the bartender the cost of any damage would be covered by the U.S. Marshal Service, as well as Southland's burial.

The men stopped at the livery stable to retrieve their horses and get one for Nik. They rode out to the site where the storm had washed away Charlie's chuck wagon.

As they approached the Arkansas River, a lone horse was spotted grazing on a hilltop.

"Glory be," Nik said, recognizing the horse, "Lincoln survived the storm.

"You boys head on down to the river to see what you can find there. I'm going to wrangle my horse," Nik called out, as he rode in the direction of the grazing storm survivor.

Blue Feather led the way to the campsite where the wagon had been when the flood started washing it away. As they drew near, the canvas covering came into view, and there was a general feeling of relief that at least some of the chuckwagon was still intact.

The wagon had been carried by the water into the grove of trees near the river's edge and was wedged between two cottonwoods. A large pile of debris and mud had built up against the wagon where the wheel had come off the axle. A great deal of slush had also flowed into the buckboard covering the gear inside. Roger found Nik's saddle nearby, but Roger's saddle was nowhere to be found.

Nik rode up with Lincoln in tow and surveyed the damage.

"Any sign of that wagon wheel that came off?" Nik asked.

"We haven't checked up by the campsite where we were," Roger said. "If the wheel is still around, it might be lying up there."

Nik gave Lincoln's rope halter to Charlie, while he rode up to the original campsite. Borchers and Roger started digging the mud away from what was left of the wagon. After a brief survey of the washed-out campsite, Nik returned.

"The wheel was still there, covered in muck," Nik said. "But what's interesting is I discovered this," Nik said and held up a short stick with an arrowhead attached.

"What's that?" Borchers asked.

"I think it's the reason the wagon wheel came off last night," Nik said, giving the broken arrow to Charlie. "My guess is those two Indians that got away from us at Iron Bear's hideout may have substituted the wheel's lynchpin with a piece of one of their arrows."

"Why would they do that?" Roger inquired.

"Lynchpins are made of iron," Nik explained. "My guess is those two warriors of Iron Bear substituted the iron lynchpin with this broken arrow in hopes we'd break down and be stranded somewhere. I'm surprised we did not discover it earlier."

"Arrow made with hickory, very strong," Charlie said, handing the small arrow shaft back to Nik. "Likely Choctaw arrow, but not Choctaw trick."

"So, who would have done this?" Nik asked.

"Not know why Comanche have arrow. Maybe found and used for lynchpin," Charlie surmised.

"Or I'm just trying to put two and two together and come up with three," Nik said, staring at the fractured missile. "It maybe we'll never know what happened. The wheel may have been that way for some time, and we never noticed."

"It's going to take a lot more than a lynchpin to put this wagon together again," Borchers said, "but at least there's enough left of it to get the job done. Once we get this thing back to Wichita, Charlie and I can work on it with the local blacksmith's help. Meanwhile, I've got an assignment for the two of you," Borchers added, looking in the direction of Nik and Roger.

It took a couple days to get what was left of the wagon and the recovered gear back to Wichita. After putting the blacksmith to work on restoring the conveyance, Borchers told the men to store the mud-caked equipment and clean it later. The chief marshal then took Nik and Roger back to the hotel and into Room 101.

"Boys, I'm going to have to send you back into Oklahoma and Texas, but not the Llano Estacado, so you won't need Charlie's help," the marshal said. "There's a group of desperados raising hell along the Red River. Not sure who they are. Some say Southland was a part of this group, but he split off to join that cattle drive."

"How many men would we be facing?" Nik asked.

"I'm not sure how big the outfit is, but according to reports they operate in small groups of three to four," said Borchers. "They strike and then disappear."

"Where and what do they strike?" Roger questioned.

"Banks, trains, settlers and whatever presents something they need or can be turned into a profit," the marshal continued. "That's part of the problem. It's hard to determine where they'll strike next."

"If they're splitting up like that, they could actually hit two different places as the same time," Nik chimed in.

"Precisely, and that's part of why we can't seem to track them down," Borchers said. "I'm going to ask you boys to put your badges in your saddlebags and pretend to be drifters looking for work. Find out what you can, even if you don't catch up to any of them.

"Nik, I'm not sure what kind of reception you'll get in Texas, the state did secede from the Union," Borchers continued. "I've been told most of the folks in the northern counties joined with Governor Houston and were against that, although there was some trouble in Gainesville before the war."

Borchers was referring to a Confederate uprising in Cooke County, Texas, that occurred when a few residents decided to support the North. Confederate troops rounded up nearly two-hundred suspected Union sympathizers, of which forty-one were hanged.

"I've dealt with those Jed South types before," Nik said. "Many parts of Texas have more black settlers than whites. I think I can handle it."

"At any rate, you need to be careful. I don't want to lose you," the chief marshal said, then he turned to Roger. "Deputy, if there's any trouble, I want you to step in and let people know Nik's with you."

Nik gave Roger a playful shove, enjoying the responsibility put on his brother.

"It would be my pleasure, sir," Roger answered. "I would love to do something for Nik, for a change."

Borchers began instructing his two deputies on the different sites the gang had hit, how they operated and where they seemed to go afterward. The three worked out a travel plan in hopes of running across one of their outlaw parties. They also started loading up supplies and were given enough money to cover expenses along the way.

"I plan to visit Paris, Texas, in a few weeks," Borchers said. "The new chief deputy marshal will be taking over that office and I've been asked to give him a hand. If you guys are in the vicinity, come by and let me know what you've found out."

"Hopefully we'll have something for you by then," Nik said. "We'll stay in touch."

Summer was now creeping into fall, as Roger and Nik set out and again headed south into Oklahoma Territory. Although Borchers and Nik knew most activity would decrease with the change in weather, including criminal activity, they felt it was still worth conducting the investigation. The coming winter season meant folks would head inside, making it easier to track down witnesses. With luck, they could find someone with knowledge of the raids who possibly knew members of the outlaw gang. There was speculation some of the Red River desperados could have ridden with Quantrill's Raiders during the Civil War. It was reported that Quantrill, a notorious Confederate bushwhacker, and some of his men hid out in Sherman, Texas, after the conflict.

***

Some cattle outfits were still moving their herds up the Chisholm Trail, hoping to reach the railroad in Abilene, Kansas, before winter weather arrived. When coming across a cattle drive, the two deputies would engage each trail boss in conversation, eventually asking about trouble with cattle rustlers or other outlaws. They kept their identities hidden by posing as cowboys with jobs awaiting them in Texas. What they learned was rustling had slowed because of the changing seasons, although shorter days and longer nights presented problems.

As rain became more frequent, rivers swelled, making it more difficult for migrating herds to cross. Even Nik and Roger discovered safe places to ford were becoming scarce. Inclement weather could delay the deputies' trip to Sherman by a week or more.

The duo followed the Arkansas River into Oklahoma. After several days' travel with the weather unseasonably pleasant, they reached Fort Gibson, where they replenished their supplies. They headed southwest after that through Choctaw Nation, perhaps the friendliest Indians in Oklahoma Territory. They headed across the high plains of Choctaw country toward a town called Boggy Depot.

"This will likely be the most boring part of this trip," Nik said. "It's not quite as bad as Llano Estacado because you'll see a lot more grass here."

"That's good for the horses, right?" Roger commented.

"If it's not wet," Nik said. "Eating wet grass isn't good for horses and tall grass can be difficult to walk through. What is in our favor are the Choctaw villages. Choctaw go out of their way to be friendly."

It did not take long for a rainstorm to roll in, forcing the men to don rain gear. Like Nik said, the damp grass made travel more difficult. After coming across a small stand of trees, the deputies decided to camp there for the night.

"We'll just have to pray lightning keeps its distance from these trees," Nik said, as the two made their way into the grove's center. "Chances are lightning would strike trees on the grove's periphery."

Fortunately, the night was uneventful, and the sky cleared by morning. After a couple hours' ride, they came upon an Indian Village and retrieved their badges to let the tribe know they meant no harm. After an introduction in broken English and what little Choctaw Nik knew, they were invited to spend the night in the village.

Nik did his best to solicit information from the tribe's chief, but little was learned. The chief said outlaws rarely ventured into Indian Territory because there is little to benefit them. However, the chief had heard of the "dark man" who had brought an end to Iron Bear's savagery. Although there was peace between the Choctaw and Comanche, most tribes were opposed to renegade warriors causing trouble on the reservation.

After several days of riding, camping and a few more storms, the two men reached Boggy Depot in Oklahoma Territory.

"There was a time when this little town used to be a thriving community," Nik said, as the two rode through the small village. "But the railroads bypassed it some time ago, and that reduced its importance. It's now a nice place to hang out if you don't want to be noticed."

"I guess things are changing," Roger said. "The railroads have sure made a difference out here, much like they did in the war."

"Some things for the better, and some things that turned out not so good," Nik replied. "We shouldn't run into any trouble here if we watch our step. But we just might pick up some useful information from those who pass through here."

"What would 'watching my step' entail?" Roger asked.

"Be friendly, but don't offer too much information. People here are suspicious of those who talk too much," Nik answered. "Offer no more information than you ask for and leave the impression the less they know about you the better it is for them. Don't go for your gun, if you can avoid it, but always keep it at a moment's reach."

"Sounds like a place to avoid," Roger murmured.

"Not if you're looking for directions," Nik countered, "and we are. This trip has us looking about as seedy as those we'll run into, so we'll be all right."

Boggy Depot wasn't much to look at. A recent rain had turned main street into a symbol of the town's name. A few horses were tied up in front of the Trading Post Saloon, along with a buckboard wagon parked just across the street. Boggy Depot had once been the center for trading in its day, but those times were well in the past.

Nik led the way through the swinging doors and scanned the room with a non-threatening look. Roger followed and felt much like he did during the saloon encounter he and Nik had in Wichita. Nik eyed everyone in the place as he headed toward the bar and drew looks in return.

"Whisky," Nik said, upon reaching the counter.

The bartender, an older gentleman who appreciated customers of all types, paid little attention to Nik or Roger. He turned and grabbed a bottle from the back bar along with two glasses. He set them on the counter and poured two drinks. Nik threw back his shot of whisky, while Roger continued to stare at the one in front of him.

"Ah, do you have any beer?" Nik asked the barkeep. "I guess the long ride has made my partner too thirsty for whisky right now."

The bartender stared at Roger for a moment and then said, "I've got Choctaw Beer, if you want that."

"That should do," Nik said.

The bartender poured a draught of "Choc" beer for Roger and set it in front of him. Nik slid Roger's whisky glass over to his side.

"Better drink up and look as if you like it," Nik said under his breath. "We can't afford to look any more suspicious than we do."

Roger took a drink of beer and worked to keep his face expressionless. He set the beer down and swallowed – hard.

"You don't seem very thirsty," the bartender said, a little sarcastically. "How long have you been on the trail?"

"Too long," Nik said. "My partner's just a little slow in adjusting.

"Drink up," Nik said to Roger. "Knock back some of that trail dust, or maybe I should say trail mud," he added for levity.

Roger complied and tried to drink the rest of his beer in a single effort but came up short. Nik finished his second glass of whisky and asked the bartender for two more beers.

A rather grizzled-looking man wearing buckskins walked up and leaned on the counter next to Nik.

"You two new in these parts?" the man asked.

"Been riding since Kansas," Nik said.

"You want to buy some furs?" the man continued. "It's going to be getting cold pretty soon."

"You have furs?" Nik asked.

"In the wagon across the street," the man said, "buffalo mainly, bear, some beaver."

"Sounds inviting," Nik said. "But we're out looking for work. We really don't have the money to buy fine furs like you apparently have."

"Humpfh," the man said gruffly. "If you change your minds, I'll be here for a spell."

"Don't go just yet," Nik said. "We're new here and could use some advice. Right, Roger?"

Roger had finished his first beer and was looking down at his second one.

"Huh, oh yeah, we could use some advice," Roger said, turning to look at Nik.

"We'd be happy to buy you a drink for your help," Nik said to the man. "What did you say your name was?"

"I didn't," the man said, "but I'll take that drink. Gad's the name, Gad Hastings."

"Nik, Nik Brinkman," Nik said, nodding to the bartender to get the man a drink. "This is my partner, Roger, ..." Nik hesitated before saying anymore, not wanting to attract any more attention to the Brinkman name.

"Nik and Roger, okay, let's sit at my table," Hastings said, picking up his drink and walking toward the table in question.

"Where'd you get your furs?" Nik asked, as the men each pulled back a chair at the table. Nik looked across the room at three men sitting around a separate table. They stopped their conversation, turning their attention on Nik's gaze. He touched the brim of his hat and looked down to avoid making the men uneasy, as he slid into his chair.

"Mostly in Colorado and along the Canadian River," Hastings said. "Buffalo hides I bought from the Choctaw, so the price on those is a bit high."

Roger was nursing his second beer, feeling a bit unsteady after trying to quickly down his first.

"We're cowboys, not trappers," Nik said. "I… we've shot a few buffalo, but not for a living."

"It's getting tougher," Hastings said. "I wouldn't recommend the fur trade to anyone who hasn't been at it for a while. Now I guess it's mostly cattle or farming."

"We can do cattle," Nik said. "Do you know of a ranch or a drive going through these parts?"

"Getting late in the year," Hastings answered. "You wouldn't have had any trouble a month or so ago."

"How about you fellas?" Nik called to the men across the room. "Do you know where a couple ranch hands could sign on in these parts?"

The men stared at Nik for a moment and simply shook their heads to answer no. They leaned forward and began to talk in low tones.

Nik shrugged his shoulders and turned his attention back to Hastings, as the men at the other table concluded their private conversation and left the saloon.

"Do you know who those guys were?" Nik asked Hastings.

"Nope, they didn't want any hides either," Hastings said. "They weren't the friendly kind and made it clear they didn't want my company."

"You know, Nik, I don't think I want this other beer," Roger said, adding his first comment to the conversation.

"I'll take it," Hastings said.

"It's yours," Nik answered, and slid the beer over to Hastings.

"So, where will you go from here?" Nik asked.

"Not sure," Hastings said, "maybe north, maybe west. They might still be trapping in Canada, or I'll see if there's any more gold in California. It ain't like it used to be around here."

"I'll say," Nik added. "I guess my partner and I will have to try our luck elsewhere, as well.

"Thanks for your time, Gad. Perhaps we'll meet again, sometime."

"Maybe, thanks for the drinks," Hastings said.

"C'mon, Roger, we'd better be getting along, ourselves," Nik said.

As Roger rose to his feet, he felt a little unsteady but did his best to maintain his balance.

"Your friend's not a drinker, is he?" Hastings said to Nik.

"He's a good cowboy, but he's not used to the hard stuff," Nik replied. "Thanks again for your help."

Nik put his hand on Roger's shoulder as a friendly gesture but knew it would also assist to steady his brother. They left the saloon, mounted their horses and headed south.

"Are you okay?" Nik asked.

"Yeah, my head's beginning to clear," Roger responded. "What the heck was in that beer?"

"Alcohol, brother, alcohol," Nik said with a chuckle. "I think those three cowboys headed south, and I'd like to stay on their trail."

"Where did you learn to drink like that?" Roger quizzed his brother.

"In case you have forgotten, there was a war not long ago," Nik said, emitting a low chuckle. "To keep our spirits up, our commanding officers would occasionally supply the troops with spirits. You just happened to be on the wrong side."

"Yeah, we were just happy if we got enough food and water each day," Roger replied, thinking back on the difficult conditions the South suffered. "All the good stuff went to the officers."

The three men who left the saloon in Boggy Depot were not hard to follow. The early September rains had washed away most of the tracks of previous cattle drives but clearly marked the trail of the three riders. The cattle drives were traveling north, while the trio from the saloon were headed south.

The weather held up for the next few days, and the deputy marshals tracked the three to just outside an old, abandoned fort known as Fort McCulloch. It had been used as a Confederate outpost during the war but had since been decommissioned. Nik and Roger held up, keeping just out of sight of the outpost. The deputies decided to wait and watch for their departure to pick up the trail again.

"Do you think we ought to try and sneak up on the fort to see if we can hear or see anything?" Roger asked.

"Too risky," Nik said. "And besides, we really don't know anything about those men. They could be desperados, or they could just be drifters like we're pretending to be.

"No, I suggest we wait and see what their next move is," Nik added. "My guess is they will spend the night in there and move out in the morning. We'll check out the fort after they leave."

The deputies stayed down behind a small knoll not far from the fort. They made camp there and even built a small campfire.

"What if they see our smoke?" Roger asked.

"We aren't doing anything more than making camp and traveling south," Nik answered. "Besides, it's not likely they can see beyond the walls of that fort."

The two lawmen would sneak up the hill on occasion to see if there was any activity at the former outpost. By nightfall, there was no sign the three riders would leave the old fort, so the two marshals laid out their bedrolls for the night.

"Do you want me to stand watch?" Roger asked.

"No, we'll check it out in the morning," Nik said. "If they're still there by sun-up we'll just wait a bit and then approach the place."

"Won't that stir up some trouble?" said Roger.

"Naw, if they're still there, we'll just tell them we spotted the fort and decided to check it out," Nik said. "We'll make it look like a coincidence. They have no reason to think we're following them."

That next morning, the two deputies woke early and headed up the hill just in time to see the three men ride out from the gate. The riders paused briefly to discuss something, and then two rode off in the direction of the rising sun. The third turned and continued his journey south.

"What now?" Roger asked.

"Well, partner, we split up. You follow the two riders going east, and I'll stay on the single rider's trail," Nik instructed. "It'll be easier for you to follow those two but keep your distance. Nobody's done anything wrong, yet."

"Wow, on my own," Roger said. "I guess I'd better get used to that."

"You'll do just fine, Roger," Nik said, trying to reassure his brother, as well as himself. "I'm sure you'll do just fine."

Once the three riders were out of sight, Nik and Roger rode up to the fort and made a hasty inspection of the place. The three men left nothing of significance behind, so Roger and Nik said a few parting words before going their separate ways.

"Are you sure you're up for this?" Nik asked, turning in his saddle. He had confidence in his brother but could only hope his decision to separate was the right one.

"I would say this is the only way to find out. I can't marshal in your shadow forever," Roger said. "What about you? You may be able to hide your badge, but you can't hide from hate and discrimination. And now I won't be there to help."

"You're absolutely right, brother," Nik answered, comforted by Roger's expression of confidence. "We both have our crosses to bear so we best get used to it."

"Godspeed," Roger said. The two exchanged expressions of kindred pride before turning and riding off in opposite directions.

***

After two days' travel, Nik was now certain his man was headed for Sherman, Texas. Sherman had turned into a hostile town when Confederates from nearby Cooke County raided the village shortly after the war started and threatened many of its abolitionist residents. Finding The town hospital to their cause, Quantrill's Raiders were also known to occupy the settlement. However, it had been said that Sherman righted itself after the war, but Nik knew a black man would still attract attention there, regardless.

Nik needed information and the sooner he secured it the sooner he could join Roger. Nik realized his brother needed to do some solo work as a deputy marshal, but he couldn't help but feel uneasy about Roger working alone. Since becoming a deputy, the only living thing Nik had seen Roger shoot was a snake.

After reaching the town, the subject Nik was following entered Sherman's tavern dubbed the Hanging Tree Saloon. Despite the town's reputation, Nik knew it would be a great place for information despite the likelihood of a less-than-cordial atmosphere.

As he entered the Hanging Tree, Nik made a quick glance around the room, not letting his eyes settle on any single person. The room was crowded. Some heads looked up to see who had just come in, and there were a couple stares of disdain, but for the most part, his entry was treated with indifference.

Nik quickly moved over to the bar and was pleased to see the barkeep was Mexican. Mexico and Texas were often at odds over the issue of slavery. Where many in Texas promoted the practice, Mexico did not. Nik requested whisky.

The bartender quickly brought him a glass and poured the liquor. The place was busy, and Nik could see the man behind the bar had little time to chat or express any opinions. Nik sipped his drink slowly, wanting a better look at the crowd without staring at anyone. As luck would have it, there was a huge mirror above the back bar where he could scan the room behind him. He spotted the cowboy he'd been following looking in his direction, but Nik avoided returning his gaze. Periodically glancing at the mirror, Nik noticed the man he'd been tailing get up from his chair and head toward him. The man squeezed in between Nik and the customer to his left.

"Didn't I see you a couple days ago in Boggy Depot?" the intruder asked.

"You may have," Nik answered, without looking at the man. "I was there no more than two days ago."

"I thought you was," the man said. "Where's your partner? There was another fella with you, as I remember."

"Just someone I met after finishing a drive in Kansas City," Nik answered. "We agreed to travel together back down south to look for work. I came this way in hopes of signing on with another outfit.

"My companion decided to try farming for the Choctaw," Nik continued. "He was more of a farmer than a rancher, so he decided to stay behind when I left Boggy Depot."

"Seems you'd be more suited for farming than that fella," the man said, with a sly smile as he took a drink from his whisky glass.

"Okay, let's knock off the small talk," Nik said, putting down his glass. "I'm looking for Jed South. Do you know him?"

"I'm Jed South," the man said. "Who, might I ask, is looking for him?"

"My name's Nik," Nik said. "You don't look the way South was described to me."

"Maybe you got a bad description," the man posing as Southland said. "What do you want with… me?"

"I was told South had a deal going on, and I'm interested in learning more about… your 'deal,'" Nik answered, playing along with the stranger who called himself Jed South. "I'm open to a lot more things than driving cattle."

"Really, like what kind of things are you looking for?" the man asked.

"Whatever brings in money," Nik countered. He downed his drink and pushed his glass forward on the bar signaling the bartender for another.

"Pour one for me," Nik said, when the bartender approached, "and one for my friend here, as well."

"Much obliged," the man said. "Perhaps we should move over to my table where we can talk in private."

After the two men sat down at "South's" table, the man spoke.

"To be quite honest," said the man, "I work for an outfit run by a man named Sockeye Sammon. Oh, sometimes the work isn't always on the up-and-up, but we haven't had any trouble with the law over it."

"I'm listening," Nik said, controlling the exhilaration he felt at the mention of Sockeye.

"I'm not making any promises, mind you," offered the man, "but it's possible we could use someone like you. If you're interested, I'll mention you to Sockeye.

"What's your last name?" the Jed South imposter asked.

"Rogers, Nik Rogers," Nik said, jumping on the first name that came into his head, hoping it wouldn't prove to be a choice he would later regret.

"Well, Nik Rogers, do you plan to be in town for a while?" the man asked.

"I can be if there's money in it," Nik answered.

"Where are you staying?" the man inquired.

"I'm not sure. Can you recommend a good place?" Nik inquired.

"The Red River Lodge down the street is your best bet," the imposter said. "Owned by a German. They take all kinds."

"Good to know. I guess I'll check into that lodge and wait to hear from you and this..., what did you say your boss's name was?"

"It doesn't matter, right now," the man answered. "I'll let you know if he's interested in talking to you."

Nik picked up his whisky glass and motioned a small toast. The man complied, and both finished their drinks. Nik rose from his chair, tipped his hat, and exited the saloon.

Chapter 22

Although a little nervous about being on his own, Roger Brinkman was doing a respectable job of keeping up with the two men he was directed to follow. They were headed southeast from Fort McCulloch and did not seem to be in a big hurry. They traveled along the Boggy River and then appeared to head off in the direction of the Red River, and perhaps Texas. Since the country was open land, Roger could keep his distance without danger of losing their trail. When his supplies started to give out, he would visit a Choctaw village and use his badge to gain confidence. The badge seemed to work, but Roger didn't know if it was because they accepted him as a lawman or thought he had killed a lawman to get the badge. He would mimic Nik's tactics to barter for food, since the Choctaw were self-sufficient farmers. He sometimes offered money, but it was often rejected and the food given out of goodwill.

Along with their produce, the Choctaw gave him buffalo and venison jerky, which kept him going while in pursuit of the riders. Roger was pleased he was able to replenish his supplies without Nik's help.

The two men eventually led Roger to Fort Towson, now abandoned, where they spent the night. The sky let loose a downpour, making miserable Roger's night outdoors. He slept little but dozed off when the rains stopped a few hours before morning. However, that kept him from waking up early enough to see the men depart. Disappointed, Roger approached the old outpost looking for a clue as to which direction they went. The mud in front of the fort's gate, from the previous night's rain, made it easy for the deputy to pick up the hoof prints of the two men's horses, now familiar. The tracks were still leading southeast so he set out in that direction. Although discovering the tracks was routine, Roger still felt pride in having done it on his own.

He eventually came to Rossdales Ferry on the Red River, where he inquired about the two men he was tailing. After giving a description, Roger was relieved to hear the two had crossed the river on the ferry just a few hours ahead of him. Roger then paid his fare and boarded the ferry that took him into Texas.

***

In Sherman, Nik was aroused by a sharp knock on his hotel room door. The deputy rolled off the bed where he had been lying, wondering if he would get to meet Sockeye. He felt fortunate the "Jed South" he had been following mentioned Sockeye, but he did not know if it would amount to anything. There was also an uneasy feeling his true identity was known, and he was being set up for a fall. Nik was also concerned South may not have bought his story about Roger staying behind to farm for the Choctaw. He cursed himself for not devising a better alibi as to why Roger was no longer with him – and "Nik Rogers?" What a blunder that could turn out to be.

Nik opened the door to see three men standing in the hotel hallway. The front man was the man who identified himself as Jed South, the man behind was wearing a black coat with a broad-brimmed hat to match, which covered much of his face. The last man of the three was much bigger than the other two, but had a cherub face, although it rested on a large, lantern jaw.

"Mr. Rogers, may we come in?" the first man asked.

"By all means, gentlemen," Nik answered, while stepping aside. "Please make yourselves at home, although this small room isn't very accommodating."

The Jed South character stood, along with the large cowboy, who now seemed even bigger once he entered the room. The middleman in the broad-brimmed hat sat down at the small table near Nik's bed, removed his hat and motioned to Nik to sit opposite him. Nik pulled up a chair and sat down.

With the man's hat removed, Nik could see that the man's right eye was somewhat sunken into his head. There was a large scar over that eye that nearly erased his right eyebrow. Nik tried to avoid staring.

"I'm Sockeye Sammon," the man said.

It wasn't hard for Nik to figure out where the man's nickname came from.

"I hear you're looking for work?" Sammon said.

"I am," Nik answered. "I was on my way back from a cattle drive and ran into Mr. South, here," Nik nodded in South's direction, "and he told me you might be able to use me."

Sockeye laughed, "Lupe told you his name was South?" Sockeye said, while still laughing.

"I just assumed…" Nik started.

"No, Lupe here's been a part of my outfit for some time," Sockeye said. "He doesn't like to give out his name unless it's absolutely necessary.

"So, how do we know you ain't a lawman?" Sockeye continued, centering his one good eye on Nik.

Nik's blood ran cold, but he maintained his composure. "I'm a black man from the South. How many lawmen do you know who fit that description?" Nik answered.

"Don't tell me you fought for the Confederacy," Sockeye said.

"What else was I to do?" Nik answered. "I can't say that slavery suited me, but I didn't know much about what was going on. I was handed a rifle and told to shoot anyone wearing a blue uniform or get shot myself – from behind."

"I guess you've got an ax to grind," Rogers. "How particular are you about how you grind it?"

"Let me put it this way," Nik began. "I was told to shoot, and I did. It wasn't until later I realized the Yankees were fighting to free men like me, but once I was free, they didn't want nothing to do with me.

Neither side would have me, so I am on my own. And since I was not paid by either the Union or the Confederacy, I'm not beholden to either one as to how I get the back-pay owed me."

Sockeye hesitated a moment, then pushed his chair back from the table and said, "Well, boys, what do you think?" Sammon returned his hat to his head.

"Sounds okay to me," said the man now known as Lupe.

"Huh, huh," grunted the larger man.

"Tell you what, Rogers," Sockeye said. "I'll get back to you with a proposal, and we'll go from there."

"I hope it won't be too long," Nik said with a smile. "I'm getting a little short on cash."

With that Sockeye reached into his coat pocket and pulled out his wallet. He extracted a one-hundred-dollar bill and placed it on the table in front of Nik. Smiling, Sammon said, "Let's see if this will hold your interest until we get back to you." Sockeye's smile made his injured eye look even worse.

"That'll hold me tighter than a jail cell," Nik said, looking down at the money.

"We'll be in touch," Sockeye said, getting up from his chair. He pushed the chair back toward the table and led his entourage out the door.

Nik watched as the men walked out and closed the door behind them. "Damn," he said under his breath.

***

The Red River was now swollen with winter rain and, as Roger disembarked from the ferry and realized there had been several riders crossing the river there that day. The tracks on the other side were mixed and led in several different directions. He was afraid he had blown his assignment until he spotted a small trading post not far from the dock on the Texas side. He rode over to the post and inquired as to whether anyone had noticed the two men as Roger described them.

"This isn't the first time those men have been by this way," said an older gentleman occupying a wooden chair inside the small establishment. The man was spry and somewhat mischievous in his manner. He sat up and seemed almost nervous as he eyed Roger and then glanced at the man behind the counter.

"Hold on, old timer," the post proprietor said and then turned his attention on Roger. "What's your concern with those two men?"

"Ah, I've been inquiring about work and was told those two cowboys could help me," Roger said, striving to sound sincere. "I've been trying to catch up with them since Fort Towson."

"Sounds strange," the proprietor said. "I've never known those two to offer work."

"Ten-to-one they're headed into the backwoods of Sulphur River Canyon, several days south of here," the old timer said, spitting the words out in rapid succession, "just below Clarksville, it is."

"All right, Scudder, that's enough," the proprietor said to the old man. "There's a few homesteads down there, but I doubt you'll find much work."

"Guess I'll just have to take my chances," said Roger. "What have I got to lose?"

"Suit yourself," the proprietor said, giving Roger the once over.

Roger thought it a strange conversation but tipped the edge of his hat and stepped outside. He mounted Brinker and headed south. It was not long before he came upon the familiar tracks of the riders he was tailing. The old man was a big help, despite the proprietor's objections. Oklahoma was new to Roger, but he had Nik with him. Now he would have to navigate Texas on his own. Trees were in abundance, as were small creeks and tributaries. Following the two men would be more difficult now, but if he could find his way to Clarksville, he could get directions to Sulphur River Canyon from there.

The traveling was almost pleasant and the occasional homesteads he came to were often hospitable. Roger was prepared to use his badge to put folks at ease, but his appearance was non-threatening, and he was seldom turned away.

Assisted by the directions the homesteaders offered, he soon reached Clarksville. Roger sought out the sheriff's office and was unsure if he should keep his identity from the sheriff or not. He decided to put his badge in his pocket just in case.

After introducing himself to the sheriff, Roger used his name but did not reveal his purpose right away. He feared blowing his cover could mean failing to complete his first solo mission as a U.S. Deputy Marshal.

"So, you want to visit the Sulphur Fork River, and do what?" said Curtis Packard, Clarksville's sheriff. "I have to warn you that place has a bad reputation and not typically a place where someone looks for work."

"I guess it does sound a little strange," Roger said, doing his best to act naïve. He was aware his cover story began falling apart after he reached Texas. "I've just been trying to catch up to a couple guys who might hire me on."

"Young man," Packard started, "unless you're an outlaw you're not going to get hired by anyone in the Sulphur Fork area."

"I don't understand," Roger feigned.

"What I'm trying to tell you is that area is crawling with bad guys," Packard said. "Those fellows you've been chasing are likely outlaws. Even I won't venture into that forest."

Roger stared at the sheriff for a few minutes and then blurted out, "I'm a U.S. Deputy Marshal and I've been tailing those guys all the way from Boggy Depot in Oklahoma Territory." He then pulled his badge from his pocket and presented it to the sheriff.

The sheriff just smiled and said, "Why didn't you just say so?"

"I am supposed to be undercover, and I was trying to remain that way," Roger said. "I'm sorry. I debated whether or not to be up front about it."

"You're a bit new at this, aren't you, deputy? Packard said.

"Yes, I have a partner, but we had to split up when the men we were following parted company and set off in different directions," said Roger. "I really wanted to get this thing right."

"Deputy Brinkman, I've been the sheriff of Clarksville for some time now. I have a bit of a special unspoken relationship with some of the desperados who hang out in that area – I don't bother them, and they don't bother my town," Packard said. "So far it's worked."

"I can respect that, sheriff, but I don't want to fail at my first job. All I really need to do is find that place and whether those men are there or not," Roger said. "If I do that, my job is done. I don't need to shoot it out with anybody."

"I can tell you how to get to Sulphur Fork Canyon, son, but I'm afraid I can't do more than that," Packard cautioned. "Like I said, I've got a special relationship with those river dwellers."

"I understand that, sheriff, and I am not asking for anything more than directions," said Roger.

"I will give you that and a piece of advice. If you reach a place where you can see where those men went without getting shot, turn around and hightail it out of there," Packard said. "I don't want to have to inform the U.S. Marshal Service that they have a man missing. I'm asking that you report back to me once you've fulfilled your assignment."

"Thanks, sheriff. I will be careful," Roger promised. "But just in case, I work out of the Wichita, Kansas, office under Marshal Ned Borchers."

Sheriff Packard wrote Roger's information down and gave the deputy specific directions, while wishing him luck. Roger then checked into the local hotel to plan his next move.

Roger could not help but feel excited about finding the possible hideout of the gang Borchers was looking for. It really would not matter if the cowboys he had been tailing were there or not. He could give Borchers the location and tell him what Packard had said about the desperados hanging out there.

The next day, Roger put his badge back in his saddlebag and followed Packard's advice by working his way south along a road out of Clarksville. He had lost the two men he was following but finding a potential hideout should certainly make up for it.

He rode south a few hours before coming to Little Mustang Creek, where Packard told him to leave the road and follow the creek. It would lead him to the Sulphur River. From there, the sheriff said he was on his own.

The forested area did provide cover, but it also made it difficult to see very far in any direction. Still, Roger stayed with the creek until it emptied into the Sulphur Fork. The river was swollen because of the frequent rains that often showed up without warning. Some of the riverbanks were cut deep with steep drop-offs. Fortunately, he could stay well within the shelter of the trees and still follow the river by sight and sound – suddenly, Roger heard horses walking on river rock nearby.

His heart was pounding when he dismounted and covered Brinker's nose to keep him quiet. Roger tied up his horse and quietly made his way toward the river to get a clearer look. He reached an area where he could see two riders in a shallow part of the river splashing their way toward a ridge. The men did not resemble the two he had been following, but he assumed these men were in the river to cover their tracks.

Using the skills Nik taught him years ago, he stealthily reached the top of the riverbank. He was several feet above the water on a ridge that followed the river and made a sharp turn to the right. Roger saw the two riders make the turn and disappear. He hurried to reach the bend to try and pick them up again. He came out in a small clearing that ran for several feet along the crest of the ridge. The deputy crouched down on all fours and virtually crawled to where he could look down on the river from above – all he saw below him was water.

The two riders were gone. Roger carefully raised up to get a better look and spotted a small, narrow path leading down the ridge to the water's edge some twenty feet below. He hesitated, thinking it dangerous to go down that far. But following those men to the hideout could mean his first mission would be a success.

Rains made the path slippery, so Roger grabbed rocks and small plants protruding from the ridge to help maintain his balance. As he inched his way along, a shot suddenly rang out, and a bullet shattered a rock just inches from his head. Roger quickly tried to reverse directions but lost his footing and plunged into the river.

***

When Nik entered the hotel in Sherman, after finishing his breakfast, the clerk informed him of a note left in his mailbox. It read: "Meet at the Hanging Tree tonight." Nik assumed it was from Sockeye, and he wasn't quite sure how he was going to deal with the situation, but he was determined to follow through with his undercover scheme. His greatest concern was for Roger, realizing the two men riding with Lupe were likely a part of Sockeye's outfit.

Nik confined himself to his hotel room for the day, figuring the less he was seen around town the better. He ran a million scenarios through his head, hoping to devise plans for each contingency. Some ideas seemed reasonable, and some too risky to even consider.

After a light dinner that evening, Nik left the eating establishment and headed for the Hanging Tree. Upon entering, he spotted Sockeye and his two companions at a table near the back of the saloon. Not wanting to appear obvious, Nik sauntered up to the bar and ordered a drink. It wasn't long before Lupe approached and invited him over to Sockeye's table.

After sitting down, Nik raised his glass to Sockeye in a friendly gesture. Sockeye just nodded.

"You've had some time to think about working for us," Sockeye said, "still interested?"

"One-hundred-dollar bills go a long way in holding my interest," said Nik.

"We still don't know too much about you, so we would like you to meet the rest of the boys – at our 'ranch.'" Sockeye said, with a sly smile.

"Is it near here?" Nik asked.

"No, it's several days' ride," Sockeye said. "I'm sure you'll like it, though."

"I'm anxious to find out about that," Nik said. "May I ask exactly where we'll be riding to?"

"I'd prefer to not say, just yet," Sockeye said, "but it takes a while to get there so be ready to travel."

"Fair enough," Nik said. "When do you want to leave?"

"In the morning," Sockeye answered. "We don't want to burn too much daylight."

"I'll check in at the livery stable in the morning to make sure my mount's ready to ride," Nik replied. "He threw a shoe getting here and might have come up a bit lame. However, if that's the case, I'll be able to buy another steed with your seed money."

"Whatever is necessary," said Sockeye. "We'll meet you for breakfast and then head out from there."

"Look forward to it," Nik said. He finished his drink and saluted Sockeye and his two companions before getting up to leave.

Nik's mind was now burning as to what he was getting himself into. Several days' ride may not be a problem, but depending on where the "ranch" was, could be. Would it lead him to Roger or away from him?

It nagged the deputy that his brother could be trailing two of Sockeye's men, since they were obviously associated with Lupe. But even if they were a part of Sammon's gang, there was no guarantee they were headed for Sockeye's ranch. And Nik knew it was possible someone at the ranch would recognize him.

After checking in at the lodge, Nik asked the clerk if he knew Sockeye Sammon. The clerk said he knew Sammon, but that he usually stayed at the other hotel in town. Nik thought it unwise to ask too many questions, for fear it could raise suspicions.

After a long night of scheming, Nik decided riding with Sammon was not a good idea. It would be less risky to follow Sockeye and his men and stay out of sight. But the only solution Nik could come up with was to end up behind bars.

The following morning, the deputy made a quick trip to the livery stable to ready his horse. He casually asked the proprietor if he knew Sockeye and the stable owner said he did.

"I'm supposed to be heading out to his ranch," Nik said. "Do you happen to know where that is?"

"Hard to tell," the stable owner said. "He and his boys come into town from all directions and leave that way. Sockeye and his bunch don't talk much about their comin' or goin'."

With that, Nik put his plan into action.

"Sir," Nik said, addressing the stable owner, "I've got ten dollars in my pocket for you if you will get the sheriff for me. And if anyone asks, you're just doing the sheriff a favor."

"Ten dollars?" said the proprietor. "What's this all about?"

"I can't tell you right now, but trust me," Nik said. "I'll have the sheriff fill you in later – just hurry."

Nik pulled out ten silver dollars and gave the proprietor five of them to let him know he was on the level. The stable owner took the money and made a hasty exit, while the deputy fished his badge out of his saddlebag. The proprietor returned within minutes with the sheriff in tow.

"What's this all about?" the sheriff asked, echoing the stable owner's sentiments.

"Sheriff, my name's Nik Brinkman." Nik pulled out his badge and presented it to the sheriff. "I'm a U.S. Deputy Marshal and I need you to arrest me and escort me to your jail. And I would like you to make the arrest look as real as you can."

"Now see here…," the sheriff started.

"I haven't got time to explain," Nik interrupted, handing the stable owner the five remaining silver dollars. "I'll fill you in on all the details in your office, but a man's life could be at stake, and I need you to make this look good, and I need you to do it now."

"Well, all right…" the sheriff said, with a growing look of bewilderment. "Since you are a deputy marshal."

"Pull out your gun and put it in my back," Nik demanded. "Take my gun and march me over to the jail in broad daylight."

Although skeptical, the sheriff complied and escorted Nik at gunpoint to his office. Once inside, Nik insisted he be put in a jail cell, where he would fill the sheriff in on all the details.

After turning the key to lock the cell door, the sheriff repeated, "Now, what's this all about?"

"Sheriff, tell anyone that asks I am being held for a murder committed in Kansas," Nik began, grasping the bars of his cell and leaning his head between them. "Do not tell anyone that I'm a deputy marshal. Please telegraph U.S. Marshal Ned Borchers in Wichita and ask him to confirm that I am who I told you I was. I'm working undercover and arresting me will do the United States Government a big favor, as well as me."

"All right, I will go along with this since you do have that badge, but if you're trying to pull a fast one on me..." the sheriff started, still uncertain about the situation.

"I'm on the level. Please wire Marshal Borchers as to my identity," Nik said. "His reply should put your mind at ease. And, besides, if I'm lying you already have me in jail."

The Sherman sheriff did as he was asked. It did not take Borchers long to respond, satisfying the sheriff that Nik was telling the truth. When the sheriff returned from the telegraph office, Sockeye and his men were waiting for him.

"Sheriff," Sockeye said, "I understand you arrested a man this morning. I think I know the fellow. Could I speak with him?"

"You're Sockeye Sammon, right?" the sheriff asked.

"That's me, sheriff," Sockeye said. "Sorry about the intrusion, but I think the gentleman you arrested was someone I was doing business with."

"I'll check with the prisoner to see if he wants company," the sheriff remarked. "Hey, Brinkman," the sheriff called out, "do you want company?"

Nik's blood ran cold. He forgot to tell the sheriff he identified himself to Sammon as Rogers.

"Brinkman? Did you call the prisoner Brinkman?" Sockeye asked.

"Sheriff, I'll explain it to them," Nik shouted. "Let 'em come on back."

"What's going on here," Sockeye asked, as he approached Nik's cell. "I thought you said your name was Rogers."

"Just a precaution, like Lupe did," Nik said, while attempting to look disgusted by the situation. "I seldom use the same name in any town I visit. It helps to keep the law confused, and I really didn't know anything about you when we met."

"I guess that makes sense," Sammon muttered. "So why were you arrested?"

"They're trying to pin a killing on me in Kansas and Brinkman was the name I used up there," Nik said. "I'll beat this thing, sorry about the delay."

"Sheriff," Sockeye shouted, "how long are you going to hold Rogers, er, Brinkman here?"

"I notified the U.S. Marshal in Wichita," the sheriff answered. "I don't expect him for at least a week or two. Then, I guess, he'll be turned over to the marshal for escort back to Kansas."

"Well… Nik, I guess we'll have to catch up to you later," Sockeye said.

"Maybe at his hanging," Lupe said, with a laugh.

"Sorry about the money," Nik responded, casting a perturbed look at Lupe. "I have most of it on me if you want it back."

"Keep it," Sockeye said. "You'll need it to hire yourself a good lawyer. If you do beat this thing, look me up.

"Let's go, boys," Sockeye said to his companions.

Sockeye thanked the sheriff, and the men left the office.

"Sheriff," Nik said, "can I have a word with you?"

The sheriff neared Nik's cell. "Yeah, what's up?"

"Sheriff, I need you to keep an eye on those men, especially Sockeye. When they leave town, let me know in what direction they go," Nik said. "I have to follow them because I think they could lead me to my partner and Sockeye's hideout."

"By the way, Marshal Borchers wired back to say he was heading for Paris, Texas, by train," the sheriff recalled. "He said in his confirmation telegram that he would be helping a new chief marshal get settled there."

"Where is Paris?" Nik asked.

"It's two counties east of here," the local lawman replied. "It's in the middle of Lamar County. I can get you in touch with the sheriff there if you like."

That would be great, sheriff," Nik responded. "You now know me. What's your name?"

"Lane, Fred Lane at your service," the sheriff answered, with a chuckle.

Chapter 23

Johnny "Mac" McLaughlin loved to fish and enjoyed spending most of the morning doing so. Although the seasonal rain had muddied the Sulphur River, the young boy was determined to help put food on his family's table by catching a string of bass. Over the last two days, the weather had been sunny and dry, and Johnny Mac was certain his luck would change this day. However, he was not prepared for the change that was about to unfold.

The lad worked his way through the trees to one of his favorite fishing spots. It was where the river came around the bend near his parent's homestead. The river created an eddy in that area where it had undercut the bank and formed a nice pool where the fish would gather. The flowing waters also unloaded silt on the opposite side of the river just below the eddy, making a nice beach when the water receded in the summer. The river had dropped a little with the calmer weather, and Johnny Mac noticed there was something lying on that beach just at the edge of the water. Driven by his curiosity, Johnny Mac moved downstream to get a better look at what it was that appeared to have washed up on land. When he drew close enough, he saw it was a man, lying motionless, as if dead. Frightened, Johnny Mac dropped his fishing pole and sprinted through the forest back in the direction of his family's farm.

"Mom, come quick!" Johnny Mac shouted as he approached the house.

Always concerned whenever her son was down by the river, especially when the water was high, Johnny Mac's mother hurried out the door to see what had her son so excited.

"Mom, come quick! There's a man lying down by the river," Johnny

Mac called out. "I think he might be dead."

Loretta McLaughlin threw aside the towel she had in her hand, as her son reversed direction and began to lead her back to where he had found the body lying on the silted shore. After a hasty trip through the woods, the two came upon the stretch of sand where the lifeless body was. Loretta put her hand on her son's shoulder to slow him down, exercising caution now that she could see what it was that had her son so excited.

"Take it easy, Johnny," his mother advised. "We don't know if the man is dead or not. He might just be sleeping."

After a slow approach, Loretta could see the lifeless figure wasn't sleeping or awake. She built up her courage and knelt next to him. She could see he was breathing, although his breaths were slow and shallow. After the woman determined there was no danger, at least not immediate, she instructed Johnny Mac to go back to the farm and hitch the horse to the crude sled her husband used to skid timber. She turned the unknown visitor onto his back. Unbeknown to the woman, the man was a U.S. Deputy Marshal. The unconscious stranger coughed up some water. and the woman turned his head to let it drain out. However, the man did not come to. She then waited on the beach until Johnny Mac returned with the horse and sled.

They loaded the man on the sled and managed to get him back to the family cabin.

***

Nik's staged incarceration did excuse him from riding with Sammon to visit his ranch but not the cost of his meals. He paid for those out of pocket to keep the sheriff's record clean. But Nik had been in jail for three days, and Sammon and his bunch still had not left. The deputy marshal was concerned their eventual departure could go unnoticed.

"Not to worry, deputy," the sheriff assured Nik. "I have spotters located around town."

"Terrific, Fred" Nik replied.

"Whatever I can do to help," the lawman answered. "But I suggest you refer to me as sheriff. It avoids suspicion."

Despite Nik's concerns, Sockeye, Lupe and Levi were saddling up that very day to leave.

"What do you think of that Nik fella?" Lupe asked, as he swung into the saddle. "Can we trust him?"

"Lupe, I don't even trust you," Sockeye said, with a slight laugh, as he mounted up. "I never rely on trust. I rely on what a man's willing to do and provide the leverage that keeps them loyal, at least as long as I need them."

"I'm loyal, boss," Lupe said, as the three riders headed out of town.

"I know," Sockeye replied, "and that's why you're still alive to talk about it." Sockeye laughed out loud at that remark. As the three spurred their horses into a gallop, Nik heard the sound and jumped onto his bunk to peer through his barred window.

"Sheriff, they're leaving," Nik called out loud enough for Lane to hear.

"Just hold on, my spotters will report in soon," Lane answered, as he approached Nik's cell and unlocked the door. "None too soon, as far as I'm concerned. I don't cotton much to this spy stuff."

It was not long before a spotter arrived to report that Sammon and two riders left town in a northeasterly direction.

"Sheriff, one more favor," Nik said, as he stepped out of the cell.

"What now?" the sheriff drawled. "Just so you know, I'm not going to stage a hanging," he joked halfheartedly.

"I appreciate that," Nik said, picking up on the levity. I do need you to bring my horse around behind the jail so I can ride out without being seen, if that's possible,"

"We'll work it out," the constable replied, "and I hope this all works out for you and your partners."

After the sheriff left the office, Nik strapped on his pistol and checked to make sure he still had his badge. He slipped out back as soon as the sheriff brought Lincoln around. He mounted up and looked down at the lawman.

"Much obliged, sheriff," Nik said. "The service won't forget what you've done."

"Just take care of yourself, deputy," said the sheriff. "Let us know if we can be of any more help."

With that, Nik spurred Lincoln in a northeasterly direction, avoiding the main road.

***

Back at the McLaughlin's homestead, Loretta and Johnny Mac managed to get the stranger into the bedroom. Loretta pulled off the half-drowned man's jacket and shirt and loosened his pants. She then put a blanket over the unconscious deputy and had Johnny Mac remove his boots and trousers. Loretta then pulled back the blankets on the bed, and she and Johnny managed to lift the unexpected visitor into the bed and covered him up.

"He's not dead, is he Ma?" Johnny Mac asked.

"No son, he's not dead," his mother answered, as she inspected a nasty gash on the stranger's head that, fortunately, was not bleeding. "I would not be putting a dead man into your parents' bed. Now fetch my medicine bag so I can dress this wound. Then we'll have to wait for him to wake up."

When Roger Brinkman came to, he found himself in an unfamiliar bed in a room he'd never seen before. He also discovered his head was bandaged and he had a tender spot just behind his right ear. When he touched the area with his finger, it caused his head to ache.

"Hello!" he called out and then groaned from the pain that followed.

His call brought Loretta McLaughlin into the room.

"So, you're awake," she said, as Johnny Mac followed behind her. "You suffered a rather severe blow to your head. I wouldn't try to do too much right now – just rest."

In spite of the confusion of where he was or who this woman and boy were, he could not help but take her advice.

"What am I doing here?" he groaned.

"We'll discuss all that when you're feeling better," Loretta advised. "I don't know how long it's been since you've eaten, but when you're strong enough you'd better eat something. Meanwhile, just take it easy.

"Johnny Mac, stay here with Mr. … Stranger, just in case. I'll leave the door open so you can call if you need me."

The McLaughlins' patient did not respond to the term "stranger," since the woman and boy were strangers to him, as well.

Loretta McLaughlin then left the room and busied herself preparing some soup. The deputy found that closing his eyes helped to relieve the agony. Roger was hungry but had no desire to do anything to increase the hurt in his head. He could feel the young McLaughlin boy watching him but made no effort to engage the lad in conversation. After a brief time, Loretta returned with some soup.

"Try to eat some of this," she said. "I will ladle it for you. Just take it in and swallow. I don't want you to do anything too fast."

The deputy opened his eyes to see the soup in front of him and his stomach churned in anticipation of nourishment. Loretta positioned herself on the edge of the bed so she could assist feeding him. The taste of the soup tempted the patient to grab the bowl and swallow the soup in big gulps, but just the thought caused Roger enough discomfort to dismiss the impulse. After several servings of soup, Loretta withdrew and instructed her unexpected guest to rest.

The next day, the pain in Roger's head began to diminish, although his head wound was still tender to the touch. As he looked around the room, he found nothing familiar, other than what he had seen the previous day.

Loretta was a handsome woman, strong and quite capable. She seemed well versed on to how to care for someone in Roger's condition. When she deemed it necessary to inspect his wound, she did not hesitate to remove the dressing and replace it with a fresh one. She wore a cotton dress typical of that worn by most women struggling to maintain a household in the growing, but untamed, state of Texas.

Johnny Mac, as he was called, was a bright boy and filled with curiosity. He had been cautioned by his mother not to engage the stranger in conversation, as the man was not yet ready for a barrage of questions from a 12-year-old boy. Johnny Mac was energetic, willing to help and assisted his mother in whatever way he could. He obviously was growing, as the legs of his suspendered trousers barely covered the tops of his scuffed boots. He had dark hair like his mother's, though Loretta's was dispersed with gray.

Roger had every reason to believe there was a man's presence in the house other than his own. He also had several questions he wanted to ask, but Loretta's stern tone forbidding conversation was enough to keep him quiet. She also supplied him with a steel bedpan and cover and told him how to use it. It was not what he wanted to hear. But he was a stranger in a strange place and in no condition to argue.

On day three, Loretta came into the room and started the conversation.

"I believe you might be well enough to talk. How do you feel?" she asked.

"Just sitting here in a bed, I have to say I feel pretty good," her guest answered, with a grateful smile. "However, I have no recollection of how I got here."

"You were brought up from the river, where Johnny Mac found you lying on the beach below the river bend," Loretta said. "Can you tell me who you are?"

The man looked at the woman for a short while and then his gaze dropped.

"No, Ma'am, I can't," he said.

"You can't or you won't?" Loretta inquired.

"I'm afraid I can't. I really don't know who I am any more than I know how I got here," the deputy said, with a little trembling in his voice. Although Loretta and Johnny Mac posed no threat to him, the fact Roger had no memory of his past frightened him.

"Amnesia," Loretta said, as Johnny Mac entered the room. "Relax and take it easy. It could be temporary. I'll show you some items you had in your pockets and maybe that will help you remember."

She left the room and returned shortly with the man's clothes and his gun belt. There was no gun in the holster.

"Do these look familiar?" Loretta asked.

Roger stared at the clothes for a moment and then reached out to gather them to himself. He looked them over carefully, but nothing about them gave him any notion of his identity.

"I'm sorry," he said. "I just can't remember. These clothes do look familiar, but that's about all." Roger Brinkman's anxiety grew realizing he could not recall anything about his past.

"In which case, we're going to have to keep you a little longer, at least until you get well," Loretta said. "So, what shall we call you – Stranger?"

"No, Ma, his name is Jonah," Johnny Mac said.

"How do you know his name is Jonah?" Loretta asked her son.

"Because a big fish must have thrown him up on the beach," Johnny Mac said. "You know, like Jonah and the whale."

"I'm sorry, you'll have to forgive Johnny Mac. He has a vivid imagination," Loretta said to the man dubbed as Jonah. "I have to teach Johnny his lessons, and the Bible is about the best book we have to do that."

"I know that story," Roger said, with some delight in his voice. "I don't recall having been swallowed by a fish, but if you want to call me Jonah, I'm all right with that."

"So, how is it you know that story?" Loretta asked. "Were you a preacher of some sort, despite that gun belt you had around your waist?"

"I don't know," Deputy Brinkman said. "I don't think so, but… do you have a Bible?"

"Sure, we've got the one Johnny Mac learns from," Loretta said. "Son, fetch the Bible for Mr. … Jonah, here."

Johnny Mac retrieved his Bible and brought it to the amnesia-stricken deputy, who began to thumb through it. The book, the chapters and verses were all familiar to him, but the memory of his past was still a blank.

"Do you know what the story of Jonah and the great fish is about?" Roger asked Johnny Mac.

"Sure, the sailors on the boat that Jonah was on threw him overboard because they thought he brought a curse on them," Johnny Mac said. "Then God lifted the curse and the fish saved Jonah from drowning."

"That's very good," Roger said. "I just hope I haven't brought some curse upon this home."

"Not if you're a good man," Loretta said. "We don't know your past, but if you get better and behave yourself, we'll have no reason to throw you back into the river."

Johnny Mac laughed at his mother's comment, and the levity brought a smile to Roger's otherwise concerned face.

That evening, the deputy sat up much of the night thinking. What if he wasn't a decent guy? What things in his past could he have done wrong? Would he harm this family in some way if he could recall who he was? He felt no malice. In fact, he felt tremendous gratitude that this woman and her son had taken him in and were nursing him back to health.

On the other hand, if he was a law-abiding person, what in the world was he doing on that beach? Had he, like Jonah, been running away from God or the law? He apparently had a gun at one time since he was wearing a gun belt when he was found. But there was no other clue as to who he was. He did remember the story of Jonah and the great fish and recognized scores of stories when he leafed through the Bible. Had he been a preacher? Why was the Bible so familiar to him? He sat up and thought most of the night and then drifted off to sleep.

The next morning, Roger woke up and tried to put on the now dry clothes he had been wearing when found. He suffered a dizzy spell, but it passed rather quickly. After getting his clothes on, he didn't bother putting on the gun belt, since he had no gun and it wouldn't have been appropriate, anyhow. He could hear Loretta working in the kitchen, so he ventured out of the bedroom and pulled up a chair at the kitchen table.

"So, you're up an around," Loretta said. "Are you feeling well enough to have a cup of coffee?"

"That would be wonderful," said Roger. "I appreciate what you said about keeping me until I was well. Since I cannot remember who I am, I don't know what 'well' would be."

"Well enough to ride," Loretta said. "We'd have to get you to town to see a doctor and then the county seat to see if they can find out who you really are."

"I noticed a closet of men's clothes, Loretta. Is there a man of the house?" the deputy asked.

"There is, but he's away for a bit. Should be back soon," Loretta answered, a little uncomfortable with the question. "Does that concern you?"

"Not really, I just feel so out of place, yet I'm so very grateful to you and Johnny Mac," Roger said. "I don't mean to be a burden like this."

"Quite honestly, while Arthur's away I feel a lot more secure with a man around," Loretta said, setting a cup of coffee in front of Roger. "I can't help but think you're a good man even if you cannot remember who you actually are."

"Arthur? Is he…" Roger started?

"Yes, he is my husband. He had to go into Mount Pleasant on business. This little farm has been difficult to maintain," Loretta said.

"Mount Pleasant? Where exactly am I?" the deputy asked.

"You're in Bowie County, Texas," Loretta answered, "but I couldn't tell you where you came from, other than the river, that is."

"Do you think I somehow floated down that river and washed up on that riverbank?" Roger asked.

"With that wound you have on your head, I'm amazed that you made it out of that river without drowning," said Loretta. "Depending on how far you traveled, it's something of a miracle that you survived. Maybe Johnny Mac was right. You may have been vomited onto that beach by a big fish."

"Did I smell like a fish?" Roger asked, only half jesting.

"Can't say as you did, but the shock of seeing you there, and alive, may have been enough to cover up what you smelled like," Loretta said. "You were a mess, though."

Roger took a big gulp of coffee, as it was starting to cool down. "Is there something I can do around here to help?" he asked. "I feel as if I ought to at least try and earn my keep."

"You're not ready to do too much yet, but you could help Johnny Mac with his studies," Loretta said. "You seem to know your way around that Bible pretty well."

"I'd be obliged to do that," Roger said. "You say this is a farm? I know a little bit about farming, too."

"Well, at least there are some things you remember," said Loretta. "That's good. We'll work up to that. When Arthur gets back, maybe you can help him as well."

"I'd like that. Does he know I'm here?" Roger said.

"No, but we're a Christian family," Loretta said. "When Arthur learns of your predicament, he wouldn't have us doing this any other way."

"I'm not surprised that you married a good man," Roger said. "Arthur has a wife to match."

"Kind words, Jonah, but it won't get you out of doing your fair share around here, once you're feeling better," Loretta said, with a chuckle.

"Just one last thing," the man called Jonah inquired. "How is it you know so much about taking care of a body like me?

"I served as a nurse in the war," Loretta said. "I'm quite familiar with men suffering from conditions like yours. After Johnny Mac was born, the war started. Arthur marched off to battle, and I took a position as a nurse at the local hospital. It didn't pay much, but it kept Johnny Mac and me going."

"The war, you say," Roger repeated. "Was there a war?"

"They called it a civil war, but to my way of thinking, there was nothing civil about it," Loretta remarked.

"Maybe I was vomited out by a fish, you being a nurse and all. It all seems like one big miracle," Roger said, finishing his coffee and searching his mind for any recollection of a "civil war." "Where's Johnny Mac? I'm ready to get him started on his studies."

After leaving Sherman, Nik rode east until he came to a small creek. The deputy marshal then followed it north until he reached the road he figured the Sammon group was following. Nik eventually came to a small town. Not wanting to enter it for fear of running into Sockeye and his boys, Nik circled around the small community and approached it from behind the structures that lined the main street. He tied up his horse behind what he believed was the livery stable and cautiously moved through an alley bringing him in sight of the main road through a limited business section. He did not see any sign of Sockeye, his men or their horses. Nik made his way along the front of the livery stable and peeked inside.

"Can I help you?" a man called out from within the stable.

Nik quickly stepped into the building out of the sunlight to let his eyes focus on whoever it was that had called to him. To his relief, an older gentleman was approaching whom he did not recognize.

"Sorry, I was looking for some friends of mine," Nik said.

"Ain't nobody here but me," the gentleman said. "Are you looking for anybody in particular?"

"There were three riders, I believe, who were headed this way. Did you happen to see them?" Nik asked.

"Yeah, I saw three men ride by earlier," the stable attendant said. "Were they the friends of yours you spoke of?"

"As a matter of fact, yes, I think so," Nik said. "Do you know if they stopped in town or were they just passing through?"

"Passing through, best I could tell," the stable proprietor said. "Are you sure they're friends of yours? The way you snuck up here I was thinking you didn't want to be seen."

"Oh, that... yes, I had hoped to surprise them," Nik said, attempting to come up with some excuse for his stealthy approach. "I was supposed to be riding with them, but I got delayed in Sherman. So, I was sort of thinking I could kind of catch them off guard and surprise them.

"By the way, did you see which way they left town?"

"I reckon they was headed to Bonham, a day's ride southeast of here," said the gentleman.

Nik was relieved to hear that. It would mean Sammon's bunch was not headed north to Oklahoma and Fort McCulloch. Sockeye was still headed east, in the general direction Roger had gone when he left the fort trailing the two men.

"Much obliged," Nik said. "I'll try to catch up to them in Bonham." Nik left and made his way around to the back of the stable where he retrieved his horse. From there he rode past the livery stable in the direction of Bonham, hoping the three men he was following would lead him to the two riding with Lupe when he and Roger split up.

***

It had been two weeks since Roger washed up on the shore of the river. He no longer needed medical care and had moved into the hayloft of the barn, allowing Loretta to reclaim her bedroom. With his strength returning, he began working the farm. He knew his way around a plow and had no trouble assisting Loretta and Johnny Mac with whatever needed to be done. He had become comfortable with his new surroundings but still had no memory of his past or who he really was.

One day, Roger was splitting wood while Johnny Mac gathered the pieces and hauled them over to a wooden storage box located near the kitchen door. After dropping an armload of wood into the box, he noticed a wagon approaching the house.

"Ma, Ma, a wagon is coming," Johnny Mac shouted, as he rushed in through the kitchen door. "Someone in a wagon is headed this way."

Loretta dropped what she was doing and hurried out of the house to see if her husband was finally returning from Mount Pleasant. Roger buried the ax into the chopping block and looked up to see what the commotion was all about. Assuming it could be Arthur, he hoped his presence would not raise any suspicion in the homesteader's mind.

"It's our wagon, Johnny Mac, but I don't think that's your Pa driving it," Loretta said. "There's also a horse tied to the back. My God, I do hope Arthur isn't in some sort of trouble."

Roger's anxiety about meeting Arthur diminished, but he shared Loretta's concern as to why the McLaughlins' wagon was returning without Loretta's husband. As the wagon approached, they could see the driver was a younger man, and he tipped his hat in a friendly gesture as he drew near. The wagon was filled with sacks of planting seeds, food sacks and other implements of farming.

"Howdy, mam," the young stranger said. "He also nodded a greeting toward Roger and Johnny Mac. "My name's Lester Suggs, mam. I've been asked to deliver your wagon with these goods. I have brought along my horse so I can return to Mount Pleasant and leave you your transportation."

"What about my husband, Arthur?" Loretta asked.

"Oh, yes mam, he gave me this note to give to you," Suggs said, as he pulled out an envelope from his pocket and handed it to her, while climbing down from the buckboard. Loretta tore open the envelope and anxiously read the letter.

"Dear Loretta and Johnny Mac," the letter read. "I am sending you these supplies as I am not yet able to return to the farm at this time. I have more business to attend to. I hope to finish and return home as soon as possible. In the meantime, please keep doing the best you can.

Best Regards, Arthur."

"Mr. Suggs, do you have any idea what it is that's keeping my husband so long?" Loretta said.

"I'm real sorry, mam, but I do not know. I was just given instructions to deliver this wagonload of supplies to you," Suggs said. "But Mr. McLaughlin seemed to be in good health."

"Well, that's a relief," Loretta said. "Thank you, Mr. Suggs.

"Johnny Mac, we need to get this wagon unloaded," Loretta said to her son.

"Loretta, I'll take care of unloading the wagon," Roger said. "Johnny Mac, why don't you unhitch the horses and take care of them, while I put away these supplies?"

"Yes sir, Mr. Jonah," Johnny Mac responded and began freeing the horses from the wagon.

"Thanks, Jonah," Loretta said. "You can put the goods and grain in the storage cellar and the farming equipment in the barn."

It was obvious Loretta was concerned about her husband, and the letter did not seem to help much. Roger wished he could do more to help her feel more at ease, but he was at a loss for words.

As he emptied the wagon, he noticed a few sacks of winter wheat. Roger had worked some of the wheat fields around Bordertown, Missouri, and still held an instinct for growing it. Although he had no memory of actually planting and harvesting wheat, the techniques he learned remained with him.

"Loretta," Roger stated as he entered the house. "I noticed your husband purchased some winter wheat seeds. Were you planning to grow wheat?"

"Arthur mentioned switching from cotton to wheat because the price of cotton has been dropping since the war ended," Loretta said. "However, we have never grown wheat as a crop before."

"If that is Arthur's plan, I can help you with that," Roger said. "I don't know why, but I have knowledge of how to grow wheat."

"First a preacher man and now a wheat farmer, Jonah," Loretta said. "What else are you going to come up with that you know how to do?"

"I cannot say," Roger answered. "Although I have very little memory of where my information comes from, I seem to keep stumbling onto certain things I am familiar with."

Loretta explained that the family was prosperous in the beginning by growing cotton. The price for the crop had been going up steadily until the demand for it plummeted sharply after the war.

"Confederates said emancipation was to blame because the plantations no longer had slave labor to do the work," said Loretta. "Arthur and I were able to hire some former slaves who came west looking for work, but as the bottom continued dropping out of the market, we eventually could no longer afford them."

"Do you think that's why Arthur is apparently planning to plant wheat?" Roger inquired.

"It's possible, but I don't know why that decision is taking him so long," Loretta answered. "He's already sent us the seed, telling me he's made up his mind. No, I'm afraid the business he's tending to is something else."

"In the meantime, I can get started planting this wheat," said Roger. "Winter wheat needs to be planted soon if you're to have a crop by spring. I'm sure whatever Arthur's business pertains to he'll be able to clear it up soon."

"I hope so," Loretta said. "I truly hope so."

Wanting to waste no time, Roger began plowing the fields to prepare the soil for winter wheat. Once he had the ground plowed, he used water from the river to flood the planting area in preparation for sowing the seed. The weather was getting colder and rains on top of the flooding delayed the planting. After a brief dry spell, Roger taught Johnny Mac how to plant the seeds, and within a week the planting was done.

Chapter 24

When Nik reached the outskirts of Bonham, he dismounted and led Lincoln into a small stand of trees. After securing the animal, Nik went on foot to see if he could spot the horses of Sockeye and his men. He made his way between two buildings where the evening shadows gave him cover. As he inched closer to the center of town, he saw a huge man leading three horses to the livery stable across the street – it was the giant who was with Sammon when they visited his room. He watched as the big man unsaddled the mounts and began grooming them. Apparently, the three men planned to spend the night in Bonham, so Nik decided to do the same, only not in the comfort of a hotel.

Returning to Lincoln, Nik moved a little deeper into the wooded area and spent the night. In the morning, he went back to where he could see the livery stable and waited until the three men retrieved their horses and headed east out of town. Once they were out of sight, he proceeded to a local store and bought some food, including some carrots for Lincoln.

"What is the next town east of here," Nik asked the store clerk.

"Paris, in Lamar County," the clerk replied. "It's about a two days' ride."

Nik paid the clerk and made his way back to his campsite where he and Lincoln enjoyed a quick breakfast and set out to pick up Sammon's trail.

It became apparent the three men were on the road into Paris, making it easy for Nik to follow. All he had to do was remain out of sight, staying close enough to observe them turning off the main road.

Keeping his distance, Sockeye and his companions led Nik to within sight of Paris. The deputy surveyed the situation and decided to again approach the town while avoiding the main road. Nik remained out of sight until after dark. He then rode into town until coming to the Paris Sheriffs Office. He dismounted and entered.

"Excuse me, I'm looking for the U.S. Marshal's office," he inquired of the man at the desk.

"You looking for Marshal Ken Oliver?" the man asked.

"I do believe I am," Nik replied. "This is my first time in Paris."

"And you might want to make it your last," the man said. "Paris is, shall we say, unfriendly to your type."

"I can't say as I'm surprised, but I do have business with the marshal," Nik advised.

"Suit yourself," said the man, "but if you're looking for accommodation you might try the livery stable. A negro serves as the blacksmith there."

"Much obliged," Nik offered. "Where do I find it?"

After receiving directions to both the marshal's office and livery stable, Nik departed. Good fortune smiled, as the blacksmith was the only one working at the stable.

"Excuse me, sir" Nik started.

"How can I help you, cowboy?" the well-muscled blacksmith inquired.

"I was told I and my horse might be able to spend the night here, out of the rain," Nik asked.

"I don't own this place, just this shop," the blacksmith responded. "A good man who owns it, so I guess it would be all right. You got money?"

"I do," Nik said. "I'm Nik Brinkman, by the way."

"Hammer Stiles. Real name's Julius, but folks call me Hammer."

"I can see why, Hammer," Nik said, smiling.

"You can bring your horse in and both bed down here tonight. I'll be closing up soon, but I'll be back in the morning," Stiles said. "You can pay me the two bits then."

"I'll be waiting," Nik said. "One other thing, I understand there were three men who came riding through today. Did they stop by here?"

"If you mean the one with a bad eye and his friends, they did stop by needing my assistance," Hammer offered. "The big man's horse had thrown a shoe, and I replaced it."

"But it appears they did not leave their horses for the night?" Nik asked.

"No, they went on up to the Plantation Hotel," Hammer explained. "It has a stable as well."

"Do you know U.S. Marshal Ken Oliver?" Nik continued.

"I do. Another good man," Stiles remarked. "You 'specting trouble?"

"I certainly hope not," Nik answered. "No, I just have business with the man. I'll see you in the morning."

The next day, Nik paid Hammer and saddled Lincoln. He rode in the direction of the marshal's office, while avoiding the Plantation Hotel. He stepped inside and introduced himself.

"Deputy Nik Brinkman," Marshal Oliver said, after introductions. "Chief Borchers told me you might be in the area. Come in and sit down."

"Is Ned here?" Nik asked.

"Not yet. He's due on the afternoon train," Ken Oliver said. "Have a seat and tell me what you've been up to."

Nik explained his dilemma of wanting to follow Sockeye and his men but was worried as to his brother's situation.

"I have not heard from him and fear he could be in trouble," Nik said. "Ned said he was coming to Paris to help you get settled in and I was hoping to get his help, as well."

"I do not have a deputy, or I would put a tail on this Sockeye character and his consorts," Ken suggested. "I'd be happy to see if anyone at the hotel can tell me where they're headed."

Nik accepted Chief Deputy Oliver's offer and waited for his return, which did not take long.

"They took off early this morning, and the hotel clerk told me they planned to stop in Clarksville," Oliver said. "It's less than a two-day ride from here, just across the line into Red River County."

"If those men my brother was following are a part of Sockeye's group, where would you suggest I could pick up his trail?" Nik questioned.

"You say you were both north of the Red River in Oklahoma when you split up, right?" Oliver quizzed.

"Yeah, and the two men Roger tailed were headed east," Nik replied.

"I would suggest checking Rossdales Ferry, just south of Fort Towson," Oliver offered. "The road from there leads to Clarksville."

"If you're willing to spare him for a few days, I'd like to take Ned with me to check that out," Nik said. "I think Roger might have been close to something."

"Certainly," Oliver offered. "Anything I can do to help is what I'm here for."

That afternoon, Borchers' train arrived, and the three marshals laid out a plan to both find out what happened to Roger and where the outlaws conducting raids in Texas could be hiding out.

The road leading northeast out of Paris led directly to Rossdales Ferry. Upon reaching the ferry, Nik and Ned stopped in at the local outpost. The only man there at that time was the one called Scudder.

"Excuse me, we're looking for a lone rider who may have passed through here sometime back," Nik said, giving a description of what Roger was wearing when they parted.

"Yep, came through a while ago. Chasing a couple outlaws, I think. Not sure if he wanted to arrest them or join them," Scudder said. "Anyways, I sent him off to the Sulphur River down by Clarksville."

Just then, the outpost proprietor returned.

"Can I help you gentlemen?" the man asked.

"No, I think we got what we need," Borchers said, looking at Nik, who nodded in the affirmative.

The proprietor glared at Scudder. "What did you tell these gentlemen?" the proprietor asked the older man.

"No more 'an what they asked," Scudder said.

"I hope he didn't steer you wrong," the outpost owner said to the two marshals. "Scudder, here, has a tendency to do that at times."

"No, I think… Scudder, here, told us exactly what we need to know," Nik answered, as the proprietor again glared at the old man.

Nik and Ned remounted and set out for Clarksville just as an approaching storm rolled in. The storm delayed the travel of the two marshals, but they eventually reached Clarksville and checked into the local hotel. They inquired of the clerk, giving Roger's description. The clerk confirmed that such a man had stayed at the hotel about a month or so ago, but they had not seen him since. After a brief discussion, Nik and Ned decided to see if Roger had checked in with the local sheriff.

"That young marshal did come into my office inquiring about two men he'd been following," said Sheriff Packard. "I asked that he report back to me after completing his investigation, but I never saw him again. That was quite some time ago."

"Did you go looking for him?" Ned asked.

"We did, to a certain extent," the sheriff answered, "but he was going where the law isn't welcome, at least not with the few lawmen we have available in these parts. However, we did find what we think was his horse, because it had a marshal's badge in the saddle bags. I think it's the one he showed me when he was here," Packard said, handing the badge to Nik.

"That's Roger's badge, all right," Nik said. "So, he told you who he was?"

"He wasn't going to at first," said Packard. "But he suddenly came clean as to his true identity and what he was doing. I warned him about that Sulphur River area, but he seemed to think he would be okay.

"Too bad, if something's happened to him," the sheriff continued. "He seemed like a good man. I liked him."

"So, how do we find this Sulphur River area?" Borchers asked.

Sheriff Packard gave Ned and Nik the same information he'd related to Roger. He also cautioned the two marshals as to the danger of the area and why, as the sheriff of Clarksville, he couldn't be of more help. The two marshals then left the sheriff's office.

"It seems a shame to be a lawman and not want to go after outlaws, don't you think, Ned?" Nik said, as the two men crossed the street to their hotel.

"It's not unusual for a local sheriff to do only what is necessary to ensure peace in the communities they serve," Borchers answered. "They only chase after desperados if it's personal. Otherwise, they leave that job up to men like us or the Texas Rangers to do. Sheriffs live longer that way."

"I never should have sent Roger after those two men," Nik said, as the thought of losing his brother began to sink in. "I don't think he was ready to set out on his own, but I thought it would be good for him – at the time."

"You did right, Nik," Borchers said. "I know the possibility of what might have happened to Roger is grim, but he was proud to be a U.S. Deputy Marshal and going out on his own had to happen sometime. His assignment was easy enough, but he may have taken it too far. Don't beat yourself up over it. You're too valuable to me."

"It's hard to believe I might be the only Brinkman left," Nik said, as he lowered his head in thought.

"You don't know that yet," Borchers corrected. "In this business, we have to be sure before we jump to conclusions."

Nik nodded and gave Ned a knowing smile.

The next day, Nik claimed Roger's horse, tack and saddlebags and paid the livery stable proprietor to continue their keep. Afterward, he and Ned had a quick breakfast and headed south toward the Sulphur River. When they reached it, they decided to split up with each riding on the opposite side of the flowing waters. They would stay close to the river to keep track of each other in case one of them came across anything, or anyone, of interest.

After riding for some time, Nik, who was on the river's south side, signaled to Ned that he had spotted something. He waved to Ned to go back upriver where there was a spot shallow enough to ford. Nik also moved back into the cover of the woods and waited for Ned. When Ned arrived, Nik explained that he picked up the sounds of horses. Nik and the marshal tied up their mounts and walked in the direction of where the deputy said the sounds were coming from. They continued to where they could see a small cabin in a clearing and a nearby corral containing several horses. There were also three additional horses tied up outside the cabin and Nik recognized them as the ones Sockeye and his men had been riding. Ned signaled to Nik to retrace their steps back to where their horses were.

"I think we've found out where the Sulphur River hideout is," Ned said, once the two men had reached their horses, a safe distance from the hideaway. "But we have no idea how many men are in that cabin, and we don't have warrants for any of them, as far as we know."

"And it's possible Roger might be in there," Nik said, drawing some comfort from the thought his brother might still be alive. "If only I could have kept my cover I would be in there too. I'm afraid I acted too hastily back in Sherman. However, I still don't think they know for sure who I am."

"You did fine, Nik. There's no way of telling who's in that cabin and if one of them might know your identity," Ned said. "At this point, we can't be sure whether Sockeye knows who you really are, and we also don't know how big this outfit is. There were at least a half-dozen horses in that corral."

"It's just going to dog me until I find out what happened to Roger and it's possible someone in that cabin knows," Nik said.

"We'll head back to Clarksville and see what Packard knows about this gang. With enough information, we might be able to round up a posse to force out whoever is in that cabin," Ned said. "For now, at least we know where this place is."

After arriving back in Clarksville, Ned and Nik paid a visit to the sheriff's office, only to find Packard was not there. An administrative deputy said Packard left town and said he would not be back for several days. The news made the two marshals a little suspicious, but they were cautious not to jump to conclusions.

The two then retrieved Roger's horse from the livery stable and began a two-day ride back to Paris, weather permitting. Conditions turned out to be on the deputies' side, as they reached Paris the afternoon of the second day.

"Ken, we believe we may have found where that bunch of desperados is hiding out. It's located along the Sulphur River in Red River County," Ned said. "We believe they may have harmed one of our agents or are holding him hostage."

"I have heard of this group, but I'm afraid I know very little about them," Oliver said. "I've been busy with administrative matters, and I've been using the seasonal weather to get it done."

"The sheriff in Clarksville gave us enough information on this bunch to lead us to the place where they might be holding up, but that's all we have," Ned continued. "We thought maybe we could get a warrant to investigate the place," Borchers concluded, "but we'd need a posse to do the investigation."

"Our circuit judge isn't due here for another week, so unless you want to track him down elsewhere for that warrant, it's going to take some time," said Oliver. "I have an itinerary for him, but he's always subject to delays, since there's no way of knowing where he'll be needed next or for how long."

"Nik and I can help you with the admin work," Borchers said. "With Nik here, I can get back to Wichita earlier, and he can stay on here with you. That way he can continue looking for Roger."

"I appreciate it, Ned. I'll do just that," Nik replied.

"I could use the help," Ken stated. "I found temporary lodging, and Nik can stay with me. I plan to buy a place and move my family here before Christmas."

Circuit court judge Victor Giles Kensington did not make it back to Paris for a full two weeks. Kensington was known for serving in areas of strife. Places where outlaws ruled, Indians raided, and homesteaders struggled to make ends meet. He was not gregarious, but many felt him generous, too generous when it came to adjudicating crime. He took his own carriage and bought only the finest horses to pull it. He hired a driver whenever traveling the circuit, and his attire was such that when visiting outlying areas, he was sometimes mistaken for European royalty.

Nik visited the judge's office and presented his case to Kensington, in hopes of securing a warrant to search the Sulphur River cabin.

"What exactly do you hope to find there?" the judge inquired.

"We have reason to believe the site might be home base for those roving gangs of desperados spreading crime throughout Texas and parts of Oklahoma," Nik began. "And I have reason to believe they might be holding a U.S. Deputy Marshal hostage there."

Judge Kensington put his elbow on his desk and put his fist to his mouth for a moment. "You say it 'might' be the home base for these desperados, as you call them, and you 'believe' they may be holding a hostage there," the judge said, removing his fist to speak. "What actual evidence do you have of that?"

Nik spelled out how both Roger and he tailed suspected gang members believed to be in that hideout. He added that Roger's whereabouts were now unknown. Clarksville's Sheriff Packard was too intimidated to even visit the place.

"I can sympathize with your concern for this deputy, who you say is your brother, but did you see his horse at this… 'hideout?'" Kensington asked.

"No, sir, but Sheriff Packard did locate Roger's horse when he went looking for him in that area," Nik responded.

"The way you describe it, this cabin is some distance from Clarksville," the judge began, "that tells me any number of things could have happened to Deputy Brinkman that would have nothing to do with this cabin or its inhabitants.

"As for this Sockeye Sammon you mentioned, has he done anything wrong that you know of?" Kensington continued. "And, I can tell you, Sheriff Packard runs a pretty tight ship in Clarksville and has had no trouble with this 'gang' you claim is in that cabin."

"I know my evidence is circumstantial, but my broth…," Nik started.

"Your evidence is less than circumstantial, deputy," Kensington interrupted. "I would say it is nonexistent. Unless you can come up with something more compelling, I am going to have to deny this warrant.

"But, your honor...," Nik stammered.

"I am sorry, deputy," the judge said, stopping Nik in midsentence. "However, I truly hope you find your brother and that he is all right. Good day."

Discouraged, but no less determined to find out what happened to his brother, Nik felt his being reassigned in Paris would facilitate his efforts to find the evidence necessary for a warrant.

After Ned left for Wichita, Nik and Marshal Oliver caught up on the administrative work.

"Ken, I could sure use your help in finding Roger," Nik requested. "It's possible we could find out more about this Sulphur River gang, too."

"I would be happy to do that if you'll help me move into my new home," Ken said. "I just put a down payment on a house and will be moving my family here soon."

"This sounds like a family affair all around," Nik remarked, with a smile. "It would be my pleasure."

The late November weather had cleared. The next morning, the two went straight to Packard's office and found him in.

"Sheriff, I think we may have found that Sulphur River gang's hideout," Nik said, after introducing Marshal Oliver to the sheriff. "Marshal Borchers and I came upon a cabin in an isolated clearing not far from the river. Three men I had been following had their horses tied up there and there was a corral nearby containing six more. But I can't get a warrant to investigate further without more evidence."

"I would like to help you, Deputy Brinkman, but what I've told you is about all I know," Packard said. "I know only a few faces from that group and through agreement, I rarely see them in Clarksville. And when I do, they cause me no trouble."

"Well, if you don't mind, Marshal Oliver and I would like to poke around to try and get some more information," Nik said. "I really would like to find out what happened to Deputy Marshal Brinkman."

"You boys share the same name," the sheriff commented. "Is that a coincidence?"

"No, he's my brother," Nik said.

"You don't say," Packard responded, with unspoken curiosity in his expression. After Nik explained how he and Roger came to be brothers, Packard continued, "That's quite a story. You'll get no argument from me if you want to poke around some more. Just be careful. I hope you find out what happened to your… your brother."

"Thanks, sheriff, we will watch our step," Nik said.

Nik and Ken left the sheriff's office and stopped in at the local dining hall to eat.

"Do you trust this Sheriff Packard?" Marshal Oliver said between bites.

Nik looked at him for a moment and said, "Funny you should ask that. There is something odd about him and this 'arrangement' he has with the Sulphur River bunch. What are you thinking?"

"I'm thinking he knows a lot about you and what you're up to. I assume he knew plenty about your brother, as well," Oliver said. "But I'm just speculating. I guess it's my nature to be suspicious about folks, even sheriffs."

"Corrupt lawmen are nothing new," Nik said, finishing his meal, "as if this job wasn't tough enough without being unable to trust those who are supposed to be on your side."

"Like I said, I'm just speculating," Oliver repeated, "but I suggest we take the sheriff's advice and be extra careful."

"If Packard is in cahoots with Sammon and his band of likely outlaws, my cover is blown," Nik said. "But if my brother is in that cabin, I don't care if they know who I am."

Nik and Ken mounted up and set out for the Sulphur River. They left the road at Mustang Creek and were soon parallel to the rain-swollen stream. They found an area where they could cross and continued according to Nik's directions.

"I take it the hideout is somewhere around here," Ken said.

"It is, but if Packard is protecting this bunch to help keep his town safe, they may be expecting us," Nik said. "That makes me a little nervous."

"They don't know me," Oliver asserted. "If you can get me in sight of the cabin, I can approach and simply ask for directions."

"That's a bit risky, don't you think?" Nik stated.

"Not unless they shoot strangers on sight," Oliver responded. "I doubt they know who I am, and I'll leave my badge with you."

"Okay, but I don't like it," Nik argued. "I'll stay in the trees and give you cover, just the same."

Nik led Ken to the cabin and stayed well out of sight as the marshal approached. There were no horses in the corral and no sign of activity. Ken rode up on horseback, dismounted and knocked on the door – no answer. He paused to look around before remounting and returning to where Nik was waiting. Ken just nodded when he approached, and the two retraced their steps back to the river, crossed over and continued on.

"Did you learn anything," Nik asked, when they reached the main road.

"Not really, but I felt I was being watched," Ken said. "The door was locked, and there were curtains over the windows. I was going to circle the cabin but thought that might raise suspicion if anyone was watching."

"Wise decision," Nik said. "I thought I caught a glimpse of the sun reflecting off something on that bluff above the river. But I did not see it again."

"It's a creepy place, but I found nothing that will help us secure a warrant," Ken added, as the two rode along. "Sorry about that, Nik."

"I won't rest until I get to the bottom of this, even if I have to go over the judge's head," said Nik.

The two men returned to the hotel in Clarksville to spend the night. In the morning, they checked out and headed back to Paris, frustrated that their trip turned out to be a bust.

***

After several days of planting, Johnny Mac came running into the house yelling, "Ma, we got all the wheat planted and Jonah said it should grow just fine."

Roger followed in behind Johnny Mac and said, "If we get a fair winter, we'll have a pretty good crop come spring."

"Thanks, Jonah, but I can't get over the fact that Arthur still hasn't come home," Loretta said. "If he's not home by week's end, I'm going to Mount Pleasant to find him."

However, near the end of the week, Lester Suggs showed up in a buckboard with another load of supplies – and another letter. It read:

"Dear Family,

Sorry about the delay in my return. Sending more supplies to keep you going. Stay on the farm until my return. Don't look for me.

Regards, Arthur"

"Did you see my husband, Lester? How did he look?" Loretta asked the driver.

"No, mam, I didn't see him. The store master just told me to deliver this load of supplies and that letter to you like I did before," said Suggs. "I'll need to take this wagon back, so I'll help you unload it."

Roger could see Loretta was stressed, as tears ran down her cheeks. He felt totally lost now. He did not know who he was or the circumstances that brought him there, but ever since his arrival, the McLaughlins had been getting nothing but dreadful news. After unloading the wagon, Roger thanked Lester and sent him on his way and entered the house.

"Loretta, I am going to have to go look for your husband," Roger said. "The stress of seeing you like this and Johnny Mac doing his best to be the man of the house has me feeling about as low as I can get. I've got to do something."

"Jonah, you still do not know who you are. How are you going to communicate with folks when they ask you to identify yourself?"

"I'll just tell them I'm Jonah. They'll have to figure it out from there," Roger answered.

"And what if you find Arthur? What will you tell him?" Loretta said, the emotion in her voice rising.

"That I'm a friend and that he needs to come home," Roger lamented.

"You've been very helpful around here, Jonah. I don't know if I could have made it this far without you," Loretta started. "But if you wander off and get lost, then I've got two people missing that I've come to depend on. Johnny Mac's a blessing, but he's just a boy.

"A few more days and then I'm going to Mount Pleasant," Loretta added. "Maybe we'll all go. I think you need to see a doctor about your condition, anyhow."

Roger felt a little better thinking he could go along and still be of some help. It was possible they could find Arthur and Roger could discover his real identity.

***

With the trail of Roger's disappearance growing cold, Nik busied himself with some of the more mundane tasks of being a U.S. Marshal. Judge Kensington gave Marshal Oliver some homestead foreclosure notices. Ken asked Nik to cover the homesteads near Sulphur River, since that was an area he was now familiar with.

The day Loretta had planned to go into Mount Pleasant looking for Arthur, the sky opened up and brought down too much rain to travel in a buckboard. It was a day to stay inside and brood. To take his mind off the situation, Roger took Johnny Mac into his room and assisted him in reading the Bible.

Loretta occupied her time by preparing some stew using some fresh venison that Roger had killed, using the McLaughlin's muzzleloader. Roger found a spot where the deer would come down by the river to drink. He picked out a nice young buck and harvested it with one clean shot. Something flashed across his mind the instant the shot rang out. Roger paused, trying to recall the vision but his effort was in vain.

Later that evening, there came a knock at the door and Loretta, surprised by the knock, hurried to answer it. When she opened it, there was a man wearing a duster and his hat was so drenched with rain that the brim of it virtually covered his face.

"I'm powerful sorry, mam, I am a U.S. Marshal and I have to serve you with this notice," the man said.

"What notice? Oh my God, something's happened to Arthur," Loretta exclaimed.

"No mam, I don't know no Arthur. This is a foreclosure notice on your property," the man said almost apologetically.

"A what?" The news left Loretta faint and shaken, and she turned and placed her hands on the table to remain standing.

Roger heard Loretta's cry and moved to the doorway of Johnny Mac's room. The man delivering the notice removed his hat to express his regrets for the intrusion. He looked up and glanced at the figure that had emerged from Johnny Mac's room.

"Roger?" said Deputy Nik Brinkman. "Is that you!?"

Nik nearly broke into a run to get closer to the brother he had almost given up for dead.

"Roger, it is you! My God, you're alive!" Nik said, embracing Roger, wet coat and all. Nik then stepped back to get a better look.

Roger looked bewildered for a moment and then said, "Who are… Nik? Nikkumbaba Brinkman, it's you!" Roger said with a shout. "Oh, my Lord, I now know who I am!" Roger grabbed Nik and gave him a monster hug. Tears welled up in the eyes of both men.

Loretta, who was sitting down on one of the kitchen chairs, could only stare at the two men. Johnny Mac walked past Roger and stood by his mother's side to try and comfort her, as he watched Roger and Nik's reunion in wonderment.

"I'm Roger Brinkman!" Roger said out loud. "Loretta, Johnny Mac, I now know who I am. Here, meet my brother, Nik Brinkman."

Loretta tried to get up, but her head was in a whirl. Johnny Mac put his arm around his mother's shoulders to help steady her and keep her seated. Roger then threw his arm around Nik's shoulders and paraded him over to the table where Loretta was sitting.

"Loretta, this is my brother, Nik Brinkman. I'm Roger Brinkman and we're both U.S. deputy marshals," Roger said, with a smile that nearly reached the expanse of his face.

As Roger explained to Loretta who he and Nik were, he also tried to tell Nik about Loretta and Johnny Mac and how he ended up living on their farm. After Roger's monologue was nearly finished, Loretta spoke up.

"Believe me, I'm happy for you, Jonah, I mean Roger, but what about this?" she said, holding up the foreclosure notice.

"Let me see that," Roger said, taking the notice from Loretta's hand and reading it. "Nik, what's this all about?"

"I'm not sure, Roger," Nik started. "I was just given this notice and told to deliver it. It's also a part of our job and not the most pleasant one."

"But this is a homestead. It's protected by law," Roger said.

"It is, but it's not necessarily protected from foreclosure against a loan," Nik answered.

"Loretta," Roger began, "do you know anything about this? Do you have a loan out on this property?"

"Not that I know of," Loretta said, with tears now in her eyes. "Unless..., unless that's the business Arthur went to Mount Pleasant to do. He never mentioned it to me."

"Nik, we can't let this happen," Roger said. "This family has been put through too much, not to mention nursing me back to health. We've got to check this thing out."

"Well, I guess we could dig a little deeper," Nik said, "but we haven't much to go on."

"Loretta, would you be so kind as to lend me one of your horses?" Roger said. "Nik and I will take this notice back to Mount Pleasant in the morning and find out what's behind this. And, with a little luck, find Arthur as well."

Chapter 25

Loretta McLaughlin was more than happy to offer a horse to Roger, now that she knew who he was and would return it. She had come to trust him even before learning he was a U.S. Deputy Marshal. Assured of their intent to help, she insisted they stay for supper and depart in the morning, weather permitting.

After supper, the three adults discussed their plans for the following day, as Johnny Mac listened intently.

"Since I'm the bearer of bad tidings as to this foreclosure notice, I will contact the lender listed on the notice to see what this is all about," Nik volunteered.

"I'll go with you," Roger chimed in. "The lender might be our best source for finding Arthur, as well."

"Can I be of any help with this?" Loretta asked.

"It would be a long ride for you," Roger responded. "You would have to take Johnny Mac, since you can't leave him here alone. Besides, I'll be using your horse and taking the wagon would just slow Nik and me down."

"He's right, Mrs. McLaughlin," Nik interjected. "Roger and I can handle the foreclosure issue and get a lead on your husband's whereabouts. As soon as we find out something, at least one of us will be headed back this way to return your horse."

"That makes sense," Loretta said. "I'll get the promissory note, it stipulates when we will have fulfilled our five-year obligation. As for you, Roger, please visit the doctor in Mount Pleasant and have him check you out. You seem fine, but it's best if you get a professional opinion."

"I'm not sure a doc could do for me what you and Johnny Mac

haven't done," Roger said, smiling at Loretta. "If all else were to fail, I think you could have a promising career in medicine."

"You're too kind, Roger, but we're going to miss having Jonah around, right Johnny Mac?" Loretta said, turning to her son with a laugh.

"Right, Ma," Johnny Mac answered, sharing the levity.

"Just the same, you see the doc when you get to Mount Pleasant," Loretta advised.

"Okay," Roger promised. "It would be foolish for me to ignore your medical advice now."

Loretta said she did remember Arthur receiving a letter in the mail before he left for Mount Pleasant. He told her the letter requested he come to Mount Pleasant to finalize the deed on the homestead.

"Arthur seemed disturbed by the letter, but insisted there wasn't anything wrong," Loretta recalled, "but he seemed awfully anxious when he left. Now, I think I understand why."

"There's got to be something wrong here," Roger said. "Arthur would not send home supplies if he thought he was losing this property. And why plant winter wheat if he didn't plan to be around this spring?"

"What's the status on that situation?" Nik asked.

"Johnny Mac and I got the winter wheat planted, and if we have a mild winter, there ought to be a good harvest in the spring," Roger said. "There's little to do now, but wait until then, except for getting this situation worked out."

"Gentlemen, I appreciate what you're doing for us, but you're going to have to excuse me," Loretta said, as the hour grew late. "I'm exhausted over all this and now I'm even more worried about Arthur's wellbeing. I'm going to go to bed and hope the future looks a little brighter in the morning – Johnny Mac, get ready for bed now," Loretta instructed.

The rain had let up some as the two men stepped outside. Roger helped Nik move Lincoln into the barn where he had been staying, and the two deputies set up their own sleeping arrangements in the hayloft. The McLaughlins' barn was small, but solidly constructed and watertight. The family had two horses and a milk-producing cow. Roger had been looking after the animals and helping Johnny Mac with the milking. The loft had plenty of hay and Roger had set up his "room" to make it quite comfortable.

"Nik, I'm not sure why, but I think there is more to this foreclosure business and why Arthur hasn't come home," Roger said. "The fact supplies kept arriving tells me he's okay, but this notice is troubling."

"We'll get to the bottom of it, Roger," Nik offered. "I'm just relieved I still have some family left. My insides kept telling me I should give up on you, but my heart just wouldn't let me. How did you survive in that river, anyway?" Nik asked.

"I honestly don't know, Nik. Maybe I was swallowed by a fish and vomited out on that beach, like Johnny Mac suggested," Roger mused, smiling as he spoke. "I remember nothing after hitting that water until I later woke up in the McLaughlins' bed. At that time, I couldn't remember anything except the Bible and how to farm."

Nik listened intently and said, "I think I may be every bit as relieved as you are and anxious to get back to work." He then leveled out some loose hay and lay his bedroll over it. "We'd better get some shut-eye. We've got a big day ahead of us tomorrow."

It took only a few minutes before Nik was fast asleep. Roger had too much running through his mind to sleep, not the least of which was knowing who he was. Everything had been set right for him, but the McLaughlins' farm had been in disarray since his unexpected arrival. He prayed for help in setting things right for the homestead family, as well as the others involved. As Roger plotted his strategy, he too drifted off to sleep.

The next day, Roger and Nik saddled their mounts in preparation for the trip to Mount Pleasant. They enjoyed one of Loretta's breakfasts and afterward Roger retrieved his gear, including his empty gun belt. Nik suggested he pick up a new pistol in Mount Pleasant and replace the cartridges as well, since they were likely damaged after being in the river.

"Johnny Mac," Roger said, turning to the young McLaughlin. "You know how to take care of the livestock around here and you're going to have to do your father's chores, now that I'll be gone."

After directing his attention to Loretta he said, "After we find out what this foreclosure is about, I will look for Arthur. Nik will work on getting this foreclosure cleared up."

"I'm grateful, gentlemen," Loretta said. "Johnny Mac and I will be all right. We have neighbors less than a day's ride from here we can call on if necessary."

"If they haven't been foreclosed on as well," Nik said, reminded that he had other foreclosure notices to deliver.

"What!?" Loretta and Roger said, almost in unison.

"I didn't think of it earlier, after the shock of finding my brother alive and well. But I have several foreclosure notices affecting several homesteads in this area," Nik continued.

"You mean, we're not alone in this thing?" Loretta asked. "None of this is making any sense."

"That's an interesting bit of news, Nik," Roger said. "That makes me think something is more amiss than a foreclosure notice."

"I didn't give it much thought at first. deputy marshals deliver such notices all the time, it's part of the job," Nik said. "I'm guessing, but it's possible all these foreclosures are for the same reason."

"'Nuff said," Roger countered. "Let's get on our way before it gets any later."

After saying their goodbyes, the now united Brinkman brothers set out for Mount Pleasant. The sky was clear, and the only vestige of the passing storm was the constant dripping of water from the surrounding rain-soaked trees.

Pushing themselves, Roger and Nik reached Mount Pleasant in less than two days. Although there wasn't a regular bank in that town, the local mercantile served as the community's financial facility. Basil Gobles was the store's owner and handled the town's banking affairs.

Gobles was a man in his fifties. He was bald on top with a parietal ridge of hair around his head. He also wore a pair of spectacles that hung on the end of his nose. He had been a banker back east, but when his wife died, he decided to move out west and start a new life.

He established the mercantile store and decided to expand when he found the community needed a bank. Mercantile banks were not uncommon in Texas.

"Yes, my business is the one that made the loans generating those foreclosures," Gobles said, speaking deliberately and almost apologetically. "Judge Kensington said it was probably the only way I was going to recoup my losses."

"Kensington was involved?" Nik remarked, raising an eyebrow.

"Yes, it seems the trouble started when a land office going by the name of Confederate Enterprises opened here, oh I'd say, about three months ago," Gobles continued. "It alleged to have a speculation deed encompassing many of the homestead properties in this area. Confederate's proprietor said the deed was granted prior to the homestead claims, as compensation for service in the war."

Gobles said Judge Kensington looked over the deed and declared it legal and binding. However, Confederate Enterprises did not want the properties and offered to sell its interest, based on each homestead's value. Gobles said the enterprise put up its own speculation deed as collateral.

"I knew those local folks needed help and their patronage is what keeps me in business. So, I offered to loan five hundred dollars on each one. That covered the purchase price, plus a little extra to help the homesteaders get back on their feet." Gobles explained. "I also structured the loans so no interest would be charged for the cash exceeding the land purchase."

"That sounds more than fair, so what triggered all the foreclosures?" Roger asked.

The mercantile banker removed his spectacles and began cleaning them with a handkerchief. "Almost all the homesteads that applied for the loans were within months of fulfilling their five-year occupancy requirement. Those who were a year or more away decided to move on," said Gobles, "but there were only a few of those folks."

"Where is this land office?" Roger asked.

"It was just down the street from here," Gobles continued, replacing his spectacles. "But as soon as Confederate Enterprises got its money, the office closed, and the proprietor moved on. Oh, I'd say he left town about two weeks ago."

"What was his name, do you know?" Nik asked.

"Curtain," the mercantile banker said. "Gabriel Curtain, I believe."

"Curtain!? Curtain was the one with the speculator deed?" Nik said.

"Claimed he was an officer for the Union Army and his military service compensation included the speculation deed," Gobles said. "Not sure why he called his business Confederate."

"Did he go by Colonel Curtain?" Roger said.

"He could have," Gobles replied. "I'm not sure what his military rank was, but Judge Kensington said all matters were in order."

"This doesn't sound right," Roger said, shaking his head. "Do you have any idea where this Curtain went to, or why there were so many defaults on these loans?"

"Well, that's when the trouble started," Gobles stated, leaning forward in his chair and narrowing his eyes. "The homesteaders were preparing to return to their farms when it was discovered the speculation deed was a fraud."

Nik's jaw dropped. "And Kensington didn't bother to check this out?" the deputy asked.

"It appears he eventually did and that broke the story. The judge claimed he'd been snookered," said Gobles. "Once the homestead folks heard that they formed a posse to go after Curtain."

Gobles said the judge advised him to file foreclosures. It would be the only way to recoup any of his losses. Gobles added that he asked Kensington not to serve the notices to anyone making a conscious effort to honor their loan.

"I'm surprised he had you issue notices so soon," Gobles said to Roger, assuming he was the deputy in charge. "I really don't want their properties."

Gobles assured the deputies the only reason he filed early was because the judge did not come around that often.

"I was also taken aback when the judge offered to buy some of those default properties if I'd agree to a short sale," Gobles added. "Kensington said it was the least he could do to help me recoup some of my losses."

Nik and Roger shared a quick glance at one another and then Roger asked, "So, which way did those homesteaders go when they went after Curtain?"

Gobles said the posse split up, each group taking one of the six roads leading out of Mount Pleasant. Unfortunately, no one knew which direction Curtain had gone.

"Were there other men working for Confederate Enterprises?" Nik asked.

"Not sure about that," Gobles said. "Some said he had help, but I understand most transactions were done by Curtain himself."

"I'm specifically looking for a man by the name of Arthur McLaughlin," Roger interjected. "Do you know if he went after Curtain?"

"I'm pretty sure he joined one of those groups," Gobles said, rubbing the back of his neck. "He purchased some goods from my store with some of his loan funds."

"Do you happen to know which road he took?" Roger asked.

"I don't know that for sure, but I do know most of them met at the Titus Saloon before heading out," said Gobles. "Someone there might be able to help you."

Roger and Nik thanked Gobles for his time, but before departing the mercantile store Roger replaced his Colt .44, along with a couple of boxes of ammunition. Roger also purchased a hat to replace the one he lost when he fell into the river.

"I kind of hate to leave Gobles hanging, but these homesteaders are not to blame," Roger surmised, as the two deputies left the store. "I have to admit that Kensington's part in this seems a little bizarre, as well."

"Judge Kensington knows this is a fraud," Nik said, analyzing the situation. "The U.S. Marshals Office ought to be able to file an injunction to stop those foreclosures. And what's up with Kensington's offer to buy those properties at a discount?"

The two deputies continued their conversation on the way to the Mount Pleasant Livery Stable to get Roger a replacement horse for McLaughlin's.

"I can return the horse to the McLaughlins, since I have to go back that way to pick up the notices I delivered," Nik said. "I'll just hang onto them since they're no good 'til served. That should at least delay things for a while."

Nik added he would ask the U.S. Marshal Service to pick up the tab for Roger's expenses, given those items were lost in the line of duty.

"Nik, I'm going to keep my promise to Loretta and stop in to see the doc," Roger said. "Why don't you go on over to the Titus Saloon and find out what you can about Arthur?"

Nik set off for the local tavern and found the establishment nearly empty. He asked the bartender as to the homestead posses and specifically Arthur McLaughlin. Fortunately, the saloonkeeper had a copy of which direction each homesteader rode off in case anyone inquired.

"McLaughlin was with the two men who went northeast of here, toward Boston, Texas," the barkeeper said, handing the list to Nik. "He took to drinking after the news. I had to cut him off so he could ride, and before he spent all his money."

"Appreciate that," Nik replied, about the time Roger walked. "I guess he took the news pretty hard. Thanks for your help."

Nik explained to Roger where Arthur was headed and asked about his brother's checkup.

"Doc said I was fine. Now I'm anxious to get on Curtain's trail, as well," Roger said. "Let's get started while we still have some daylight left."

Leaving Mount Pleasant, the Brinkmans were able to ride part way together, as both were riding northeast. Travel was easier now that the storm had passed, leaving behind blue skies to connect the horizons. The late-autumn temperature was cool but not cold, making their ride through the Texas countryside enjoyable. When they reached a point to go their separate ways, Nik raised his concerns.

"The last time we split up, you ended up in the river half dead and suffering from amnesia," Nik cautioned. "Are you sure you'll be okay this time."

"Give me credit, Nik," Roger remarked. "I may have botched my assignment, but I did survive."

"I wish I could take comfort in that," Nik said. "I don't want to go through that again."

Nik explained being assigned to the Paris office and suggested Roger contact him there when he concluded his search for Arthur. Upon departing, Nik turned north toward the McLaughlin homestead towing their horse behind.

Roger continued on the road to Boston. It took the deputy more than a day to reach the small town, although it was the seat of Bowie County. It proved little more than a wide spot in the road but featured a small saloon where Roger could inquire about Arthur.

Roger was still without his badge, but he wasn't looking to arrest anyone, just take someone home.

Roger entered the dimly-lit tavern, where the smell of cigar smoke filled the air. He approached the bar, as his eyes adjusted to the darkness.

"What can I get you," said the bartender, as Roger leaned on the counter.

"Ah, nothing, thanks," Roger said. "I'm looking for someone and was wondering if you might know of his whereabouts."

"Who're you looking for?" said the barkeep. "Lots of people pass through here on their way to who-knows-where."

"I'm looking for a man named Arthur McLaughlin, who may have passed through here with a few other riders from Mount Pleasant," Roger said.

The proprietor looked at Roger for a moment and then tipped his head in the direction of the far end of the bar. Roger looked, only to see the top of a black cowboy hat with an arm stretched out from beneath it, holding a half-empty glass of whisky.

"He's been in here a couple of days," the bartender said. "His companions have come and gone."

"Thanks," Roger said, as he moved to where the man was sitting, his head hanging over the counter.

"Arthur McLaughlin?" Roger questioned but got no answer. "Arthur McLaughlin!" Roger said in a louder voice, drawing the attention of a couple patrons sitting around what few tables furnished the place.

The man in the black hat raised his head. His eyes appeared swollen and half asleep. He was unkempt, unshaven, and seemed unaware of where he was. He turned to look at Roger.

"I'm Arthur," he said, spreading the air with the smell of stale whisky as he spoke.

"Arthur, I'm here to take you home," Roger said.

"I ain't got no home. Lost it," Arthur said with a bit of a slur. "I ain't got nothin' no more."

"Yes, you do, Arthur," Roger continued. "You have a wife, a child and a farm to tend to."

"I've got nothing,' I tell you," Arthur repeated. "Go away and let me alone."

"Barkeep, would you get this man something to help him sober up?" Roger asked.

The saloonkeeper complied, setting a cup of black coffee in front of Arthur.

"Drink up, Arthur. You've got to sober up because I'm taking you home," Roger said.

"Why don't you let the man alone?" said a voice from somewhere in the dark room.

"I can't," Roger said, responding to the one speaking. "I'm here to return this man to his wife and child."

"I would say he's in no condition to be returning to anybody," the speaker continued, with a slight laugh. "Let him drink himself to death in peace."

"I'm sorry," Roger said. "Who are you?"

"Sammon," the man answered. "Not that it's any of your business."

Roger stiffened when he heard the name. All thoughts of Arthur were suddenly turned on the voice in the darkness.

"Would you be Sockeye Sammon?" Roger asked as he moved toward the voice. When he drew closer, he could see a man sitting at a heavy oak gambling table, together with two other cowboys.

"Yeah, and you're disturbing our game here," Sockeye said, smirking as he glanced at those sitting at the table. "Since you're so inclined, take that miserable drunk with you and vamoose. You're bothering the rest of us."

"Excuse me, do you know Gloria Fenton?" Roger inquired, as he continued his approach without thinking about what he was saying.

"Who?" Sockeye said. One of the cowboys sitting with Sammon leaned over and whispered something to him.

"Gloria Fenton," Roger repeated. "She was the daughter of a couple settlers whose wagon was attacked near the Llano Estacado."

"I might know of her, so what?" Sockeye said, glancing over at the cowboy who had whispered to him.

"Besides finding Mr. McLaughlin, here, I'm looking for her also," Roger said, keeping his eyes focused on the man called Sockeye.

Sensing that Roger apparently suspected him of having a hand in the incident he was referring to, Sockeye slowly drew his pistol from his holster. Keeping it under the table to avoid detection, he aimed the gun in Roger's direction. "I suggest you get your drunken friend and get out of here," Sockeye said. "I don't know no woman named Gloria."

"I think you do," Roger continued, as his emotions began to rise. "I think you killed her parents and I'd like to know what you did with their daughter."

"Are you accusing me of murder?" Sockeye said, quietly cocking the hammer on his pistol.

"The Comanche Iron Bear told us what you had done before he died," Roger said. "Now I'd like to know what you did with their daughter, Gloria."

"I've had about enough of this," Sockeye said, as he pulled the trigger on his gun. His aim was accurate, but his bullet struck the thick, oak table leg that stood between him and where Roger was standing. Wooden splinters flew into the air. Sockeye attempted to raise his pistol above the table but hit the edge, causing the second bullet to fire into the floor, barely missing his leg.

Roger drew his pistol and fired. In the dim light, he could see the white of Sockeye's functional eye widen as his chair tipped back. The chair remained still for a moment and then fell over backward, crashing to the floor with Sockeye's dead body still in it. Roger turned his gun on the other two men at the table, who were stunned by what had taken place.

"Don't either of you move," Roger said, with his heart beating so hard it felt like it would come through his chest.

Both men raised their hands above their heads.

"We don't want no trouble," one of the men said.

"I saw you whisper something to Sockeye when I mentioned Gloria Fenton's name. What did you tell him?" Roger demanded.

"I only know Sockeye once sold a white woman to the Comanche," said the man who had whispered to Sockeye. "That's all I know."

Roger backed up toward Arthur, who was starting to sober up from the coffee and the shock of what he just witnessed. Roger kept his pistol trained on the two men, as he looked about the room to see if anyone else was threatening to make a move against him.

"Barkeep," Roger said. "I'm a U.S. Deputy Marshal. Do you have an undertaker in this town?"

"We have someone who can take care of the body, if that's what you mean," the barkeep said.

"That's what I mean. I'll be back for the body, and I'll settle up when I return," Roger said, continuing to look about the room. He reached back and grabbed Arthur by the arm and pulled him close. He walked slowly toward the saloon doors with Arthur in tow and his pistol pointed into the darkness. "Barkeep, do you know where this man's horse is?" Roger asked.

"Tied up outside," the saloonkeeper said. "You may want to get that poor animal some water. He's been out there for some time."

Arthur was sober enough to identify his horse. Roger helped McLaughlin to get on his mount, while he untied his own. The deputy led both horses to a watering trough where the horses drank their fill. Roger then mounted up while hanging onto the reins of Arthur's horse, leaving the rider to hold onto the saddle horn. Roger and Arthur then slowly rode out of town in the direction of Mount Pleasant and the McLaughlin home.

As nightfall approached, the two were within sight of the farmhouse. Loretta spotted them through the kitchen window when they were about a hundred yards away. She called to Johnny Mac and they both came out of the house and began running toward the riders. Loretta was crying when she met up with them and she literally pulled Arthur off his horse and began embracing him. Arthur protested somewhat because of his condition, but when Johnny Mac wrapped his arms around his dad's waist and held on tight, Arthur began to sob and hug back.

"Let's get you into the house and get you cleaned up. You smell like whisky," Loretta said, looking into Arthur's face through the shadowy light of the evening. She turned to see Roger politely nodding to her, but he smiled to let her know everything was okay.

Loretta instructed Roger to stay for dinner and that his hayloft bedroom was still available for the night.

Arthur's appearance improved markedly once he was cleaned up and Loretta had filled him full of black coffee.

"I cannot tell you how grateful I am to you and your brother, Nik," Loretta said. "Nik told me he thinks the foreclosure notices likely won't hold up in court."

"The lender will likely suffer some, since he was swindled out of quite a bit of money," Roger stated. "It might help if you homestead folks helped keep him in business by patronizing his store."

"We do that, anyway," Loretta said. "I don't know him personally, but he seems like a good man. Do you think we'll have to repay the loan?"

"What loan?" Roger began. "Most of the money went to the crook with the fake deed. The deeds you homestead folks hold on your properties are the legal and binding ones. I understand the judge who ruled the swindler's deed legal has offered to buy some of the properties abandoned before news of fraud broke. That should help."

"I can't thank you and your fellow deputy enough for what you've done for us," Arthur said. Roger had filled McLaughlin in on the details during their ride home. "I like Gobles, he's a good man," Arthur continued. "I can't say the same for that judge. When we protested the Confederate's deed, he refused to listen to us. Now he wants to buy the land left behind by those who panicked and left."

"I don't think my brother, Nik, cares for him either," Roger said. "I just hope everything works out okay."

After dinner, Roger said his goodbyes, telling the family he would be leaving early. He assured both Arthur and Loretta that he, Nik and the U.S. Marshal Service would do all in their power to clear up the land fraud. As for the details concerning "Colonel" Curtain and the shooting of Sockeye Sammon, Roger would leave that up to Arthur.

Last, but not least, Roger thanked Loretta for nursing him back to health and gave her the doctor's report. He concluded by requesting God's blessings on the McLaughlins' farm.

"You should have been a preacher, Roger," Loretta said.

Roger only smiled and nodded his head. He put on his hat and stepped out into the night in the direction of the barn.

It was when he was alone and settled into the hayloft for the night that the past incident and shooting of Sockeye Sammon began to play on his mind. He felt proud to have dealt with a known killer, but the killing took him back to the first time he shot a man, a Union soldier years ago. He closed his eyes as if that might make such thoughts go away.

"Feels a little different when it's personal, doesn't it?" said a kindly-looking man in bib overalls and wearing a floppy-brimmed hat. He was chewing on a stalk of straw and was sitting across from Roger. "It comes with the territory, you know."

"The man was a killer and besides, he shot at me first," Roger answered.

"So why aren't you feeling proud of what you did?" the stranger said. "You also reunited Arthur with his family, and it appears you will help save their farm. Nik's a good man. He'll straighten things out."

"I just can't get it out of my mind the look on that character's face when he went over backward in that chair," said Roger. "I actually felt a surge of satisfaction I have not felt before. Now, I'm not so sure I still feel that way."

"You've been marshaling with Nik for quite a while now," the stranger continued. "He's had to uphold justice at the point of a gun several times, many more times than what you've seen. How do you think he feels?"

"Nik's different. He seems to take his job in stride no matter what he has to do," Roger said, as he lied down on the hay. "I just wish I were more like him."

"No, Nik is who he is and you are who you are," said the stranger. "You've been through a lot, Roger Brinkman, and you're going to go through a lot more before it's all over. Just remember who you really are, and you'll be all right."

"Just be who I am," Roger said, almost in a whisper. "I'm not even sure I know..." with that Roger drifted off to sleep.

Chapter 26

The next morning, before anyone was stirring in the McLaughlin house, Roger saddled his horse and rode out in the direction of the river. He quietly followed the Sulphur River and imagined himself floating with the current while unconscious. He knew he would eventually come to the spot where a shot narrowly missed his head. It likely was close to where Nik and Borchers discovered what they surmised was a hideout. The area was perfect for hiding an outlaw gang that Sockeye Sammon was affiliated with. Nik said he'd seen Sockeye's horse tied up there.

Using caution, Roger found a place to cross the river and turn due north. He continued until he came to the trail running into Clarksville, where he would take care of business before heading onto Paris.

When Roger reached Clarksville, he stopped at the sheriff's office to let Packard know he was still alive.

"My good Lord, I think I'm seeing a ghost," Packard said with genuine surprise. "I thought you were dead and gone."

"There was a time when I was as good as gone," Roger said, smiling at Packard's astonishment. "For more than a month, I didn't know who I was or anything about my past. It remained that way until my brother, Deputy Marshal Nik Brinkman, found me and restored my memory."

"Restored your memory?" Packard said. "What in the world happened to you?"

"Oh, it's a long story," Roger said. "I'll fill you in sometime. But for now, I'm doing fine."

"Happy to hear that. Your brother and the marshal out of Paris stopped in here looking for you a while back," the sheriff explained. "He gave me a brief explanation as to why the two of you are brothers, I hope what he said squares with you."

"Yes, he is my brother, adopted, you could say," Roger replied. "I know people wonder about brothers of different shades, but he's as much a Brinkman as I am."

The sheriff nodded, acknowledging Roger's explanation. "We did find your horse with your badge still in the saddlebags. All those things were turned over to your brother and the Paris marshal."

"I'm grateful, sheriff. I just stopped by to let you know I was okay," Roger repeated.

"And I'm glad to know it," Packard replied. "Brinkman and the Paris marshal went looking for you and I guess when they returned, they came back here, but I was away on business. My deputy said they took your horse and other stuff back with them."

"I appreciate that, sheriff," Roger said. "I'll check in at the local hotel and then be off to Paris in the morning."

"Well, if I don't see you for a while, have a safe trip," Packard said.

"Oh, you'll see me again, soon," Roger said, "I have to return this way on my way to Boston after I wrap things up in Paris."

"Boston? What's going on in that little town?" Packard said.

"I have to pick up a body," Roger answered. "I had a little skirmish up there while looking for someone."

"A body, you say. Anyone I know?" Packard inquired.

"I'm not sure," Roger said. "Do you know a man named Sockeye Sammon?"

"Did you say Sockeye Sammon?" the sheriff remarked, with surprise in his voice.

"Yeah, did you know him?" Roger asked.

"Oh, ah, no, I didn't really know him," Packard answered. "I knew of him. He had quite a reputation in these parts. At any rate, I'll be looking for you when you return, deputy. Take care, now."

Roger bid the sheriff goodbye and walked across the street to check into the Clarksville Hotel. He then visited the telegraph office and wired a message to the marshal in Paris: "Riding to Paris tomorrow from Clarksville. Need to claim body of Sockeye Sammon in Boston. Will explain later. Roger Brinkman, USMS."

A telegram came back instructing him to turn his horse into the livery stable on behalf of the U.S. Marshal Service and take the train to Paris, instead.

No further instructions were given, so the next day Roger did as he was told and boarded the Memphis, El Paso & Pacific Railway heading west.

Nik met Roger at the Paris Depot, with Roger's horse and saddle in tow. Roger greeted Brinker with enthusiasm and asked Nik why he was told to take the train?

"Too risky for you to ride alone all that way," Nik said. "What's this about Sockeye's body in Boston?"

"I shot him, Nik," Roger said as stoically as possible. "I found Arthur in a saloon where Sockeye was sitting. He drew on me and missed, but my bullet found its mark."

"Roger! I'm proud of you! But when we read you were going to pick up Sammon's body in Boston, that's when we figured it best if you took the train rather than riding up here alone," Nik said. "Did anyone try to retaliate after the shooting?"

"No, in fact, one man sitting at Sockeye's table told me Sammon may have been the one who sold Gloria to the Comanche," Roger said. "I brought that up to Sockeye, and the killing of the Fentons, and that's what provoked the fight."

"What about Sheriff Packard in Clarksville," Nik asked. "Does he know?"

"Yeah," Roger stated. "I dropped by his office to let him know I was alive and told him I'd shot Sockeye."

"Borchers and I don't trust Packard and neither does Marshal Oliver. That's part of the reason why we instructed you to take the train," Nik related. "When Ned and I went looking for you, we stopped in at his office shortly after you went missing. We got suspicious of when he seemed to be awfully cozy with that Sulphur River bunch. He said he had a good relationship with them so's they wouldn't bother his town."

"Yeah, he told me the same," Roger replied. "So, you think he might be in cahoots with those desperados?"

"It's tough out here, Roger," Nik said. "One never knows who one can trust… unless they're your brother, of course." Nik concluded with a laugh.

Nik then confirmed that not only was Curtain's deed fraudulent concerning the homestead properties presented to Judge Kensington in Mount Pleasant, but Confederate Enterprises was also a fraud. Nik said he corresponded with the Department of the Interior and no such speculation deed was ever issued. The department also had no other deeds under the name of Confederate Enterprises or Gabriel "Colonel" Curtain.

"That was pretty shoddy work on the judge's part, don't you think, Nik? Roger said.

"There is something strange about that," Nik answered. "To adjudicate a deed to be valid without checking with the Interior is highly irregular, especially one requiring a payoff from each homestead on that land."

"You don't suppose the judge was in on that deal, do you?" Roger asked.

"Very little surprises me anymore," Nik said. "It's not easy to try and investigate a judge in these parts. There are so few of them. And the adjudicators that do monitor those circuit judges tend to side with their own. U.S. marshals work for them, not against them.

Nik continued, "But I've got to admit I was disappointed in Kensington when he would not give me a warrant to investigate the Sulphur River hideout."

"He turned you down for that?" Roger said. "What was the reason?"

"Lack of evidence," Nik stated. "I argued that evidence was what I would be looking for, but Kensington brushed that off. I figured I'd have some clout being a deputy marshal, but it didn't carry any water with him."

"Is there anything you can do?" Roger asked.

"I plan to get Borchers to approach the Department of the Treasury concerning this judge controversy, but I'm not going to get my hopes up," Nik answered.

The next day, Nik and Roger picked up a buckboard and two drive horses to begin the journey to Boston to retrieve Sockeye Sammon's body. They both had their pistols and rifles, and Nik even brought along a shotgun and his saddlebags. They carried extra rounds of ammunition in case they ran into trouble if Sockeye was indeed connected with the Sulphur River outfit.

Last, but not least, they put their saddles in the wagon and tied Lincoln and Brinker to the back of it.

"You think we're going to need our horses as well?" Roger commented.

"If we end up in pursuit of outlaws, we can't very well do it in a buckboard," Nik replied. "Just part of being prepared for any contingency." They also tossed in a load of hay to keep the animals fed.

The trip took most of a week to reach Boston. The town didn't look much different, despite being short one outlaw. They stopped at the saloon to find out where Sockeye's body was taken.

"You boys are a little late, aren't you?" the barkeep said. "There was a couple of deputies through here about two days ago claiming the body."

"A couple other deputies?" Nik exclaimed. "We're pretty much the only deputies in these parts."

"No, I'm pretty sure they said they were from the U.S. Marshals Office because the embalmer released the body to them," said the saloonkeeper.

"Okay, thanks for your time, but we'd better check with the mortician, just the same," Nik said.

"Suit yourselves," the bartender responded, and then busied himself with washing glasses.

"Something stinks about this," Nik said, as the two deputies left the saloon. They climbed onto the seat of the buckboard and rode up to the local mortuary. The undertaker was out, but his wife said that the body had been turned over to two men who identified themselves as marshals. The woman said her husband was given a letter authorizing the two men to claim the body.

"Do you know who signed that authorization?" Nik asked.

"I don't rightly know, but it gave my husband a reason not to doubt their word," said the mortician's wife.

After leaving the undertaker's office, Roger said, "Sorry, Nik, I guess we rode all this way for nothing. I told the barkeep who I was when I left the saloon that day."

"I don't like this," Nik said. "We need to take another way out of Boston because I think we might be riding into trouble."

"There is a trail that leads more south of here, near where the McLaughlin homestead is," Roger said. "It was the way I came looking for Arthur."

"Let's head that way," Nik said. "Not only should it be safer, but it gives me an idea."

Nik's plan was to reach the Sulphur River and then work their way upstream until close to the hideout. Nik remembered seeing a bluff near the place, where Nik and Roger could position themselves to spy on the cabin without being seen. From that vantage point, Nik was hoping he could see if Sockeye's body was there and make an arrest based on the false claim of Sammon's remains.

"What if there's too many of them for us to handle?" Roger asked.

"We've got plenty of ammunition and the law on our side," Nik said. "One thing you have to know about being a deputy marshal: You'll always be outnumbered. Our saving grace is that most outlaws are cowards and would rather run than fight."

Nik and Roger eventually reached the Sulphur River and stopped in at the McLaughlin homestead. The McLaughlins agreed to hang onto the deputy's wagon, as the two deputies saddled Lincoln and Brinker. After a brief conversation concerning Nik's plan, the two deputies packed up their arsenal and headed up the river.

After a couple hours' ride, the bluff Nik spoke of came into view. The two deputies rode into the woods and dismounted after reaching the bluff. They left their rifles and shotgun with the horses, taking only their gun belts to make the climb easier. Nik also retrieved a pair of field glasses he maintained in his saddlebags.

"There could be a sentry on that bluff, so we need to be cautious," Nik said. "If we find the coast is clear, we'll gather our hardware and approach the cabin."

Fortunately, as the deputies reached the top, they found no one there. From that vantage point, Roger and Nik could see virtually all the area surrounding the hideaway. Roger also spotted the narrow path along the ridge where he was climbing when a bullet struck close enough to cause him to fall into the river.

"I wonder if this is where the shot came from," Roger mused.

"If so, it's probably why the shot missed you," Nik said. "It would take a sharpshooter, like you, to hit a target at that distance."

Also in view was the hideout. Nik used his binoculars to scan the cabin. There were two horses in the corral next to the structure, encouraging Nik to think the odds now favored approaching the hideout.

"Two horses is a good sign, but are you sure there are only two men down there?" Roger remarked.

"I can't be sure, but we may never get a better chance than this to find out," Nik said, raising his field glasses to take another look at the area.

"Wait a minute," he said. "I see a rider approaching."

"Those odds don't sound so good now," Roger remarked.

"I'll be damned," Nik muttered. "Here, take a look at who just came into the clearing," Nik said, handing the binoculars to Roger.

"That's Sheriff Packard," Roger whispered. "Your suspicion of him appears correct.

"Wait, there's someone else I don't recognize," Roger added. Another rider emerged from the woods following Packard.

"Let me take a look," Nik said, taking the glasses from Roger.

"Now I'm double damned, "Nik exclaimed in a low voice. "That's Judge Kensington. I knew there was something fishy about him. He and Packard are a part of this gang."

"We don't know that for sure," Roger said. "Maybe they're investigating the place."

"Judges don't investigate, and Packard said this place was off limits to him," Nik continued. "Hold it. A couple of guys just came out to meet them."

Nik could see the two men greeting the sheriff and judge, as the two dismounted. Neither of the two men from the cabin were familiar. Once the horses were tied to the corral fence, Packard and Kensington followed the men into the cabin.

"This is too good to pass up," Nik said. "Come on, let's get our horses and move into position to confront these polecats. I want to see that judge squirm. I'll bet he's in on that land fraud, as well."

Nik put the binoculars away and headed off the bluff, with Roger close behind. They reached their horses and began loading their rifles and filled their gun belts and pockets with extra cartridges. Nik also double-checked the pistol in his boot and decided to take the shotgun, as well. When finished, the two deputies walked their horses closer to the hideout for quick access should the situation grow more hostile than the two could handle.

Nik and Roger tied up Lincoln and Brinker where they couldn't be seen from the cabin and advanced on foot to the edge of the clearing surrounding it. Once in a safe position, Nik fired his rifle into the air.

He called out, "Come out with your hands over your heads!"

Inside the cabin, Judge Kensington looked at Packard. "Who the hell is that?" he said.

"I can't see anybody," said one of the men in the cabin, looking out of a window.

"I recognize that voice," Sheriff Packard said. "I think it's that Negro marshal."

"So, what do we do?" the judge asked anxiously.

"I'm not sure," Packard said. "We could go out. It's not against the law to be here."

"That doesn't necessarily pertain to us," said the second man who had greeted Packard and Kensington outside the cabin. "If there's only one of them, I think we could take him."

"That's much too risky," Kensington said. "What about Sammon's body? What have you done with that?"

"We're planning to dump it in the river when it rises with the next storm," the second man said.

"So that means the body is still here," Packard cut in. "That's not good, I've told that marshal that I never come near here. Now he would have evidence to the contrary."

"Packard! Kensington! I know you're in there," Nik called out. "Come on out, and no one gets hurt."

"Do you think he's alone?" Kensington asked.

"His brother could be with him," Packard said. "He's a white guy, and we don't know how much he knows. I sent him down here some time ago thinking he wouldn't make it back alive, but he did.

"Willie," Packard said in a hoarse whisper, to the man by the window. "Stall, tell whoever is out there they've got nothing on us. See what he says."

"Show yourself," Willie yelled. "Let us know who you are and what you want."

"I'll show myself when you come out with your hands in the air," Nik said. "I have a warrant to investigate your cabin."

"That's a lie," Kensington said to the men in the room. "I turned that marshal down when he asked for the warrant."

"Seems we have two choices," Packard stated. "Go out with our hands in the air and take our chances we can talk our way out of this or open fire and see how many men are out there. If there are too many, we'll surrender if necessary."

"I like that second one," Willie said and fired his pistol in the direction of Nik's voice.

Nik fired back, shattering the window where Willie stood.

"Hold your fire, Roger," Nik said, speaking in a low voice. "They don't know you are here. I'm going to run through the trees to try and get them to shoot at me. When they do, you fire a volley in the direction of wherever those shots come from. They won't be expecting it."

"Nik, that's crazy," Roger said. "You could get shot."

"I've been shot at before," Nik said. "Don't forget, I fought in the war, too."

"So why go through that again?" Roger demanded, under his breath.

"Roger, we're U.S. deputy marshals. Those guys in that cabin are outlaws," Nik said, sending his brother a stern message with his expression. "This is what we do! Now, cover me." Nik began running through the trees.

Willie fired at Nik but missed. Roger raised his rifle to his shoulder but did not pull the trigger. The other man who had come out with Willie to greet the sheriff and judge poked a rifle barrel out a second window and fired in Nik's direction. Nik plunged face-first onto the ground.

"Nik!" Roger called out, his mind nearly boiling over with a multitude of thoughts fueled by the fear that his brother had been hit. Roger turned his rifle on Willie's window and drove him from it by firing off two quick rounds. He then took careful aim and shattered the hand stock on the rifle protruding from the second window. That was enough to cause the weapon to disappear back into the cabin.

In a blind rage, Roger began running toward the place, firing his rifle as he ran. When empty, he dropped the rifle, drew his pistol and hurled himself into the cabin door with enough force to knock it from its hinges. Roger rode the door to the floor and rolled over in time to see Packard and Kensington making an escape out the back. Roger then turned to fire at Willie but saw he was leaning against the wall with his hand over a bleeding shoulder wound. Roger ducked and rolled in the other direction to take aim at the second shooter, but no one was there. The deputy then jumped up and ran to the back door and shouted at Packard and Kensington.

"Halt, or I'll shoot to kill!" Roger yelled.

The two men stopped in their tracks with their hands in the air. As Roger stared at them, he failed to hear a door open behind him that allowed enough room for a pistol barrel to poke through and take aim. A loud blast rang out.

Roger spun around in time to see a huge hole blown through the open door behind him and a body being propelled from it. Roger turned to face the light pouring in from the broken front door. He could see the shadow of a man framed in the doorway who called out before Roger could act.

"Roger! It's me, Nik," said the silhouette

"Nik!" Roger responded.

"Yep, I always wanted to use this thing," Nik said, as he walked into the room smiling and holding the smoking shotgun.

"Nik, I thought you might be dead," Roger said excitedly. "I saw you go down when a shot was fired from the cabin."

"It was close," Nik said, "but that was what I wanted you to think. I had to see what you would do if you thought you were on your own. However, I didn't think you'd do this."

Nik then walked over to the door with the hole in it and observed the man lying lifeless behind it.

Suddenly, they heard two horses galloping away.

"It's Kensington and Packard! They're getting away!" Roger shouted.

When Roger turned away from the door at the sound of the shotgun blast, the judge and sheriff decided to break for their horses.

Roger ran back to the doorway to catch them, but he was too late.

"Never mind," Nik called, looking over at Willie leaning against the wall of the cabin. "We've still got this one, and I have a hunch he could tell us plenty when we get him fixed up."

After a search of the hideout and surrounding area, Nik and Roger found what they assumed was the embalmed body of Sockeye Sammon lying in a buckboard hidden in the nearby trees. They hitched up that wagon to the two horses in the corral and loaded the dead man next to Sammon's neatly wrapped mummy-style corpse. They patched up Willie's shoulder as best they could and loaded him into the wagon. Nik drove the team toward the McLaughlin farm, while Roger rode behind the buckboard towing Nik's horse and keeping a watchful eye on Willie.

Once they reached the McLaughlins, Loretta skillfully took the bullet out of Willie's shoulder, bandaged the wound and put his arm in a sling to help prepare him for travel.

"By the way, cowboy, what's your name?" Loretta asked.

Willie was thin and his blood-soaked shirt hung on him like a drape. He was unshaven, but his mustache was full and curled around a mouth shaped as if he had no teeth. His expression was one of anger, although his persona was nonthreatening.

Willie had withheld his name from Nik and Roger, thinking it would serve his cause in some way, but Loretta's care for him broke down his resistance.

"Willie," he said reluctantly, disappointed knowing the deputy marshals could hear his response.

The two deputies gave the McLaughlins the outlaws' wagon and horses, compliments of the U.S. Marshal Service. They loaded up the two dead men into the deputy's wagon the McLaughlins had kept for them. They helped Willie settle into position alongside his former companions.

Nik and Roger decided to head for Mount Pleasant where they could get their other dead passenger embalmed, along with having the local doctor prepare Willie for further travel. From there, they could head back to Paris, without passing through Clarksville.

Chapter 27

Roger, Nik, and Willie rode for several miles, quietly lost in thought. After more than enough time to contemplate the situation, Nik decided to break the silence.

"We'll ride due east to Tarrant. It'll take us two to three days at this pace, but it should be pretty much trouble free, right, Willie?" Nik said, making sure Willie realized he was a part of the conversation. "Say, whatever happened with Lupe and the silent giant that Sockeye was riding with?"

Willie didn't speak, as he absorbed each bump the buckboard encountered. He was feeling much better now, but his left shoulder was still plenty sore. He knew he was headed for trouble because it would not be hard to link him to the gang responsible for many of the crimes taking place across Texas. The fact the deputies discovered Sheriff Packard and Judge Kensington at the hideout would likely prove to be a disaster, too.

"We have a long way to go, Willie," Nik said. "You might as well make yourself comfortable and enjoy the ride and the conversation. You know, Willie, turning state's evidence can go a long way in making things easy on yourself."

"You mean squealing?" Willie muttered. He winced when a jolt to the wagon threw his left shoulder against the sideboard.

"Call it what you like, but I think the way the law expresses it is your best bet," Nik continued. "Besides, telling us what you know could mean you wouldn't have to worry about the folks you're afraid of – they'd all be in jail," said Nik, laughing at his remark.

"With what we saw, Packard and Kensington are aware they're headed for a rough time," Roger said, while nudging Brinker closer to where Willie was sitting in the wagon.

"That's right, Willie," Nik chimed in. "Do you think those two won't sing like songbirds if they think that could save their hides? Besides, they sort of have the law on their side, you and your desperado buddies don't."

"Why don't you just shut up?" Willie said, with a snarl. "You've already shot me, isn't that torture enough?"

"Oh, Willie, Willie," Nik said lightheartedly. "I think before this ride to Paris is over, you're going to find we're the best friends you've got."

As they rode along, a fine rain began to fall, forcing Nik to don his duster and Roger to put on the old poncho he brought with him from Missouri. Nik, in anticipation of foul weather, had picked up a canvas tarp for the wagon in Mount Pleasant to cover up Willie and the bodies.

Although the drizzle was steady, there was no thunder or lightning in the area. Nik found a grove of trees where they were able to camp for the night. They dined on food purchased in Mount Pleasant and a few leftovers from what Loretta had prepared for them.

After checking to make sure Willie was secure for the night, Roger and Nik laid out their bedrolls under the wagon. They laughed, recalling the time they were caught in a downpour near Wichita while sleeping under Blue Feather's chuckwagon.

Despite the situation, they managed to get a reasonable night's sleep, but the rain had not let up by morning. Roger and Nik harnessed the horses to the wagon and untied Willie to let him move around a little before resuming their journey.

The small creeks nearby were swelling, and the two men were not familiar with the rivers they would have to ford near Tarrant, but they were destined to soon find out.

Even with the rising waters, the two deputies were able to cross the first creek they came to without any trouble. However, as they drew closer to Tarrant, they came to Whiteoak Creek, which was already overflowing its banks.

"Roger, you'll have to ride out into the river to see if we can cross here," Nik called out to his brother, as they approached the swift-flowing waters.

"I'll give it a try, but this does not look like such a good spot," Roger answered.

"No, but it's where this trail leads," Nik said. "I have to assume this has to be one of the typical places where travelers cross."

Roger rode out into the creek, but by the time he reached the middle of the stream the water was nearly filling his boots. He turned and rode back toward the wagon.

"We'll never get that wagon across here," Roger said. "We're going to have to look for another location."

"Turn south and follow the creek," Willie commented in a matter-of-fact voice.

"Do you know this area?" Nik called out to his prisoner.

"Well enough," Willie said.

"Let's turn left," Nik shouted to Roger, as the rain grew heavier. "What have we got to lose?"

"Just about everything if we try to cross here," Roger answered.

Although the overflow of water obscured the creek's banks, after traveling a short distance south of the main trail the riders could see the creek then turned in a westerly direction. After splashing through a couple of smaller tributaries, the rain let up somewhat, as the men came upon a wide spot in Whiteoak Creek that offered the riders some hope.

"Roger, try it again here," Nik shouted. "Otherwise, we may be following this thing all the way to Mexico."

Although the stream was spilling over its banks and the current rapidly flowing, it wasn't deep. Roger made it to the other side, then turned and rode back.

"I think we can cross here," Roger said. "But we had better do it soon."

"Take your rope and tie it to the harness. Do the same with the rope on my saddle," Nik called out, jumping down from the wagon to assist. "Use Brinker and Lincoln to help pull the wagon. It's risky, but it's probably our best shot."

After getting the two ropes tied to the wagon's harness, Nik secured the other ends to both horses. Roger took Nik's horse in tow and started into the water. The system worked nicely, as the wagon neared midstream. Lincoln and Brinker had reached shallower water and were approaching the opposite bank when, suddenly, Willie rolled out of the wagon. Unable to swim with his wounded left arm, he tried to stay afloat by rolling onto his back.

"Son of a…, he's making a getaway," Nik called. "Roger, keep pulling us onto the other side."

Roger spurred Brinker as the two lead horses cleared the water and pulled the drive horses and wagon out of the creek.

"Untie these ropes!" Nik yelled. "We've got to get Willie out of that water before he drowns."

Once the ropes were free, Nik jumped onto his horse and signaled Roger to follow. "Come on, leave the wagon," he shouted. "The other two bodies in there aren't going anywhere."

Nik and Roger took off at a full gallop, as the current carried Willie back in the direction they had come. When they reached the spot where the creek turned north ahead of Willie, Nik reined in Lincoln and Roger followed suit. Both men dismounted and Nik took the rope off his saddle and told Roger to shed his poncho and sit on it. Nik then grabbed Roger's foot and began taking off his boot.

"What are you doing?" Roger asked.

"Removing your boots! Take off your gun belt, as well, and put the loop of my rope around your waist," Nik said, while pulling off Roger's second boot. "Make sure that rope is secure and wade out as far as you can to catch Willie as he comes by. I'll use Lincoln to pull you out of the water when you've got ahold of him."

"Are you sure about this?" Roger shouted. "I'm not a good swimmer."

"You were better than I was, as kids, and I haven't improved a lick since then. Now get going," Nik said.

Where the creek turned north, it widened forming an eddy slowing the current. Roger was able to wade out most of the way, ignoring the rocks and waterlogged sticks under his bare feet. When he reached where the heart of the creek was, he turned and looked upstream. He could see Willie floating into view, but the outlaw was no longer on his back. Roger jacked up his courage and lunged into the deeper part of the stream, gasping as the near-freezing water closed in around him. As Willie's floating body drew near, Roger was able to grip his left arm, pulling it from the sling that supported it. The pain aroused Willie who grabbed for Roger, pushing the deputy underwater. Fortunately, Roger's feet hit the bottom of the creek. Refusing to panic, he walked along the bottom of the stream toward shore while reaching up to tow the wounded prisoner above him.

Fearing for the safety of his brother, Nik spurred Lincoln, attempting to pull Roger to the surface. Willie had swallowed too much water to fight. Soon, Roger was able to get his head above the surface, drawing in a deep breath of air. He began dragging Willie toward the creek bank and, with a mighty heave, shoved the outlaw toward shore. Nik had jumped off Lincoln and was wading into the stream to help pull both men to safety. Close to exhaustion, Roger fell onto his back and lay in a supine position on the bank gulping in air.

Nik began pounding on Willie's back, as the water-choked prisoner regurgitated fluid and struggled to catch his breath.

While the three men sat in mud gathering their wits at the water's edge, the rain started to let up and soon stopped.

"Great job, Roger," Nik said.

"You almost drowned me," Roger replied.

"Yeah, but we got Willie, and I think he's going to be all right," Nik said while stroking his mustache to wick away the moisture.

"Thanks," Roger said, giving Nik a look that said otherwise.

The sun finally began to peek through the clouds, and the floodwaters started to recede.

"Why did you do it?" Willie said between coughs. "Why did you rescue me?"

"We've already got two dead bodies to deliver. We have no intention of making it three," Nik answered.

"What do you care?" Willie continued. "All you want to do is see me hang."

"I think Roger answered that for you," Nik said. "Tell me, was his effort to save you the actions of a man who wants you dead?"

"If you think I'm going to help you by ratting on the others, you've got another think comin'," Willie said, between coughs to help clear his lungs.

"Our mandate is to save lives," Roger said, as his breathing returned to normal. "The killing is only in self-defense. Remember, you guys shot at us first."

"Yeah, and look what that got me," Willie said. "You guys will walk away from this as free men, and I won't end up free either way."

Roger and Nik looked at one another with expressions of hope. Willie's perception of his situation could mean the prisoner would prove helpful after all.

After recovering from the rescue, Roger gathered up his belongings. He placed Willie's arm back into the sling, still hanging around the prisoner's neck, and helped the recaptured escapee climb onto Brinker, while Nik held the horse's reins. Roger positioned himself behind Willie, and the three men rode back toward the wagon.

"Did you fight in the war, Willie?" Roger asked.

"I did my part," Willie said.

"Which uniform did you wear?" Roger continued.

"Does it matter?" Willie answered.

"Not really. Would you believe that Nik, here, fought for the Union?" Roger said.

"Figures," Willie grumbled.

"And I fought for the South," Roger continued, "and Nik and I are brothers."

"That's what Packard said," Willie started, "doesn't make sense, but what does that matter?"

"It means brothers can actually reconcile after choosing different sides," Roger said, "even in war. However, we're both on the same side now."

"I was with Quantrill's bunch," Willie stated, as the men reached the wagon. "Satisfied?"

They found the horses were still hitched to the buckboard and the wagon was in one piece. The two mummy-wrapped bodies were also where they had left them. After the deputies pulled themselves together, Nik and Roger put Willie back into the wagon with his former companions. The trio then rode on to Tarrant, where they stayed the night.

Tarrant's hotel was owned by an elderly couple who used the accommodation largely as a residence. Tarrant was in transition after the state decided it would move the Hopkins County seat from there to Sulphur Springs. Business in Tarrant had dropped off, and the proprietors were grateful for whatever business they could get, even that of a man they assumed was a former slave and another being held in custody.

Their room was clean but in need of improvements that likely would never be made. However, it was dry and had beds plus a hot meal provided by the matron of the hotel. After eating, the men prepared for a night's sleep.

"Why do you have to tie me to my bed?" Willie grumbled, as Nik and Roger secured him to it. "Where would I go with this busted shoulder?"

"You did try to go swimming with it, so why not running?" Roger remarked. "Your legs are okay."

Satisfied their prisoner was not going anywhere, all three men, exhausted, were soon asleep.

The next day, the storm had passed and the men departed Tarrant on the trail that led to Paris. Their progress was slowed a little by the mud and debris left by the rain, but the night in a hotel bed made the trip considerably less stressful.

As the sun dried out the road ahead of them, traveling became easier and the temperature was quite comfortable. Nik and Roger took turns driving the buckboard while the other would ride along behind.

They came to the North Fork of the Sulphur River and decided to make camp for the night and, if the trip progressed without mishap, they would reach Paris the following day. There was no threat of rain, so they were able to make a campfire and enjoy a pleasant meal with the few provisions they had purchased in Tarrant.

"Willie, what will you do with your life once you've been cleared by the law?" Roger asked the prisoner.

Nik, who was preparing the meal, glanced over at Roger and smiled.

"What do you mean 'cleared by the law?'" Willie said.

"I don't know all that you could be found guilty of but depending on how you handle yourself you may get a short sentence or none at all," said Roger.

"I know what you're trying to do," Willie said. "You're trying to get me to talk."

"That I am," Roger said. "But you don't have to tell me anything if you don't want to. You seem like a decent enough fellow. Whatever made you want to become an outlaw, anyway?"

"Like I said, I rode with Quantrill," Willie said. "I wasn't proud of what we did, but after that, I was a fugitive, so what else was I to do?"

"Pay your dues and move on," Roger said. "Have you ever read the Bible?"

Willie looked at Roger for a moment. "What's that got to do with anything?" Willie asked.

"I'm guessing you weren't always bad," Roger said. "Didn't your Ma and Pa take you to church when you were growing up?"

"Yeah, my Ma took me a few times," Willie muttered. "Pa was usually in jail."

"Then you were given a pretty good idea about the difference between right and wrong, correct?" Roger said. "What made you choose wrong?"

"Life wasn't easy for me," Willie began. "My family didn't have much money, so we were always moving from place to place because of my Pa's reputation. It was tough in the South, because all the places that had work also had slaves. They weren't open to hiring nobody."

"Yeah, the slave idea worked for some but not for everyone," Roger said. "Right, Nik?" Roger called out to his brother.

"It worked for the wealthy," Nik said, "but that's about it."

Willie looked over at Nik. "How did you go from being a slave to being a lawman?" Willie asked.

"I was smuggled over on a slave ship, but I never became a slave," Nik said. "Roger's Pa bought me at an auction when I was just a kid and the Brinkmans adopted me into their family. I fought for the Union and then turned to the law when the war ended."

Willie then turned to Roger. "So why did you join the Confederacy?" he asked.

"Because a Union Colonel and his men killed our family," Roger said. "A Colonel Gabriel Curtain, ever hear of him?"

"Yeah, he tried to join up with us when I was riding with Quantrill," Willie said in a softer tone, while looking at the ground. "So why did you go Union?" Willie said, again looking up at Nik.

"Because I don't think Curtain was a colonel, and I don't think he was a member of the Union Army," Nik answered.

"No, I don't think so either," Willie said. Nik then approached the prisoner with a cup of coffee in his hand.

"Here, have some coffee, Willie," Nik said, handing the man the cup.

"Thanks," Willie said, taking the cup with his good hand. "Quantrill didn't care for Curtain either, although Curtain was probably more Confederate than Union. I think he really was just a marauder."

"Any idea what happened to Curtain after the war?" Roger asked.

"No," Willie answered, "but I heard the judge mention his name. Seems they had some kind of land deal going on, but I don't know nothin' about it.

"Sockeye, there, could have told you more," Willie added, nodding toward the wagon.

Nik and Roger glanced at each other but looked away quickly in hopes Willie wouldn't notice.

"I'll bet you guys would like to catch up to this Curtain, fella, right?" Willie said, "having killed your family and all."

"Willie, if you could tell me where to find Curtain," Nik said. "I'd be tempted to let you go right now."

"Sorry, I don't know," Willie said, "but maybe I am getting a little tired of running. Got anything to eat?"

"You bet," Nik answered, as he strolled back to the campfire to serve up some dinner.

The final day's journey to Paris progressed without incident, with all three men riding along lost in their thoughts. The traveling was easy, but the two deputies couldn't help regretting the administrative work they would have to face at the journey's end. Willie's concerns, on the other hand, were centered on the outcome of his uncertain future.

"Do you really think they'll go easy on me if I tell what I know?" Willie said out loud.

Nik, taken a little by surprise by their prisoner's sudden question, said, "Willie, I'm going to be as honest as I can with you. Roger and I cannot guarantee anything, but I will tell you this. If you're the brains behind whatever has gone on with this Sulphur River gang, then it's best you say as little as possible. However, if you were just one of the boys the odds are very much in your favor if you cooperate."

"Well, I sure wasn't the brains of the outfit. That was pretty much Sockeye here," Willie began, glancing at Sammon's wrapped body. "However, Kensington came up with most of the plans. That's why the judge showed up at the place the other day after he heard Sockeye had been killed. With Sockeye gone, it meant we'd need someone else to lead us."

"What about Sheriff Packard," Roger asked, steering Brinker closer to the wagon.

"First time I'd ever seen him," Willie said. "I guess he was friends with the judge."

"Now, I know Lupe and his giant partner were a part of this gang. What happened to them? Why weren't they there at the hideout?" Nik asked.

"They was out to ambush you two coming back from Boston, but apparently you decided to head our way rather than go back to Paris," Willie answered, as Nik and Roger looked at each other.

"What I don't understand," Roger said, "is why those guys pretended to be marshals and took Sammon's body?"

"That was just a dumb idea on Lupe's part," Willie said. "He thought that would somehow mess up your plans, for whatever reason. And, besides, he was pretty shook up when he heard about Sockeye getting killed. He organized the ambush as well. He had no idea you two knew where we was hidin' out."

"Who is the other man that was in the cabin with you?" Nik asked.

"That was Buster Morgan," Willie said. "Too bad about him. He was a lot like me. He had nowhere to turn so he fell in with Sockeye, as well."

"I'm sorry I had to put a bullet in you," Roger said to Willie. "But when I thought you had killed my brother, here, all the thoughts of what Curtain did to my family came rushing back to me. That's why I acted as I did."

"I'm just glad I wasn't standing on the other side of that door when your brother showed up with that shotgun," Willie said, looking at Morgan's mummy-like remains.

About then, Paris came into view and the three men were again lost in the silence of reflecting on what was ahead.

Nik pulled the wagon up in front of the U.S. Marshals Office in Paris and brought the horses to a halt. Roger dismounted and tied Brinker's reins to the hitching rail in front of the office. The deputy then approached the wagon and leaned against the side where Willie was sitting.

"Just be true to yourself," Roger said to the prisoner. "Nik and I only want to help bring law and order to the territory. We have our personal issues but not with you. We think you were drawn into this as the only thing available to you, and we do not begrudge you for that. In fact, Nik and I will do all we can to see that you get a fair trial and fair treatment.

"I have a spare Bible if you would like one," Roger concluded.

"Thanks, deputy, but I don't read so well," Willie said. "I'm not sure what good that would do me."

"I understand," Roger responded. "But I'm going to give you one, anyway. Hopefully, you'll get an opportunity to learn to read, and there's no better book to learn from than the Bible."

"Much obliged," Willie said. "I ain't never had a book before. Just havin' it could make some folks think different of me."

Roger stepped over to his saddlebags and pulled out a Bible and gave it to Willie. Nik entered the office to get some help with the bodies. He emerged with two office assistants.

"These fellas will take the wagon over to the coroner to complete the record," Nik said to Roger. "Willie will come inside with us for processing."

After helping Willie out of the back of the buckboard, the two assistants drove the wagon down the street to the coroner. Nik and Roger stepped inside the marshal's office with Willie and explained the situation to Marshal Oliver. Willie took a seat across the desk from the chief marshal.

Nik began, "We've got nothing more on Willie, here, than the gunfight that erupted at that cabin in the woods by the Sulphur River. He was hit in the shoulder, and we took him to a kind lady, a former nurse in the war, who patched him up. After a visit to the doc in Mount Pleasant, I think he's close to healing, but I don't think the long ride helped any."

"What's your last name, Willie?" Ken asked.

Willie sat silent for a moment and then looked over at Roger. Roger nodded in an affirmative manner and motioned for Willie to answer.

"Warneke," Willie said. "William Warneke."

"Thank you, Willie," Ken said. "We'll check our records to see what warrants may be out for you. In the meantime, we'll have to keep you locked up here until we've had time to process this situation."

Ken, Nik and Roger walked Willie into the back room where three iron-barred holding cells were located. Marshal Oliver unlocked one of the cells and motioned to Willie to enter. Willie did so, looking a little forlorn, and took a seat on the small bunk in the cell.

"I'll have the doc come over to take a look at your wound, Willie," Ken said. "If you're hungry, I'll have some grub sent over."

"Not hungry just now," Willie answered, and he lied down on the bed and stared at the ceiling.

The marshal turned, unlocked a second jail cell and spoke to Nik.

"I'm sorry, deputy, but I'll have to lock you up, too," Ken said.

"What?" Nik exclaimed. "Why me?"

"Seems Judge Kensington filed a complaint against you," Ken said. "Something about an unlawful assault on the Sulphur River cabin without a warrant."

"Unlawful assault!? I just asked everyone inside to come out peaceable-like," Nik lamented.

"Complaint says you were the one who started the shootin'," Ken said.

"Nik just fired his gun in the air to get their attention, that's all," Roger offered in Nik's defense.

"I'd hang onto that testimony," Ken said to Roger. "For whatever reason, you weren't included in the complaint.

"Sorry, Nik," Oliver continued, motioning for Nik to enter the cell, "but until this thing gets cleared up, I have orders to put you under arrest."

Nik took off his gun belt, handed it to Ken and entered the cell. Roger then turned to Willie's cell.

"Willie, you know what happened, right?" Roger said.

Willie sat up and looked at Roger, then down at the Bible he had beside him on the bunk. He again looked up at the deputy and gave him a slight smile. Roger wasn't sure what that smile meant. He could only hope the effort Nik and he made during their journey had influenced their prisoner in a positive way.

"Oh, Nik, by the way," Ken said, "I received word that the Treasury Department has an agent who is going to look into that homestead matter that involved Judge Kensington. He should be here in a couple of days."

"Looks like this is a standoff between two forces of the law," Nik said. "Unfortunately, I'm the deputy and he's the judge."

"So now what?" Roger asked Marshal Oliver as the two left the cell room and entered the office.

"We wait," Ken said. "Unless we come up with some mitigating evidence, my hands are tied."

"Well, mine aren't," Roger said. "How can I help in this case?"

"The quickest way would be to get Kensington to drop his complaint," Ken said. "I wish I could tell you how to go about that, but I'm afraid I really don't know."

"Kensington isn't going to be the judge presiding over this, is he?" Roger asked.

"It depends on judge availability," Ken said. "It wouldn't be the most prudent situation to have Kensington adjudicate this, but I would hate to see Nik sit in jail until another judge could be brought in.

"However, if the Treasury agent turns up anything, they would likely suspend Kensington and appoint a new judge to the territory," Ken mused. "You might speed things up by helping the Treasury agent do his investigation."

"I will do that, but there is something else," Roger said. "How can I get my hands on Willie's record, providing he has one?"

Just then, the two office assistants returned.

"These two guys can help you," Ken said. "Try the courthouse. My assistants are fantastic at poring through the paperwork."

Taking the marshal's advice, Roger and the two assistants visited the courthouse and found that Willie was, as he said, a raider with Quantrill's outfit that included being on a list of crimes he was implicated in. He was also implicated in a possible bank hold-up in Dallas during the previous year and he had been seen in the company of outlaw Denton Sammon, otherwise known as "Sockeye." After spending the afternoon viewing the records with the assistants, Roger then caught up with Marshal Oliver in his office.

"Ken, Willie may be able to help us if we help him," Roger said.

"Do you think you can persuade him?" Ken asked. "I'm not sure how much we can do for him."

"Willie has a warrant for minor war crimes, having ridden with Quantrill, and a possible bank hold-up. However, the evidence is circumstantial at best," Roger started. "That means, even if he's convicted of anything, he's likely to get off with a light sentence. We can present him with what we have and tell him we'll work to get his name cleared if he helps us. He will know we have the goods, but only he knows the extent of his guilt and may jump at the chance to turn state's evidence.

"Secondly, if war crimes are his biggest concern, we could possibly get the Treasury agent to plead for clemency in Willie's case since he was under Quantrill's thumb.

"Third," Roger continued, "if Willie is willing to testify on our behalf, could you let Nik out in my custody?"

"One and two are easy enough to do, but I would have to petition Judge Kensington to get the third one done," Ken said.

"If Willie speaks on Nik's behalf, it might be that Kensington would want Nik out of jail rather than here under your protection," Roger said. "I know it's risky, but we're aware that some of the men from the Sulphur River outfit were already planning to ambush Nik and me. If Kensington thinks he can get those men to carry through with that, I would bet he'd rather see us dead than on the witness stand."

"Sounds like you have a handle on this," Ken said. "I've already sent word to Marshal Borchers about this. He will also be showing up here in a day or so."

"Excellent, Borchers is definitely an ally," Roger replied. "Now, if I may, could I speak with Willie?"

"Sure, I'll let you in," Ken said.

The marshal let Roger into Willie's cell, while Nik sat on the bunk in his cell and watched, assured that his brother was working on his behalf. Roger sat down next to Willie and picked up the Bible.

"Willie, we found your record and know what you are wanted for. Although there are federal crimes you are facing, we feel confident we can help you," Roger advised. "But it's important that you cooperate because Washington, D.C., likes cooperation, and the federal government has the power to pardon you."

With that, Roger opened the Bible.

"Willie, you said your Ma took you to church, so I'm going to assume you know who Jesus is, right?" Roger asked.

"Yeah, I know who He is," Willie said, looking at Roger.

"So let me read you a passage from St. John," Roger began. "Then Jesus said to those who believed in him 'If ye continue in my word, then are ye my disciples indeed. And ye shall know the truth, and the truth will make you free.'"

Roger continued "'Verily, verily, I say unto you, whosoever commits sin is the servant of sin,' but 'if the Son shall make you free, ye shall be free indeed.'

"Jesus has put you on the road to recovery, Willie," Roger concluded. "Please let Him, and us, help you."

Roger closed the Bible and gave it back to Willie, while looking directly into the prisoner's eyes.

"God bless," Roger said and then turned and called to the marshal. "Ken, I'm ready to go now."

Ken returned and let Roger out of Willie's cell. Roger glanced at Nik, who was still sitting on his bunk, but with a slight smile on his face. Ken and Roger then left the cell area and returned to the office.

"Hopefully I planted a seed," Roger said to Ken. "Now all we can do is wait."

Chapter 28

The next day, Roger got out of bed, dressed and crossed the street to enjoy a hearty breakfast before heading back to the marshal's office. After eating, he walked into the office only to see Oliver, Borchers and Nik sitting at the marshal's desk.

"What have we here?" Roger said, with an expression of bewilderment on his face.

Nik jumped up, grabbed his brother by the shoulder and gave him a grateful slap on the back. "You did it, brother," Nik said.

"It worked," Ken commented. "Willie called me in last night, after you left, and explained to me what happened. Nik confirmed what he said and indicated you would too. Ned said Nik could be released on the chief marshal's recognizance by the authority of the U.S. Marshal Service."

"But we've got some work yet to do," Ned said. "The Treasury agent arrives today by train, and we'll work out a method to proceed. Meanwhile, you two watch your backs," Ned said to Nik and Roger, "when the word reaches Kensington, he's sure to let Sockeye's gang know."

"Just one more thing," Roger said to Ken. "I would like to speak to Willie again, if I may."

"You certainly may," Ken said, while getting up from behind his desk. "You seem to have a way with him."

Ken then let Roger into Willie's cell and returned to the office.

"Willie, you just took a huge step forward in your rehabilitation," Roger said, as he sat down on the bunk. "And I just want to say, there is much more work to be done. And I want you to know that you, Nik, me and marshals Oliver and Borchers are in this thing together.

"You may not be able to read, but you have an incredible capacity to understand." Roger concluded. "I extend my gratitude and look forward to better days to come."

Roger shook Willie's hand and detected a new sparkle in the prisoner's eye. Roger called out to Ken to let him out of the cell.

As Roger was going out of the cell door, Willie said, "Marshall, you forgot to say, 'God bless.'"

Roger turned and said, "I may have forgotten, but God never does." Both men smiled.

The next day, the four lawmen met the Treasury agent at the train depot. The agent was neatly dressed in a gray jacket, gray pinstriped pants, plus a black vest, highly polished black boots and a black classic bowler hat on his head. He was also carrying a brass-tipped walking cane.

"Gentlemen, from the reflection of your badges, I assume you are the local constabulary come to greet me," the man said, smiling. "Allow me to introduce myself. I am Special Agent Sebastian Mason, Department of the Treasury."

The four lawmen grinned back at the agent, shook his hand and introduced themselves. Ken checked the agent into the local hotel and then the five men made their way to the marshal's office to discuss strategy. Little did the lawmen know they were being watched as they walked across the street to the marshal's office.

"I recognize the black cowboy. Sockeye tried to talk him into riding with us, but who's the guy in the fancy duds?" Lupe Rodriguez peered at the men from his second-story room window of the Plantation Hotel.

"The black cowboy is actually a deputy marshal. He and the other deputy are brothers," said a voice from behind Lupe. "I fear the man in the fancy duds is a federal agent from the Treasury Department. I wouldn't mind seeing him dead, either. Marshal Oliver is probably onto us now, as well."

Lupe turned around in the direction of the voice to face Judge Kensington and said, "There's four marshals and a Treasury agent? You know killing all those lawmen is going to cost you plenty."

"If you fail, it could cost us all plenty," the judge said. "It could even cost you your life. I'm not too worried about the other marshal, who Packard said is from Kansas. I don't think he knows us. But they will all come after you if you come up short, so suit yourself."

Lupe turned and looked out the window once again and then let the drape fall, obscuring the view. "I'll talk to the boys, but money talks even louder," he said. "I'll come up with a plan, but I doubt I'll get much support if I can't back it up with cash."

"I can get my hands on a grand," the judge said. "That's going to have to tide the boys over until I can return, but I'm not coming back until the job is done."

"That's not much," Lupe said. "Although, those who hung around after Sockeye's death are killers."

"Fine, those who say no are out of luck. Anyone who declines means more for those who go along," said Kensington. "I'm not the only one who would benefit from a reduction in law enforcement."

"Where you goin', anyway?" Lupe inquired. "How can I convince the men that you're coming back with the final payment?"

"Where I'm going is none of your business," Kensington answered. "If the job is done properly, I'll still be the judge in these parts. That's reason enough for me to return. Besides, you boys might need me on the bench until this thing blows over."

"I don't necessarily like it," Lupe said, "but with Sockeye and you gone, our only choice is to get the job done. Who else are we gonna turn to?"

"You'll do fine, Lupe," Kensington said. "I always thought you were the brains of the outfit. Sockeye just happened to be the man with the guts to follow through."

Lupe had been loyal to Sockeye and didn't respond to Kensington's flattery but changed the conversation to how the judge figured to get him the money. The two men settled on the arrangements and then Judge Kensington departed.

Some other men were also making plans, those in the U.S. Marshals Office.

"Gentlemen," Agent Mason began, "the Treasury Department has reason to believe that local Magistrate Kensington may have been involved in a number of shady land deals. Our thanks go to Deputy Marshal Brinkman's effort to bring it to our attention."

Mason said Kensington had been moving up through the ranks by volunteering to serve as circuit judge in remote areas where homesteading was practiced.

"Following Deputy Brinkman's lead," Mason said, "we found Kensington was often the ruling magistrate where these incidents of land fraud occurred."

Mason said a sham land office would approach the judge with a speculation deed that Kensington would sanction. The deed always claimed the existing homesteads legally belonged to the counterfeit land office, which demanded payment for them. Some vacated their homesteads, but those nearing their five-year commitment paid up.

"Those who remained took out loans and paid the land office," Mason continued. "Shortly thereafter the land office would close up and disappear."

The Treasury agent added that Kensington would claim fraud and offer to buy some of those abandoned homesteads at a discount. The judge claimed he was doing it to help make up for his oversight.

"What we need is evidence he received money in those deals," Mason concluded. "That's what we hope to find here."

"What did he do with those properties he bought?" Roger asked.

"He would promptly sell them and then put in for a transfer," Mason answered. "As it stands, he can claim that is where he got his money, but it doesn't explain his lavish lifestyle."

"He does put on the airs," Marshal Oliver chimed in. "So, what do we need to arrest Kensington?"

"We need evidence he received monetary kickbacks," Mason said. "Without that, we cannot prove guilt."

"So far, great work, Sebastian," Borchers said. "And you too, Nik and Roger, for putting the Treasury Department onto this scheme."

"By the way," Mason said, "how is it that you deputies are both Brinkmans. Is there a connection?"

"Yeah," Nik said, "we're brothers."

"I see," Mason mused, looking a bit puzzled while the others broke into laughter. Nik and Roger then explained to Mason how their "brotherhood" came about.

Then Roger asked, "What about those phony land office proprietors?"

"We have yet to find one," Mason said. "But it does appear they were drifters, for the most part. They used their actual names to make things look more legal. I'm sure Kensington insisted on that, so if questioned, he could say he acted in good faith."

"They could easily adopt an alias afterward and use the money to travel to parts unknown, like Mexico," Oliver surmised. "Without catching them in the act, law enforcement would have little to go on."

"Men, we've got to be on our guard," Borchers said. "Kensington knows we're onto him, and the word has probably spread to the other members of the Sulphur River outfit. There's no telling what they might try."

"Willie also indicated to me that there are outlaws in that gang we don't know about," Nik said. "And I noticed Agent Mason doesn't wear a gun, either."

"Not quite true," said Mason, who raised his arm and a double-barreled derringer suddenly appeared in his hand. "I am not as harmless as I may look," the agent added with a smile, while tucking the mechanized weapon back up his sleeve. "I might add, it may look like a small pistol, but I assure you it will dispatch a man at twenty meters."

"Anything else we need to know about?" Ken Oliver asked.

"Although you have my utmost trust, gentlemen," Mason continued, "there are some things best left unsaid. Now, let us formulate a plan."

Roger and Sebastian were assigned to find the whereabouts of Judge Kensington and locate, if possible, any of the judge's land office co-conspirators. Nik, Ned and Ken agreed they would make it their job to determine where the rest of the Sulphur River gang could be. It was decided that Oliver would check in and around

Paris in case any of the outlaws had come to town while Nik and Borchers set out for Clarksville to pay Sheriff Packard a visit.

Lupe Rodriguez rode out of town and met Judge Kensington at Rock Creek. Curtis Packard was waiting there with him.

"Did anyone follow you?" Kensington asked, as Lupe rode up to the judge's carriage.

"No, why's the sheriff here?" Lupe asked.

"He's here to see that I get my money's worth," Kensington answered. "He'll be your contact to let me know when the job is done. Just so you understand, there's a grand apiece for you and those who help when I get back." Kensington reached into the back of his buggy, brought out a canvas bag and handed it to Lupe. "Here's your thousand dollars in small bills. Use it wisely, there's more where this came from."

"This won't tide us over for long," Lupe said, "but I don't expect this job to take us more than a few days."

"Curtis will inform me when it's safe to come back," Kensington said. "Once those lawmen are out of the way we can get back to business."

Lupe took the canvas bag and glanced inside. He then nodded, touched the tip of his hat and rode off in the direction of Paris.

"Do you think you can trust him?" Packard said, once Lupe was out of earshot.

"Too much is at stake not to," Kensington said. "Besides, I got word to Levi that I was giving the money to Lupe. The Leviathan will see to it that Lupe plays his cards straight."

"Yeah, Lupe wouldn't want to cross Levi," Packard remarked.

Roger and Sebastian stopped by Judge Kensington's office only to find a sign in the window indicating the judge would be away and to leave any notices for the magistrate at the Lamar County Courthouse or office of the U.S. Marshal.

"Why don't you check the land records at the courthouse, and I'll visit the local bank to see if there were any recent foreclosures," Roger said to Mason.

Roger walked along the street in Paris, unaware that the man riding by him on horseback was Lupe Rodriguez. Upon seeing Roger, Lupe tugged the brim of his hat to shade his eyes, not knowing if Roger could identify him. Lupe relaxed a little in his saddle when he noticed Roger had paid him no attention.

A spokesman at the bank told Roger there were no recent foreclosures that he knew of in Lamar County. The bank owner said that as far as he knew none of the homesteads were in any kind of financial trouble.

Roger again met up with Mason, who also found no land deals that would cast further suspicion on the judge.

"I am not surprised that Kensington didn't involve himself in any shabby real estate deals here," Mason said. "His office is located here, and I imagine he has a home in this area, as well. It is likely he practiced his foul trade in places that have yet to establish a reliable archive of public records."

"When Nik and I passed through Tarrant a few days back, it was a county seat in transition," Roger said. "The seat was being moved to Sulphur Springs. I think that's where I'll try next."

"Then I shall tag along," said Sebastian.

"It's a two-day ride on horseback," Roger said. "Do you want to rent a buggy?"

"My dear deputy," Mason began, "I rode with General Hampton's cavalry."

"You fought with the Confederacy?" Roger exclaimed.

"No, dear fellow, I was part of a reconnaissance unit assigned to Hampton and was given pretty much free rein," Mason said. "I would then take Hampton's plans and deliver them to the nearest Union encampment. I ended up in a Union uniform after Hampton caught onto my shenanigans."

"All right, let's get you a horse," Roger said.

The two set out for Sulphur Springs early the next morning, Sebastian was still wearing the suit he arrived in. He also exchanged his walking cane for an umbrella, with a unique head curved in the shape of a dolphin. A drizzle was starting to fall, so Sebastian unpacked an overcoat and opened his umbrella while Roger donned his poncho before they rode off.

They were unaware that ahead of them were Lupe and Levi, the silent giant. They were also headed for Sulphur Springs.

"I don't know, Levi," Lupe said, "seems to me we have the money. I think we ought to just head west and forget about starting a war with those lawmen."

"No," Levi said.

"But we don't owe that judge nothing," Lupe pleaded. "We never got this much money from Sockeye."

"No!" Levi repeated, this time with more conviction.

The storm started to increase, so the two found a wooded area where they planned to camp for the night. A few miles behind, Roger and Sebastian continued to ride through the storm. Roger was holding his poncho tightly around his neck against the rain. The deputy could see that Sebastian was at home in the saddle, although he looked almost comical holding his umbrella over his head.

As they rode past where Lupe and Levi were camped, Sebastian's horse neighed and snorted, picking up the scent of the outlaw's horses. Levi's horse responded with a neigh, but Lupe quickly stepped over to quiet the animal. He then signaled to Levi to look after the horses while he worked his way to the edge of the trees to get a better look at the trail.

"Did you hear something, Roger?" Sebastian asked, patting his mount on the neck.

Roger, who had been listening to the rain fall on his hat, said, "Just your horse."

Spotting the two riders and realizing who they were, Lupe quietly returned to where Levi was waiting.

In a low voice, Lupe said, "It's two of the lawmen. We'll wait for a bit and then follow them. We may get our chance to earn some of this money the easy way."

As Lupe watched, Roger and Sebastian made their way into a nearby grove of trees to make camp. They found a spot with enough shelter to at least get them out of the direct downpour. The storm continued, giving every indication that it was not going to be a night to get much rest.

Roger didn't bother to start a fire. The two men found a downed tree and were able to construct a makeshift shelter. They then dined on jerky and water. After the scant meal, Mason produced a flask of brandy. He removed the cap and used it to pour a shot of the liquor. After consuming the capful's contents, he offered some to the deputy, who politely declined.

Assured of where the two lawmen made camp, Lupe told Levi they would wait until just before dawn to move in. Lupe positioned himself where he could see if their quarry decided to leave earlier than that. The storm let up as the night wore on, and with the parting clouds, the sky was beginning to brighten. Lupe and Levi quietly approached the lawmen's camp and made their presence known.

"Time to get up, boys," Lupe called out to the sleeping lawmen. "It's the end of the trail."

Both Roger and Sebastian sat up shaking off a fitful night's sleep only to see Lupe pointing his pistol at them, accompanied by a hulk of a man who stood without a weapon.

"If you're looking to rob us, we don't have much," Roger said, glancing at his gun belt lying next to him.

"Don't get any ideas of going for your gun," Lupe commanded. "And you," he said, looking at the agent, "get your hands in the air."

Mason complied, releasing the derringer into his hand, and he immediately fired. The round caught Lupe in the midsection and the outlaw staggered back and fell on his backside. Roger seized the opportunity and grabbed his gun as Levi lunged at the two men. The giant managed to knock Roger's gun away, but Sebastian sent his second shot into Levi's knee. When Levi reached for his wounded knee, the agent came around with his umbrella and hit the enormous assailant on the side of the head. The blow knocked him to the ground unconscious. Roger quickly retrieved his gun, pointing it at Lupe, who was now lying on his back.

"Let me get a look at the downed man's wound," Sebastian said, while quickly moving to Lupe's side. The agent tore open Lupe's shirt to see that the slug had caught the outlaw in the side.

"I may have missed any vital organs, which means this man should live," Mason said. "Gather up the weapons because I think the big fellow will be coming to, presently."

Roger picked up the pistol that Lupe dropped and found no weapon on Levi after frisking him.

"I've got to admit, you may not look it, but you do come prepared for just about any situation," Roger said. "I'm surprised you didn't break your umbrella over the giant's head."

"Not much chance of that," Mason said. "This umbrella contains a .44 caliber, 1860 Henry rifle barrel, accurate up to one-hundred yards. Unfortunately, it's just single shot."

"Unfortunately," Roger repeated, sarcastically. "You agents come equipped with everything, don't you?"

"We have to, old chap," Mason said. "There really aren't many of us to go around and we're hard to replace. By the by, who are these men?" Mason asked.

"I really don't know," Roger answered, "perhaps just a couple of road agents or maybe guys from the Sulphur River gang."

"Fascinating," Mason said, "judging from whatever their vocations, the big fellow seems to eat well."

About that time, Levi let out a groan.

"I'm glad you only wounded him," Roger said. "Otherwise, I don't know how we would have gotten him back to Paris."

"I typically do not shoot to kill," Mason added. "Wounded men can be a fountain of information, whereas dead men don't talk."

Roger let Sebastian's last remark sink in and gently nodded his head. After their conversation, the two men patched up their assailants as best they could. They retrieved their horses from where the outlaws had left them and discovered the canvas bag of money.

"Sebastian, look at this," Roger said, pulling the bag off Lupe's saddle. "This thing's full of money."

"Spectacular, Brinkman," Mason said. "That money may tell us quite a bit about these two."

"How so?" Roger asked.

"Serial numbers, deputy, serial numbers," Mason replied.

Lupe's wound had stopped bleeding. He was weak but strong enough to ride. Levi said nothing and cooperated with whatever he was asked to do. He used his uninjured leg to mount his horse and sat upright in his saddle.

"Poor creature," Mason muttered, sizing up the horse selected to carry the huge man.

Once in their saddles, the four men made their way back to Paris, with the sun shining bright in a clear blue sky.

After reaching Paris, both prisoners were taken to the local doctor's office to treat their injuries. The doctor removed the bullets from both men and skillfully bound their wounds. From there, Roger and Sebastian took the men over to the U.S. Marshals Office and jailed them in cells opposite Willie. The two outlaws did not notice Warneke, but Willie's face indicated knowledge of them.

Roger looked in at Willie and mouthed the words, "Do you know them?"

Willie nodded slightly, looked down at the floor and then back up at Roger. Roger winked.

Sebastian took the money to the local bank for identification. The Treasury agent learned the money had been drawn out of Judge Victor Giles Kensington's account the day before. Kensington had taken out all the money from his account – ten thousand dollars. The agent recorded several serial numbers and sent a telegram to Basil Gobles, the banker in Mount Pleasant. Within hours, a telegram returned identifying the serial numbers as loan money given to the homesteaders whose properties had fallen into foreclosure. Mason now had the evidence needed to tie Kensington to conspiracy to commit land fraud.

The lawmen were also able to put two and two together to explain how it was that money drawn from Judge Kensington's account ended up in Lupe's possession.

When Nik and Ned returned from Clarksville, they were more than surprised to find Lupe and Levi in jail. Nik explained to everyone who the two former companions of Sockeye were. Ned then mentioned that their trip to Clarksville was in vain. They were told by Packard's assistant that the sheriff was away on official business and wouldn't be back for some time.

"My guess is, the cash in Lupe's bag was blood money," Borchers concluded.

"Hired assassins," Mason chimed in. "Undoubtedly employed to terminate with extreme prejudice."

"You mean, kill us," Roger said, grinning at Sebastian.

"Deputy Brinkman, I have no doubt you shall become a fine lawman one day," the agent said, with a hearty laugh shared by the others. "But I caution you all, there was only a thousand dollars in the possession of Lupe and that behemoth. That means there is nine thousand dollars in someone else's hands."

"Good point, Mason," Borchers said. "We could still be targets for others out there."

"Unless," Nik began, "that scoundrel Kensington took off with the rest of that money with no intention of returning."

"We will have to keep up our vigilance," Oliver added. "But knowing Kensington, I'm inclined to agree with Nik."

The deputy marshals were now aware others may be in on the blood money but did not know how many could be involved. Special Agent Sebastian Mason wired Washington, D.C., to inform officials there of the need for a new circuit judge for the territory. With his work done, Mason was scheduled to leave that evening on the train. He expressed his pleasure over the opportunity to work with the U.S. Marshal Service.

"One other thing," Mason said, "I'm guessing the judge had other bank accounts scattered throughout the district he adjudicated. I would venture ten thousand dollars was not the full extent of his ill-gotten gains. I'm sure Kensington has set about closing all of his accounts, but it would serve justice to know just how many he had."

Mason shook the hands of each officer and offered his farewell. He took leave and returned to the hotel to gather his things.

Borchers announced he would be leaving the next day as well, returning to Wichita. He told Roger and Nik to continue assisting Marshal Oliver in the search for Kensington until further notice.

"Ken can use the help, but all of you need to remain vigilant," Borchers cautioned. "I'd put a high priority on finding Kensington."

The four men decided to have one last dinner together and went across the street to the diner to eat and discuss the day's events.

"Well, Roger, are you ready to saddle up to go after Kensington?" Nik asked, wiping his mustache with his napkin.

Roger stared down at his plate and paused before speaking. "Nik, Ken, I would like to help out with this, but something has been eating at me that I simply have to do. I have to try and find Gloria Fenton, and I won't rest until I do. I have information she may be held by Comanches in Indian Territory.

Nik explained to the others who Gloria was and the circumstances of her disappearance.

"Ned, I understand if this is out of line, and I will turn in my badge, if you would like," Roger said.

"I see no reason to do that, Roger," Borchers commented. "I will simply record this as a missing-person's search. When do you plan to do this?"

"Soon," Roger said. "Though I'm not prepared to do it right away."

"In that case, I suggest you wait 'till spring," Borchers advised. "Winter is upon us, and you don't want to be alone in Indian Territory this time of year. Besides, if Miss Fenton is with the Comanches, she'll still be there in spring."

"I tell you what fellas," Ken said. "I will make arrangements so you and Nik can stay with me and my family until winter blows over. We can celebrate Christmas together. What do you say?"

"That would be terrific, Ken, but we don't want to put you out none," Nik said. "But it has been a while since the Brinkmans spent a Christmas together."

"Then it's settled," Ken said. "I'll let Mary and the kids know you'll be moving in. I have some chores around the house you can help me with, as well."

"One other thing," Borchers added. "I can't spare Nik for your quest, Roger, but I can commission Blue Feather to go with you. He spends his off time in Wichita Village. I'll send word to him of your plans and when you make your decision to leave here, let me know and I'll inform Charlie when to expect you."

"Thanks, Ned," Roger said. "Nik, I'm sorry to drop this on you, like this."

"No problem, brother," Nik began. "I've known this was going to happen. Sorry I can't go with you, but there's no one I would rather see go in my place than Charlie Blue Feather."

After dinner, Ken headed for home and Marshal Borchers secured rooms at the Plantation Hotel for himself and his deputies.

Chapter 29

It had been years since Roger and Nik had celebrated the Christmas season together. The Oliver family welcomed the two deputy marshals into their home and soon the Brinkman brothers felt less like guests and more like part of the family. The Olivers had three children, a boy and two girls. The boy, Stephen, was nearly a teenager, and the two girls, Sissy and Darlene, were two and four years younger. Darlene reminded Roger and Nik of Dolly Brinkman and they could not help but show a little favoritism toward her. However, the other children either didn't mind or did not notice their little sister getting more attention from the two adopted lawmen.

Roger also took time to visit Willie in his cell and help him with his reading. Warneke was a little slow at first, but his enthusiasm over learning how to read accelerated his progress. Reading the Bible proved beneficial, but much of the Scriptures had to be explained. Roger enjoyed doing that but knew his pupil needed something more secular to become proficient. Roger began bringing Willie other books that were easier to read to improve his comprehension. However, Roger still encouraged Willie to continue his Bible study. The other bright spot was that Willie's shoulder was healing nicely, and he was beginning to regain full use of it.

Although Roger, Nik and Ken engaged in a concerted effort to find Judge Kensington, they were hampered by winter weather, with no clue as to where the judge-turned-fugitive may have decided to hide out.

As the winter moved through January, the weather turned too cold for rain.

"Why don't you boys ride into Clarksville and see if you can find Sheriff Packard," Ken Oliver said, addressing the two deputies. "Chances are he's staying closer to home these days."

"What do you say, Roger?" Nik said. "I think Packard could be a fountain of information if we asked the right questions."

"Like, what he was doing that day at the hideout and where he disappeared afterward?" Roger remarked. "He knows far more about us than we do him."

"He's shrewd that way," Nik replied.

Marshal Oliver sent the deputies by rail, as traveling by horseback was difficult in winter. After reaching the depot at Clarksville, a light snowfall greeted Roger and Nik, as they made their way to the hotel and checked in. From there they went straight to Packard's office. Much to their surprise, they found him, and he had a warm fire going in the facility's potbelly stove.

"Well, if it isn't my two favorite deputy marshals," Packard said, when the Brinkmans walked in. "I did not expect to see you this time of year."

"Business is slow, and we were hoping you could help give us a head start on spring," Nik said, removing his hat and brushing off a few flakes of snow. "Chief Marshal Oliver suggested we call on you to help in our investigation."

"I'll help in any way I can, boys," Packard said, waving his hand at two chairs in the office. "Have a seat."

The two deputies apprised the sheriff as to the charges being brought against Judge Kensington and opened by asking Packard if he knew of the magistrate's whereabouts.

"I wish I knew where Judge Kensington was," Packard said. "We need a judge in this town, and I suppose we won't get one until spring."

"I'm afraid this isn't one of the more popular districts to serve," Nik replied. "Chief Borchers and I came by to see you last month, following our unfortunate meeting at the Sulphur River hideout. But you weren't here."

"That meeting was unfortunate," Packard remarked. "But to make a long story short, after Kensington and I got back, I asked him to adjudicate a prisoner I had locked up here.

"However, Kensington said he had an urgent matter to attend to and boarded a train back to Paris," Packard concluded. "I haven't seen him since."

The local lawman added that he sent a telegram to Kensington, asking when he would return to hold court.

"I did not get an answer, so I had to transport my prisoner to Upshur County to catch the circuit judge there," Packard explained. "That took a while and was probably about the time you and the marshal showed up here."

"I have to ask why you and the judge were at the Sulphur River hideout that day Roger and I came upon the place," Nik said, studying the sheriff's face.

Packard explained that Judge Kensington arrived in Clarksville shortly after hearing of Sockeye's death and insisted the sheriff take him to the Sulphur River hideout.

"Did Kensington say why he wanted to visit the hideout? I thought you had an understanding you would not go near their place if they stayed out of Clarksville?" Roger inquired.

"Kensington didn't say why he wanted to go there," Packard continued. "I agreed to go because Sammon was the one behind my hands-off agreement with that group," Packard said, with no hint of anxiety. "I was hoping to find someone else with enough clout to maintain that arrangement."

"Why did you open fire on us and then try to run?" Nik questioned.

"To be quite honest, I suggested we simply come out peaceful-like. We hadn't broken any laws, but the two men we found there seemed determined to fight. When all hell broke loose, the judge grabbed me and pulled me out the backdoor."

Packard looked at Roger and said he thought the trouble had ended when Roger ordered them to stop, but the judge took off again when another shot rang out.

"I don't know why I went after Kensington when he mounted his horse. It wasn't until later I realized I should have stayed to make sure you guys were all right," the sheriff offered, with a look of genuine concern. "I guess I kind of felt it was my job to stick with the judge. I'm sorry about that, but thankful you boys are obviously okay. I hope you don't suspect me of being mixed up in anything."

"We weren't sure, Curtis," Nik remarked. "A lot happened that day, but it wasn't you we were concerned about. It had more to do with your ties to Kensington, not the Sulphur River gang."

"As I said, I needed the judge to handle my prisoner's case," the sheriff responded. "I had no idea he was part of some land deal."

"We're just glad you're on our side," Roger chipped in. "Our official visit was to find out what we could about Judge Kensington."

"By the way, you don't happen to know how many men were connected to that Sulphur River bunch, do you?" Nik asked.

"Other than Sammon and those we ran into out there, no," the sheriff replied. "I'm sure there were more than those three, though."

"There were, but just how many we don't know," Roger said, turning to his brother. "Nik, do you have any more questions?"

"Not really," Nik said, extending his hand to shake Packard's. "I truly appreciate your help, Curtis."

"Anytime, gents," replied Packard, taking the time to shake Roger's hand as well. "The last thing I want is trouble, especially from the U.S. Marshal Service."

Nik and Roger then crossed the street to their hotel room.

"I still don't trust that man," Nik said. "I've got to admit his story was pretty good, although I'm curious why he didn't find out Kensington's reason for visiting that hideout before taking him there. There's just something about Packard that bothers me."

"Maybe you're just too suspicious," Roger said, thinking back on previous encounters with the sheriff. "If he's crooked, he certainly knows how to cover his tracks. However, he did say his agreement was with Sammon, and earlier he told me he didn't know Sockeye other than by reputation. Think we ought to pay another visit to that hideout?"

"I was going to say no," Nik said, "but I think if we go there, and

Packard knows we're going, it could lead him into making a mistake. If that doesn't happen, it may help me to set aside some of my suspicions."

"Let's do it, then," Roger said. "We'll get a couple horses from the livery stable tomorrow and tell Packard what we're going to do. That way it'll look more like we're cooperating with his authority."

"Smart," Nik said. "You might make it as a marshal after all."

"Why not, I've had one of the best mentors in the business," Roger said, with a grin.

The next morning, the temperature warmed a few degrees and a storm rolled in, complete with lightning and thunder. Anticipating the worst from the seasonal weather, the two deputies had brought along their winter gear and dressed appropriately. They made certain they had plenty of ammunition, including bullets for Nik's boot pistol. They still had no idea how many desperate men were using that hideout.

They checked in with Packard, and he seemed unconcerned, other than to tell them to be careful and check in with him when they returned. The sheriff lent them two rifles to add to their arsenal in case there was trouble. After leaving the sheriff's office, Nik and Roger secured two horses from the Clarksville Livery Stable and set out in the storm to make their way to the Sulphur River. The deputies used the cover of the forest along the river to avoid detection, then dismounted and approached the cabin on foot. As soon as they were in sight of the structure, they stood in the rain with disbelief on their faces.

"What in the world...," Roger began. "What happened to the place?"

The cabin had been burned to the ground. They approached cautiously and spent some time sifting through the rain-soaked debris and rubble but found nothing that gave them any clue as to who started the fire or why the cabin had been torched.

"Somebody wanted to put an end to this chapter of the Sulphur River gang," Nik commented, kicking over a charred piece of wood. "I can understand abandoning this place, knowing it was compromised, but why burn it to the ground?"

"There must have been clues we missed after confronting Willie and that Morgan fella," Roger suggested. "I assume whatever it may have been has since gone up in smoke."

The Brinkmans returned to their horses and rode back to Clarksville, offering different scenarios of where their combined investigations had taken them.

"We've made some progress," Nik said. "Sammon and one outlaw is dead and three are in jail. However, Kensington is still at large."

"Unfortunately, I think Packard was our best hope for finding the judge," Roger surmised. "Wherever Kensington is, he's probably safe from us for the winter."

"Packard was no help, and the hideout is now a heap of ash," Nik mused. "I believe the Sulphur River saga is at a dead end now."

"That makes Packard's involvement in all this moot, as well," Roger surmised. "Now we wait until spring."

"When you will be on your way to Comanche country in search of Gloria," Nik added, as the two lawmen continued their ride toward Clarksville.

After reaching the town, the two men stopped in at the sheriff's office to report their findings, but as usual, Packard was absent. Nik scribbled a note and left it with the sheriff's assistant, and they departed to have dinner.

"Where do you suppose he's gone now?" Nik wondered, poking at his food, and lifting his head to look at Roger. "I'm beginning to detect a pattern here. First, Packard sends us on a wild goose chase, making us promise to check in when we return. When we do, he's nowhere to be found."

"It's as if he picks our brains and then takes what he knows to someone else," Roger surmised. "Do you suppose he relates all this to Kensington? Sockeye's out of the picture."

"It would not surprise me if he were doing something like that," Nik replied, tossing his napkin on the table. "But I don't know what he could tell the judge, other than the fact we're after him but have no clue where he is."

"Not having a clue as to where Kensington is could be all the judge needs to know," Roger offered. The two men nodded in agreement, paid their bill and returned to the hotel.

They checked for messages, but there were none. They went up to their room to wait for some word from Packard, but it never came.

The next morning, they packed their gear and made one more attempt to find the sheriff, only to be told he'd left town without leaving word as to where he was going. Weary of the run-around, the two deputies boarded the train for Paris.

"I had hoped our visit to that hideout would help to explain some things," Nik said, as the two men took their seats. "Now I'm more conflicted than when we arrived."

"I think I've had it with Sheriff Packard," Roger replied. "He seems so helpful when you talk to him, but when we need him, he vanishes."

"Why does he keep asking for us to check in with him?" Nik mused, stroking his mustache. "It's obvious he really doesn't care."

After returning to Paris, the two deputies resumed looking for leads concerning Judge Kensington's disappearance. They grilled Lupe and Levi, but neither had much to offer, other than their displeasure over sitting in jail.

"Look at it this way, gentlemen," Nik stated. "Once you're sentenced for attempted murder, you'll get credit for time served."

Marshal Oliver would allow Willie Warneke to leave his cell when the deputies agreed to keep him in their custody. Lupe would shout warnings at Willie about the consequences of "squealing," but Willie learned to ignore them. Ken Oliver had put them in adjacent cells so they would not have to look at each other. Willies' cell was also closer to the office door so his coming and going wouldn't be as noticeable.

When the weather permitted, the deputies would either dig for clues on Kensington or help the Olivers build onto their home. Ken was also constructing a stall for horses. His son, Stephen, proved a skilled carpenter, helping when not in school or doing homework.

"What do you plan to do when you grow up?" Roger asked Stephen one day as they stacked logs for the corral.

"I'm not sure," Stephen answered, struggling as the pile of wood grew. "My Pa wants me to go to college, but I'm not so good with book learning."

"You should get Nik to help you," Roger said from above, where he was helping Ken nail down the roof of the stall. "He started school several years behind me and learned so fast that he almost finished before I did. He's a smart guy."

"Is that right, Mr. Nik?" Stephen asked, as Nik started a new log pile.

"Don't let my brother kid you," Nik said, while stacking the timbers. "He's the college boy. I only appeared to learn fast because of Roger's help, but I would be glad to assist you where I can."

The Brinkman brothers' assistance around the Oliver home made the winter go faster. They helped Stephen with his schoolwork and Ken to complete his home improvements. Although the search for Kensington had stalled, they got a breakthrough on the judge's paid assassins.

To keep from alerting Lupe and Levi, Willie requested a bathroom break. After entering the main office, he informed the marshals of what he'd learned from his former outlaw companions.

"I asked Lupe if he knew where the rest of the gang had gone," Willie said, as he sat by Marshal Oliver's desk safely out of earshot of the jail cell area. "During the conversation, Lupe said Kensington asked him to talk to the others about his plan. But Lupe never said what the plan was."

"So, there are others?" Ken asked.

"Only if the judge met with 'em," Willie said, lowering his voice just in case. "Lupe and Levi never caught up with the others. Lupe thought killing Deputy Brinkman and that Eastern dandy would mean more money for him and Levi, but that plan backfired."

"That means Agent Mason and I were the first on the hit list," Roger chimed in, as Willie signaled for him to speak softer. "Sorry," Roger whispered. "But it means the others likely never knew of Kensington's plans."

"And I'll bet Kensington took off with the rest of the money," Nik interjected. "My guess is he figured Lupe would foolishly do his dirty work for a thousand bucks, and with us out of the way, the judge would get away scot-free."

"Great work Willie," Roger said. "Ken, can this be entered to help in Willie's defense?"

"I'll say," Oliver responded. "Willie should be considered for a citation, not a trial."

Willie could not hold back his sheepish grin as Roger and Nik patted him on the back.

***

Spring finally arrived, and both deputies were anxious to return to their tasks at hand. With the weather warming and the leaves returning to the deciduous trees, it came time for Kensington's replacement to arrive.

"Gentlemen, Judge Beauregard J. Lewis at your service," said the distinguished-looking magistrate disembarking from the train. "I trust you are my welcoming committee?"

"I'm U.S. Chief Deputy Marshal Ken Oliver and these are deputies, Nik and Roger Brinkman," Oliver said, extending his hand to the new judge. "Welcome to Paris and the great state of Texas."

"Thank you, marshal," Lewis said, then turned his attention to Nik and Roger. "The Brinkman brothers, agent Mason told me about you boys. Roger, I guess you and Sebastian had a pretty close call while he was here."

"Yes, but thanks to Sebastian's remarkable weaponry we were able to fight our way out of it," Roger said, offering an expression that resembled relief.

"Circumstances are a bit different back East," Lewis said. Nik and Roger picked up the judge's bags as the men walked in the direction of a large carriage. "The agents have to be especially careful because the times are a-changing, and so is the profession of criminal behavior. Out here, I understand, enforcing the law is more a matter of courage and marksmanship."

"We also have to employ some clever tactics, on occasion," Nik said, thinking of the pistol hidden in his boot. "Although our outlaws are probably less sophisticated than, perhaps, they are back East. Being the fastest draw doesn't always favor the lawman."

"And, I would say in Judge Kensington's case, a more sophisticated brand of crime is also moving out West," Lewis said, as the bags were loaded onto the carriage and the men climbed on board. "Sorry to hear that about Victor. I always thought he was a good magistrate."

"Our hands are kept full, with renegade Indians and die-hard rebels," Oliver remarked, snapping the reins. "I'm afraid Judge Kensington has introduced us to a side of law enforcement we're not that used to."

"Hopefully, between the four of us, we can start to change that," said Lewis. "I'll inform you as to the wiles of the East and you can teach me the wilds of the West."

The men shared a laugh over the judge's remark, and they departed for the office now abandoned by Kensington.

As March turned to April, Roger sent word to Borchers that he would be heading out on his search for Gloria Fenton. Borchers wired back to say Charlie Blue Feather would be alerted as to the deputy's plans and wait for Roger in Wichita Village, located in Comanche Territory. Roger planned to ride Brinker and tow a second horse packed with provisions for the trip. Charlie would have his wagon available, and Roger's second horse would then become part of the wagon team. That meant faster traveling through the potentially hostile Llano Estacado.

However, before departing, Roger joined his brother in a meeting with Judge Lewis to clear the complaint that Kensington had filed against Nik. Due to Roger's and Willie's testimonies and the fact Kensington was nowhere to be found to back up the complaint led Lewis to formally dismiss the charge.

With that completed, Roger submitted to a deposition concerning the three prisoners and concluded by giving a glowing recommendation of Willie Warneke.

On Marshal Borchers' request, the trial of the three Sulphur River outlaws was scheduled for late spring. That allowed Nik time to accompany his brother west, as far as Gainesville, Texas, searching for Kensington. Their itinerary took them through several towns, where they hoped to pick up his trail. Gainesville was where Roger would head north following the Indian Trail.

Nik assumed the judge was aware of his fugitive status and the possibility he could even be a target of what remained of the Sulphur River gang. That suggested Kensington was probably headed for Mexico.

Once satisfied as to where the judge was headed, Nik would have to return to Paris in time to testify in the trials of Warneke, Rodriguez and Levi, who apparently had no last name.

***

During an investigation, Marshal Oliver learned that Levi had been enrolled in an orphanage in Arkansas when, as a baby, he was left at the front door of the local sheriff's office. The child grew so rapidly the caretakers of the orphanage dubbed him a Leviathan and gave him the name Levi. The other children in the orphanage teased the overgrown boy to the point he ran away. He was taken in by a homestead family because of his size and ability to work the farm. They were unaware of his age and rarely engaged him in conversation, which suited the quiet giant just fine.

Levi's education was what the farmer taught him. While he continued to grow physically, his training was restricted to the use of his hands and strength. When the homesteaders gave up the farm, the huge man was let go. He later met up with Lupe Rodriguez, a Mexican immigrant. The two became good friends, as Lupe loved to talk, and Levi was content to listen. As drifters, they worked at odd jobs until catching the eye of Denton "Sockeye" Sammon, who introduced them to a life of crime.

***

The weather was warming in north Texas, and Roger was anxious to begin his search for Gloria. Judge Lewis scheduled the trials of the Sulphur River trio in late spring on request from Marshal Borchers. That gave Nik enough time to accompany his brother.

The early spring storms dampened the Brinkmans' progress but not their determination. In Bonham, they found some folks who knew the judge, but no one there had seen him in more than a year.

When they reached Sherman, Nik stopped in to see Sheriff Fred Lane and thanked him again for his assistance in dealing with Sockeye.

"Sheriff Lane helped me when I was in a tight spot with Sockeye and his boys," Nik said, introducing Roger to the sheriff. "Roger is the one who had it out with Sammon, and I'm happy to report Sammon lost.

"I can't say as I'm sorry to hear that," Lane replied, extending his hand to Roger. "I was never happy about having that bunch in town."

Nik filled the sheriff in on the details of Kensington's case. Lane said Kensington was in town several months ago but did not come by the office.

"I expected him to inquire about my possible need to hold court, but he never showed up," Lane said. "I know he was in town because he spoke to some of the locals. You may want to check with them."

After leaving Lane's office, the deputies followed up on the sheriff's leads. Several people had seen Kensington sometime before Christmas, but none knew where he had gone. A storekeeper, who waited on Kensington, said he remembered the judge being in a hurry.

"He was here buying supplies," the storekeeper said. "I remember him leaving in the direction of Gainesville, which was odd because that town's not in his district."

Satisfied with what they learned, Nik took Roger to the Red River

Lodge to check in for the night. Nik requested the same room in which he met with Sockeye, Lupe and Levi.

"I led them on hoping to find out more about them. When I said I was broke, Sockeye fronted me a hundred dollars. I had to take it to avoid suspicion, but I knew I was getting myself into a jam," Nik recalled, as the men entered their room. "But the money helped me buy my way into jail and avoid riding with them. Once I gained Lane's trust, all I had to do was follow them, hoping they would lead me to you."

"You did a heck of a job as an undercover man," Roger said, removing his hat and sitting down. "I'm afraid all I did was botch the operation."

"You certainly didn't botch the second time we paid a visit to the Sulphur River gang's hideout," Nik remarked, sitting on the edge of one of the beds. "You know, you cleaned up that mess almost singlehandedly."

"Well, we really don't know how many of their men were missing that day," Roger said. "It bothers me that some of those men are still running wild."

"Never fear, brother dear," Nik started, getting up and moving over to the washbasin. He removed his hat and hung it on the mirror frame. "If they continue working outside the law, we'll eventually hear about it. Besides, they probably hunkered down for the winter much like we did."

"Do you ever feel you're climbing a topless mountain in this job?" Roger said, somewhat rhetorically, while leaning forward to stretch his back.

"Not really," Nik answered matter-of-factly, while pouring some water in the basin. "If we were able to reach the top of that mountain, we would be out of a job."

"I just hope I can find Gloria," Roger said, paying little attention to Nik's answer.

"With Charlie at your side, your chances are better than good," Nik said. "That is, if Gloria is out there to find."

"I hope that cowboy in Boston knew what he was talking about,"

Roger remarked pensively. "He said Sockeye sold Gloria to the Comanche, but he didn't know any of the details. I'll not rest until I find her."

"Or find out what happened to her," Nik said, speaking between efforts to splash water on his face. "I hate to say it, but the Comanche could have turned around and sold her into Mexico."

"Then I need to know that," Roger said. "If I have to, I'll go to Mexico."

"You won't have any authority in Mexico," Nik cautioned, drying his face and tweaking his mustache in the mirror. "There are some bad hombres hanging out down there."

"Then I'll have to turn in my badge," said Roger. "I've got to settle this."

"Well, let's hope it doesn't come to that," Nik said, moving over to open a window and looking out. "You're becoming quite a lawman."

"As long as I have help," Roger said, with a smirk.

"You always have help," Nik replied, retrieving the washbasin and emptying it out the window. "As long as I've known you, you've had an angel riding on your shoulder."

"It sure doesn't feel that way at times," Roger said, reflecting for a moment on the past, as he straightened up and clasped his hands behind his head.

"Hey, just because you're a Christian doesn't mean life's going to be easy," Nik quipped, replacing the basin. "In fact, just the opposite, but take into account you and I are still here and since our boyhood days our lives have been anything but easy."

Roger looked over at Nik and gave him a knowing smile.

"Hey, wash up and let's grab some dinner," Nik said, throwing Roger the towel.

The following day, they arrived in Gainesville, which had grown considerably since the end of the Civil War. A large group of former slaves had moved into Gainesville and were assimilated into the community during Reconstruction. The town's sheriff was a former slave and soldier in the Union Army. Quite a contrast considering the town's reputation, something the community was trying to live down and doing a good job of it.

"Nik Brinkman," Nik said, introducing himself to the sheriff, while extending his hand, "and this is Deputy Roger Brinkman."

"Welcome, marshal, deputy," said Silas Brown, the town sheriff. "What brings you two to Gainesville?" Brown shook the hands of both men. He paid little attention to the disparity of the two brothers, familiar with relationships between southern masters and the women they owned.

"Sheriff, we're looking for a Victor Kensington. He was the circuit judge over in Paris, Lamar County," Nik said, giving the sheriff a brief description.

"I would like to say you're in luck, you say he was a judge?" Silas queried. "There was a gentleman here a couple of months ago who fits your description, but he was here only a short time. He rode in a nice carriage, but he traded that in for a buckboard wagon and two horses. He loaded that wagon and then set off following the old Butterfield Overland Trail.

"I think he was headed for Fort Belknap, but that fort's about to shut down," the sheriff concluded.

"Did you get to know him?" Roger asked.

"No, he made no attempt to visit my office," Silas said. "Peculiar, now that you mention he was a judge. Since he caused no trouble, I had no reason to confront him."

"He probably wanted to steer clear of you, worried that you might recognize who he was," Nik said. "He's wanted for land fraud, and we have to assume he's on the run."

"Land fraud, you say?" Silas mused. "It seems you can't trust anybody these days, at least not out here, anyways."

"You've been most helpful, sheriff," Roger said.

The sheriff pointed out the local hotel and set off in the direction of his office.

"What are you going to do now, Nik?" Roger asked.

"All I can do is go after him," Nik answered, looking around at the town and back at Roger. "I at least have some idea where Kensington was headed, and I still have time to go after him.

"I wonder why he traded in his buggy for a buckboard?" Nik said thoughtfully.

"That is puzzling, all right," Roger said, "but as you mentioned, we have no jurisdiction in Mexico."

"No, but I would at least like to confirm that's where he went," Nik replied. "Until I do, it's possible he could still be in Texas, for all we know."

"Wish I could help you," Roger offered, putting his hand on Nik's shoulder.

"Not to worry, Roger. It sounds like Kensington is traveling alone," Nik said, wrapping his fingers around the handle of his holstered pistol. "If I catch up to him, I doubt I'll have any trouble bringing him in – one way or another."

The deputies checked into the hotel, had dinner and retired for the evening. The next morning, they said their goodbyes.

"You take care of yourself," Nik cautioned, as the men entered the livery stable to saddle their horses. "Don't go near any Indian Villages unless invited. They will know of your presence but should leave you alone if you pose no threat. There are renegades, so keep your rifle handy. And if you run into any army patrols, let them know who you are and what you're doing. They will help you."

"Wow, I wish I had a similar litany of advice for you, brother," Roger remarked, grabbing Nik's forearm. "I'll just offer, Godspeed."

"Nuff said, brother." Nik replied, grasping Roger's forearm. "Good luck and tell Charlie I said hello." Nik turned to go, but then turned back, with a broad smile on his face. "By the way, tell Gloria I said hello, too."

Chapter 30

Roger laughed and tipped his hat farewell, as Nik mounted Lincoln. Nik brushed the rim of his hat and rode away. Roger watched him for a while before mounting Brinker, with his packhorse in tow, and headed north.

Following the Indian Trail out of Gainesville, Roger was able to find an area to cross the Red River, now swollen by spring rains. The deputy could almost feel the change in atmosphere as he crossed into Indian Territory. There had been Cheyenne and Comanche raiding parties in the area, and the U.S. Army was kept busy between fighting with renegades and struggling to keep the peace among friendlier tribes. Riding alone, Roger would not have been a lucrative target, but angry braves seeking revenge could see him as easy prey.

He passed several Indian villages but kept a low profile and attempted to stay out of sight, per Nik's advice. He resisted the temptation to approach in peace and inquire about Gloria. Not only would it be naïve, he also did not have enough command of Indian languages to get his point across.

For the most part, the four-day trip was uneventful, except for a few thunderstorms. Roger arrived at Fort Arbuckle about midday. The scuttlebutt was about a corporal leading a small detachment of soldiers to break up a band of former Confederate outlaws near Sherman just weeks before Nik and Roger got there. For some in Texas, the Civil War was not yet over.

Although Fort Arbuckle was under the command of Philip Sheridan, the general was in the field on campaign. The post was left under the temporary command of a red-headed Irishman,

Sergeant Buck Bushmill.

"Aye, marshal, long journey, no?" Bushmill asked upon greeting Brinkman. Bushmill sat behind a small desk that featured little more than a bottle of liquor and a glass.

"Yes, but no trouble along the way," Roger answered.

"Perhaps you would enjoy a little corn squeezins to quench your thirst?" Bushmill asked, producing a second glass. "There's not many of us left in ol' Arbuckle, but we've got plenty of corn and hay for the horses, so you're welcome to fatten up your steeds while you're here."

"You know, I will have some of what you're offering," Roger said, feeling sociable.

Bushmill poured the deputy a glass and one for himself. It was a bit stout, but Roger had made up his mind he was going to have a friendly drink with the sergeant.

"So, what are ya' doin' in these parts?" Bushmill asked.

"I'm here to report to the one in charge, which I assume is you," Roger said.

"Not much to command here any longer," Bushmill said. "I am the ranking officer, so to speak. Most of the men have moved up to Fort Cobb, where the Indian raids have been taking place."

"I am searching for a white woman," Roger continued, "who I believe was kidnapped and sold to the Comanche somewhere in these parts."

At the mention of Fort Cobb and Indian raids, Roger choked down a few more sips of liquor. As the conversation progressed, the deputy was feeling much more relaxed and enjoying the newfound sensation.

"I don't envy ya' wanting to find a white woman among the Comanche. If they have 'er they're not likely to want to give 'er up," said the sergeant. "Was she your wife or something?"

"No, just a friend, but a close friend," Roger said. "I guess she could have been my wife, but I had too much on my mind to consider settling down. However, I do owe it to her to find out if she's okay."

"Do you know what Comanche tribe has 'er?" Bushmill asked.

"I really don't know who has her, for sure," Roger confessed. "I have reason to believe the kidnapper sold her to Comanches in this territory and that's why I'm here."

Roger was now beginning to feel a little woozy, so he set his glass down and concentrated on putting Bushmill and the conversation into focus. Bushmill finished his drink and poured himself another. Before Roger could protest, the sergeant also refilled the deputy's glass.

"So how long will you be staying here?" the sergeant asked.

"I have to get to Wichita Village soon as I can," Roger said, trying to control his tongue. "There-san Indian meeting me there. Good man."

"Well, you're in luck," Bushmill said. "We have a detachment heading out that way in the morning. Drink up and we'll get you fed and feed your horses."

Roger raised the glass to his lips. The liquor was going down easier now, but he wisely put the drink down before finishing it.

"Oooh, I think I've had enough," Roger said, doing his best to control his speech. "The room seems to be moving. I guess I have been on the trail too long."

"I understand, marshal. A little grub will help to clear your head," Bushmill said. "We'll take care of the horses for you." Bushmill stood up and started for the door. He turned to see Roger still sitting in his chair.

"Are you coming?" the sergeant asked.

"I would like to," Roger said, "but I don't think I can stand up."

"Let me help ya," Bushmill said, with a laugh. "I guess you have been on the trail too long."

Realizing the condition Roger was in, Bushmill helped Roger up from his chair and steadied him while leading the deputy to the quarters where he could spend the night.

"Are ya' hungry?" the sergeant asked, after sitting Roger on an empty bunk.

"I think I'd better just lie down for a while," Roger said, "perhaps later."

"I'll fix ya' a plate and leave it here in case you get hungry later because the mess hall may be closed later on," said the sergeant.

"Fine," Roger said and put his head on the pillow and felt the room spinning around him. It turned into a long night.

The next morning, after falling asleep for a short time, Roger woke up and smelled the food left for him the night before. He rushed out of his quarters and deposited what was left in his stomach on the fort's main grounds. He did not feel like riding.

"A rough night, deputy?" Bushmill asked, as he approached. "Sorry, I didn't know you would be reacting this way. Let's go to the mess and get you something to eat. That should help."

Roger gathered himself and was able to down some black coffee and a biscuit.

"A wee bit of the corn squeezins might make you feel better," Bushmill said.

With that, Roger rushed from the mess hall and added the coffee and biscuit to the fort's grounds, as well.

Despite his hangover, Roger braced himself, readied his horses and joined the small detachment leaving the fort. He bid Bushmill goodbye and apologized for his lack of discretion. Bushmill laughed and wished the deputy a safe trip.

The detachment was led by Corporal Chester Naughton, a slightly built soldier, who rode tall in the saddle. He was by the book and expected Roger to be the same. That did not make the trip any easier.

Naughton took the Indian Trail out of Fort Arbuckle, which followed Wild Horse Creek. The rains had kept the creek flowing, much to Roger's delight since he could not seem to take in enough water that day, much to Naughton's annoyance. After a couple hours' ride, the deputy began to feel more like himself, as the detachment neared the end of Wild Horse Creek south of Signal Mountain.

They eventually reached Beaver Creek, and Naughton told the men they would camp there for the night. Roger ate heartily that evening and the next morning he was feeling great.

The detachment, consisting of six horse-soldiers and Naughton, turned north and followed Beaver Creek. The stream flowed from an area near Wichita Village and after almost a day's ride, Corporal Naughton halted his men.

"We head west from here," Naughton said, "but Wichita Village is farther up the creek. You'll come to a small feeder tributary flowing from the east. Follow that and you'll come to the village."

"I appreciate you letting me tag along, corporal," Roger said. "I have a good idea where the village is and should have no problem making my way from here.

"By the way, where are you headed?" Roger asked.

"There's a new fort being established just west of here," Naughton said. "We've been assigned to help complete that job."

The two men bid each other safe travel. Roger thanked the soldiers in the detachment and began making his way along Beaver Creek. After traveling a short way, he heard shooting and shouting coming from the direction where he left the detachment. He turned Brinker around, dropped the towrope of his packhorse and began galloping back in that direction. He crossed the creek and came up over a knoll in time to see Naughton in hand-to-hand combat with a warrior, who was part of a band of Indians that had descended on the corporal and his men. While the soldiers had formed a small circle to hold off the more than a dozen renegades riding around them, Naughton was pinned to the ground a short distance from his unit. Roger pulled up and drew his rifle from its scabbard.

Chapter 31

The Indian who had the corporal pinned down was raising his tomahawk to make the kill. Roger took careful aim, fired and hit the renegade below his raised arm shattering the warrior's shoulder. The Indian fell, and Naughton finished the fight with his knife.

Roger again fired at a mounted attacker who had broken ranks and set his lance to spear Naughton. The Indian fell back and toppled from his horse. The raiding party then broke away and rode south, with the soldiers still firing. Roger then rode up to the site of the battle. Naughton was standing, somewhat shaken, but for the most part unhurt. Two of his men were lying dead and one had an arrow protruding from his leg.

"Are you okay?" Roger shouted at Naughton.

"Yes, thank you. You saved my life," the corporal said, as Roger approached.

"I guess it was fortunate I wasn't among your ranks when the attack occurred," Roger said. "I think my return after the fight started gave me an advantage."

"Nonetheless, that was lifesaving shooting," Naughton said. "I'm indebted."

"Where did this group come from?" Roger asked. "What Indians were they?"

"Judging from the two who attacked me, one appears to be Cheyenne and the other Kiowa," Naughton said, turning and walking in the direction of where his soldiers were tending to the injured man. "There could have been others, but we were taken too much by surprise. I lost two men and one wounded."

"I'm sorry I wasn't able to get here quicker," Roger said, noting the dead and wounded soldiers. "Is there anything else I can do?"

"No, its best you continue on your way while that bunch is still on the run," said Naughton. "No telling if they might come back for more. If they do, we'll be better prepared this time, despite our losses."

Roger put a couple more cartridges into his rifle and returned it to its scabbard. He rode back to where he had left his packhorse, which fortunately had not run off during the heat of battle. Roger took the packhorse in tow and once again continued north on Beaver Creek toward Wichita Village. With the day drawing to a close, Roger spurred Brinker ahead to reach a stand of trees several miles in the distance. He felt if he could camp there for the night, it would afford him a strategic position should that raiding party come looking for him.

Reaching the wooded area at nightfall, Roger set up camp. There was plenty of grass for the horses, the creek was nearby, and the night was warm enough to eschew a campfire and settle for a cold dinner of jerky and hard biscuits.

The night passed without incident and Roger made haste to reach Wichita Village the next morning. Upon arrival, he was met by Charlie Blue Feather and a few other tribesmen coming out to greet him.

"Welcome, Deputy Roger Brinkman," Charlie said. "I have told my friends about you. We have been expecting you."

Roger swung out of his saddle and stepped forward to greet Blue Feather. He was introduced to Charlie's friends and was pleased to find they all spoke English, although some of it broken. Charlie led Roger and his friends to his dwelling, where the Wichita women had prepared a meal for them. They sat around eating and discussing Roger's plans as to the best way to conduct a search for Gloria Fenton. Roger also related the attack of renegades on the patrol he was with the day before.

"There are braves that have left their tribes to seek revenge on blue coats," Charlie said. "They say too many white buffalo hunters poaching on Indian land."

"Why pick on the army, then?" Roger asked.

"They protect white buffalo hunters. Say that protects settlers moving west," Charlie said. "Either way, army little help to Indians."

"It's a political problem," Roger reflected. "Different commanding officers have different ideas on how to deal with keeping the peace between the Indians and white men. I'm afraid some officers think Indians are simply the enemy."

"That make Indians the enemy. Wichita too small to fight, we too were relocated from homelands," said Charlie. "Now we defend against army and renegades."

"I know the solution, Charlie, but I do not have the power to implement it, only suggest it," Roger said, drawing from his knowledge of the Bible. "I'm afraid a man's peacemaker rides in a leather holster. Only the hand of Providence can keep it there."

"Providence?" Charlie said.

"Yes, the Great Spirit, I believe is how you think of Providence," Roger said, "an immortal creator of all things."

"I think you ask this Providence to guide you," Charlie said. "We ask the Great Spirit to protect us. We are sometimes not protected, and your Providence does not keep guns in white man's holsters."

"That's an interesting way to put it, Charlie. Perhaps you're onto something I did not learn in school," Roger said, smiling at Charlie. "Perhaps the real answer is hidden in the difference between the two."

"Perhaps," Charlie said, smiling back. "Now, as for search," the guide continued. "I suggest we go to Fort Cobb. There Wichita and Comanche live in peace. Perhaps we find answers there."

"My plans exactly," Roger said. "When do you want to get started?"

"Daybreak," Charlie said. "Tonight, we ask for guidance and protection."

That evening, the Wichita put on a great ceremony, calling on the Great Spirit to be with both Roger and Charlie. Roger knew the task ahead was not going to be an easy one, but a companion such as Blue Feather was a great substitute when his brother, Nik, wasn't available.

The next day, Roger removed his supplies from his packhorse and harnessed the animal to the wagon alongside Charlie's horse. With all provisions in the wagon, Charlie started north on the Indian Trail past the Wichita Mountains, crossing a tributary of the Washita River in the direction of Fort Cobb. Along the way, they were greeted by a small party of friendly Comanche. Charlie explained their mission and the mounted braves led them into their village. Using Charlie as an interpreter, Roger described Gloria and asked if they had seen her. Unfortunately, no one in the village had. Roger and Charlie spent the night in the Comanche village and then set out for Fort Cobb the next day.

They reached the fort by evening and were greeted by Captain George Holbrook, the same officer Roger, Charlie and Nik ran into when struggling to find their way back from Iron Bear's hideaway.

"Captain Holbrook, here," said the officer, extending his hand in greeting. "You men look familiar, have we met?"

"I believe so," Roger answered. "You're the officer we ran into after our encounter with Iron Bear, a year or two ago. I think you were a lieutenant then, right?"

"Yes, I was, and now I remember you. Wasn't there another deputy marshal with you at that time?" Holbrook said.

"Nik Brinkman, my brother, was the deputy you spoke to," Roger answered.

"Of course, the one with the mustache," Holbrook said, recalling Nik. "As for me, I was promoted to captain shortly after my patrol ran into you.

I'm sorry that General Sheridan was not here to greet you, but he is on campaign in Kansas. I'm afraid we've been having problems keeping a few tribes on their designated reservations.

"Wonderful folks, the Wichita," the captain said, looking toward Blue Feather. "We've had no trouble with that tribe," Holbrook concluded.

"Nor will you," Charlie said. "Marshal Brinkman is looking for white woman believed held by Comanche. We need help, can you spare it?"

"I'll be happy to do what I can, but right now we're kept busy shuffling between here and Camp Supply," Holbrook said.

"It's just that we need to file an itinerary with you, so if you do not hear from us after a certain amount of time, it will alert you," Roger broke in. "We can use all the help we can get, but we understand the strain the U.S. Army is under right now."

"We have known of white women held captive and we negotiated for their release," Holbrook said. "Sometimes we get lucky, and then there are times when the women choose not to come with us. If they're in Comanche hands it can also mean they've been bought and paid for, and that makes it a tough negotiation."

"I understand," Roger said. "I'm not sure how this will turn out, or if I can even find the woman I'm looking for. But it is something I must do, no matter what the odds."

"I don't envy you," Holbrook said. "Who are you looking for?"

"Miss Gloria Fenton. Her parents were killed, and we believe she was kidnapped by whoever did the killing," Roger said. "I have reason to think she was taken by a gang of murderers, rustlers and thieves and sold to the Comanche."

"I remember now," Holbrook said. "There was talk that Iron Bear had done that killing, but I guess he was not involved?"

"We found the man who did the killing, and he was definitely not Indian. He was a white man who is now dead," Roger said. "However, we only have someone's word that she was taken by that man and sold to the Comanche."

"I wish you well, marshal," said the captain. "Why don't you men get some rest, and we'll work out an itinerary in the morning. There's plenty of grub in the mess hall."

Roger and Blue Feather thanked the captain. They took care of their horses and stopped in for a hot meal. After that, they retired to their quarters.

The next day, Roger and Charlie met with Captain Holbrook in the fort's main office. The captain had a map laid out with a proposed itinerary.

"Now the Fentons' wagon was found southwest of Fort Gibson

along the North Fork of the Canadian River. We figure they were following the wagon trail south and for some reason headed due west along the river," Holbrook began. "That area is Creek Indian Territory and one of the reasons we don't believe the Indians had anything to do with the attack. The Creeks have shown no hostility since the war.

"If the woman you search for was taken by outlaws and sold to the Comanche," Holbrook continued, "they likely traveled due west, passing through Seminole Country. The Seminole discourage intermarriage so it is unlikely they would have had any interest in the woman you seek. So that means the territory west of here is your best bet to find her," the captain concluded.

"Sounds well thought out, captain," Roger said. "What route should we

travel?"

"I suggest going southwest of the fort to a small Comanche village near here. You may have passed it on your way," Holbrook continued. "Although I doubt they have Miss Fenton, the village has been quiet and they may be able to help in determining which village does have her.

"However, avoid the Wichita Mountains. It's a favorite refuge for renegade bands. We received word about the war party that attacked you and the Fort Arbuckle detachment. Those warriors were probably from those mountains.

"Depending on what you find out from the Comanche village, leave word with Owl Tree. He's supposed to be a descendant of former chief Old Owl. Owl Tree isn't a chief, but he is a spokesman for the camp. Leave word with him as to where you plan to go after that.

"Also, there will be patrols crisscrossing that area. Should you run into one, identify yourselves and send word back as to your location and heading."

"Thanks, captain, for all your hard work," Roger said. "We appreciate it."

"It's our duty to keep folks as safe as we can and hopefully maintain the peace," Holbrook said. "Just be careful because not every

Indian out there is friendly. It'll help having Blue Feather along."

Roger and Charlie thanked the officer again and left to load up their gear. By late morning they were headed toward the Comanche village located more southwest of Fort Cobb than the camp they visited on their way to the fort. It was a tribe Blue Feather was quite familiar with, and he was acquainted with Owl Tree. They arrived at the camp in late afternoon, and Charlie introduced Roger to the Comanche spokesman.

"Welcome, Deputy Brinkman," Owl Tree said, displaying an excellent command of English. "Come and sit where we can talk."

Charlie and Roger followed Owl Tree to a small clearing in the village where they sat on blankets placed on the ground.

"Blue Feather tells us you are looking for white woman?" Owl Tree said.

"We believe she was taken by white outlaws more than a year ago and sold to the Comanche," Roger said. "Any help you could offer as to her location would be greatly appreciated."

Owl Tree conferred with Blue Feather in a language accompanied with sign language. Owl Tree then turned to Roger.

"We know not of this woman but suggest Comanche camps where sun sets is best choice," Owl Tree said. "Comanche there have white women in camp."

The information was about as expected, but Owl Tree also gave advice on route of travel. He told of where water could be found and how to avoid war-like bands of Comanche-Kiowa that hide out in the Llano Estacado.

"Cross the Red River and go west until Elm Creek," Owl Tree instructed. "You will come to a place where a river flows in from the northwest. Then turn and follow it to a village known as Old Comanche Camp."

Roger and Charlie expressed their appreciation to Owl Tree and remained in the village for the night. The next day the two travelers set a course heading west, allowing a wide berth of the Wichita Mountains. The trip to the North Fork of the Red River took the better part of three days. After crossing the North Fork, they turned southwest with hopes of reaching Elm Creek by the second day. The weather was warm, but occasional showers slowed their progress.

"After Elm Creek, two days to Middle Fork," Charlie Blue Feather said, as the two men dined on salt pork and beans. "Comanche Camp located on river."

"What kind of reception do you think we'll get?" Roger asked.

"I do not believe Comanche in Old Camp hostile," Charlie said, "We cross the river with white flag on wagon. Let them know we come in peace."

The deputy and his guide crossed Elm Creek and traveled to within a half day's ride from the river and Comanche Camp. They dined on sturgeon cooked Blue Feather style and discussed their entry into Comanche Camp.

"It best we put guns in wagon," said Charlie, as the two men washed their dishes in a nearby stream. "Like white flag, it is sign of peace."

"I'm okay with that, but I'll stay close to the wagon until we can be certain they know our intentions are peaceful." Roger said, shaking the water off his dish. "I hope we do not run into trouble. I want this mission to be a success."

After reaching Middle Fork the next day, they stopped to assess the Comanche village on the other side. Charlie pulled his wagon up to the water's edge and Roger moved up where he could be seen. Two small boys down by the river saw them and ran into the village.

"I guess our presence is about to be announced," Roger said.

"Wait to see response, then proceed," Charlie replied.

Three men walked up onto the riverbank and stood watching. Charlie then urged his team into the water and Roger followed. Once they reached the other side, Roger could see one of the braves was darker than the others.

"State your business," said the darker man in English.

"In search of white woman," Charlie responded.

"There is no white woman here," the spokesman said. "There has not been one here for at least a year now."

Charlie climbed down from the wagon and signaled for Roger to dismount. Charlie spoke to the three braves.

"This U.S. Deputy Marshal Brinkman. I Charlie Blue Feather. Please tell more about white woman," Charlie requested.

"They call me Comanche Joe," said the darker man. "This is Light Crow and Crying Wolf," he added, introducing the two braves.

Comanche Joe explained he was originally known as "Joe" and was a slave of the Comanche. When slaves were emancipated, Joe was adopted into the tribe and renamed Comanche Joe.

"There were six or seven men, one with a very bad eye. I was told the wounded eye was the result of being in the war," Comanche Joe continued. "He was trying to trade that white woman for horses, but we did not have the horses he wanted."

Comanche Joe described the woman as best he could. Roger was convinced it was a description of Gloria, despite some adjectives to the contrary that included cuts and bruises.

"We suggested the group go west, deeper into the Staked Plains where Comanche with superior horses have camps," the former slave said. "But that is hostile territory."

Charlie looked at Roger, as if to say, "what now?"

"I've got to find her, even if I have to fight my way there to do it," Roger said. "If you want to turn back, Charlie, I understand."

"If you go, I go," Charlie said, his facial scar reminding Roger of Blue Feather's encounter with Iron Bear. "I think it best we keep weapons handy."

"You're going to need Charlie," Comanche Joe said. "Many of those Llano Estacado warriors do not speak English or even want to."

The two travelers were welcomed into the camp and spent the night there. It was a restless evening for Roger, knowing he may now be on a path to find Gloria. He also worried about what he was dragging Charlie into. Roger was not that concerned about himself, but Charlie really had no stake in the ordeal. In the morning they were directed to head west until reaching the base of a plateau and then to turn north. Once they came to the end of the plateau, they were to turn west into Comanche territory.

It was still late spring, but as the temperature warmed up, the storms became more severe.

Shortly after departing Comanche Camp, Roger and Charlie met up with a company of U.S. soldiers led by Lieutenant Andrew Edwards. Corporal Naughton was with the patrol and related to the lieutenant Roger's mission and his assistance in the Indian attack.

"Appreciate what you did," said Edwards. "So, you are seeking a white woman?"

"Yes, I realize we're in potentially dangerous territory and Captain Holbrook has asked that we leave word with you as to our progress," Roger said.

"You will likely see warriors observing your movements from atop the escarpment," said the lieutenant, pointing in that direction, "but they made no attempt to engage us. Hopefully, they will give you and your scout the same courtesy."

After confirming with Edwards their intentions, Roger and Blue Feather continued toward the plateau. The patrol was headed back in the direction of Comanche Camp.

After reaching the escarpment and turning north, strong, dry winds made the trip less than pleasant. When the wind was strong enough, it kicked up the dust and sand making it necessary to either find shelter or cover the faces of both men and horses.

Charlie's meals were still appetizing, enhanced by the occasional grouse, rattlesnake or rabbit. The pair spotted a few buffalo during their travels but knew killing one would not be wise in Comanche Territory. And there were times when mounted Indians could be seen high atop the escarpment watching the wagon with Roger trailing close behind.

One night, when the two travelers were having their meal, Roger asked about the sentries watching from above.

"Do you think those Indians watching us will cause us any trouble?" Roger asked, pouring himself some coffee.

"By now they know who we are and what doing here," Charlie said, finishing his dinner. "Will not face warriors until turn west into Comanche territory. I do not think they attack because we are no threat with nothing they want – maybe horses."

"Would they attack us for our horses?" Roger asked.

"Do not think so," Charlie said, rising and collecting their empty plates. "Attack could alert army. They do not want blue coats against them for gain of three horses."

Although it was comforting for Roger knowing Charlie was a Plains Indian, Charlie's association with the white man did not make him popular among hostile Indians. In fact, Iron Bear would likely have killed Charlie had it not been for Nik's quick action. Roger and Charlie tried to get some sleep knowing they could reach the end of the escarpment the next day and the potential danger that could be waiting for them.

As they set out in the morning, the wind was at their back making travel a little easier. The men scanned the top of the escarpment for signs of anyone watching them, but they saw no one. That would have made them feel at ease except for the fact the end of the high plateau was now in sight. Finding a small playa lake, they stopped to water their horses and discuss what to do if a band of Comanche and Kiowa were around the bend to greet them.

"If we are met by a band of hostiles, what's our best plan of action?" Roger asked Charlie, while allowing Brinker to drink from the lake.

"If tell us to leave, it would be best to do," Charlie answered, holding a bucket for one of the wagon horses to drink from. "If they attack, we surrender or fight. Depends on how many warriors."

"If we surrender, I tell them I am responsible for intrusion and to send you back," Roger said, feeling the dread of guilt at dragging Blue Feather into the search.

"They likely hate me more than you," Charlie said, putting the empty bucket into the wagon. "I make decision to ride with marshals long ago. This not your doing."

Roger swung back into the saddle and watched as Charlie climbed up onto the driver's seat of the wagon. The Indian guide gave Roger a sly smile, snapped the reins and began rolling the wagon toward the end of the plateau.

Chapter 32

Prepared for a confrontation, the two travelers made their way to the trail that led west running alongside the Canadian River. After entering the trail, they were relieved to see no war party was waiting for their entry into Comanche and Kiowa territory. Emboldened, they continued looking for a safe place to camp for the night. They came to a bend in the river where they saw a lone Indian woman sitting quietly by the river.

"It looks like we've come across the first one to welcome us," Roger nervously quipped.

"I think woman spirit talker," Charlie said. "She not look at us."

"A spirit talker?" Roger asked.

"Spirit medicine," Charlie answered. "Believe woman seeking spirits, perhaps sees us through them."

The woman was sitting in the shade of several cottonwood trees. Her dark hair was parted in the middle with long braids that flowed over the front of her buckskin dress. The leather was embroidered with colorful beads. Visible around her neck was a feathery amulet that she held in her hand as she slowly rocked back and forth.

"Shall we approach her?" Roger asked, in a low tone.

"We wait," Charlie said. "She may have words for us, but not bother now. When woman beckons, now welcome. Good to hear woman's words."

Roger and Charlie turned and made their way to the river where they watered the horses and enjoyed the cool of the location to wait for the spirit talker to acknowledge their presence. After about an hour, she turned and signaled to Charlie and Roger to approach.

"What do we say?" Roger inquired, as the two men made their

way through the cottonwoods toward the lone Indian.

"I speak first," Charlie said. "Then deputy ask woman for guidance."

Charlie knelt by the shaman and spoke in low tones to the spirit talker. After a short conversation, Roger was invited to join them.

Using Charlie as translator, the shaman told Charlie she understood that Roger was looking for a white woman.

"Spirit Talker say she knows of you and your search," Charlie said, turning to Roger.

"Tell her I have reason to believe the woman I seek may be among the Comanche," Roger said, speaking to Charlie, who related it to the shaman.

"I know reason," the woman said, bypassing Blue Feather's translation. "You have things of who you seek?"

"No," Roger said.

The shaman took Roger's hand and spoke through Charlie to have Roger think of the woman in question.

While holding Roger's hand, the shaman closed her eyes and began to breathe in a slow deep rhythm, listening to the sounds of the river to quiet her thoughts. Roger shut his eyes and concentrated on images of Gloria. After a brief time, the spirit talker appeared to mumble to herself. She then fell silent and eventually opened her eyes and looked at Roger. She then spoke to Charlie in her native tongue.

"She say you are a man of good medicine. She say you have spiritual power," Charlie relayed.

"I believe in God," Roger answered, speaking to Charlie.

"I know your God," the shaman said. She then spoke with Charlie once more.

"The woman you seek is not far," Charlie offered. "She say follow river and it will lead to Comanche village. She sent word we come in peace. But…,"

"But what?"" Roger asked.

"She say message is dark, but spirits not reveal why," Charlie answered.

"I guess I'm not surprised," Roger said. "I just wish I knew what to prepare for concerning this darkness."

"Already prepared," Charlie said. "Can do no better."

Roger then expressed his appreciation to the shaman, as did Charlie, and the two men returned to their wagon.

"Do you really think Gloria will be in the village the spirit talker mentioned?" Roger asked.

"Shaman use your power to make sure woman there," Charlie answered.

Roger could only hope Charlie's interpretation was correct.

The two men made camp, and Charlie boiled some salted meat for dinner. The spring evening was calm and the river's high waters were already beginning to recede. In the morning, they found the shaman was gone.

"Darkness or no darkness," Roger said over a cup of coffee, "there is no turning back for me now. If you would rather not come with me," he said to Charlie, "I will understand."

"Shaman say we come in peace," Charlie said. "Put guns in wagon. I put up white flag, we proceed as shaman say."

Roger undid his gun belt and put it into the wagon, along with his rifle. Charlie tied a white cloth to the brake handle next to the driver's seat. He then boarded the wagon, turned and nodded to Roger, who mounted Brinker, and the two set off following the river.

After about two hours' travel, the trail led between a grove of trees on one side and on the other a low, long-running ridge. As the wagon and trailing rider continued, soon a mounted Indian appeared out of the woods and one also approached from the other side, coming over the ridge. The Indians said nothing and made no attempt to engage the two travelers. Two more braves soon approached on horses, one from each side. This continued until there were six Comanche on both sides riding parallel to the wagon and Roger. The trail turned to the left and the village came into view. Charlie glanced at the first rider who appeared, and the warrior indicated to continue into the village. As the wagon reached the edge of the encampment, the twelve Indians crossed in front of it and Charlie reined in his horses. The leading rider motioned to Charlie and Roger to get down and proceed on foot. Once they did, the Indians again divided with six on each side of them. A chieftain-looking warrior wearing a feathered bonnet and a colorful robe approached, walking toward them. The chieftain spoke to Charlie in Comanche, and they both looked to Roger.

"Chief know we come in peace," Charlie said to Roger. "Chief take deputy to woman deputy wanting to see. I wait here."

Roger then followed the chieftain, who led Roger through the village and down to the river where a woman was standing beneath a growth of trees. He could see her skin and hair was not dark like the other Indians. She wore buckskins skillfully embroidered with colored beads, much like the shaman was wearing, and she wore moccasins with the same beading. As Roger approached, he knew immediately it was Gloria.

Overcome with emotion, Roger attempted to speak but struggled to find the right words with which to begin.

"What is it you want, Roger?" Gloria questioned in a subdued tone.

Roger's heart was beating faster now, as a thousand thoughts ran through his mind as to how to answer, he blurted out, "Gloria, I'm so sorry for what happened, and I've come to take you home."

"Take me home? Take me home where, Roger?" Gloria asked.

"Ah, back to civilization where you belong," Roger said, surprised at Gloria's demure attitude.

"Civilization? You mean Bordertown? Is that civilization to you?" Gloria continued, her tone less subdued.

"Look, Gloria, I'm just trying to help, here," Roger said, now flustered by the unexpected course of the conversation. "I know this has been a horrible experience for you. I just want to help and maybe make it up to you."

"Make it up to me? Do you mean you want me to come with you?" Gloria continued. "Do you plan to marry me and make me civilized again?"

"Well, I don't know about that necessarily, Gloria," Roger stammered, surprised by the question. "I just thought you might want to be back among your people."

"Roger, I am with my people," Gloria said. "Do you know what I've been through and why I agreed to meet with you like this?"

"I thought it was so you could come home?" Roger queried, his face contorted by a dialogue seemingly going in circles.

"Roger, there is no home for me out there. My parents are gone, my past is gone. I was ravaged by that horrible man with one eye, and I wanted to kill myself," Gloria began. "The abuse continued until I was dragged into this village where they wanted to sell me. I looked so terrible the villagers thought I had a disease, and they wanted nothing to do with me. That is until the medicine woman spoke to them on my behalf. After that, the chief brought several horses to the men in exchange for me."

"But you look fine, Gloria. Other than you look a little Indian-like in that dress," Roger offered.

"Roger, Roger, out to save the world," Gloria stated, her tone softening a bit. "How did you feel, Roger, when you found out your parents had been killed? Did you fall on your knees asking God to give you the strength to forgive those who murdered your family? No, you joined the army vowing to kill those responsible. I didn't understand then, but I do now. If I had had a gun, I would have killed that one-eyed bastard and then taken myself out of this world. I was totally empty, empty like you were. But these people took me in, took care of me, and the medicine woman befriended me. She eventually healed my soul and allowed me to be me again."

"But didn't you have that faith when you attended my father's church in Bordertown?" Roger said. "You were one of my father's favorites."

"Of course I did," Gloria replied. "But I was younger then, and God was in your father and in his church. Out here, it's different. These people find God in a different way, not in a building. But either way it's based on faith.

"The medicine woman and I shared our faiths," Gloria continued. "Our mutual understanding of God led to my healing and why she could send you here in peace. She is the reason I am now at peace.

"Go back, Roger," Gloria said. "What has passed is in the past. I am fine and have found a new life with these people. You know, if you would let your guard down a little, you might be able to quench the fire that rages in you – and not have to do it with a gun."

"So, you don't want to come home?" Roger again stated, looking as if Gloria had spoken in a language he could not understand.

"I am home, Roger," Gloria replied. "And I pray you find your home as well. Our lives have changed and we now live in two different worlds.

"Goodbye, Roger," Gloria said and then walked past her longtime friend.

Roger was left staring at her as she went. He had found Gloria Fenton but failed to recognize what she had been through. His experience had driven him into war and the law, her into a culture he little understood. The difference, she had found peace while he was still looking. Roger watched as Gloria disappeared among a people she now called her own, and the past Roger hoped he could recapture disappeared with her.

The chieftain was standing at the edge of the village where Gloria had passed, waiting for Roger. As the deputy's thoughts began to untangle, he made his way to where the chieftain was standing and followed him back to the wagon. Charlie had turned the wagon around and the twelve warriors were again in position to escort the two men out of the village. Roger mounted Brinker and the procession began to put the village behind them. As they rode along, the warriors disappeared two by two, much like they had appeared earlier upon the wagon's arrival.

Now alone, the two men rode along in silence, making their way back to the edge of the escarpment where they would turn south and head back to the fort. The temperature was warm as the day wore on, but the weather was becoming more erratic. Hot wind was followed by rain, then sunshine and humidity led to more hot wind, sometimes strong enough to bring the dirt and sand with it.

They spent the night along the North Fork of the Red River. The two men spoke little. Roger did not know what to say, and Charlie thought it best to say nothing. The next day, they replenished their water supply, removed their weapons from the wagon and continued their journey. The wind was particularly hot, and dark clouds began to form overhead. A light rain began to fall, only to let up momentarily. The sky then opened with a downpour that eventually turned to hail. Fortunately, the hail was not large enough to injure or do damage, so the riders pressed on. Then, as suddenly as it started, the hail stopped, as did the wind, except for a growing, rushing sound in the distance. The cloudy sky seemed to change color, as the harsh sounds of wind began to grow louder and, suddenly, in front of the two men a tornado began to descend less than 500 yards away.

"Great wind!" Charlie called.

"Oh my God!" Roger said. "It's a twister, and it's headed our way. Quick, Charlie, free the horses from the harness!" Roger shouted, as he dismounted from Brinker. He and Charlie released both horses, and the tornado began throwing dirt, brush and rocks in their direction.

"Over there is a gully! Roger shouted. "Run, run for that and get down below the bank!"

The two men slapped the horses and raced for the gully as the tornado appeared to gain speed, tearing up whatever was in its path. Roger could see that Charlie wasn't going to stop in the gully, so he tackled his Indian companion and lay over the top of him as the roar of the cyclone grew deafening. Then, as suddenly as it appeared, it was gone and with it the wagon.

The two men lay quietly prone for a time, with their arms over their heads. Then Roger girded his courage and looked up. The clouds were parting, and sunshine again fell on them.

They stood up and dusted themselves off. They looked around, and to their amazement, all three horses were grazing nearby in a patch of damp grass.

"Roger have great medicine, like shaman say," Charlie said, with a grin creasing his scarred face.

"I'm not sure what I have," Roger mused. "I'm just glad we're alive and hope whatever it is gets us home safely."

The two men made a search for what remained of the wagon. They recovered a few items thrown from inside, but the wagon and the rest of the supplies were nowhere to be found.

After rounding up the horses, the two travelers were able to make better time without the wagon, but their provisions were gone. Retracing their route, it eventually led them to water.

Roger also bagged a wild boar with his rifle. Unfortunately, the wild pork turned out to be as difficult to eat as boot leather. Charlie had no trouble making a fire, but without the wagon and its contents, there was nothing to season or tenderize the meat. However, hunger is a good substitute.

The travelers arrived at Old Comanche Camp after a few days' ride and were greeted by the same trio that met them before.

"You made it!" Comanche Joe said, obviously surprised. "Lieutenant Edwards stopped by shortly after you left and expressed concern for your safety. However, he was expected at Fort Cobb and had to move on."

"Actually, things went well, as far as the trip was concerned," Roger said.

"Did you find the woman?" Comanche Joe asked.

"We did," Roger answered. "I'm glad to report she is well, but she also has no intentions of returning to the world she was torn from."

"Was she family?" Comanche Joe asked. "Is that why you were so determined to find her?"

"A family friend," Roger said. "She and her parents, God rest their souls, were members of my Pa's church."

"She lost her parents?" Comanche Joe questioned.

"She did, but she now seems to have a new family and is quite happy with them," Roger said.

"Although that's not always the case," Comanche Joe replied. "Still, a lot of white folks would be surprised how the Indian culture can grow on you."

"And me among them," Roger said. "It's remarkable to me how

little we understand about those we do not take the time to know.

"Say, you guys wouldn't have something to eat, would you?" Roger asked. "We lost our grub in a storm, and we're plumb-near starved."

Comanche Joe chuckled a bit at the remark, and he and his companions led Roger and Charlie into the village, where a meal was prepared for them. The following day, the people of the camp helped Roger and Charlie load up their packhorse with supplies and prepared the men to set out the next day, again the two were cautioned about the Wichita Mountain Range.

"Safe journey, gentlemen," Comanche Joe remarked. "Just steer clear of the Wichita Mountains. Follow Elm Creek east and you should be fine."

"May we look forward to the day we can all live in peace," Roger replied, shaking Joe's hand. "I've been east and west, and it seems war follows me wherever I go."

With their packhorse in tow, Brinkman and Blue Feather followed the Middle Fork of the Red River in search of where it met Elm Creek. The temperature was warm, and the two riders had soon lapsed into a dream-like state. Elm Creek's water flow came in from the opposite side of the Red River and had diminished. Consequently, both failed to see the confluence and ended up farther south than intended. After traveling for some time, Roger noticed the Wichita Range appeared closer than it should.

"Charlie, did we miss something?" Roger asked, startled by the nearness of the mountains.

Blue Feather pulled up and began to look around. "We should not be here," he said. "Elm Creek farther north."

Realizing their mistake, they crossed the Middle Fork to the east side and headed north, but they were now exposed to an escarpment running east of where the North Fork flowed. The two nervously scanned the escarpment, searching for anyone watching from there.

***

Nik Brinkman had followed the Overland Mail Route out of Gainesville, which led to Fort Belknap. After two days' travel, the deputy met a detachment coming from Belknap, commanded by Major George Trundell, on their way to Fort Arbuckle. Nik inquired as to the buckboard and whereabouts of Judge Kensington.

"Funny you should ask," Trundell remarked, whose sergeant had halted the troops and joined the major. "It just so happens Sergeant Fetterman discovered the remains of such a wagon but nothing more. Right, sergeant?"

"Yes sir," Fetterman replied. "It was probably a week ago or more. While on patrol we came across the burned-out remains of a buckboard, probably thirty miles southwest of here. We scoured the area but found no signs of an attack. There were tracks of what appeared to be two horses, but the rains had washed away any hint of where they led."

"Indians, perhaps?" Nik suggested.

"We ruled out a raid by Comanche or Kiowa. They've moved north," Trundell said. "That's why we're pulling out of Belknap."

"No bodies or evidence of a struggle?" Nik offered.

"None," the sergeant said. "It was like someone decided to abandon the wagon and light out on horseback. Second horse, if there were two, probably used as a pack animal."

Nik thought for a moment and decided against going on farther. If Kensington was on horseback, he had too great of a lead to catch him, and the burnt remains of the buckboard would be of no use.

"Which way are you headed, major?" Nik asked.

"Gainesville, then on to Arbuckle," Trundell answered.

"Mind if I join you? Nik asked. "I think my work here is done."

"Not at all," the major said. "Sergeant, let's move out."

Nik would have liked to follow the soldiers all the way to Arbuckle, but he needed to get back to Paris to testify as one of Willie's arresting officers.

***

After stopping to make camp, Roger and Blue Feather decided against a campfire and dined on jerky and flatbread.

"I apologize, Charlie," Roger said, nervously scanning the ridge still glowing in the waning sunlight. "I should have been paying more attention as to where we were going."

"Mistake mine," Charlie responded, also eyeing the plateau. "I the one asked to guide."

"I just hope we can avoid trouble," Roger remarked, turning to his Indian companion. "Perhaps we should sleep in shifts while one keeps watch."

They camped in an area by the river surrounded by buttonbush plants. They gathered feed for the horses so they could stay inside the camp. The night was without incident but offered little sleep for the duo. Although tired, they rose early to get a good start on the day. Roger noted that Brinker seemed restless, and Charlie was having trouble getting the other two horses to settle down.

"What's with these animals," Roger remarked, rubbing Brinker's nose to calm him.

"Danger near," Charlie called out. "Need guns."

But before either man could unsheathe a weapon, a shot pierced the air. Two mounted warriors emerged from the bushes, with one shouting orders in a language Roger did not understand but he had a good idea what was being said.

"Iron Bear's braves," Charlie said. "The two who took our rifles."

Drawing closer, one of the braves spoke to Blue Feather.

"Do they know who we are?" Roger inquired.

"Yes," Charlie said.

The renegade, not speaking, stepped forward and gathered the rifles and Roger's pistol. He did a thorough search of both men, including Roger's boots.

"They learn fast," Roger quipped to no one in particular.

The Indians signaled for Roger to saddle Brinker and both to mount their horses. With their rifles butted against their thighs and pointed skyward, the warriors positioned themselves, one on each side of their captives.

The two Indians led them in the direction of the escarpment. Charlie was silent, but Roger could see they were headed directly for the Wichita Mountains.

Roger knew they would not survive once they reached the Wichita Range. At first, he thought he could bargain with them, since neither he nor Blue Feather were directly responsible for Iron Bear's demise. But it did not take long to abandon that idea. These were renegades bent on avenging Iron Bear's death, and it did not matter who they killed.

After a two-hour ride, Roger and Charlie were led to a small ravine in the plateau. It reminded Roger of Iron Bear's hideout and he had to admire how well these braves knew their territory. The four men turned onto a small path that led north along the ridge ascending to the top.

"Charlie, is there any way we can bargain with these two?" Roger asked.

The Indian spokesman shouted something, and Charlie just shook his head, "No." Roger could see Blue Feather was assessing the situation, but he had no idea what he was thinking. Roger tried imagining himself as Nik and what he would do, but prayer was all he could come up with.

They reached the top of the ridge and traveled in a northeast direction toward the other side. Once there, another trail led down in a similar pattern to the one they ascended. He could see the Red River below and another plateau east of it. They were descending into what appeared to be a canyon.

The late-morning sun was shining brightly on them now. The trip down the escarpment was slow, with one brave in front and the other following. Roger could see the Wichita Range to the south and knew he would have to come up with something before they reached the mountains, so he prayed.

The lead brave raised his hand to stop the procession and was peering at the ridge across the river. He turned and spoke to the second brave, who shook his head. After the exchange, the lead rider continued his descent.

As they reached the bottom of the plateau, the river created a divide from where the trail appeared to come out on the other side. They approached the flowing waters, and the lead brave suddenly came to a stop. On the other side, an Indian stepped out from the brush and knelt on the river's edge to cup a drink of water into his hand.

The warrior escorts seemed puzzled and focused on the Indian, as did Roger. Suddenly, Charlie kicked the horse of the rider next to him and took off at full gallop into the river. Roger glanced over to see the renegade on his side was raising his rifle to shoot at Charlie. Without thinking, Roger dove into the side of the brave, and both went crashing to the ground. All he heard after that was shouting and gunfire.

Roger had his man on the ground and was ready to deliver a blow when he heard someone call his name. He held up and looked around. It was Nik.

"Nik! What the blazes are you doing here?" the astonishment in his voice ended in almost an elated laugh as he stared at his brother not more than a few feet away.

"Thought you might need some help, so I decided to drop in on you," Nik said, with a grin that stretched his mustache to its limits.

"Thank God," Roger said, as he lifted himself off the man he just tackled. "I don't understand," he blurted.

"I'll explain it all later," Nik said, helping his brother to his feet. "For now, dust yourself off and meet someone I think you know."

Lieutenant Edwards and Corporal Naughton walked up to Roger and Nik, as another soldier led the Indian away. The warrior whose horse Charlie had kicked was already in custody with his hands tied.

"This is quite a reception," Roger said, shaking the hands of both soldiers.

"As luck would have it," Nik started. "I met Lieutenant Edwards after reaching Fort Cobb."

"You were at Fort Cobb?" Roger asked. "Why?"

Nik explained that after he gave his testimony in Paris, he was told to return to Kansas.

"Borchers sent word to Marshal Oliver that he wanted us back in Wichita, so I set out for Fort Cobb hoping to find you," Nik answered. "While there, Lieutenant Edwards told me he had run into you. After discussing your situation, the lieutenant suggested we assemble a unit to go looking for you and Charlie. It appears it may have been a very fortunate suggestion."

"I'll say. Thanks, lieutenant," Roger said, smiling at Edwards. "But how did you know we would end up here?"

"By Providence, we took a route closer to the Wichita Range thinking if you ran into trouble this is where we would find you," Edwards explained. "Corporal Naughton was the one who recommended we follow the very trail over the escarpment you were on."

"We scanned the ridge to make sure it was safe and by fortune spotted the four of you," Naughton chimed in, as Charlie Blue Feather approached the conversation. "Knowing where you would come out, that's where we set our trap."

"So, Charlie, what prompted you to kick that warrior's horse?" Roger asked.

"Deputy Nik's signal," Blue Feather answered.

"Signal, what signal?" asked Roger.

"Before you became a marshal, Charlie and I devised a method to warn each other of trouble if separated," Nik interrupted. "It's nothing more than reflecting the sun off metal or glass to let the other know our whereabouts."

"So, when did that happen?" Roger asked, incredulously.

"When lead Indian stop on trail and speak to fellow warrior," Charlie said. "He saw flash. I saw it too but did not let on."

So, when the Indian scout came down for a drink of water, you knew it was time to act?" Roger questioned.

"Yes," Charlie said, with a rare smile. "You did good knocking brave from horse."

"You actually saved that warrior's life," Nik added. "If you hadn't tackled him, we were ready to shoot."

"I hate to break this up," Edwards said, "but we need to be on our way. These gunshots will attract attention."

After a hasty return to the saddle, the patrol was on its way to Fort Cobb with the last of Iron Bear's renegades in tow.

The patrol approached a small Wichita Indian village shortly after sundown. Charlie Blue Feather entered the camp as liaison to assure its council the patrol posed no threat. The tribe agreed to let the patrol bivouac nearby.

The next morning, Roger took a short walk outside the camp.

"So, how are things going so far?" said a voice from behind the deputy. Roger turned to see an Indian sitting on a rock shaving a hickory stick into an arrow shaft.

"I don't know, things are kind of confusing right now," Roger answered, as he lowered his head.

"They've been confusing for quite a while, haven't they?" the Indian said, pausing his whittling. "What's it going to take to get yourself back on track?"

"I've done a good job. At least I think I have," Roger said, as he looked out over the landscape. "But I've got to admit there are some things I've had to do that I'm not real comfortable with."

"Well, that's kind of a recipe for life, don't you think?" said the Indian, peering down the shaft of the arrow.

"It's not that I assume my life should be any better than anyone else's," Roger answered, turning his attention on the brave. "But I'm just not sure I'm going about it the right way."

"Not surprising," said the Indian. "That sounds like the plight of a whole lot of people."

"Everything seemed so neat and right when I left for school several years ago," Roger said, reflecting on that day. "Then, everything unraveled."

"So, you thought everything was going to run as smooth as summer waters, right?" the Indian said, pointing his arrow shaft at Roger. "I'm afraid life isn't like that. You've done the right things, put some new skills and experiences in your quiver. Nothing wrong with that."

"So now what, more gunplay, hostility, kidnappings and killings?" Roger quipped.

"Perhaps," the Indian said, as he resumed shaving the arrow. "But you should be better able to handle those situations now, even if you follow a different path," the warrior commented and looked up. "No life is immune, but it's important to seek the path that best satisfies you, despite the occasional setback."

Roger looked up at the sky, with the feeling another change was likely on its way.

"Who are you talking to," said a voice behind the deputy. Roger turned to see Nik approaching.

"Ah, just..." Roger turned toward the Indian, who was no longer there, "just myself. I figured I'd come out here and collect my thoughts."

"Well, come on back to the village and collect your gear," Nik said. "We'll be pulling out soon."

Chapter 33

The detachment arrived at Fort Cobb early in the afternoon, where the two renegades were sequestered in a room guarded by two soldiers. Roger, Nik, Charlie, Lieutenant Edwards and Corporal Naughton reported to Captain Holbrook concerning their activities and the capture of two of Iron Bear's outlaw warriors. Nik announced that Roger, Charlie and he would be departing for Wichita, Kansas, as soon as they could secure a wagon for Blue Feather. Captain Holbrook instructed his aide to request a replacement for the conveyance and then show the men their quarters where they could stay until the wagon arrived.

"So, we won't be returning to Texas?" Roger said as the men entered their quarters.

"No, I gave my deposition concerning our three prisoners in Paris," Nik said. "After you left Gainesville, I ran into a troop moving up from Fort Belknap. They told me of a buckboard wagon they found, basically burned to the ground. However, no remains were found of a man or animal, so there is no certainty as to what happened to the judge."

"Is there any evidence he was attacked by Indians or outlaws?" Roger asked.

"Nothing for certain," Nik said, looking down and shaking his head. "There was speculation the judge unhitched his horse, burned the wagon, and rode off with the money hoping it would be assumed he was dead.

"I located the carriage he traded for the wagon," Nik continued, with a less-than-satisfied expression, "but there was no evidence of value left in it, either."

"In other words, justice still hasn't caught up with the judge," Roger said, rubbing his forehead.

"It appears that way," Nik remarked. "For that reason, Marshal Borchers has asked that we return to Kansas for further orders."

The wagon requisitioned for Charlie arrived, but it was larger than the one destroyed in the tornado. So the men had to add another two horses for a team of four to pull it. Still, it was sturdy and capable of getting them to Wichita. After loading the wagon with supplies, the three men started north following the Washita River.

The men traveled easy, encountering no trouble along the way. They eventually crossed over to the east side of the river to gain a more direct route to Kansas. As spring moved into summer, the days were getting longer and hotter, and the team moved slowly. After reaching an area where the Antelope Hills divided and the trail turned east, they passed between two ridges. The terrain consisted of rolling plains dotted with mesas. The flora was mostly tall grass, small scrub trees and patches of wild sunflowers. Once clear of the hills, the three turned north again, heading for the Canadian River. The travelers stopped at the Canadian and brought out fishing poles they had added to the equipment in the wagon. Using cheese and small pieces of jerky for bait, they landed a few good-sized catfish for dinner. Charlie then added beans, fried potatoes and biscuits to the riverside dining experience. All three men slept comfortably that night.

The next day, they crossed the river entering the outlying area of Seminole Territory, where members of the former Florida tribe had been relocated. The trio continued north, eventually reaching Camp Supply. After a short stay and the addition of more provisions, Roger, Nik and Charlie set out and eventually crossed the Red Fork of the Arkansas River at the edge of Creek Country. The Creek Indians were forced out of Georgia over a controversial treaty with the United States.

There was little threat from the tribes in this territory, as most of the fighting involving the U.S. Army had been with the Kiowa, Comanche and Cheyenne. The men also passed through Cherokee and Osage territory on their way to Wichita. The Cherokee were driven out of their previous territory in the Southeast, partially because of a grudge held against the tribe for siding with the British in the Revolutionary War.

The Osage migrated west into Kansas following conflicts with the Iroquois Tribe, but like the Wichita, the Osage were resettled from Kansas into Oklahoma Territory. The Osage were described as the tallest Indians in America.

After being on the trail for almost two weeks, the three men came to the Little Arkansas River and made camp. Charlie worked on putting together the evening meal.

"You two haven't told me about your trip into Comanche Territory," Nik said, looking at Roger. "Charlie has filled us in as to his tribal neighbors and you about Bushmill's whisky and Naughton's ambush. But let's hear more about your search for Gloria."

"I suppose I should be talking like a jaybird, considering what I've been through since Charlie and I first left Fort Cobb," Roger said, staring at Charlie's campfire. "There's just so much running through my mind right now, I cannot string enough thoughts together to make sense."

"How was Gloria? Was she okay? You haven't said much about her," Nik questioned, stirring the fire with a stick.

"She was doing okay, but it surprised me how well she had adjusted to life with the Comanche," Roger said, looking up. "I thought she'd be anxious to come back into the white man's world, but she wanted nothing to do with it. I think part of the problem is that I was so intent on finding her that I hadn't given much thought as to what to expect or what to say when I did."

"You mentioned she had a rough go of it, but you didn't elaborate," Nik said, putting down his stick.

"It's part of why I've been lost in thought. You know, we pretty much grew up with her going to the same church and studying at the same school and all," Roger said, inching back a bit from the fire. "I guess, I kind of thought that familiarity would make things like old times once we met up again."

"Old times," Nik said, chuckling a bit. "As I remember, you and Gloria were an item in Bordertown before you went off to college. What happened after that?"

"After our family was murdered, everything changed for me," Roger said, picking up a small stick and scratching meaningless images in the dirt. "We had talked of marriage until then, but after that incident, my feelings went cold. That's when I told Gloria I was joining the army in hopes of killing Curtain. She took it hard."

"I can understand that," Nik replied, watching Charlie move about. "So, the Fentons headed west to homestead while you were looking after Lee?"

"Lee was a man molded by time," Roger said. "I often wondered why he fought for the South while expressing patriotism. He just had a different vision for America than Lincoln had.

"And yes, the Fentons eventually lost their farm and migrated west."

"What did she have to say about her family being killed?" Nik asked.

"She went through hell until Sockeye sold her to the Comanche. While there, she met a medicine woman who apparently helped her get past that ugly ordeal," Roger answered, pulling his knees up and wrapping his arms around them. "Charlie and I met her before reaching the camp where Gloria was. Apparently that medicine woman did wonders for her."

"Spirit Talker," Charlie cut in, stirring his stew pot. "Woman a shaman, had powerful medicine."

"Spirit Talker," Nik repeated, "I've heard of them. I understand they have some means of dealing with the spiritual world, right?"

"Apparently so," Roger said. "So, whatever went on between those two certainly lifted Gloria's spirits."

"So, she was happy?" Nik asked.

"Not so much happy, as content," Roger said, taking a plate of stew from Charlie. "She seemed to be in a better place than where I was coming from."

"And now?" Nik inquired, also accepting a plate from Charlie.

"I don't know, Nik," Roger said, turning toward his brother. "It's like everything I've gone through should have brought me closer to the contentment Gloria now seems to have. And yet, I think I'm more confused than ever."

"Fortunately, we're in friendly Indian territory," Nik said, with a slight smile. "Otherwise, you wouldn't be much use to Charlie and me in that state of mind."

"My apologies," Roger said, shaking his head.

"Food should help clear deputy's mind," the camp chef commented to Roger.

The following day the team was back on the trail. The two deputies and Blue Feather eventually pulled into Wichita and passed by the hotel where the marshal's office had been.

"Are we not going to stop here?" Roger asked.

"Nope, the service finally got the jail Ned had been pushing for," Nik said. "I understand Ned really likes it."

They eventually halted in front of a new building at the end of town, with a sign out front displaying "Office of U.S. Marshal." Nik grinned, as Roger and he dismounted and waited for Charlie to climb down from the wagon. They entered the marshal's office.

"You're finally here," Marshal Borchers said, getting up from behind his desk. "I was beginning to wonder if you'd gotten lost."

The men shook hands, and then Ned called to someone in the next room. Willie Warneke walked out with a big smile on his face.

"Willie?" Roger said, taken by surprise. "What are you doing here?"

"I'll answer that," Borchers said. "Willie is going to join the Marshal Service. Judge Lewis ruled Willie's time served in the Paris jail was punishment enough for his crimes, except for putting him in my charge for six months."

Ned explained how Willie helped Nik search for Kensington until the trail went cold.

"I put Willie on a train for Wichita, accompanied by Ken's new deputy, following the investigation," Nik chimed in, removing his hat and placing it on the back of his chair "That's when I decided to follow your trail."

"When Willie's probation is up, we'll make him a deputy," Borchers concluded.

"And I owe it all to you, Deputy Marshal Brinkman," Willie interjected, extending his hand to Roger.

"I don't know about that," Roger said, glancing over to a grinning Nik.

"And may I announce," Ned began, "Nik is up for promotion and will have his own district," Borchers continued, turning to Roger. "You'll be the one to replace Nik and mentor Willie."

"Man, I don't know what to say," Roger started. "No, wait. I do know what to say. Ned, as grateful as I am to you, Nik and the service, I can't accept the position. In fact, I'm turning in my badge," Roger said and then removed the shield from his shirt and put it on the marshal's desk.

"I'm sorry to hear that, Roger. You've been a terrific addition to the service," Ned said, picking up the badge. "Yours will be a big hole to fill."

Roger then pivoted to face Nik, who was still grinning from ear to ear. "I'm sorry, brother."

"Not me," Nik said. "I knew your mind was changing. I just didn't know when you would come to that conclusion. I'm happy for you, Roger, depending on what you have planned next."

"I'm planning to return to seminary," Roger said. "My failed quest to catch up to Curtain has softened my need for revenge. As much as I have enjoyed my experience as a deputy, it's not the life for me."

"That's the plan I hoped you'd make," Nik said, grabbing his brother around the shoulders and patting him on the chest. "You've come full circle and did it magnificently. I could see the change coming over you."

Willie cut in and said, "After you introduced me to the Bible and Jesus, I thought I might want to be a preacher, too," said the aspiring deputy, with a laugh, "but I'm afraid seminary needs folks who read a heap better than I do. But I'll be as pleased as all get out to wear a badge, instead."

"You'll do great, Willie," Roger offered and turned to Marshal Borchers. "I hope my decision isn't going to mess you up, Ned."

"Not at all, Roger. Nik and I had discussed this possibility some time ago and we were pretty much prepared for it," Borchers said. "Nik will train Willie to take over the spot you're vacating. After that, Nik will receive his promotion.

"Now I think this all calls for a drink."

Roger's stomach churned a little with that suggestion, but it was too big of an occasion not to savor the moment. Charlie was not one to drink in public and offered to take the wagon and horses to the livery stable and care for them.

"Forgive me for not going to celebration," Charlie said to Roger. "Now offer that Deputy Brinkman's spirit is great. I respect deputy's plan to follow new path. May Spirit of my people go with you."

"Thank you, Charlie," Roger said, taking Blue Feather's hands and clasping them in his own. "Let me just say that you and your people have opened my eyes to things that have helped me in ways I would otherwise never have known."

The five men then departed the marshal's office, with Roger, Nik, Willie and Ned heading for the saloon.

"When did you make up your mind to go back to seminary?" Borchers asked, as the men sat around a table in the tavern, each with a beer. Roger found that if he sipped on the brew, it went down smoother.

"I would say the process had been working in me for some time," Roger answered, "but I would add that things really began to change during my recovery following my fall into the river and the McLaughlins fishing me out. It was during that period I suffered amnesia, I didn't know who or what I was, and I did a lot of soul searching then."

"That was a miracle in itself," Nik said. "Not just surviving that trip down the river but having no memory of who you were until I stumbled across you at the McLaughlins' homestead."

"I was helping the McLaughlins' son, Johnny Mac, with his Bible studies and the fact I could remember so much scripture kept me wondering why," Roger said. "I don't know if my memory would have come back to me if you had not shown up, but I knew I must have gotten the knowledge of those Bible stories from somewhere."

"Maybe it was Pa who was reaching out to you from the Good Book," Nik said, taking a long pull on his beer and stroking his mustache.

"Maybe," Roger replied, "but my decision didn't finalize until Ned spoke of the promotions. It was then I realized my search was over, and it was time to go home."

"No matter the road you travel," Ned said to Roger, "I'm proud to have served with you as chief marshal and truly hope all goes well for you.

"What do you plan to do after seminary?" Borchers asked.

"I've given that some thought, as well," Roger responded. "I'm inclined to take my degree, my Bible and head west."

"A circuit rider?" Ned asked.

"Yes, I'm afraid I've got the West and wanderlust in my blood now," Roger said, taking a sip of beer and breaking a smile. "Who knows? Maybe I'll even have you guys in my congregation one day."

"If you're in these parts," Willie said, "you can bet I'll be there."

That brought a laugh, as the men finished their celebration and returned to the office to finish up the rest of their administrative work.

Borchers told Roger to hold off on his resignation until word arrived that Concordia had accepted his application. Roger also corresponded with the Tillotsons. They assisted with his reapplication and offered him his old room back. Roger accepted their offer and sent a telegram as to the time of his arrival.

There had been outlaw attacks on the railroads and stage lines, so Roger's last official duty would be as a marshal en route to St. Louis. Before his departure date, Roger turned Brinker over to the U.S. Marshal Service.

"I know you're going to miss him," Borchers said, as Roger and Willie led Brinker into his stall. "You can reclaim him if you're ever back this way."

"I promise to take good care of him," Willie replied, stroking the bridge of the horse's nose."

"And I promise he will take care of you," Roger, said, as he wrapped his arm around Brinker's neck to give him a hug.

When the day arrived for Roger to board the train for St. Louis, Nik rented a buggy to take him to the depot. For a brief time, they said nothing until Roger broke the silence.

"It seems I'm always leaving someone behind," Roger remarked. "When will I ever find a home?"

Nik drew the horse to a halt and turned to his brother.

"Your home is in here," Nik said, pointing to Roger's heart. "And in here," he repeated, touching his own chest.

"Maybe you're the one who should be going to seminary," Roger said, laughing.

"Who knows what the future will bring? I'm just happy you're making the decision Ma and Pa wanted you to," Nik continued. "And one more thing. When you're ordained, I want you to baptize me."

"Pa didn't do that?" Roger quizzed.

"It was scheduled for the Sunday following that fateful day in Bordertown," Nik answered, looking straight ahead as he spoke.

"That will give me another reason to look you up when I return," Roger said, eyeing his brother's profile.

They pulled up to the depot and both got out of the buggy. Nik grabbed Roger's bag and Roger his rifle. The seminary-bound deputy also felt the handle of his holstered pistol and checked to make sure his badge was in place. Both men walked onto the station platform.

"It's been quite a journey the way we've gone in and out of each other's lives," Roger said, as Nik put down the luggage and Roger laid his rifle on it. "I'm going to miss you, brother."

"Don't go sentimental on me," Nik chided. "I love you, but I don't envy you. Becoming a preacher is a privilege, but it's not for me."

"You're not bitter, are you?" Roger asked, with a surprised look on his face.

"Bitter? Not the way you may be thinking," Nik responded. "Roger, we were raised as brothers in the same loving family under completely different circumstances. You just happened to know where you were going – once you figured it out – but I've had to go wherever I was sent."

"And do you resent that?" Roger replied, as his puzzled look continued.

"No, I don't resent that. In many ways I'm better off than you," Nik said, smiling as he spoke. "You've been given the responsibilities, and I've been given the challenges. I've met my challenges, now it's time for you to meet your responsibilities."

"I… I don't know," Roger stammered, turning his head as the sound of a train whistle shrieked in the distance.

"That's what you're doing now, don't you see?" Nik put his hands on Roger's shoulders and looked into his eyes. "It has taken you a while, but my glory is knowing my brother is finally doing the right thing."

"But what about you?" Roger said as the churning of the engine could be heard.

"I'm being promoted!" Nik said, tossing his head back as he laughed. "How about offering me congratulations!?"

"Richly deserved, but what about Curtain?" Roger noted.

"To hell with Curtain," Nik continued grinning. "God will take care of him in due time. We're family, and that's what matters."

The train chugged into the station, hissing as it billowed clouds of steam. Roger just stared at Nik for a moment and then wrapped his arms around him and hugged as hard as he could.

"Hey, don't break my ribs," Nik wheezed. After Roger released him, Nik picked up Roger's rifle and luggage. They hurried to where passengers were boarding, and Roger stepped onto the car's platform.

Nik handed Roger his bag and shouted over the noise, "Our journey isn't over. This is just another step along the way."

As the train began to move, Nik handed Roger his rifle, "Here, don't forget this."

"Not the usual way one departs for seminary," Roger said with a laugh, while grabbing the gun.

The brothers watched each other as the train began to put distance between them. Nik waved as Roger raised his rifle in salute and stepped inside.

He sat in the first empty seat he found and let the memories of his life as a U.S. Deputy Marshal fill his mind. Like before, he spent most of the journey looking out the window watching the countryside hurry by. The trip was peaceful, and the deputy had no cause to use either weapon. Finally, the train pulled into St. Louis. He stepped from his car with his gun belt strapped around his waist and a rifle in his hand.

"My goodness," said Pastor Tillotson, "were you expecting trouble?"

"Not armed like this," Roger said with a wide grin.

The Tillotsons' son, William, had graduated from Concordia and was serving as assistant pastor in Boston, Massachusetts.

When Roger entered his old room, he felt like he was stepping back in time. As he looked around, he spotted a smooth, white stone lying on his desk. He sat down, picked it up and placed his elbows on the desk. While examining the keepsake, tears began to flood his eyes. He folded the stone in his hand, bowed his head against his fist, and surrendered to the loving memory of his family.

The following day, there was a new bounce in Roger's step, and he wore a broad smile that surprised him when he looked in the mirror. It was one he had not seen in years.

Roger borrowed the Tillotsons' buggy and visited the U.S. Marshals Office and officially turned in his badge and rifle. The agency allowed him to keep the pistol and gun belt because his was lost in the line of duty. He stored them in one of his dresser drawers, where they remained out of sight.

Concordia College was in the process of building a new classroom facility and dormitory, but otherwise the campus was pretty much the same. Now in his mid-twenties, Roger was a little older than many of the other students, but he paid that no mind.

"Welcome back," said his advisor, Professor Ulrich Duttenhoffer. "I understand you've had quite a career since leaving here."

"Thanks, professor, it's good to be back" Roger said. "There were a lot of issues I had to work through, and they took me down a path I thought I would never have to follow."

"So, you now think life in the service of the church is what you want?" the counselor asked.

"I have, perhaps, a greater motivation than I've ever had," Roger said. "I now have a much better understanding of what is out there and why my new decision is the right one."

"Perhaps you could be of service to the school as a student-teacher, as well," Duttenhoffer said, half questioning.

"A student-teacher?" Roger said. "What would I teach?"

"Life, Mr. Brinkman – life," the professor answered. "Your student profile tells me you are a fountain of it."

Advisor Duttenhoffer's words were prophetic. Because of Roger's eagerness to learn, he was able to balance his studies with his job as student-teacher. When the word spread of Roger's class, fighting in the Civil War, and marshaling in the Wild West, it became so popular Concordia had to limit the class to upper-tier students.

Roger's time at school passed quickly. His years at Concordia seemed more like months and before long he was graduating.

"Roger, it is time for you to indicate what you plan to do with your degree," Professor Duttenhoffer said. "Once you are ordained, you can begin working in the field or stay on here as a postgraduate. You could easily qualify."

"I appreciate all Concordia has done for me," Roger said. "But my calling is out West. I loved teaching here, but my heart yearns for the wide-open spaces of this great country and the people settling it.

"My father was among those who helped establish this school and, had he not had a family, he would have likely become a circuit rider," Roger added. "I feel that is my calling."

"A traveling clergy, I envy you in many ways," Duttenhoffer said. "Maybe when you have completed your calling, you will return and instruct our students as you did so brilliantly while you were here. You should have many more stories by then."

"Maybe I will do that, professor," Roger said, "maybe I will do that."

Chapter 34

The circuit riders in the West were dwindling, as some pastors began to settle into towns and establish their own churches. This forced those known as saddlebag preachers to move farther west to find a flock scattered over partially settled areas. Pastor Roger Brinkman began his traveling clergy career along the Rio Grande River in Southwestern New Mexico. It was an area where both mining and farming were the dominant means of making a living. A number of Chihene Apache also inhabited the area. The Chihene were a tribe less hostile than most Apache and willing to trade goods with the new settlers. However, the peace between the Indians and the settlers was still an uneasy one.

Moving up and down the Rio Grande, Pastor Brinkman developed remote parishes through individuals willing, and often eager, to serve as elders. The elders would hold services in their homes or wherever space was available, whether indoors or out. Roger would ride the circuit and meet with these elders and spend the weekend hosting services for local congregations. On occasion, some among the Chihene would attend, leading Roger to consider finding an English-speaking Apache willing to serve as an elder among the tribe.

With the evening shadows spreading, Roger approached a modest, well-constructed house. The façade was log, complete with a porch. The occupants had built onto the home, as the family grew. Most impressive on the property was a two-story barn. The community of Palomas, New Mexico, needed a barn. But the homesteads there could only afford one, so they chose Paul Zimmerman's property on Palomas Creek to build the barn because of its central location.

With the arrival of Pastor Brinkman, that barn also doubled as the local church.

"Pastor Brinkman, good to see you," said Paul Zimmerman, stepping off the porch, as Brinkman rode up.

Zimmerman was nearing middle age. He had moved from Missouri and tried settling in Texas. Difficult circumstances in Texas had prompted him to move his family farther west, settling in Palomas. Farming in the deep Southwest was also challenging, so Paul tried prospecting to supplement the family income. Some miners in the area had success working claims along the small tributaries of the Rio Grande, but Zimmerman's true talents remained farming and harvesting souls for the church.

***

Roger got off his horse, Brinker II, which the new pastor affectionately called "B-two." After seminary, Roger traveled to Wichita, Kansas, to reclaim Brinker, but found the horse had grown too old for travel in the backcountry of the Old West. Chief Marshal Borchers had pastured Brinker at a farm near Wichita since the U.S. Marshal Service was no longer using the horse. As payment, Roger donated the animal to the farm's family.

***

"It is so good of you to bring the Gospel to these parts," Paul said. Roger and Zimmerman teamed up when the pastor started his ministry and Paul proved to be his number-one elder. "We're getting the barn ready for Sunday's meeting. A lot of folks are coming to hear you preach."

Brinkman's circuit covered nearly two hundred miles and took in Fort McRae and Fort Craig along with the towns and settlements in that area.

"That's encouraging, Paul," Roger said. "You've done a fine job in this area and deserve much of the credit for establishing this church."

"Well, thank you, Pastor," Paul said. "Now come on in and make yourself at home. Sally's got some coffee on, and we've made up a place in the barn where you can sleep during your stay here."

"Much obliged, Paul. You know, without families like yours, I'd probably be preaching to the birds and squirrels instead of solid folks like you Zimmermans," Roger said.

"It's our pleasure, Pastor Brinkman," Paul replied. "Sally and I look so forward to your visits. My boys are out working right now. They'll be glad to see you when the day is done."

"I look forward to that," Roger said as the two men entered the house.

"Well, if you ain't a sight for sore eyes," Sally said, as Roger walked in. "We do cherish the time you are able to stay with us."

Sally was the perfect match for her husband. They both threw themselves into maintaining their homestead and were also bedrocks of the church. When Pastor Brinkman was not in town, she and Paul would deliver sermons Roger helped them write during his visits.

"That feeling is mutual, I assure you," Roger said.

"Sit down and enjoy a nice cup of coffee," Sally said, retrieving the coffee pot from the stove. Although the Zimmermans included plenty of ventilation in their home, Sally's face was always reddened by heat from the woodstove. "I've got some pie, as well."

"Oh, no pie for me right now," Roger said. "It'll spoil my appetite for one of those fine meals you cook up."

"The boys should be bringing in a batch of catfish for tonight's feast," Paul said. "They usually head down to the river to fish after they finish work."

"Catfish is a favorite of mine," Roger said. "Our former cook was handy at cooking up cats over the campfire during my marshaling days."

"Speaking of marshaling days, Pastor, the local folks are having some land issues, and we were wondering if you could help out," Paul said. "There's someone claiming to own a lot of local properties backed by a homestead speculation deed. He says the locals owe him payment for their farms."

"Now that sounds familiar," said Roger. "Just who is this speculator?"

"I would tell you more, but I've stayed out of it. It's mostly the folks north of here," Paul said. "If you'd be willing, those folks would like to get some advice. I've set up a meeting in town tomorrow with the farmers' spokesman, but no obligation, you see. If you don't show up, he'll know you were unable to make it. However, he may be in church Sunday."

"I'll tell you what," Roger began. "I'll be glad to make that meeting. I just might be able to help and encourage him to attend church."

When Peter, Matthew and Andrew, the Zimmermans' sons, showed up with a beautiful string of catfish, Roger promptly offered to help clean them in preparation for supper.

After the meal, including some of Sally's pie, Roger retired to the barn's hayloft where he usually slept. After looking after Brinker II, he lay out his bedroll and hung his gun belt on a hay hook attached to a wooden column. Despite his new profession, Roger continued to wear the pistol for protection, and no one in the West seemed to pay it any mind. He did, however, remove it for church services.

The next day, Roger set out for the town of Alamosa, a few miles north of the Zimmerman farm, to meet up with the troubled farmers' spokesman. There was a small eatery and saloon in the town, where Roger was told he would find a man named Carlos Sanchez Santana. Santana served as a voice for the farmers, having good command of English, Spanish and Apache languages. The homesteaders in question had joined forces to fend off the speculator who claimed the farmers owed him for their properties. When Roger entered the eatery, there was a man of apparent Mexican descent, fashionably dressed, with a smile made brighter under the man's black mustache.

"Ah, Señor Brinkman, I assume?" the man said, getting up from the table where he was sitting. He removed his hat and held it in one hand while extending the other. "Won't you join me?"

"If you're Carlos Sanchez Santana, I would be happy to join you," Roger said, removing his hat and returning the smile. The men shook hands and then sat down at the man's table. The table was small, so both men put their hats back on their heads.

"Reverend Brinkman, I know this is not a typical question for a preacher, but Señor Zimmerman said you were a lawman in your earlier days," Carlos said.

"I was," Roger answered, "and not that long ago."

"There is a man who claims he has a deed to many properties in this area where many farmers have made their homes," Carlos began. "He said he is willing to give up the land but demands payment. Many here do not have the money, and there is no bank to borrow from. This man said we can pay in gold or work in his mine for payment."

"He has a gold mine?" Roger asked.

"We do not know for sure," Carlos said. "We think if he does, he probably jumped the claim of some poor prospector. He also said he would take payment in horses, which we think he either sells to the Apache or in Mexico. The farmers here cannot give up their horses."

"Who is this man?" Roger asked.

"He claims he is a colonel and said he was given the deed for this land for his service in the war," Carlos said. "He said his last name is like ... Cortina, or as you might say Drape. I think his first name is Gabe."

Roger felt a little dizzy after hearing Santana's attempt to recall the name. He reached over and laid his hand on Carlos' forearm, which the spokesman had resting on the table.

"Could his last name be Curtain, by any chance? Colonel Gabe Curtain?" Roger asked.

"Si, that is it Señor Brinkman, Curtain, Colonel Curtain," Carlos responded. "Do you know him?

Roger's head was now spinning. Was it possible he had finally come across the man whose name matched that of the one who killed his parents? He instinctively reached down to feel his .44 Colt.

Roger began grilling Carlos for information. At first, the spokesman was a little taken aback by Roger's aggression, but then out of enthusiasm began answering the pastor's questions as best he could.

"Is the local sheriff or judge involved in this man's claim?" Roger asked.

"Señor Curtain presented a letter to our sheriff signed by a judge claiming the deed was valid," said Santana. "Because of the letter, the sheriff said the matter was out of his hands. Our sheriff is a farmer who knows very little about the law."

"Do you know the name of the judge who signed that letter?" Roger said, leaning forward to look into Carlos' face.

"I have not seen the letter, so I do not know," Santana answered.

As their conversation continued, a rather large figure filled the doorway of the cantina, but neither Roger nor Carlos noticed him until the man spoke.

"Sanchez Santana, I'm getting tired of waiting, and I think you're the one holding me up. If these farmers don't pay up, I'm going to have to use force," said the man in the doorway.

Both men at the table turned to look at the figure silhouetted in the door frame.

"Señor Curtain?" Carlos said, his voice cracking a bit.

Roger pushed his chair back to get a better look at the intruder.

"Sorry, parson," the figure in the doorway said, "but I have urgent business with the company you happen to be keeping."

"Well, that affects me, as well," Roger said. "This man is a member of my parish."

"This is real business, Parson, not church business," the man said. "You can talk to Santana on Sunday, if he lives that long."

Roger slowly rose to his feet. "Now that's mighty strong talk, Mr. ..." Roger started.

"It's none of your damn business who I am, Preacher. Now get out of the way!" the man said in a louder tone.

"Tell me, are you Colonel Gabriel Curtain?" Roger asked as he squinted at the figure before him. Roger moved away from the table to get a better look at the intruder. He could see the man's clothes were a mix between a businessman and a cowboy. He was wearing a gun and kept his hand close to it. He was rather large, but more round than tall. His face sported a beard that somehow made him look bigger than he was.

"What does it matter to you what my name is?" the man said. "My business is not with you."

"It might be," Roger responded. "Are you the man with the speculation deed and are you Colonel Gabriel Curtain?"

"I am, so what's that to you, Preacher? I am not a member of your church nor do I intend to be," the man now known as Curtain replied.

"I once knew a colonel who rode with Quantrill's Raiders. That colonel was known as Curtain, and he committed murder. He was also involved in a land swindle in Texas, much like what I'm hearing from Mr. Santana, here," Roger said in a steady tone. "Would that be you?"

Roger's eyes had adjusted to the contrast in light and could now see Curtain's expression changing from one of annoyance to growing anger.

"You're starting to get on my nerves, Parson," Curtain said. "My quarrel is not with you, but you are beginning to try my patience."

"Because if you are that man," Roger started, "then I'm going to have to ask you to turn yourself in to the law."

Curtain now looked dumbfounded. "The law!" he bellowed. "Preacher, I'm going to give you to the count of three to get out of the way. Don't force me to go through you to get to that Mexican dirt farmer behind you."

Pastor Brinkman did not move.

"We can settle this peaceful-like," Roger said. "If your claim is real, then you should have nothing to worry about. If you are who you say you are, then you may need a lawyer."

Roger forced himself to remain calm. He was now convinced he was facing the man who killed his parents and sister. Though it was his nature to avoid violence, his experience told him intimidation was the best way to get a coward to back down. So, he slowly pulled his coat back past his pistol to let the man know he was serious, and added, "I advise you to do as I asked, and no one will get hurt."

Colonel Curtain's eyes seemed to flash red. Suddenly, he reached for his gun without bothering to count. Roger drew and fired before Curtain's pistol cleared its holster. Curtain stepped back, hesitated, and then fell backward into the street. Roger watched the scene for a moment and then approached the fallen man. He knelt beside the body and pulled back Curtain's collar. There on his neck was the burn-type scar Nik had mentioned. Knowing he had killed the right man, Roger made the sign of the crucifix over him and silently prayed before rising.

He turned to Carlos Sanchez Santana sitting at the table behind him. "Carlos, when you see your sheriff, please let him know what happened here. Colonel Curtain was a wanted man," Roger said, and added, "Hope to see you in church Sunday."

Carlos could only stare momentarily at Curtain lying dead and then up at Roger. Roger tipped his hat to Carlos, then approached Brinker II, mounted, and rode off in the direction of the Zimmerman farm.

As Roger rode back from Alamosa, New Mexico, he was conflicted. His intention was to relinquish his quest to find Colonel Curtain, but the haunting memory of what the man did to his family remained. As a pastor, he had genuinely hoped Curtain would turn himself in, but he could not let the man just walk away. Roger pondered how Nik would take the news. Would his brother be disappointed to hear Curtain died from a single bullet? Roger also wondered what his parishioners would think of their pastor gunning down a man they barely knew.

Roger's mind drifted back to Gloria Fenton, Sockeye Sammon, the conversion of Willie Warneke and the narrow path that lay ahead. He had come a long way since his boyhood days in Missouri. Would killing the man who turned his world upside down free his soul or simply open a new chapter in his troubled life? Was it over or just starting?

Eyeing a quiet spot down by the river, Roger steered Brinker II off the trail that led to the Zimmerman farm. He found a shaded area where the river ran deep and wide, making almost no sound as it drifted along. The pastor dismounted and, while holding B-two by the reins, sat down by a tree and thoughtfully watched the water flow by.

As the sun was setting, he arose and tied Brinker II to a tree and began gathering wood to build a small campfire. He retrieved his Bible from his saddlebags and began going through the pages. Roger used the light of the campfire to read by, as the evening shadows closed in. His mind began to focus while reading to himself.

"A little trouble today?" said a man from across the campfire dressed in heavy pants held up by red suspenders. He was slight of build, wore roughed-up boots and a hat pushed up in front. The stranger stirred the fire with a stick and the flames flared up even brighter than before.

"Show off," Roger muttered, offering but a glance at the man. "Is this how it's going to be?"

"What did you expect? Did you think once you were ordained that everything would come up roses?" said the man, looking like someone who had just climbed out of a mineshaft. "It's still the same world, although you were probably hoping yours would be different now."

"I've wanted to kill that man since I heard what he had done to my family," Roger said, as he lowered his Bible and stared at the stranger. "Now that I have killed him, the satisfaction isn't what I thought it would be."

"Would you feel better if you were still a lawman?" the stranger asked, as the flames of the campfire threw dancing light across his face.

"Now, why would that make a difference?" Roger asked. "It would still be me, whether wearing a badge or wearing a collar."

"So now that you're a traveling clergy, you think everywhere you go will result in peace and tranquility?" the stranger questioned. "I don't recall that happening in my time."

"But I'm supposed to be different now, not a hired gun," Roger said. "How am I supposed to live with that?"

"Like everyone else does, son, taking life one day at a time," said the man. "Don't worry, you'll do far more good things than those you find distasteful. But let me remind you, this world is still ruled by the Devil."

With that, Roger snapped his Bible shut and rose to his feet. He drew his pistol and began firing into the darkness until his Colt ran out of bullets.

"You'll never stop Satan with that," the fading stranger's voice echoed in the night. "The weapon you need is the one in your other hand."

Roger looked down at the words on the book he was holding – "The Holy Bible." His gun hand dropped to his side and tears began to roll down his cheeks. He stood for a time attempting to regain his composure. He holstered his weapon and turned to kick dirt onto the campfire. He mounted Brinker II and made his way back to the Zimmermans' place.

"Pastor, we thought you would be back long ago," Paul said as he came out onto the porch of the farmhouse holding a lantern as Roger approached. "We were beginning to worry about you."

"Sorry, Paul. It's been a long day," Roger answered, riding up to the porch and dismounting.

Paul handed a lantern to his oldest boy, Peter, and instructed him to take Brinker II into the barn.

"Come on in. Sally's got dinner waiting for you," Paul said, as Peter led the horse away. "She kept the stove going to keep it warm."

"She shouldn't have gone to that trouble," Roger said, knowing how warm the inside of the house must now be. "I apologize for my thoughtlessness."

"Not at all, we know the responsibility you carry. It must weigh heavy on you," Paul said. "We're just happy to help.

"By the way, we heard what happened in Alamosa," Paul added.

"Word travels fast," Roger remarked, "even out here."

"This is rough country, Pastor," Paul said. "It's important that folks stay in touch."

"So, is anybody going to show up for church Sunday?" Roger asked as Sally set his dinner on the table.

"As far as we know. Ain't no one said otherwise," replied Paul.

"Don't fret, Pastor," Sally said. "Folks out here are way tougher than they are back East. Being back there may have softened you some."

"Not nearly as much as I thought," Roger said. "You're right. I need to face this thing and the folks. I will try to make the best of the situation."

While Roger ate his meal in silence, Sally and Paul sat quietly keeping him company. Roger slid his chair back and looked at his hosts.

"I am deeply indebted to you both," Roger said. "Let me help with those dishes."

"Nonsense," Sally said, springing up to gather his plate. "You have enough to do already. We still have to set up the barn for church, so we all need to be up early. Matt and Andrew are already in bed, and Peter will join them when he finishes with your horse."

"God bless you both, and the boys too," Roger said, as Peter entered the house and headed for bed. "I'll see all of you in the morning," the pastor concluded, donning his hat and stepping out to make his way to the barn. The evening was pleasant with a full canopy of stars overhead. Fatigue began to replace Roger's thoughts and, after settling into bed, sleep came easily.

Roger rose early Sunday morning and began preparing the barn for services. Paul had constructed a wooden platform to keep the hay dry and used it to place the altar and pulpit he had built. There were also a couple of chairs on the platform for the pastor and elder to sit on. Paul and the boys had rolled splitting logs into the barn and placed planks across them for folks to sit on. Roger climbed into the loft and opened the large doors for loading hay to let sunlight would flow in from above. When the time for church approached, people began filing into the converted barn in large numbers. It was a clear day and not too warm.

"Good morning," Paul said as he approached the podium. "I am pleased to see so many of you were able to make it today. It is an honor to have our circuit pastor with us. We don't get to see him that often. The real good news is you won't have to hear me deliver the sermon today."

After a hearty laugh from the congregation, Paul led the church in a hymn of praise. Paul then gave way for Roger to take his place at the pulpit. Roger had removed his gun belt but had his Colt tucked into his pants. Taking a deep breath, he approached the podium and removed his Colt and placed it on the platform next to his Bible.

"Brothers, sisters and the wonderful children who join us today," Roger began. "I have to start with the story of what happened in Alamosa recently, when I went up to meet with Carlos Sanchez Santana."

Santana, who was seated near the front, turned and nodded to the others. A few folks stood up to leave, and Roger picked up his pistol and shot into the ceiling of the barn. The blast echoed throughout the building, startling everyone, including those who stood to leave.

"Sorry, folks," Roger continued, "but I need you to hear this. Please, everyone, return to your seats."

Those who were leaving did return to their seats, as Brinkman began his sermon.

"As I mentioned, Carlos and I had a run-in with a man who was trying to extort folks in this area, and I felt compelled to confront him. Some of you may have known the late Colonel Curtain, having had to deal with the man and his nefarious ways. What some of you probably don't know is that same man killed my parents and my little sister years ago, while I was away at seminary.

"That day in Alamosa, once I learned who he was, the love in my soul turned to hate, and I am afraid I did confront the man. However – and Brother Carlos can attest to this – I did ask the colonel to turn himself in to the law. As a former deputy marshal, I knew there was a warrant for his arrest. He was a wanted man. But he refused to comply with my request and attempted to draw his gun.

I cut that action short, along with his life. For that, I am not proud.

"I'm sure some of you are not disappointed that Mr. Curtain is no longer with us, but I need your forgiveness for the hate I had inside me for that man," Pastor Brinkman continued. "Yes, I've spoken to God, asking for His forgiveness and know that I have it through the blood of his Son, Jesus Christ. But what I need is your forgiveness, also.

"I need your forgiveness because my work in this territory has just begun and I need all of you – men, women and children – to help me see it through.

"My power comes from this book," Roger said, holding up his Bible, "and not from this," he added, holding up the pistol.

Roger stared at the weapon for a moment and put it back down. "The Bible is what binds us in this fight against the evils of this world," the pastor said as he raised the Good Book even higher. "A world in which we sometimes have to do what the Ten Commandments tell us we shouldn't, and believe me, I know those commandments well. But life doesn't always follow what God wrote on those tablets thousands of years ago."

Roger then replaced the Bible on the podium.

"We may not be able to change this land, but we can bring change to men's hearts and help give the Holy Spirit a chance to bring them to God," Roger continued. "What happened to me stands as testimony as to what we're up against.

"As I continue my journey," Roger added, "I ask not only for your forgiveness, but also for your prayers. You opened your homes to me in the beginning and now I need you to open your hearts to me. I need your forgiveness and blessings so I can continue what I was truly sent here to do."

With that, Roger removed the pistol from the podium and laid it on the floor. He then rose and lifted his hands high.

"May the Lord bless you and keep you. May He make His face shine upon you and be gracious unto you. May He lift up His countenance upon you and give you peace. Keep your hearts and minds in Christ Jesus. Amen."

There was a long period of silence, and then Paul stood up and announced the next hymn. Roger walked over to his chair and sat down, while Paul led the congregation in song.

Following the service, all who came to church approached Roger and committed their support to him. Roger was not able to keep tears from welling up in his eyes, as he thanked them for giving him the hope he needed.

"Pastor, I know you are torn over what happened," said Carlos Santana, "but if it helps, I shall thank the Good Lord every day that He saved my life through you. May He give you peace, as well."

"Thank you, Carlos," Roger said, shaking the man's hand. "Godspeed."

After everyone had gone home, Roger helped to restore the dais to its original purpose, a platform for hay. He then climbed up to the loft and began packing his belongings. Sally hurried into the house to put together some food for his journey, while Paul and the boys cleared the makeshift benches from the barn. Once all was in order, the Zimmerman family gathered to say goodbye to Pastor Brinkman.

"Are you sure you'll be all right?" Paul asked. "I see you're still wearing your gun."

"I'm hoping I'll never need it again," Roger said, smiling as he mounted Brinker II, "but just in case, I will keep it with me. I may preach heaven, but I still have to contend with hell."

With that, Roger thanked Paul and his family, tipped the brim of his hat and rode away.

ALSO BY TIM W. JAMES

Blood Justice
The Blind Man's Story

OTHER BOOKS BY IRON SPIKE PRESS

Tim W. James
Blood Justice
The Blind Man's Story

Reid Lance Rosenthal
Threads West
Maps of Fate
Uncompahgre
Moccasin Track

CPSIA information can be obtained
at www.ICGtesting.com
Printed in the USA
BVHW091136110922
646361BV00001B/3